TIPTOE THROU

I had the impressi the eye to fully captu under the impact of f the floor. His exclamation of surprise, pain, and rage hung in the air, as though the sound hadn't had time to dissipate in the echoes of the vast room.

And then all hell broke loose. Something tugged at me, as if the feeling between Kit and me were a taut rope, binding us heart to heart.

I never thought about it. Never made a decision to attack anyone. Never even made a decision to move. Yet as soon as Kit hit the floor, I was flying through the air.

My father, in his attempts to subdue me, or perhaps to give me an outlet for that pent-up aggression that worried everyone so much, had enrolled me in various academies which taught self-defense or martial arts. When I escaped Daddy's authority I'd learned hand-to-hand dirty fighting.

But for my money, the most useful fighting moves I ever learned came from a ballet camp in Switzerland to which Dad had sent me, apparently under the delusion that dance would tame the savage beast.

I caught myself mid-air, leaping, in graceful ballet-style, over Kit and his huddled captors and straight at the blond man. The tip of my extended foot hit him mid-chest, and took him down as I landed. I grabbed the burner from his hand before he could react. I pointed it at his head.

DARKSHIP
RENEGADES

SARAH A. HOYT

DARKSHIP RENEGADES

A Baen Books Original

Baen Publishing Enterprises
P.O. Box 1403
Riverdale, NY 10471
www.baen.com

ISBN: 978-1-4767-3617-4

Cover art by David Mattingly

First paperback printing, November 2013

Library of Congress Control Number: 2012033436

Distributed by Simon & Schuster
1230 Avenue of the Americas
New York, NY 10020

Pages by Joy Freeman (www.pagesbyjoy.com)
Printed in the United States of America

To Robert Anson Hoyt, for the future.

Acknowledgments:

Thank you to Dr. Tedd Roberts for helping with research, and to Chris Muir for letting me play with his characters in the last bit of this book.

Also, thank you as always to Toni Weisskopf for letting me do Space Opera and to my team of beta readers. In particular I'd like to single out Francis Turner, Dayna Hart, Pam Uphoff, Amanda Green, and Kate Paulk—and always Dan Hoyt—but that does not diminish the contributions of the others who helped make this book what it is.

WELCOME TO EDEN

OUT OF THE FRYING PAN

I WAS A PRINCESS FROM EARTH AND HE WAS A ROGUE spaceman from a mythical world. He saved my life three times. I rescued him from a fate worse than death. We fell madly in love.

We married and lived happily ever after.

Ever after comes with an expiration date these days. We'd been married less than year when Kit got shot in the head.

It started with our return from Earth. No. Wait, what it really started with was my meeting Kit, in the powertrees which are biological solar collectors in Earth orbit. They were put up way back when bioengineered rulers governed the Earth. And ever since the turmoils sent the bioengineered rulers—you probably know them as Mules, so-called because, of course, they couldn't reproduce—fleeing the Earth in a ship called *Je Reviens*, the powertrees have been haunted by legends of darkship thieves.

3

Which is all anyone ever thought the darkship thieves were. After all, even if the Mules really had left in an interstellar ship, and of course, there are doubts that the ship even existed, why would they come back to harvest powerpods from the powertrees—the biological solar energy collectors in Earth orbit? And why would no one else see them but powerpod collectors?

I found out the legend was less legendary than advertised when a mutiny aboard Daddy Dearest's space cruiser sent me fleeing in a lifeboat into the powertrees. Which is where I met Kit, who rescued me and took me to his homeworld, Eden.

Eden is where all the bioed servants of the Mules stayed behind, instead of going to the stars with their masters. They had had enough of being ruled by Mules, which considering what the Mules did to the Earth I couldn't really blame them for, but they also couldn't live on Earth, since this was the time of the turmoils and anyone with even a hint of bioimprovement would get killed in a horrible way.

So, they'd stayed behind in Eden, which is an asteroid they hollowed inside. Its naturally erratic orbit hides it from Earth detection. But it still needs power. And for its power it depends on darkships, which are ships built to be non-reflective and pretty much undetectable, provided they harvest while the powertrees are in Earth shadow.

Each of the darkships is piloted by a Cat—no, they are wholly human, but they are bioengineered so their eyes resemble those of cats, and also so that they have very fast reflexes—and a Navigator, whose memory, mechanical skill, and sense of direction were bioenhanced to make him or her ideal to help steer darkships, which cannot have any of its data in a form Earth might capture if Earth forces capture a darkship.

Which, until recently, was very much an unfounded fear. No darkship had ever been captured ... Then the Good Men of Earth realized that I must have been taken up by a darkship and started an all-out search for me.

At that point, I was Kit's Navigator, and married to him, a combination that's not mandatory but has grown to be expected. His catlike eyes, his reflexes, had ceased to seem alien. And when I was radiation-burned in an attempt to capture me, he chose to surrender to Earth to save me, instead of following procedure and killing both of us, and destroying the ship, leaving Earth nothing but a burned-out hull.

It had paid off for us; we'd come back out of Earth alive and I'd been healed of the radiation burn.

The problem was the return to Eden. I had no idea how Eden would react to news that not only had we failed to self-destruct, but we'd chosen to land on Earth and seek treatment. It was probably useless to try to get forgiveness for this by explaining we'd left a good portion of the Earth in flames behind us, and a revolution brewing.

Eden had been colonized by refugees of a perse-cuted people, by people who never, ever, ever again would trust any authority. I'm not saying that Eden was paranoid, because worlds can't be paranoid. But if Eden had been an individual, he'd live in a compound with motion-sensor-triggered burners at every entrance, and would fingerprint his own children twice a day to make sure no one had slipped ringers in on him.

So, three months after we left Earth, we hailed Eden on approach.

Kit has said you could land on the surface of the asteroid that contained Eden and never guess that there was a thriving civilization inside. I don't know if that's true. Never tried it. I don't like to take his word for it. He could be wrong. But I did know we could not land *in* Eden unless they let us. Well, not intact. Kit had once threatened to ram his ship into the asteroid, and from the reaction, this was possible even if it would kill us. It was impossible to get into the landing tunnels—whose covers didn't even show to radar—without someone inside letting us in. Whoever said *knock and it shall be opened* had Eden in mind.

We called on the link. Kit reached for my hand and squeezed it, hard, while his other hand pressed the comlink button. "Cat Christopher Bartolomeu Sinistra and Nav Athena Hera Sinistra, piloting the *Cathouse* on behalf of the Energy Board. I request permission to land."

My heart beat somewhere between my esophagus and my mouth. And don't tell me that's a physiological impossibility. I know what I felt. Given just a little more nervousness, my heart would have jumped out of my mouth and flopped around the instrument panel like a landed fish.

There was a silence from the other side, long enough for my heart to almost stop. I took a deep breath or two and told myself that if Eden didn't want us, we'd go back to Earth, or perhaps to Ultima or Proxima Thule, Eden's two water-mining colonies.

Not only was I bluffing, I knew I was bluffing. To make it elsewhere we'd need food and fuel, and a world that rejected us wouldn't be likely to hand over rations and powerpods. All that kept me from shaking was the impression of Kit's mind, warm and amused.

We could mind-talk, an ability bioengineered into pilot and navigator couples in his world and engineered into me for a completely different purpose. Most often it was much like talking in voice, only we could do it privately or over a great distance. In extreme circumstances, we could connect at a deep, deep level, but that wasn't sustainable. It didn't help preserve sanity not knowing which body went with your mind. But sometimes, like now, there was just the impression of feelings. And the feelings Kit was giving off were reassurance and amusement. Which meant he was lying.

But it would be a pity to waste his effort, so I managed a half smile in his general direction, as the voice of Eden's Dock Control crackled over the link: "The *Cathouse* is more than six weeks late. It has been entered in the roll of losses. Cat Christopher Sinistra and Nav Athena Sinistra are dead."

I registered the little shock I always felt at hearing Kit called by my surname. It was Eden's custom, though not mandatory, to have the husband take the wife's name.

"Not really," I cut in. I felt almost boneless with relief. I hate bureaucracy as much as anyone else, but not nearly as much as I hate exploding. That they were talking instead of burning us out of the sky was a very good sign. "Only late."

"You cannot be late. You only had fuel for a four-month trip. Three weeks later you'd be out of reserves and dead. You—".

"We were down on Earth," I said.

The silence didn't last long, but it gave the impression of being a very large silence. The type of silence that could envelop and swallow a whole fleet of darkships. Then the answer came, sounding like a clap of thunder announcing the beginning of a storm. "What?" the Controller asked. "You were where?"

Kit cleared his throat. I could see him reflected in the almost completely dark screens in front of him: his eyes bioengineered for piloting in total darkness looked like cat eyes, glimmering green and very wide open, in worry. His calico-colored hair seemed vivid and garish against his suddenly colorless skin. It was an accidental mutation caused by the same virus that had given him the catlike eyes, superhuman coordination, and speed of movement. Without the modifications to his eyes and hair, Kit would have been a redhead, so his skin was normally that shade of pale that can turn unhealthy-looking at the slightest disturbance. Now he looked white and grey, like spoiled milk. Even if he continued to lie at me with an amused and calm mind-projection and his voice sounded firm and clear, his face gave him away. "Nav Sinistra had radiation poisoning and we stopped on Earth for regen treatment."

"You *stopped* on Earth for *treatment?*"

I swallowed hard, to prevent having to grope for my heart somewhere on the control board. "Well, it wasn't that simple, but.yes," Kit said, "I'll be glad to tell you the whole story after we land."

"You'd better, *Cat*." He pronounced Kit's professional title as an insult. The term "pilot" had long since become "cat" in Eden. "And you'd better make it convincing. This is most irregular."

"Controller," I said, thinking it was time to add another consideration to his decision, "we must land. Kit's family is expecting us." Kit's birth family, the Denovos, were socially powerful in Eden. His sister Kath would have been a force to be reckoned with in any size society. It was a good thing she'd been born in Eden. If she had been on Earth, she'd probably now be sole supreme ruler of the whole world, a feat slightly more difficult to achieve on Eden, which had no rulers of any sort, much less supreme ones.

Another silence, and the Dock Controller's voice sounded dour as it came back. "Navigator Sinistra, if you delayed your collection run for personal reasons, you have to know that the Energy Board will fine you for the delay in supply, and all the boards will want to interview you for potential breaches of security. Also—"

"I *know*, Controller. Now, could you give us a dock number, please? Before I go crazy and just give my Cat instructions to dash at Eden in the area of the landing control station. We Earthworms are *so* temperamental."

Kit chuckled aloud, then stopped with an intake of breath. His mental impression wavered a little, allowing me to see some fear beneath the amusement.

"Dock fifty-five, but I want you to know that I shall have armed hushers ready and that you will be examined for any evidence of undue influence, and that—"

I flicked the comlink off. A sleevelike structure extruded from Eden and Kit piloted us into it, then leaned back as dock remote controls took over the navigation. His foot skimmed along the floor next to him, flicking up the lever that turned off our artificial gravity now that we were covered by Eden's. Not that keeping it on would give us double the gs, but one could interfere with the other and cause some really interesting localized gravity effects.

It wasn't until our ship settled into one of the landing bays that Kit released the seatbelt that criss-crossed his chest, and, without letting go of my hand, got up and said, "You know, you really shouldn't have taunted the controller."

I got up in turn. I knew. One of the first rules I'd been taught was never to pick on people. The second was probably to always be gracious.

I'd been born the only daughter of Good Man Milton Alexander Sinistra, one of fifty men who controlled the near-endless land and resources of Earth. My parents, my nannies, the heads of various boarding schools, the commanders of various military academies, and the psychological medtechs that ran several rest homes, sanatoriums, and mental institutions upon which Daddy Dearest had wished me, had all told me I had an aggression problem and must control my impulses.

If I had followed their instructions I wouldn't be alive now. And neither would Kit. Something Kit knew very well, which was why he put his arm around me and smiled as he shook his head.

We walked like that through two air locks, then waited while the last door cycled open, letting us see that we were in one of the cavernous, circular bays that admitted ships to Eden. An out-of-use bay, because there were no powerpod-unloading machines nearby. Instead, a large group of young men, all armed, stood in front of our ship's door, all aiming their burners directly at us.

To the left side and a little behind the young men stood two older men, a dark-haired one and a blond one.

The dark-haired one was the dock controller. He wore the grey uniform of the position, and he had that harassed, frustrated look of someone who was sure he'd been born to better things, but who found himself confined to an inglorious desk job.

The blond was something else altogether different. To begin with, he didn't wear any uniform, but a well-cut black suit consisting of something much like an Elizabethan doublet and leg-outlining pants, tailored to make the wearer look good, whether he did so when naked or not. The fabric shimmered with the dull shine of real silk and conveyed an unavoidable sense of wealth and sensuousness. The face above the suit was sharp and vaguely threatening. He looked like a young Julius Caesar—or at least a Julius Caesar from a world where people didn't lose their hair unless they chose to.

It was the blond man who spoke. His words had far more force than if they'd been spoken by a mere bureaucrat. "Cat Christopher Bartolomeu Sinistra," he said, each syllable dropped in place like an essential part of exacting machinery, "you are under arrest for treason against Eden."

QUIS CUSTODIET IPSOS CUSTODES?

"WHAT?" KIT SAID. THE GUNS IN THE HANDS OF THE young men holding them swung to point more accurately at him.

The man did not repeat himself. He smiled, urbanely. "If you'd please step down."

Kit didn't move, except to brace himself, his feet slightly farther apart, his shoulders pulled back, as if he expected a physical impact. "You can't arrest me," he said. His voice sounded more puzzled than outraged. "I'm a free citizen of Eden."

Eden, in addition to being paranoid, hated authority. It had no rules and no laws. Most of the things that police handled back on Earth were handled on Eden by custom, tradition and public opinion, or by a short blast from a burner. If they'd shot Kit—not that I wanted them to—it wouldn't have been surprising. Arresting him, on the other hand, should have been impossible.

12

But I grew up with Daddy Dearest. I knew one never argued with a loaded burner.

I clenched my hands. I'd get out of this alive. Or at least I'd try to make sure that Kit would.

"Ah," the blond man said, and managed to convey the sort of smiling concession that a person makes, on the way to doing exactly what he always wanted to do. "Indeed. Perhaps it would be more accurate to say you are taken in custody by the Energy Board, pending the resolution of charges of treason, willful endangerment of Eden's technologies and location, and leading your ward into similar crimes." He man smiled. There were teeth in that smile. *The better to eat you with.*

"My ward?" Kit said. "Do you mean *Thena*?"

When I'd first arrived in Eden, a stowaway in Kit's ship, the only way the Energy Board would allow me in was for Kit to become my guardian. Because in Eden, the only way to control or punish an individual was to make them pay blood money or reparation for violations of public peace and safety. Since blood geld obligations often extended to family and close associates, this meant that your nearest and dearest watched you and made sure you didn't get in trouble.

But back then I had no nearest or dearest in Eden— or, at the time, anywhere, really. I could only be controlled by making Kit and Kit's family responsible for me.

Now that I was married to him, and had the same relatives, surely I was no longer his ward? Only we'd never got around to cancelling the document. Which meant they could now use my action to make Kit's punishment more severe. Perhaps severe enough to kill him if I overreacted. Which meant, I couldn't react. At all. I could barely breathe. Kit and I had saved each other from near death more than once. I couldn't imagine life without him.

The blond man didn't even bother to answer the question, just inclined his head and cast me a look. I held myself so immobile my muscles hurt.

I kept quiet, too. If there had been only one gun pointed at me, I could have tried to make a grab for it. I'm genetically enhanced. When needed, I can move faster and more accurately than any natural human. One gun I could evade. I could overpower the bearer before he knew what hit him.

But forty armed men and some of them Cats by engineering? No. I could only take out one or two before the rest of them brought me down or worse, brought Kit down.

Besides, the forty young men holding the guns looked different from Eden's normal hushers. Hushers were an all-volunteer force, and most of Eden's young men served a few months or a year in it. Kit, himself, had at fourteen or fifteen. Most of them viewed it as a not-too-exacting social activity, which got rewarded with social approval for their willingness to defend Eden from an invasion that never came. Normally they looked like children at play.

Not these hushers.

Straggly and young, dressed in what could be called a uniform only because everyone wore blue, though there was no uniformity in cut or design, wearing all manner of hairstyles and adornment, they still managed to look like a military force.

It was obvious they would shoot at the least pretext. Or the least excuse. I looked into their gazes and realized they wanted to kill us, and I wondered what had been going on in Eden in our absence to change the young in that way.

I tightened my fists till my nails bit into my palms. I couldn't get any mind-words from Kit, only a sense of wariness.

"If you believe I'm a traitor—" he told the blond man and stopped.

The blond man smiled wolfishly. "Indeed. We should have eliminated you. But we had to decide quickly. Your com contact was a surprise. We thought you dead. We certainly didn't imagine you'd landed on Earth. We've not had the time to look through all possible implications of your actions and, frankly, your being who you are complicates things. You have relatives amid our most respected and prominent citizens, who might take offense and make trouble if we had shot you out of orbit."

"But—" Kit started.

"So we'll decide it now," the blond man said. "And execute you with due formality, if it's warranted. So no one can doubt it's proper."

Kit opened his mouth. Closed it. Mentally, he told me, *Don't question anything I do.*

I wondered what he meant to do. I trusted him implicitly. Kit knew the customs of the land, and was good at strategy. I prepared to follow his lead. With his speed and reflexes he could overpower any number of his accusers.

And he said, "I'm surrendering to the authority of the Energy Board," Kit said.

I had heard wrong. Either that or there was some deep planning involved. Kit didn't surrender to the authority of anyone. Then I thought I saw it. He'd get out of the ship, approach Blondie and, as the man let down his guard, take his burner. Then Kit could point the burner at Blondie's head, hold him hostage and demand a fair hearing.

I could visualize all this, as Kit came down from the ship, hands in view, held some distance from his body. It was hard stepping down from the ship like that, because the steps—two—were just a little too long for any normal legs.

Before Kit could recover, Blondie lifted his hand.

It must have been a prearranged signal. Four young men with Cat eyes detached from the ranks of Hushers and jumped Kit.

They did it so fast—what Kit called Cat speed—that to me it looked like they disappeared, only to materialize again, holding Kit down on the ground and handcuffing him behind his back.

I had the impression of movement, too fast for the eye to fully capture, an impression of Kit falling under the impact of four bodies, of his head hitting the floor. His exclamation of surprise, pain, and rage hung in the air, as though the sound hadn't had time to dissipate in the echoes of the vast room.

And then all hell broke loose. Something tugged at me, as if the feeling between Kit and me were a taut rope, binding us heart to heart.

I never thought about it. Never made a decision to attack anyone. Never even made a decision to move. Yet as soon as Kit hit the floor, I was flying through the air.

My father, in his attempts to subdue me, or perhaps to give me an outlet for that pent-up aggression that worried everyone so much, had enrolled me in various academies which taught self-defense or martial arts. When I escaped Daddy's authority I'd learned hand-to-hand dirty fighting.

But for my money, the most useful fighting moves I ever learned came from a ballet camp in Switzerland to which Dad had sent me, apparently under the delusion that dance would tame the savage beast.

I caught myself mid-air, leaping, in graceful ballet-style, over Kit and his huddled captors and straight at the blond man. The tip of my extended foot hit him mid-chest, and took him down as I landed. I grabbed the burner from his hand before he could react. I pointed it at his head.

Confusion reigned. In the middle of my beautiful leap, several hushers fired at me, and various others tried to follow me down with burner fire to my destination, only stopping short when they realized that killing me would risk killing their leader also.

None hit me.

Like Kit, I had been bioengineered for speed, and while I wasn't quite as fast as he was—while I couldn't give the impression of moving so fast I disappeared from one place and materialized in the other—I could and did move too fast for normal human eyes. And Blondie had taken the only four Cats in the group—the only four people who were faster than I—and used them to neutralize Kit.

But that many burners going off in an enclosed space will hit something. I could smell acrid smoke.

I didn't look to see where it was coming from. Hushers ran. I heard fabric beating against hard surfaces, and feet stomping and fire retardant spraying. I didn't turn.

I stared down at Blondie's eyes and saw fear and confusion. Whatever he had planned, I'd just made his plan go horribly awry. My late, unlamented father would have told him that I did that to plans.

"Nav Sinistra—" he started.

"Stop," I said. And no, I didn't care if he was right by the book. He didn't get to hurt Kit. Right be damned. Kit was mine to love and protect, the same way I was his. Besides, no one absolutely sure of his legal ground would have hurried to grab Kit without warning. I resisted a temptation to hit Blondie on the side of the head with my burner.

"Stop. I don't want to hear it." I barely looked up, keeping most of my attention trained on Blondie, but managing to convey that I was speaking to the four young Cats also. "You, let Cat Sinistra go. Now. Now, or I'll shoot this man." I pressed the burner harder against Blondie's temple as I straddled him, keeping him still.

"Dear lady," my captive said. His gaze was calm, his voice composed. "You don't mean that. You can't mean that. I know the amount of money your husband owes for the repairs to the ship you damaged last year. If you shoot me, you'll never be out of debt for the blood geld."

He'd just told the young Cats both that he was not afraid and that I was unlikely to shoot. The dirty rotten scoundrel. I'd bet he cheated at chess.

I swallowed hard. "Right," I said. "How about I shoot your feet off, then? Then your ankles. Then your knees. I'll set the burner on high so it cauterizes. No risk of dying and you can regen it. But you won't get anywhere near a medtech until you let my husband go."

I set my foot on his trachea. I could tell from

his look that he knew very well I could crush it with just a little downward pressure. Then I pointed my burner at his feet. His eyes showed worry, but he didn't give an inch. "Dear lady," he said, still in that soft tone, "what will you do then? Go back into space in the *Cathouse*? Surely there are easier ways to commit suicide."

And I realized we weren't on Earth. Fine, I knew that. But I hadn't realized how the differences between the two worlds and their populations changed my calculations. Was it possible to run and hide in Eden? Sure it was. For a while. But unlike on Earth, you could not hide forever.

Earth is much vaster and has a much larger population. People can move from one place to the other unremarked. No one would even care about their pasts in some places.

But on Eden there were a limited number of families and everyone seemed at times to be an amateur genealogist.

And then there was the limited physical space. You couldn't move *that* far away.

Kit and I couldn't just run and hide.

We couldn't assume different names and claim to be from elsewhere altogether. After a while our isolation would stick out. Besides, both of us were famous: Kit because of his first wife's death, myself for being the only Earther to come to Eden in three hundred years. Someone would spot us within a week. I could feel my jaw setting into what dad called my mulish look—possibly because the old bastard had a sense of humor. "Fine," I said. "Let my husband go, and replenish the ship, so we can leave."

Where we'd go, I didn't have the slightest idea. Earth, probably. Now there was a planet you could get lost in.

Blondie looked chagrined and sighed. "Do as she says," he said. But weirdly, there was an odd gleam of smug triumph in his eyes.

"No," Kit said, sitting up. "No." And then, hurriedly, "I submit to the judgment of Eden."

He must have hit his head much harder than I thought. I started to open my mouth to say so, but he was in my mind. *Drop it, Thena,* he mind-spoke, perfectly clear and far more forcefully than normal.

I closed my mouth, but managed the mental protest, *But—*

You're playing into their hands, he said. *Here they have to keep up appearances. They can't murder us. If they get us to take off, they can shoot us out of the sky. They'll be protecting Eden from suspected spies. No one will protest.*

You mean to let them arrest you? I asked, in disbelief. *I can't let them—*

No. I'll allow them to detain me. They can't arrest me. They don't have governmental powers. They don't have legal powers. They don't even have traditional powers to do this. I don't like this any more than you do, Thena, but trust me. My way is the best course.

TYRANNICAL AUTHORITY

"I WANT HIM TO DIE SCREAMING," I SAID. IT WASN'T for the first time.

Katherine—Kath—Denovo gave me a sideways glance, but didn't comment, because she knew I wasn't referring to her little brother, but to Blondie.

Kath had picked me up, in her family flyer, which smelled of candy and had dolls and toy flyers hidden in the crevices of the seats. Right now something was poking at my backside. I suspected it was the outstretched, burner wielding hand of a plastic figurine. I had no clue how many children Kath had, and I suspected that Kit was hazy on it.

In a culture where most gestation took place in bio wombs, which one could pay professionals to tend, I sometimes suspected the parents themselves forgot exactly how many children they had. I knew Kath's eldest, a Cat named Waldron, had just got married and started doing powerpod runs. But I suspected a couple of the toddlers that ran around the compound where Kit's whole family lived—benevolently watched over by his father, Jean—were also hers.

Kath looked nothing like Kit. This made sense, when you realized he'd been adopted in utero and was no biological relation. Of course, they both had Cat eyes, hers in dark blue. She now lowered her eyelids halfway as she drove unerringly through the confusion of traffic in Eden Center, where flyers crisscrossed at all altitudes and in every possible path.

I confess that when I'd first come to Eden, I was horrified that they had no traffic regulations at all, no beacons tracking altitude, no enforcement of any kind. Of course, how could they have those when they didn't have anything resembling authority? But still, I expected that they'd have accidents every three seconds. I'd swear that we barely escaped being smashed into about ten times on any run through Center. But it turned out accidents were very rare. Kit said it was because other people were actively trying not to hit us or be hit by us.

So, I knew this, mentally. But I couldn't make my gut believe it. Going through the chaos of Eden Center felt like it should be lethal and I had trouble nerving myself to fly it. But Kath and Kit could do it without even giving it full attention.

Kath seemed to be deep in thought, though not about driving, something that happened more or less automatically, as her hands tapped lightly on the controls as we dipped and soared. I suppose once you drive a powerpod collection ship through the explosive coils of the powertree ring, driving through Eden is child's play. "I agree with you," she said, "on his dying screaming, but perhaps it is actually impossible to strangle a man with that part of his anatomy." She gave me a sheepish look. "I don't think it has enough elasticity."

I tried to smile, but it wouldn't quite gel. I made myself clasp my knees, instead of balling my hands into fists, but I suspected my fingers were leaving marks on my knees through the fabric of my pants. "What is his name?" I asked.

"Who? The president of the Energy Board?" she asked.

"Is that who Blondie is?"

A fleeting smile, while she brought us out of the traffic, and took one of the side streets. No. One of the side *tunnels*, only it didn't look like it, because the tunnel was broad and showed neatly planted gardens and plots on either side of the road. Each of the gardens and plots would hide an entrance tunnel. Eden's houses were always dug down or into the raw rock of the asteroid, from the tunnels that served as streets. Made logical sense, in an environment where rain and leakage were no danger.

Above, the stone was masked by a convincing holographic rendition of a sky with fluffy clouds. It turned out humans reacted better to that than to being enclosed in rock. "I like *Blondie* as a name for him, though it might give the impression he'll be easy to defeat. He won't. There's poured dimatough under the patrician good looks."

"I gathered," I said drily.

"His name is Fergus Castaneda," Kath said. "And his family have been members of the Energy Board for as long as Eden has been Eden, though usually in minor positions. He's the first Castaneda to be president of the board."

I absorbed this. It made a certain sense. Perhaps his resemblance to Caesar wasn't simply external. When you ask why people do things and your only answer is "money," you miss that more people want power than money. To many people, power is an aphrodisiac that money could never be. In fact, to many, if not most people, money is a way to power, not the other way around.

"I still want him to die screaming," I said, sullenly.

"But only after he screams a long, long time," Kath agreed dreamily. She drove down the street, turned into another street, which brought us to the profuse and spacious garden that covered the Denovo compound.

This idea of gardens covering the entire plot, with the house underneath, had puzzled me when I'd first come to Eden. It shouldn't have. Underground houses have never quite taken on Earth for two reasons: first, because humans prefer natural light if they can get it; and second, because even with the most high-tech materials, it was truly impossible to make anything underground completely proof against the inevitable leaks. Construction on Earth was, ultimately, bound by the dictum that water flows downhill.

On Eden, water didn't flow anywhere unless you paid for it to flow. Everything was underground—or everything above ground, however you chose to look at it—since everyone lived inside an asteroid and sunlight could be piped in anywhere. That meant that everyone lived at various levels. There was no reason to have the house at street level. So, most people didn't. They burrowed under the plot—real estate contracts were for cubic space, not linear—and left a garden or a pasture or an orchard above.

We opened the door artfully concealed by rose bushes and went down a staircase enclosed in walls with niches, where fragrant plants grew. Entering the Denovo house involved going through a riot of smells, a symphony of perfume. Most of the time, just coming home made me feel better. Not this time.

Despite what Kit had said, about this being the safest alternative, it didn't make it a *safe* alternative. He'd never said he'd be perfectly fine. That was because he couldn't be sure, and my darling hated to lie.

It all felt wrong. I loved the Denovos, who had taken me into their family as if it were perfectly normal for one's son to bring home barely controlled human wrecking balls born and raised on Earth. But they were Kit's family before they were mine. And he should be here with me, when I came back. The fact he wasn't was at least partly my fault.

At the end of the entrance tunnel opened a small hall, which led into a much larger hall. The Denovo compound didn't look like any normal house on Earth. It was closer to a public park—with an even carpet of grass underneath, plants everywhere, and even the occasional statue. Though they had sofas and chairs in other rooms, in the public areas people mostly flopped down to the grass floor, children and adults alike, reclining to eat or to work. Little robots I called "turtles" roamed around picking any object left out of place and cleaning it or returning it to where it was supposed to be.

I was never sure that what was underfoot was really grass. It felt like it: cool, soft and alive. I was sure on the alive part, because Kit had once made a comment that any crumbs dropped or even skin cells sloughed off would get eaten by the floor covering. But, unlike grass, the carpet didn't seem to grow on dirt, but on some cushiony surface that gave and adapted under one's weight. And it never needed mowing.

This time, the entire Denovo family, or at least all the adults, were crammed into the tiny front hall to receive me. There was Kit's eldest sister, Anne, old enough to be his mother, who was a navigator by bioengineering and profession. Next to her was her husband, Bruno, a tall, olive-skinned man, with dark brown Cat eyes.

Then there was Kath's Navigator Eber, a man so well grounded, so thoroughly calm and self-contained that people often wondered—sometimes even in Kath's hearing—why she didn't roll over him and completely silence him. But she didn't. I'd known them now long enough to realize there was a fund of extreme stubbornness in Eber that was a perfect match for Kath's more ebullient forcefulness.

Standing just behind him were Kit's parents. Jean—his name was pronounced Je-ahn in the ancient French way and routinely butchered by strangers—looked a lot like an older, male version of Kath, but was one of those people who always gave the impression of being quietly sure of themselves. So quietly sure that they didn't need to project outward, or make a big fuss out of anything.

Not implying that he was smug. He wasn't. He was attentive to his surroundings and to his family and always sure of the course to follow. I'd been shocked when Kit had first told me that Jean had raised most of the children on his own, while his wife did water runs to Proxima and Ultima Thule. *Most*, because I understood that early on they'd simply taken Anne on their runs for powerpods. It was only after they had retired that Jean had decided to stay behind and make a stable home for the children and grandchildren while his wife preferred to make the long lonely-but-lucrative runs for the Water Board, after her vision had aged enough to make powerpod collecting runs to Earth orbit dangerous.

In retrospect, it was silly to be surprised that a man chose to or could be the care taker for his children. The biowombs had freed men too, because when women could do whatever they wanted to, so could men. Most women still raised their children, but no stigma attached to the husband choosing to do it.

Tania, Kit's mother, would have made an awful care-taking parent. She loved her children, even Kit, the non-biological one. But I suspected her attempts at keeping house and organizing family would have fallen apart between boredom with her task and finding something more interesting to do.

That she looked subdued and worried right then was a bad sign. That all the Denovos were at home was another very bad sign. In a household of Cats and Navs, who traveled for a living, this was a very rare occurrence, made more ominous as Waldron, Kath's eldest, came from the inner room, bringing his wife, Jennie, with him. If even the younger generation was home, something was wrong, beyond what had just happened to Kit.

I stared around myself at a circle of eyes, half of them normal, the other half feline-looking. They all shimmered with tears.

Suddenly Anne grabbed my arm and hugged me. Next thing I knew I was being hugged by the entire family.

I started to explain that this was all my fault. It would never have occurred to Kit to ask for Earth help, if I hadn't got myself stupidly burned. It would never have occurred to anyone in the Energy Board to arrest him if he hadn't stopped on Earth to get me help. So the trouble Kit was in was all my fault, and I hadn't even managed to prevent his being arrested.

"Shush, now," Jean said. "That's nonsense, and I suspect you know it as well as we do. First of all, I think they have . . . other motives, and could have found another excuse, or done the thing in a way that would have been far more . . . permanent. As it is, they've practically played into our hands. Judicial murder is the most difficult form of murder on Eden. It has constraints, while other forms of murder don't."

I looked around at a circle of nodding people, and started to wonder if insanity ran in my family-in-law.

MORE THAN ONE WAY
TO SQUEEZE A BUG

SERIOUS TALK WAITED UNTIL WE FINISHED DINNER. I didn't notice what we ate. We sat in the living room, on the biocarpet, and the little turtle robots were going around picking up our plates and silverware. The chit-chat that had accompanied dinner fell silent.

Jennie, Waldron's wife, took all the children to the back and left them there.

Then everyone scooted closer, until we were all drawn up in a circle. In the year I'd known Kit's family, I'd never seen them do this. Of course, it was completely possible they had done this behind my back and away from me while I was still a relative stranger.

They seemed to be waiting for me to speak, so I did. I told them about landing and what had happened. Eyebrows went up here and there through the narrative and when I finished with, "I have no idea what Kit meant by saying he would be safer if

29

I left him there. We could be on our way to Earth right now. We could—"

"No." It was Jean and he was final. Not loud. Just definite. "You couldn't have taken off again after landing. They would have shot you out of the sky. In fact, I suspect the docking operator must have had your best interests in mind when he called those hushers."

"Uh?" Clear as mud. Of course, anyone who calls a group of armed men to subdue you clearly has your best interests at heart!

Jean smiled. "No, Kit was right; the safest thing for him is for us to get a lot of people in Eden to demand a public examination of the facts." He frowned. "That shouldn't be difficult if all of us talk to our friends, who will talk to their friends. And then, if we can get him examined by Doc Bartolomeu, I mean under hypnotics—"

"We can't," I said. "Then the truth will come out. I mean . . . who Kit really *is*." I looked around the room and hesitated because I wasn't sure how many of them knew the secret of Kit's true origins. His parents knew. His sisters almost certainly. But his in-laws? His nephew? Did they know?

They knew Kit had tainted origins, of course. Everyone on Eden did. When I'd come to Eden I'd been told he was a child of tragedy, that the reason he'd needed to be adopted in utero was that his father had killed his mother and then himself. But the truth was far more complex and damning than that and not something he wished widely known.

The truth was that Kit's biological "father" and Doctor Bartolomeu, one of the family's oldest friends, and the man who'd decanted Kit from the biowomb, had both been Mules, two of the bioengineered rulers whose ruthless despotism over Earth was said to have turned a lot of it into a wasteland and oppressed the natural-born population into revolt. The same rulers who weren't supposed to be able to reproduce themselves.

Doctor Bartolomeu and Kit's "father" had been part of the planners of the exodus from Earth just ahead of the riots that supposedly killed most of their kind and anyone with even a suspicion of bioengineering. And in planning it, they had chosen to leave behind those Mules who had been created for and grown to enjoy less savory avocations: assassins and murderers, rapists and arsonists.

Created as weapons of terror, some of those Mules left behind had been very powerful under the Mule regimen on Earth, but their past and their bioengineering tainted them, so that Doc Bartolomeu and Jarl, Kit's biological "father," had thought them not fit for the confined society of an interstellar ship, certainly not while humans were on board. Among those left behind had been my...*ancestor*. Not that he was that. I was his female clone—but that is a very long story.

Their decision had probably saved many lives. One shouldn't pen together wolves and sheep. But it had created great resentment, not just among those left behind, but among the Mules who had made it onto the ship with their bioengineered servants.

Jarl and Doc Bartolomeu had chosen humanity over their own kind, and they found that they had to do it yet again. Driven by the resentment of their own kind towards them, they had chosen to stay in Eden with the bioimproved, non Mule humans. Where Jarl never quite fit in.

As far as the public knew, Kit was a human, created to be as much as possible like the Mule, Jarl, the husband of Kit's supposed mother without sharing any genetics. This was not true, and Kit knew it, had known it for years. He was Jarl's clone.

That two Mules isolated on Eden had even managed to clone one of them was a miracle. Mules had been designed by humans who wanted them to be superior, capable of doing things that humans didn't do well, *and* incapable of reproducing either the normal way or by cloning. Doc Bartolomeu, himself, was a Mule. But few, if any, remembered it. Jarl could not hide it. In his time, on Earth, he'd been a genius as famous as Einstein had been before him. He'd been a genius even among Mules, and his face had been plastered on everything from posters to clothing.

His friend, Bartolomeu Dias, less well-known, had hidden it. Eden didn't know what Doc Bartolomeu was. The few who'd known it had died. Their descendants had forgotten. His freakish longevity was attributed to random good genes, plus I suspected no one knew how old he was—only "very old" and "a fixture of Eden." Jarl had wanted to give his clone a similar chance to be anonymous, a human among humans.

But Kit knew. And worse than that, Kit knew about Doctor Bartolomeu. The first didn't worry him. My husband was sufficient in himself, and didn't care all that much what people thought of him, provided that his family didn't mind. He regretted that his true origins had blighted his first marriage and led directly to his first wife's suicide, and yet, he was not ashamed of being what he was.

Still, after his wife died in space, he'd lived under

suspicion of murder for two years rather than submit to questioning under hypnotics. Because there were no other witnesses, he had no other way to exonerate himself. And though—as he'd explained to me—he didn't mind its being known what he really was—he was afraid that his origins, if revealed under hypnotics as the cause of Jane's suicide, would expose Doc or blight his family's standing. And so he'd kept quiet. If he submitted to questioning now...

I finished lamely, "It will come out about his past and who he is..."

Jean shook his head. "In this case, Kit's origins aren't at the root of events, as they were with his first wife's death. Doc Bartolomeu will ask the questions and keep them within bounds. Our family can demand it, since he's our family physician, well acquainted with Kit's physiology and Kit is dreadfully allergic to most hypnotics."

"What?"

"Oh, he is," Jean said. He gave me a tight smile. "It's not a cover-up, though it would be convenient. No cover-up is as convenient as one that's true. We know about it, because the drugs are in the same class as drugs used to test reflexes in final Cat tests. Since the Energy Board must risk a rookie, his Nav, and a ship on a run to the powertrees just to test him, they give Cats hypnotics to make the run more difficult, and they put them in virtus. Kit gets respiratory issues and an upset stomach from the hypnotics. He passed, but that was an awfully messy virtus closet, and the test had to be carefully timed to give him the antidote before hypnotics caused serious damage."

"Oh," I said. "But if it's not safe—"

"Perfectly safe, provided it's ended in time. And it gives us an opportunity to request Doctor Bartolomeu," Jean said, "who will be careful in administering it."

"But what will a hypnotics test prove?" I asked. "I mean, you can't rig it so Kit says he didn't land on Earth after all. He did. I was there. We figured there was no way to hide it, so we might as well tell the truth, from orbit."

"You did the right thing," Kath said. "At any rate, I suspect they would have arrested him on suspicion, considering how late you were. That you confessed it up front establishes that you didn't have any ill intent towards Eden or its people."

"But then what can Kit say under hypnotics that will exonerate him?"

"Why," Tania said, "the only thing he can say. That he has no ill intent towards Eden and her people."

"But that's obvious," I said. "Why would he have any? And what difference does it make?"

"All the difference in the world."

"I still say," I said, darkly, "that this is all very confusing. It would be much easier to storm the cursed place, get Kit out and take off to space. I know places on Earth we could land. I know his eyes make him illegal, but my friends didn't care and I—"

Anne's hand rested on my arm, a light touch that managed to be both sympathetic and restraining. "Thena, on Earth he'd always be out of place. Here... don't give up yet. Remember there's more than one way to juice a bug." This was a proverb in Eden, relating to the fact that their equivalent of coffee was bug juice, actually made from the droppings of specially engineered bugs.

But I didn't want to juice bugs. I didn't even drink the stuff. I wanted my husband back.

"Trust us," Kath said. "We can get you through this, and get Kit released."

"Whether we can get Eden back too, that's something else again," Bruno said darkly, as his eyebrows came down over his eyes. To my non-comprehending look, he added, "There are some people very invested in keeping powerpods scarce and a state of emergency going on."

"State of emergency?"

"Sure," Bruno said. "When the Earthwo—" He stopped, midway through the derogatory term. "Earthers started hunting darkships—"

"That was my fault," I said. "My father was trying to recover me. He . . ."

"So? It hasn't stopped since you were caught. At least not to our knowledge. Going to the energy trees remains a huge risk, and the Energy Board maintains it's too risky to take more than one trip per couple, per year, because we're losing so many of our pilots before new ones are trained, and besides they need to take time to repair ships. They've convinced everyone—well, almost everyone—that it is somehow your fault. And Kit's fault for bringing you here." He made a face as though he'd like to spit. "So, we're all on rationed power, which means the Energy Board gets to pick who gets power and who doesn't. They can dictate that someone gets their power shut down, for *using too much*. And if you ask questions, you're suddenly using too much, and find yourself cut off. No one has died yet, but people have had to hide out with relatives and friends. It's only a matter of time, though."

"But..." I tried to reconcile this with the Edenites I knew, who were always ready to fight for the freedom to do as they pleased. Kit had once told me that if they had traffic-tower access controls installed in their ships, Edenites would just rip them out. That sounded right. This didn't. Letting people tell them when they could—or couldn't—have power didn't seem like them. "Won't people rebel against..."

"How can they rebel against scarcity? Scarcity so terrible that of course supply has to be controlled. And not just by how much you're willing to pay," Bruno said. "Because no one wants their less well-off neighbors to freeze in the dark. At least that's how it is being sold. The truth is they have switches and they can control who gets what." He looked vaguely ill. "It's the problem of a centralized supply system."

"But why is it centralized?" I asked. "Is the Energy Board elected?"

"No," Kath said. "They're not a government. We don't have elections. Jean, how did the people in the boards come to the boards?"

He frowned. "Don't remember reading about it. I think... Well, I assume they owned the ships? Somehow? It was long ago, and it worked, so it didn't seem important."

"They never tried to control Eden with energy rationing before," Anne said. "But of course, they never had an excuse before."

"And of course no one complains," Eber said. "Not even us. Because if we do, then we'll come home one day and find our home has been without energy, which drives air and heating as well, and Jean and the kiddies are all dead. No. We don't complain. Mind you, they haven't cut energy to anyone to that extent, but there have been instances of people left in the dark and without heating, with only enough power for air recycling for hours."

"And I think," Jean said, "that this is why they wanted to get rid of Kit. It's a minor miracle they didn't blast you out of orbit, and I say our family owes that docking controller a debt of gratitude."

He shook his head at what must have been my utterly blank look. "Don't you see, Thena? They've somehow figured out what Kit is. They're afraid Kit will be able to understand what we have of Jarl's writing, and be able to complete Jarl's last project—the creation of a new cluster of energy trees, and our own powerpods. That would put an end to Castaneda's power. Not immediately, but inevitably." He made a face. "Though why they think Kit can understand it . . . We're not primitive, surely they know that clones do not have the memories of the original?"

The word "clones" dropped unremarked and no surprise showed in any of the faces around me. I know. I looked. Which meant they knew what Kit was. But his family would never talk. Certainly not to Castaneda and his ilk. They had accepted Kit as their own, as if he were their genetic relative. I felt at once vaguely envious and so moved I had to swallow so as not to cry. Kit's kind—and mine—didn't have families. Having one even at a remove was more of a miracle than I ever expected.

"I think perhaps his late wife told someone," Jean said in the disconcerting way the Denovos had of answering questions I didn't ask. Of course, they were mind-readers, but their ability was supposedly restricted to their partners. I decided either I was glass-fronted or our minds worked remarkably alike. "Because a lot of people seem to know what he really is. People who shouldn't. Mind you, it's not as...certain as his confessing it under hypnotics would make it, and most people will refrain from acting on it unless they can be really sure. Because, it's such a shocking idea. Of course, as your...when you two don't have children, it will be seen as a confirmation of rumors, but it will be slow and over years, and by then there is no reason you two can't immigrate to one of the Thules before it's noticeable."

"There is no reason our marriage won't have children," I said. This time confusion showed in their faces.

Jean looked down and said, "No, look, Thena, see..." looking much like a man who finds himself forced to explain the facts of life to an innocent female.

"No, listen. Of course, humans and Mules can't reproduce." It was part of making sure they were *supermen, but not supermen who could take over*. Which was why the Mules were all male, and, for double sure, all supposedly incapable of being cloned. Though that second part had been broached both on Earth and on Eden.

I explained it to the Denovos, my voice shaking, Earth had enormous resources and some of Jarl's writing. They had scientists, both human and Mule scientists they could conscript. And twenty years after Jarl had left, some of those Mules he'd left behind had figured out how to clone themselves.

Being the kind of people they'd been created to be— not exactly the most empathetic creatures on Earth or anywhere else—they'd used this not for reproduction, but as an endless source of new replacement bodies when old ones aged beyond their prime, transplanting the brain into a new body about every fifty years, while keeping up the pretense of dynastic succession. And then the Mules, having ascended through the power ladder during the turmoils—and now posing as Good Men of an Earth in which genetic engineering was punishable with death—had labored for three hundred years or so, in secret, to create a modified clone of one of them: a female. Me.

I told Kit's family all this, as clearly and succinctly as I could, aware they'd probably think I was insane, but not knowing how to prove a discovery that I hadn't wanted to make, and which I would still dearly love to deny. I didn't want to think that I was that much like the bastard who'd called himself my father. And I didn't want to know I'd been created to be the queen bee of a new race. A race that thought itself superior to simple homo sapiens.

"I didn't want to believe it either," I said, "but . . . in the fight with my . . . with Milton Alexander Sinistra, he left little doubt I'd been created as a brood mare for the Mules."

Jean nodded. He looked resigned. "Doc Bartolomeu suspected it. He said you had to be Sinistra's . . . modified clone, unless you were a human designed to look like Sinistra, and he said that your fath—uh . . . Good Man Sinistra was not the kind to indulge in such a thing in a fit of sentimentality. And besides . . ." He shrugged. "Well, he thought it was possible. He said Jarl worked on that just before he died, even with Eden's more limited resources. On his own. And he and Jarl had come to see it was possible. He said there were loopholes the creators couldn't have seen. Their science wasn't that advanced."

I licked my lips. "My...uh...father recognized Kit for Jarl's clone, and this delusion that knowledge as well as genius is inherited must be very widespread, because he tried to make Kit read notes that Jarl left behind."

"There are notes Jarl left behind on Earth?" Jean asked. "Still available?"

"Oh, yes. They've been working off them for centuries."

"Good," Jean said. "I must call Doc Bartolomeu and tell him this. He has always said that the notes Jarl left *here*, on how to seed powerpods, would be far better understandable, if Jarl hadn't assumed he'd always be around to remember all the research he'd done on Earth. Without that, the research he did here was like...half of a jigsaw puzzle, with the important pieces missing. It's as though we've got a lot of black fur, but we don't know if it's the rug or the cat's tail. With those notes on Earth...Yes, I can see how we'll be able to spring Kit."

He got up to go call Doctor Bartolomeu Dias in private. Which was when I knew for sure that my in-laws were insane. What Jarl's notes could have to do with setting Kit free, I'd never understand. Of course they had to do with restoring power to Eden, eventually, depending on how long the powertrees took to grow, which was a matter out of the understanding of anyone alive or dead—except for Jarl. But what did that have to do with Kit and with Blondie's power play?

Kath got up too, and then Waldron and Jennie. Jennie smoothed her form-fitted dress and said, "I shall get on the buzzer and start with my family, spreading the idea that Kit owes it to Eden to answer questions under hypnotics, instead of just being secretly disciplined by the Energy Board. Since the board has talked about what suspicious characters Kit and Thena are, they should allow the public to judge in how much danger they placed Eden. After all"—she gave a crafty smile—"he was on Earth. The first one of us in three hundred years. Who knows what they told him or what he told them. Eden has to know to be prepared. It wouldn't be right for the Energy Board to do away with him." She smiled at me. "It will work. By tomorrow morning, everyone will assume that of course Kit will be interrogated in the Justice building, under hypnotics."

"That quickly?" I asked, my voice sounding odd.

"Oh yes," Jennie said. "Even not counting on Kath's powerful gossip network, I have nine gossiping sisters."

"And a mother," Waldron said, rolling his eyes, "who is a...uh...social power." He ducked from Jennie's playfully aimed slap, then gave her his hand, and they walked off.

"And we should tell Zen. If they attacked Kit, they might—" Anne said, as though speaking to herself.

"Who is Zen?" I asked.

"What?" Anne looked at me. "Oh, she's...a family friend. Recently widowed." Anne blushed. I wondered why, but I wondered about something else more.

"But why would they attack her, if they attacked Kit? Why—"

"Oh, there's no reason," Anne said, patting my arm. "I'm probably being very foolish."

I remained totally in the dark at what means they'd

use to make the Energy Board grant them a hearing or even make public opinion think they should. Surely gossip alone couldn't accomplish it?

It was true that the Energy Board didn't have the power to impose the death penalty on anyone. If they did, it would be murder, and they could be sued for blood geld or initiate a neverending chain of feuds and revenge. One even the mighty Energy Board wouldn't be immune from.

On the other hand, if the Energy Board could cut the supply of energy to anyone they wanted, and if they were willing to use that force to shut off all protests against their authority, what did their right or lack thereof mean?

Rights only exist in the abstract. That was something the old Usaians didn't seem to get with all their idea of natural rights. Or perhaps they did, since they'd made it a religious belief and therefore immune to questioning by reason.

Rights only existed if the group was willing to recognize them. And they rarely remained the same around any government. Government—any government—is simply an entity that can impose its will on the population by means of force. Whether that government is a monarchy as most of those in Earth's past were, an oligarchy as the regime of the Good Men, a democracy or a democratic republic, no matter what the system of voting—one man one vote or pay in, situational, sacrificial or negotiated—whether the government existed by consent of the governed or imposed from above, whether for the good of all or the good of a few, government meant only one thing—force.

Through police or army or other means, government

could impose its will on the rest of the people. Done judiciously and when needed, or wholesale and continuously and with intrusive caprice, didn't matter. Without force behind it, government would be only a small group of people with very strong opinions. The kind of people that populate any faculty lounge or philosophy club.

Eden had no army and no police. Each individual was supposed to defend himself and his community. The hushers were at best a defensive force against a farfetched threat of invasion by Earth.

But since the Energy Board had got hold of the lever of rationing power and stood on their willingness to use it for political purposes, they had the force they needed to move Eden. Exactly where the board wanted it.

Eden had acquired a government. And it looked to be a dictatorship or, at best, an oligarchy.

UNREASONABLE SEARCH

IF THIS KEPT UP MUCH LONGER, I WAS GOING TO happen to someone.

My night hadn't been easy. Nor the day after, nor the next night. Sleep was never easy when Kit was absent. This time it had been disturbed by tormented dreams and sudden waking-up, believing I was still on Earth and Kit was still imprisoned at my father's mercy, in the dungeon known as Never-Never. So called because once you entered it—guilty or not—release was delayed to that mythic time.

Waking up didn't make things any better, either. We were—instead—caught in a trap in a place we'd considered home; separated and threatened in a world that *should* be safe.

And then on the second morning, when the hearing was actually set to happen, Kath took forever to get me to the Judicial Center. This was a problem because mine and Kit's flyer was still parked at the arrival area, and there was no adult except Kath left in the Denovo compound. And Kath, sipping her bug juice, acted perfectly serene and completely in control. And relaxed. Way too relaxed. "Oh, they wanted to go early," she said about the rest of the family, "to make sure that Kit is all right before the hypnotics and that they don't give him too large a dose."

"Wouldn't Doc Bartolomeu know that?" I asked.

She smiled, her best renaissance Madonna smile. "Yes, but you know my parents."

Yes, I knew her parents. But there was absolutely no reason that Anne, her husband, and for that matter every other adult would have gone too, unless they weren't sure what would happen. And there was no reason for them to leave without me.

A young neighbor had come in to watch the children and had taken them to one of the back rooms, from which a vague murmur of voices reached us. But other than that, the compound was eerily silent and had that empty feeling that houses get when almost everyone is out. It spooked me. I'd never seen this home this quiet. The Denovos were a boisterous clan and the public areas normally jumped with an intersecting madness of competing personal trajectories.

I sat across from Kath, refused the offer of bug juice—I didn't like it anyway—refused the offer of the hot chocolate that Doc Bartolomeu had sent over. And I fumed. After a while, I said, "Kath, look, you don't need to come. I'll drive myself. I'll just take your flyer."

Perhaps it was the threat of my less-than-experienced hands taking her flyer through the insane traffic of

Eden Center that woke her up. She looked startled. "Oh, no, no, no," she said, "I'll take you."

And like that, she turned around, left her cup on the ground where the cleaning robots would pick it up, and hurried to the door, with me trailing behind.

Of course, by the time we arrived, it was two minutes to the start of Kit's examination, and every possible parking space in the Judicial Center had been taken up. We had to circle for ten minutes before we found a narrow and possibly illegal space, where Kath wedged her flyer, after asking me to get out so I wouldn't need to open the door once we were parked. Which was a good thing as getting out once she was between two flyers would have required me to become one with an orange flyer next to us.

We hurried up the stairs to the Judicial Center proper. No, the name made no sense, since technically it was neither. I didn't understand how it could be a judicial anything since there were no laws on Eden.

And as for Center...look, justice on Eden could take place anywhere. Probably the most common way of resolving what would have been some sort of litigation on Earth were duels. Most of these duels weren't even to the death, and many of them might involve nothing more serious than fisticuffs.

However, there was a notion of justice. For instance, certain customs determined whether society at large regarded a death as something to be punished, something to be praised, or various shades in between. Say you killed someone who had, for years, been on everyone's radar as a nuisance or worse.

If this fact were known to the entire community and if the person was so wretchedly disliked that there was no one who would avenge him, you wouldn't even be bothered over it. There was a chance, in fact, some people would thank you.

On the other hand—as was more common—if you murdered a person whose death would be regarded with relief by some and with grief by others, you would be in trouble with the person's family, his friends, and the multitude of connections who might have a reason to commit revenge murder.

But if you killed someone perceived as helpless and at your mercy, then total strangers might undertake to avenge the death. You'd find you'd become one of those "better dead" persons.

One way to circumvent this, as well as revenge for other, more or less serious crimes, was to volunteer to be examined in the Judicial Center as to your reasons and your thinking when you killed the person. Or of course to prove you hadn't done it at all.

Because interrogation was done under hypnotics, one couldn't lie, or even fudge it. I knew. I'd been interrogated once.

If, after you presented the true case, most people agreed that the death had been forced for a pressing and necessary reason, then there would be no feud in return, as that would invite retribution from practically everyone. You might still be required to pay blood geld or other compensation to the victim's family.

And when a case was prominent enough, it would attract a lot of people. And I guess this attracted still more because it involved Earth and a potential danger to Eden.

Which probably explained why the center proper—a huge amphitheater, sitting hundreds of people—was even more crowded than the parking lot. There were people seated in every one of the seats—and squeezed two to a seat, here and there—and there were people seated in the aisles that led down to the front and stage area where Kit sat and where Doc Bartolomeu hovered over him.

Walking down the aisle was impossible. Making our way to a seat was impossible. The only places we could sit were on a path near the door. It would be a complete violation of fire safety rules, if Eden had ever had fire safety rules.

As we came in, I heard Kit's voice, sounding oddly distant and wavery, boom over the amplifying system, "—to get her treatment or to give her the coup de grace. And I couldn't."

I could see the backs of the rest of Kit's family sitting in the front row, within his field of vision. Would Kit be upset at not seeing me there? I felt Kath's hand on my arm, pulling me down and I understood. Kit's family thought I would get upset and then I would get dangerous.

It took me all of a second to realize that was indeed likely, and considerably longer to convince myself that inflicting some pain on the population of Eden at large, and the members of the Energy Board in particular, would be a bad idea.

This was made harder by taking a look at my husband—or rather, at his amplified image projected on a screen behind him, I guess so people could judge his expression for themselves. His skin had gone a shade of pasty grey and his specialized inner eyelids had closed halfway. Those eyelids were similar to those of certain cat, bird, and reptile species, whose eyes were likely to be damaged by light that wouldn't hurt others.

We were in normal light and therefore Kit had his light-abating contact lenses in. He always did when not in semi-dark. Which meant there was only one reason for his nictating eyelids to show, same as in a real cat, on Earth: he was ill.

I started to get up, to take a step forward, even though walking straight ahead meant walking through the spectators row upon row ahead of us. But Kath grabbed my arm again, hard, and more or less shoved me down. Her lips formed "no," but her eyes looked amused. And though it annoyed me, it also made me feel better, because Kath would never look amused if Kit were in any true danger.

As I sat down, I became aware of what Doc was asking Kit. "...endanger Eden?"

And wondered if he had asked Kit if Kit had willfully endangered Eden. Because I knew the answer to that, and saying, in front of all, that he hadn't even thought of Eden wouldn't be likely to turn the tide in Kit's favor.

Kit seemed to struggle with the answer or struggle not to give the answer, which I knew was impossible. Except that people who'd never been under hypnotics wouldn't know that and his struggling not to speak would make them think he had something to hide. My hands clenched on my lap.

And then Doc Bartolomeu rushed over with a sickness bag and it was obvious Kit was vomiting. Which accorded with what his family had said. And gave him perfect cover for his expression—if he needed to cover. I didn't know. There are things even an intermittently telepathic married couple won't know about each other.

Afterwards, he wiped his lips to the back of his hand, and said, "There was no danger to Eden. I erased all data and disabled the alarms and the responders that tell us when Eden is near. I did it in a way that would take them decades to reconstruct."

"How could you know what must be done?" Doctor Bartolomeu asked.

"I had talked to my wife about the technology of Earth for over a year," he said. "I knew."

The interrogation continued. How he'd managed to get aid for me. I could hear both Kit and Doctor Bartolomeu, a small, olive-skinned man whose wrinkled face and interested eyes made him look like an ancient gnome out of a fairytale, skirting anything that might give away my true nature, and the fact that I was the only female Mule ever. I hoped it was not that obvious to the rest of the audience that there were vast parts of events being edged around and avoided.

The most dangerous part was when the doctor asked Kit how he'd been interrogated, and about what. Kit mentioned they had given him the writings of Jarl Ingemar to read.

The sudden, absolute hush that fell over the amphitheater—a silence so complete that I was sure everyone would be able to hear my frantic heartbeat— told me more than I wanted to know. Everyone must have heard that Kit was a Mule, Jarl's clone. And they'd think someone on Earth knew it. Why would they give Kit Jarl's writings unless they suspected him of the same capacities—of being Jarl's clone?

Doctor Bartolomeu asked Kit if he had, then, had

any idea why Earth would do this, thereby giving Kit the option of answering about what he had known at the time, which had been close to nothing. At the time, Kit had known himself to be a Mule, but of course he hadn't known that my so-called father was also a Mule, one of the original ones who'd known Jarl personally and therefore identified Kit on sight. So Kit had not had the slightest notion why he had been given Jarl's writings or why he was being interrogated about them.

Kit coughed. His face looked swollen and his breathing was labored. He shook his head and shrugged. "I assume," he said, "that on Earth they think Jarl passed his work onto the people of Eden in such a way that every one of us learns the full complement of Jarl's biological math in elementary school." He shrugged, gave an apologetic look. "Instead of most of us, like myself, not being able to understand his work even if someone spent weeks trying to teach it to us after full training in the matter. I guess Earthworms think we're all geniuses? It's probably all that explains my wife marrying me."

His expression and voice were so embarrassed and confused that there were a few chuckles in the audience. I unclenched my hands a fraction. Getting people to laugh with you is a good step towards their not killing you.

"Of course, I could tell them nothing, no matter how aggressive an interrogation technique they used."

"Did they use aggressive interrogation techniques?"

"Yes."

"Hypnotics?"

"Yes." Kit said, and the setting of his jaw, the

jutting-out of his chin, told me what I didn't want to know. That he'd had a similar reaction to the drugs, and that he'd barely survived it. And that, I thought, with a shudder, probably only because the interrogators had realized what was happening and wanted him to survive.

"Sleep deprivation and discomfort?"

"Yes."

"Pain?"

My husband's eyes swept the amphitheater, and I realized he was looking for me. I didn't know why—whether because the answer would hurt his pride and he needed my support, or because he was afraid how I'd react. He didn't find me, and his features flickered, in the split second between question and answer, between stubborn pride and resignation. "Yes." He seemed to look at the ceiling afterwards. Did he relax a little when there was no sound of my erupting?

"And yet you told them nothing?"

"There was nothing I could tell them," Kit said.

"Why not?"

"I didn't understand those equations. It was like ... being asked to translate a lost language. Biology isn't my speciality any more than linguistics is. I'm a vacuum-ship-pusher and fairly useless at anything else."

Other questions followed a trailing multitude of them, clarifying various details, but always, always, avoiding the central questions of what Kit was, what I was, and why Earth was so interested in us.

Kit vomited many times during this. His skin started to shine with sweat, and he became—if possible—paler, till he looked like he was dead except for still moving. His breathing sounded very loud in the amphitheater.

Doctor Bartolomeu periodically looked at Kit through something that resembled a large magnifying lens, but which I knew was in fact a computer that picked up and analyzed various inputs, from the way the patient looked to his heartbeat, blood pressure, temperature, and other vital signs.

After an hour, the doctor turned towards the audience and said, "I will now give Cat Sinistra the antihistamine and antidote. His allergic reactions to the hypnotics are such that, should we take any longer, we risk killing him."

There was a faint murmur, but no real protests, and the doctor injected Kit with a succession of colored injectors. Then while Kit covered his face and shook, probably in reaction to whatever the compounds were doing to him, the doctor turned to the audience. "As you can see, the accused neither willfully nor accidentally endangered Eden."

"But he didn't follow instructions!" a voice said, from the audience. "They are supposed to follow instructions and kill themselves and destroy the ship to avoid Eden being discovered. My son—" The voice cut on something like a sob.

I cringed. There would be a lot of anger about that. A lot of Cats and Navs had committed suicide to avoid revealing secrets. Their families would resent those who survived, anyway, but they would resent us worst of all, since we'd violated orders to survive.

"For the average Cat and Nav, suicide might be best," Doc Bartolomeu said. "Sorry, but with no knowledge of Earth, and considering that gen mod brings on the death penalty there, the chances of a gene-modified human being captured and emerging again, unscathed, are nearly none. And there is no reason to risk discovery—no matter how small the risk—if the result will be death to Cat and Nav anyway. But given the special circumstances, and the ability of Nav Sinistra to extricate her husband from prison and get out of the world, surely you'll admit theirs was a rational decision. There existed at least a chance, if not a good chance, that both could survive."

They weren't willing to admit any such thing, and there was much discussion back and forth. Some people said we should still be executed, or at least Kit should.

"They lived while other people died," one of these people said. "They are as guilty of murder as if they had killed those people themselves."

Kath shot up. She stood before I was aware of it. Incongruously, she wore a very feminine dress, a few scraps of fabric twisted in a way that made her look very young and innocent. But Eden is a small enough community, as I've said. Everyone knows everyone else, at least by reputation. You could hear the collective drawing of breath as people recognized her. And a deeper drawing of breath as she put her hands on her hips. "Stupid," she said. And I sensed her sneering comment applied not only to the person who'd just spoken but to everyone else who had murmured assent. I wondered if those people would all drop dead of asphyxiation, since I couldn't hear anyone exhaling. "Who spoke?" she asked, her voice full of belligerence.

A man stood, across the amphitheater. He was a short man, with blond hair running to grey and, as the camera pickup swung to get him on the screen behind

Kit, I realized he had Cat eyes in pale green. From his age, he was a retired Cat, which probably meant his children were Cats or Navs, since the occupations were normally inherited in the sense that very well paid Cats and Navs could afford the prohibitive price of genetically enhancing their children and therefore assure their future too. Which meant that there was a good chance he'd lost family to Earth's raids. I didn't think we could blame his tightly compressed lips and his flinty expression on the fact he looked somewhat like Castaneda. "I did, Cat Denovo," he said, firmly, looking up in Kath's direction.

"Well," Kath said. "Then you're barely competent enough to stand and talk, much less to have flown a ship, as I presume you have." Her hands had moved from her hips to ball at her side.

"Cat Denovo, if you weren't distraught I'd challenge you to a duel for those words."

"Oh, please," Kath said, in the tone that implied she would like nothing better than a duel. "I don't fight the mentally handicapped. As for my being distraught, at least it doesn't make me stupid."

"Cat—"

"No. Tell me in what way my brother is responsible for any of those deaths."

For the first time the man looked like he was on uncertain ground. "Well, he survived and they—"

"You can keep repeating that all you want to. The only people who assume that because two things happened together one must have caused the other, are animals and infants. Which one are you?"

"You have no right to insult me."

"I am not insulting you. Just pointing out your

mental deficiency. You accused my brother and my sister-in-law of having committed murder. How? If they had died, how would that have saved the lives of all our friends and relatives who died?"

"What?" the man said. "It wouldn't. But they had no right to survive where others died."

"No? How not?"

"Because there are rules."

Kath chuckled dismissively. "Cat . . . Verre, is it not? Are your eyes still good enough to pilot a ship?"

"I don't see where that's any of your business."

"No? Well, at your age, I suspect they're not any more efficient then standard issue eyes. I suggest you have them replaced, and then relocate to Earth."

"What?"

"Your only rationale for why my brother committed some sort of crime is that he refused to die in obedience to *rules*," she pronounced the word as though it were obscene. "That devotion to external, arbitrary imposition is better fitting an Earthworm than an Edenite. You, sir, don't deserve to live here." She must have seen something in her opponent's eyes, as the camera swung around to pick him up again, because she said, "I'll meet you any day, any time, with any weapon. But you'll have to be the one to force it on me, because my reflexes are obviously better than yours. I'm younger. I won't have it said that I took advantage of you."

"Sir," Verre said, turning around towards the podium area and Doc Bartolomeu. "Doctor Dias, you are running these proceedings. Would you tell Cat Denovo she can't simply insult people to get her way?"

"Cat Verre," Doc Bartolomeu said, "she didn't simply insult you. She demolished your argument.

You seem to believe that rules must be obeyed even when they endanger survival of self or those under one's protection. They don't. Even the most authoritarian governments on Earth made it a point of at least pretending to respect the right of self-defense. Sir, the right to continue drawing breath—unless it forces you to commit murder to do it, and sometimes even then—is the only true unalienable right anyone has. So long as they can keep it from being alienated."

The man opened his mouth as though to speak, then closed it. I swear the snap of his lips meeting and the force of his sitting down was heard all through the amphitheater. But it might have been simply an effect of his image being on the big screen behind Kit, and his expression and movements visible to everyone.

When it became obvious Cat Verre was not going to continue, the camera turned to Kit again. It was still shaking, but almost imperceptibly. He still looked exhausted, but at least he didn't look dead. His eyes were starting to focus.

"Cat Sinistra is not a murderer," Doc Bartolomeu said. "Cat Denovo, for all her brusque manner, is absolutely right. Though it seems to be an ancient mechanism of the human mind, enough to create a syndrome named after it, just because someone survives circumstances that cause the death of many, it doesn't mean he's responsible for the deaths. Survivor's guilt is an abnormal reaction and an unhealthy one. Any of you who feel otherwise are free to challenge Cat Sinistra to a duel. At least any of you who are Cats or who can get a Cat to stand for him or her. But I suspect you'd face so many revenge challenges that you're unlikely to survive, no matter how skilled."

"He's not on trial for murder," someone said. My eyes followed and the speaker was close enough for me to register he was another man, and also had blond hair. I wondered if I was only imagining the resemblance to Castaneda. "He's on trial for treason against all of Eden. And it's not necessary to challenge him to a duel. He did risk revealing Eden secrets to Earth. He should be executed."

"Executed by whom, sir?" the doctor said. "No matter what the sentiment, there is no authority on Eden that can order the execution of one of its citizens. Yes, yes, a group of you could do it, but you'll be laying yourself open to blood feuds, since I don't believe everyone thinks he should die." I noted that he asserted this, but asked for no corroboration. Was he really sure? "And he has family and friends powerful enough to inflict damage in return." The look in Doc's eyes served fair warning that he was indeed one of those friends.

A long silence fell, and then Doctor Bartolomeu said, "I will grant you, one might think that he did something dishonorable, in acting to his own benefit and marginally increasing danger to Eden. I can understand how people might feel that he needs to make restitution. But execution is well past any such reasonable punishment."

"Blood geld," a voice said from the crowd. "For every Cat and Nav who had the courage to do what he didn't." There was an avaricious sound to that voice, and I tried to calculate what the blood geld would be. Cats and Navs were expensive people to kill, as not only did their bioengineering in utero cost the family money, but they earned a lot more than normal people throughout their active years. And by the time I'd left on the last pod run, the number of couples missing and presumed dead was already well above twenty. Compensating all the families for lost wages would make Kit an effective slave to them the rest of his days and well past the age when a Cat's visual acuity allowed for pod runs—even if we were allowed to do pod runs back to back, which I understood was no longer permitted.

"No blood geld," the doctor said. "Whether Cat Sinistra should have followed the example of those who committed suicide or not, is a matter open for philosophical discussion, but he didn't cause those Cats and Navs to die. If he'd died, those Cats and Navs would still be dead. So blood geld is not appropriate in the circumstances. I meant reparations he should make to Eden as a whole for having endangered us—even if fractionally."

For a moment I frowned, furious that he'd brought that up, when it was...well, not ridiculous. I supposed we'd marginally endangered Eden. Very marginally. Either of us would have died rather than given away the location of the asteroid or how it was set up inside. On the other hand, once we were on Earth there was, of course, a chance, some of that information would have been extracted from us by drugs or torture.

On yet the other hand, Doc Bartolomeu knew better than to expect the paranoids of Eden to be rational about even a marginal danger to the security of the world. *What* did he think he was doing?

There was a long silence, and then a voice I didn't recognize spoke up from a mid row, halfway up the amphitheater. "Why don't we send them back to

Earth, on a ship designed to give nothing away? If they survive and bring us back all the notes from Jarl Ingemar that can allow us to seed our own powertrees, then we'll consider the debt paid."

"Yeah," someone else said, from another end of the amphitheater. "If they can find how Jarl grew the powertrees, maybe we can grow our own. Here and at the Thules. And then the ridiculous rationing can stop."

As a chorus of agreement rose all around, I realized two things: first, that I felt near-frozen with fear at the idea of going back to Earth. We'd barely made it out last time. Would we escape this time?

And second, that Blondie was in the crowd. I could see him, standing against the side wall, a few feet from me, looking down at Doc Bartolomeu. And though he didn't say or do anything to counter the consensus forming in the center—to send us out in search of Jarl's writings as compensation for our not-quite-rational "crimes"—he looked very much like he would like to spit.

That last made me feel marginally better. If Mr. Castaneda didn't like it, perhaps the plan wasn't disastrous for us, after all.

And then I realized yet another thing. This had been planned.

Look, I never said I was suited to conspiracy. Ever. I could be cunning enough about getting my own way. And when cornered I would always fight for the right to continue drawing breath, as Doc put it. Or perhaps even the right to have my way. But I was not the type to lay plans in advance and carefully manipulate people into my aim.

And ordering us to do what we were on trial for doing was a master stroke I couldn't have imagined at my most crafty.

Whoever had conceived this—Jean or Doc, or Tania or Kath—was clearly much smarter than I was. I could see now what the plan had been: to manipulate the crowd into deciding by obvious majority, to send Kit and me out of reach of the Energy Board, where they couldn't kill Kit openly.

OUR LIVES, OUR FORTUNES, OUR SACRED HONOR

"WHY DID YOU LET IT HAPPEN?" SOMEONE ASKED. I didn't know who, but I was grateful that, for once, I was not the last one to see the plan.

We were in the back room of the Judicial Center, the rest and recovery area, where Kit lay on a low bed, with his arm flung over his eyes, to protect them from even the residual light allowed in by his eyelids and the darkening lenses.

"Why did you let them send Kit and Thena to Earth on a life-or-death mission?" Waldron said, standing up, so I could see he was the one speaking. "And one that might be impossible?"

His question was addressed at Doctor Bartolomeu, but Jean answered, "They're not safe on Eden," he said. "And Thena wanted to go back and get lost on Earth, anyway, instead of letting Kit be detained. She might have had the right idea."

The entire family was sitting around the room, on floor and chairs. There were more people than those who lived in Jean and Tania's compound. A woman who looked much too young for it, had been introduced to me as Kit's grandmother, plus there were cousins and uncles, and in-laws. There was also a redheaded woman who sat apart from them, towards the back. She reminded me of someone, but I would not be able to say whom.

I knew that Jean meant well. But he had it all wrong. "No," I said, "I meant for us to go to Earth and live there, someplace secluded. Not for us to go to Earth and go digging through secret places for documents that might or might not have been destroyed by now. Or for us not to be allowed to come back till we find them. Why, the Good Men of Earth are likely to—"

Kit made a weird sound and said, "Thena!"

"You don't have to come back," Kath said, very calmly. She sat near me, and now reached over to squeeze my shoulder. "Oh, we'd prefer it if you did, but if you don't, it's fine. You don't have to risk your lives for Eden."

"Of course we have to," my beloved and I said at the same time, and then I shut up because, while I did know that, I had no idea why it was so. I let him continue. "We can't leave Eden like this. Eden is the only home we have. We can't let it be taken from us." He paused. "You planted the suggestion they send us away, didn't you?" he asked no one in particular. "And not just to give us a chance to escape Eden."

"We planted the suggestion," Tania said. "Mostly to allow you to escape since, as long as you're here, there will be people who will want you dead."

"*Mostly,*" Kit echoed.

"Well, there is also the undeniable fact that if it can be done—and Jarl thought it could—we need to be able to seed or transplant powertrees. We have never been able to do it, and as long as we have to go to Earth orbit for powerpods, we are dependent on Earth, the politics of Earth and the rulership of Earth—and how active they are in tracing us, and how much they mind the theft of pods. Even if the current hunt for darkship thieves subsides, it would always start up again. And because of the large investment needed to get to Earth we are also dependent on the Energy Board and its rules. We cannot allow that, because—"

"By controlling what people need to survive, they've become a government and are turning Eden into a dictatorship," I said.

"An oligarchy, I'd call it," Doctor Bartolomeu said, inclining his head marginally. "Or at least they'd consider themselves oligoi. But you're correct on the essentials. A few people who consider themselves superior wielding the power of life or death over the rest of the world." A fleeting smile turned his lips upward and rearranged his wrinkles. "Even when those people were engineered to be truly superior in every way that was considered relevant, it did not end well."

Kit removed his arm from atop his eyes, and sat up. I rushed to sit beside him and he reached out for me and squeezed my hand hard. He smelled of sweat and vomit, with an overlay of illness, and he looked like he'd been dragged through hell backwards, but he was alive, conscious and attentive. I wanted . . . something else for us. I wanted people to stop trying to kill one of us, and just let us be. I wanted to be left in peace. You never get what you want.

He said, "What you're saying, and what Thena is saying is that we can choose to come back to Eden, eventually, but to come back to Eden we must bring back the solution to Eden's energy stranglehold, which has become a power stranglehold. Because we won't be accepted back if we don't bring with us the way to remove the power..." He looked around searchingly and Doc Bartolomeu said "The room is clean of bugs. We took care of it."

Kit nodded. "The way to remove the power of life or death from the greedy hands of the Energy Board. And frankly, we won't want to come back in that case, as Eden will be no better than Earth and this being a smaller world, it will allow those at the top to control every individual at the bottom that much more tightly. On the other hand, we can choose to stay on Earth and live in hiding and forget about Eden, right?"

"Right," Kath said. "We would not force you to risk your lives for the chance of bringing freedom back to Eden. I mean, we hope you care for us, but risking your lives is a price that only the two of you can determine to pay."

"Our lives, our fortunes, our sacred honor," Kit said, in almost a whisper. Mentally he said, *What do you think?*

We do it, I said. *And we do find a way to grow the powertrees nearby, where anyone can harvest them. I want Castaneda powerless.*

He smiled. By now he probably knew better than to appeal to my higher sentiments, since I might not have any. But he still added, *And I don't want Waldron's children growing up under his authority.*

That too. But mostly I wanted to take Castaneda's toys away. And hurt him.

Kit smiled again. *My girl!* He said, managing to sound proud. Aloud, he said, "We'll do it, or die trying. We'll bring back the solution to the power rationing, a way to open the power business to everyone—or we die."

"I didn't expect any less of you, my boy," Doctor Bartolomeu said, and he did sound like he really meant it. "But you must not expect this to be either simple or easy. The Energy Board can't fight back openly, but that only makes it more dangerous. They will fight back. No one gives power up easily, certainly not someone who is as invested in holding power as Castaneda is. He is one of those for whom power is more important than material comfort, possibly more important than his own life. He must rule or die trying. I want you to realize when you pledge your life, you might very well be required to pay."

"I don't say it lightly," Kit said. "And I understand that. Doc, I'm not an infant."

"No," the doctor said. "But you must also understand that you and Thena can't go alone. The type of ship they will send you in will be more stripped and require more intensive piloting than the *Cathouse* ever did. And besides accidents, real or engineered, will happen. The Cat and Nav teams are designed to cover for each other at need, but this will require something more. I believe you will have to double up. As it is, with two Cats and two Navs we'll be straining the food and fuel and water capacity of the ship, but since we won't bring back pods, the allowance is slightly higher. Not by much, mind you. Pods aren't that heavy. And the ships are built at most for a couple and their supplies, with about a child's supply worth of tolerance. I wish you could do it alone, but we need to have four people and double every ability."

"Go with another Cat and Nav?" I asked. I tried to imagine who would do it, whom we could trust, and whom I wouldn't kill after months alone in a tiny ship. Maybe Kath and Eber, if we were all very lucky. "But any other Cat will be in danger on Earth. I mean, Kit will be too, but him I might be able to conceal. But you know, Cat's eyes are—"

But the doctor said, "I volunteer to do the turn of backup Cat. While I don't have Kit's advantages of vision, I do have the reflexes, and I can move fast. I wouldn't pilot through the energy trees, but I can pilot anywhere else." He didn't say his improvements came from being a Mule, but no one asked about it. For that matter, no one in the room, not even the extended family, showed any surprise at his volunteering, and I remembered something about the Denovos being hereditary friends of Jarl—probably originally Jarl's servants, now I thought about it, or his confidential helpers—which probably meant they all knew what Doc Bartolomeu was. He lifted a hand as Kit seemed about to speak. "If I go with you, it gives you two people who know Earth, at least somewhat. Yes, I realize it has changed somewhat in the last three hundred years, but Thena has time to catch me up on that. But having been born and raised there, I'm not going to go into a panic at the sight of the ocean or have acute agoraphobia at the wide-open spaces, which you know very well most Cats and Navs would have."

"And I volunteer to be the backup Nav," the red-headed woman to whom I hadn't been introduced said. And as she stood and took a step forward, I realized who she reminded me of. It didn't make me feel any better. Classical paintings shouldn't come to life like that, and I realized—startled—that she looked exactly like Botticelli's Venus. So, she wasn't standing on a seashell, and she had clothes on: a very practical-looking kind of coveralls, not much different from, even if obviously better tailored than the ones I wore when working on the ships' innards.

I went all defensive. I couldn't help it. There is something in every woman that makes her despise someone that much more attractive, someone who was better equipped by nature to appeal to a man who wishes to have children. I could no more have kept myself from talking than I could have stopped from breathing. "Wouldn't your Cat object?" I said. In my defense I managed not to hiss and meow in the manner of another type of cat. Also, I was right, to a point; most—if not all—Cat and Nav teams were married and used to spending all their time together. And if we had to take her husband too, then we'd end up, by accretion, taking half of Eden. I didn't think this was a good idea. For one, four would push the weight limits on the ship, as it was.

"Len died," she said, and frowned in my direction, as if she held me responsible for it. "Radiation poisoning in the powertrees. I brought our ship back alone." Her voice went all tight, as if a constriction in her throat only allowed it to squeak through. "I gave his body to space. I am without dependents or restriction on my movements."

And no doubt would hate me till the day she died because I had been similarly poisoned and survived. Right. Sure I wanted her with me on a long trip in tight quarters.

Doctor Bartolomeu stood up, went to stand by her. "Thank you, Zen. It would help," he said, then to me, "This is Zenobia Sienna," Doctor Bartolomeu said. "She's...almost my adopted daughter." This got him a little smile from Ms. Ice Queen. "She's the daughter of some dear friends. I've watched her grow up. I wouldn't ask anyone to go with us—it's not my right to command anyone to risk his or her life—but I think we should accept her services."

"Zen?" Kit said, looking at her, and smiling a little in turn. It was obvious he'd known her for years, which of course made perfect sense. Most Cats and Navs knew each other; they all grew up together. None of which meant I had to like it. "Great. Yeah. It will give us a backup if Thena is..." I could see him struggle with the idea I could die, then shake his head. "If Thena is incapacitated. It will also give you time to...well...I know what it's like. It will give you time to get better, to...get used to being alone, in a place where nothing reminds you of Len, you know?"

She inclined her head minimally. "That's what I thought."

Oh, great. Not only was she a grieving widow who would immediately awaken in my husband sympathetic feelings, because he'd been widowed himself, but he clearly knew her and liked her. That he knew her was a given, considering how small the community of Cats and Navs was. That he liked her, not so much given my husband's temperament. As he liked to put it, he didn't play well with others. But I had to get lucky right across the board. I was going to be locked in a small space with a woman who was mad at me and probably trying to make up to my husband.

While I trusted Kit implicitly—he'd risked his life for me way too many times not to—the morals of Eden were complex and fidelity might or might not be part of what Kit thought he had signed up for in marriage. I didn't trust Zenobia farther than I could throw her.

THE POISON AND THE DAGGER

I DIDN'T HAVE TO LIKE IT, WHICH WAS A GOOD thing, because I didn't.

It wasn't even the rigged examination at the center and the feeling that everyone knew something I didn't know and seemed to understand how to spring Kit from this trap better than I did. It wasn't the trip to Earth being imposed on us from above, to look for something that might or might not exist any longer. It wasn't even that Zenobia was foisted on us, or that she was a total stranger, destined to spend six months in space with us and Doc.

No, the problem was that I knew there were *other* things going on, beyond the reach of my ears and that no one was going to tell me about them. I was a stranger in Eden, had lived there for far less than a year, if one took into account my trips out with Kit.

Perhaps Kit's family thought I would blow up if I knew all that was going on, but I didn't think that was it. Not this time. At least Kit himself would know that if I hadn't blown up yet, I wasn't about to.

I'm not going to claim any great level of maturity, but it had been some time since I thought every problem could be solved by kicking it in the appropriate—Kit would say inappropriate—place. Sometimes you needed to kick it in a lot of different places. And sometimes strategy was needed. And sometimes I had to leave the strategy to others.

Only when I told Kit that, as we flew back home at last—in our own flyer that someone had fetched from the Energy Center—he shook his head, and his lips trembled upward. His eyes were oddly tender as he smiled. *Actually, Thena, I suspect there's a lot of things we won't have time to tell each other except in mind-talk. And that Doc and Zen won't tell us because they can't mind-talk us. Because most places will be bugged with cameras and sound pickups. Because the greatest authority in the world is out to get us.*

I turned this over in my mind. Having the greatest authority in the world—okay one of the fifty greatest authorities in the world (no use catering to Daddy Dearest's perception of himself particularly now that he was safely dead)—out to get me was pretty much how I'd lived my whole life. *And?*

He gave me that look again, the look he gives when he thinks I'm completely unreasonable and also extremely funny. *Thena! And what do you think? They'll have listening devices and they'll have traps.* He gave me a sidelong glance, suddenly serious, as though evaluating how I'd respond. *Surely you realize the only reason we're being allowed to go is that they think we'll never come back.*

I had been trying *not* to realize that. *I know our mission is damn close to hopeless*, I said, soberly, trying to sound as grown up as I knew how. *I saw some of the notes Jarl left behind, but they were in my father's possession and my father is...dead. Whether the next person knew what they meant I don't know. And I left behind at the broomer's lair the gems I took from my father's study. At any rate, the ones I saw were all on how to make me which I don't think anyone on Eden needs. There was nothing about powertrees. As for the ones they showed you in Never-Never...who knows what happened after the break-in. I know prisoners escaped and the lower levels, where you were, were flooded. So I think the chances of us finding powertree—*

No, Thena. Kit sounded patient and faintly amused. *No. Don't you see? It has nothing to do with how difficult the secret of growing powertrees is. We'll give it our best and I'd give that endeavor a good fifty-fifty chance.*

Not fifty-fifty chance of my understanding any of it. He forestalled my protest. *As I said, I'm just a vacuum-ship-pusher. But the chance of us bringing it back, and having the trained people on Eden decode it. These people are terrified we'll achieve it, of course, so they'd probably give us higher odds. And that's why they'll make sure something happens to us en route. So we never get to Earth, much less come back. And they can say we defected.*

Something... A monstrous idea formed in my mind. *Sabotage?* Sabotage was not a crime in Eden. But in a world as attached to the morality and rights of the individual, it seemed like they should be more moral.

Like there would be a certain basic decency attaching to their decisions, like they wouldn't simply kill us because it is convenient.

Oh, not because it is convenient, Thena. Only for the highest possible motives. They are highly moral people, don't you see that?

I don't know what my face showed looking back at him, but his lips twitched. *They are, nonetheless. At least in their own minds and whether you believe it or not. They're doing this for the good of the people.*

The good of the people! I said. *That sounds like one of Daddy Dearest's speeches. But Kit, it's impossible that they think it's for the good of the people. They can't be that stupid and there are limits to self delusion. How could starving Eden of energy be for the good of anything, except maybe the Good Men of Earth?*

Very easily, Kit said. *If you can put yourself in a frame of mind where you see yourself as knowing what everyone should do for their own good. If that were true, then being able to control who gets energy and who doesn't would mean being able to encourage certain elements of society and discourage others. You would in fact be able to design a society where only the best people had power and—*

It was all too easy to put myself in that frame of mind. I'd heard my father and his friends talk long enough that it was almost second nature to slip into that mode of thinking. Even after a year in Eden, I still wasn't sure they were wrong, for that matter. Dad and his cronies were corrupt, venal and, sometimes, evil, but they were not stupid. And so many people I met seemed too stupid to stand upright and talk at the same time. Like that man who'd got in an argument with Kath during the hearing.

I could, in a way, understand wanting to encourage the... good people and discourage the others. I could even sympathize with it. But I also remembered overhearing Daddy Dearest's policy meetings—most of the time without his knowing I was nearby. And the people that Daddy Dearest tried to encourage, half the time, were the people who were too stupid to live. They were easier to lead, you see—easier to convince of what Daddy wanted them to believe. I groaned. *The good people...* I said. *The Good Men.*

Once more, my husband gave me an amused glance. He looked vaguely feral, unshaven, wearing clothes that appeared slept in, and like he had been starved for days. This last was probably not true. Eden had no reason to ration food, and wouldn't risk starving Kit if there was a chance of Kath ever finding out.

An unholy light danced in his eyes. *Of course,* he said. *The good people always end up being the ones who do as they're told. And the Good Men—by any other name—do the telling.*

I suppose it could be argued those truly were the good people. Civilization could be said to consist of people willing to go along with others' ideas. The domesticated version of humans. But this was not a philosophic debate. We were talking about real people, people I knew... my husband's family, his friends, the place that had made him what he was. And I saw about as much chance of their going along to get along as of my growing an extra head. And—I set my jaw, remembering Castaneda—just on principle, I refused to go along.

So you're telling me, I said, *that they intend to sabotage our ship so we die in space? And you're fine with that? You still wanted them to send us out into space? Aren't there easier ways to commit suicide?*

There would be, if I had any intention of letting them get away with it, he said, and pushed his chin forward, setting his jaw. It reminded me of when he'd been near-fatally wounded and had climbed up the side of a ship, against what must have been unbearable pain, to prevent me committing suicide by Dock Control. Afterwards he'd stared at me with that sheer stubbornness in his eyes, even while a dark stain of blood spread on the side of his suit. Now the stubborn was back, as well as a definite streak of defiance. *We're going to find all their traps and all their sabotage. We're going to survive it. We're going to go to Earth and come back with a way to replant powerpods. And then we're going to make the little weasels eat it.*

I wasn't absolutely sure what he meant to have them eat: the way to make the powerpods grow? How? If in a data gem it wouldn't be that hard to eat. Perhaps he meant the powerpods? Impossible. Those were man-sized and radioactive. It wasn't really safe to ask, when Kit was in this mood. He'd probably come up with yet another cryptic utterance that would cost me sleep for days as I tried to figure the mechanics of it. So I just said, mildly, *What have weasels ever done to you?*

Which got me a puzzled look and an *I don't know. There are no weasels on Eden. Are they sort of like rabbits?*

I avoided this side-rhetorical line. I'd long ago

decided that my husband only introduced talk of Earth animals and his utter ignorance of them in order to make me laugh or distract me. I wasn't in the mood to be distracted. *You really think we can do it?* I said. *Avoid all the traps laid out for us, escape all their plotting and manage to do what the most powerful people in the world are intent on stopping us doing?*

He grinned. *We got here despite the Good Men.*

Yes, but the Earth is larger . . . there's more places to escape. Here . . .

Here we have Doc and Zen to help.

You trust them that much? And how will we communicate with them?

I trust them that much, he said, and gave me a smile that said not to worry my pretty head about it. *We'll manage it, Thena.*

I didn't like it. Look, my life had given me no reason at all to trust the judgment of others. In my experience, outside my own judgment and my own capacities, everyone was trying to pull one over on me.

But Kit was still smiling at me with that expression like the canary that ate the cat. Or in this case, perhaps, the Cat that thinks he can win over the bureaucrat. I glowered at him. *You are the most exasperating man. I don't have the slightest idea why I love you.*

The smile curved and became wicked, in a way that made my heart skip a beat. *No? Let me take a bath and I'll remind you.*

IN THE HOPPER

OVER THE NEXT FEW DAYS, THERE WAS PRECIOUS little time for Kit and me to indulge in his specialized memory-enhancing techniques.

The very next day a call from the center sent Zenobia and myself down to inspect the ship they would allow us to use. The *Hopper* wasn't so much a ship as a shell. What they told me was that the couple who had taken it out last had got badly radiation burned. Only one of them had survived the long trip home, and she had apparently decided to retire. The ship had been repossessed by the Energy Board and stripped almost to the hull to clean it. That hull had then been placed in a cavernous bay which was not used for anything else. And we were told where to find it.

Before becoming Kit's navigator, I had worked as a mechanic for the Energy Board for many months. I had repaired and reconditioned ships. I'd never seen one as bare as this. It was perfectly round, as most darkships were, and it was painted in the same dark, unreflective paint as the *Cathouse*.

The resemblance stopped there. Part of this was good. The *Cathouse* was a ship of very old vintage, which had been designed as a training ship. It had been foisted on Kit, first, because he was a Cat flying missions alone, and therefore at higher risk of losing the ship. Also, alone, he'd only been able to bring in much lower harvests, which meant that he couldn't afford to pay the fees for the rental of the better, more expensive ships.

Even when I'd joined him, they didn't trust us. I was an Earthworm, with questionable training for the job. For one, I'd never learned mechanics, or studied it consciously. It was as though I had an instinct for it. The first time our brooms, back on Earth, had needed repair, I'd studied the manual and known how to do it, and it had been the same with Eden's ships. I'd discovered, just before leaving Earth that this, like the ability to communicate telepathically, had been bioengineered into the man who called himself my father—and therefore presumably into me. But it wasn't like the Eden navigator ability, and we couldn't convince the board I was as good. So, we'd been stuck with the *Cathouse*. I didn't mind it so much, but the fact that it had been designed as a training ship, instead of a harvesting ship, presented some liabilities. The nodes for various circuitry, for instance, were easier to access for trainee navigator/mechanics than those in the more modern ships. But what made them accessible was their being on the outside of the ship—protruding out of the skin like pimples. This meant that a mishap in the powertree ring could destroy one of the nodes.

Good Cats weren't supposed to have mishaps of

that nature, and the only one I knew of had happened while I was trying to strangle Kit during our star-crossed meeting. But that didn't mean that it wasn't a greater risk.

This ship didn't have that liability. It was just a large ball, perfectly smooth, completely black, unreflective. It was in fact a ball that projected the idea that it wasn't there at all.

I walked around it slowly, while Zenobia walked purposely up to it and stuck her finger in the genlock. The door opened, which I supposed made perfect sense, as it would be keyed for us. The way the hatch doors opened on the darkships always made them look a little like they had an open mouth and were carnivorous. Normally this impression was dispelled by the exit area itself which was painted some cheerful color, and faced onto another inner lock, normally open whenever the outer door opened.

This one wasn't painted any color, but the bare, unreflective black ceramite of the inside of darkships before they were finished. It looked like a dark mouth, or a vortex of ill omen, waiting to swallow us.

Zenobia climbed up the stairs that had extended when the door opened and into the airlock space. She touched the walls, gently, as if to reassure herself of their solidity and looked incredibly out of place, with her red hair and pale skin in that almost aggressively dark space. "I guess they stripped it to its barest shell before cleaning it, then reapplied the ceramite coating," she said.

I had a feeling she was talking to herself and not to me. I said, "Maybe it was never finished," and she whirled around, to look at me, her expression surprised.

"What? Oh. No." She shrugged. "It used to be golden. Len said we really couldn't afford much, but we could at least make the entrance look like going into a palace." She stopped immediately, but she had said too much. I felt my heart sink somewhere to the vicinity of my shoes.

She was a navigator whose Cat had died. She'd limped home with her ship. Her ship. They'd given us her ship. I cleared my throat. "The *Hopper* was your ship?"

She nodded and cleared her throat, then pushed to open the membrane separating us from the inner areas.

I'll say this for the Energy Board. They might be sending us to space in a coffin, but at least it was a completely stripped, scrubbed and *really clean* coffin. Nothing in it could possibly remind Zenobia of when she had shared with her late husband. Except it obviously did. From the bare entrance hall, she wandered the corridors, touching here and feeling there, looking like a child lost in a house she'd once known, looking for something that should be there but wasn't.

I thought up some really interesting swear words, but didn't say anything. Instead, I set about inspecting the interior in a completely different way.

The navigation computers had been removed. It didn't worry me, or not too much. I—and I presumed Zenobia, who had been trained in the more normal way of Eden—could calculate a path to Earth. But some navigational computers would be needed, I thought, or one or the other of the pilots—either Kit or Doc Bartolomeu—would need to be on duty the whole time. And shift on/shift off with just two people would be exhausting.

Since Eden was on a highly eccentric orbit, it could be as much as four months or as little as two away from Earth. Usually the trip there and back took six months because what you lost on one leg, you made up on the other.

They'd told us to make lists of what we'd need, and they'd furnish it, and they'd given us weight and mass guidelines beyond which we couldn't go. I'd started making a list on a disposable electronic memo pad when Zenobia came in to the inner area.

I was once more taken aback by her resemblance to Botticelli's painting. Don't misunderstand me. There was nothing exact to this resemblance. I'm sure if I had the painting handy, I'd find her features were all wrong, and I was sure her hair was darker red than the woman's in the painting. But her green eyes had the same expression as that of Venus in the painting—the distant look of staring out at vistas invisible to mere mortals.

She was wearing a blue mechanic's whole-body suit. Not that all mechanics in Eden wore one uniform, any more than anyone in Eden was fond of uniforms. Back when I worked as a full-time mechanic, there were people who came to work completely naked, as well as those who came to work in floor-length dresses more appropriate to an Earth ballroom. But the blue mechanic's body-suit was the most common outfit, because it would fit over practically everything—except maybe the floor-length dresses—and it would protect the more expensive clothing. Also, it had deep and plentiful pockets, into which one could sink tools or parts and avoid walking back and forth to get them, or even wearing a cumbersome belt. The suits were so common for people engaged in manual labor, and so cheap, that they were sold at vending machines throughout the two docking complexes: the Energy Board's and the Water Board's.

There was no way that Zenobia should look graceful with her hands deep in the pockets of the oversized, bulky uniform, but she did. I had a fleeting thought about her having been friends with Kit since childhood, and a stab of unreasoning jealousy.

Had Kit had a crush on her? I knew he'd loved his first wife dearly, not just because he had told me, but because I knew. Once, our minds had become so intertwined that the normal barrier to the transmission of images and memories had failed; I'd got his memories of their affair.

Jean, Kit's father, called Kit's first marriage a boy and girl affair, a bad case of puppy love, because neither of the participants had known any better, or knew anything of how to make a relationship work, or even that relationships could work. Perhaps it was that. Kit's love of his first wife had that rosy nimbus quality that edged all her memories with thoughts of how wonderful she'd been. But he'd told me when he'd proposed to me that he'd had other lovers before his marriage. He'd made it sound as if they hadn't mattered at all and perhaps they hadn't, but looking at Zenobia's graceful walk, knowing that Kit never called her anything but "Zen"—surely an affectionate nickname—which Doc used also, I wondered if she'd been one of his crushes or even one of his lovers before marriage.

I've always been suspicious of women like that— naturally beautiful and effortlessly poised. Even when not doing something strenuous, I became sweaty and disheveled. The only time I looked graceful was when I used ballet moves to kick someone. The only way I've ever stunned a man with my mere presence was by adding a punch to his head.

So I might have been less than cordial as I glared at Zenobia, standing there, lost in her reverie. "Well?" I asked.

She shook a little, like someone awakened from a dream. Had she been in the past? Reliving her last trip in this ship? Or in the future, planning our trip and trying to anticipate all that could go wrong?

She looked vaguely guilty. Then she cleared her throat. "I've looked all over. There doesn't seem to be anything here that shouldn't be."

I must have blinked at her, because she looked at the pad in my hands and, without giving me time to figure out what she'd do, grabbed for it so fast it might almost have been Cat speed. She read what I had on the screen under the words "parts to requisition."

Then she typed quickly and handed me the pad back and resumed her sleep-like walking around the cabin, looking at this and touching that.

I wasn't sure what I expected her to have typed. It could, I supposed, be anything from poetry to calculations. But when I looked down, I found out that the note was perfectly rational and clearly intended for me: DON'T LET US MAKE REQUISITIONS. IT GIVES THEM A CHANCE TO SLIP SOMETHING IN THAT COULD BLOW UP THE SHIP OR WORSE. AND LET'S MAKE SURE THIS BAY IS LOCKED AND THE LOCK CODED ONLY FOR ME, YOU, KIT AND DOC BARTOLOMEU.

I raised my eyebrows at her and she looked back

at me and nodded in a way that somehow managed to ask if I was agreeable to the plan.

I was. And Zenobia had found a way to communicate that the Energy Board couldn't bug, unless they not only had mikes all around but also fortuitously aimed cameras—or had covered the interior of the ship in them.

The disposable pad I'd picked up from the children's learning room at the Denovo complex would be perfect for this. I'd picked it up because it was cheap and I didn't need to worry about returning it. But the advantage of such a simple implement, produced by the hundreds of thousands every year was that it would be very difficult for the board to know which one would make its way to our hands, much less to hack it.

I despised the way we had to think of all these things. I despised being so paranoid. But as my upbringing had proven, sometimes you really were being persecuted. And I certainly remembered how to do it.

THE TRAITOR AND THE DAGGER

TWO WEEKS LATER WE HAD ASSEMBLED MOST OF THE needed machinery for the ship. Kit and Doc—I never knew where they planned it or how they contrived it—had procured it. Now one, now the other of them showed up, bearing parts or something on our wish list.

I didn't know how the Energy Board—or Castaneda—felt about it, nor did I want to know. We'd arranged so that only the four of us could come in and out of the bay, and, because Zenobia managed to be even more paranoid than I was—a feat that ranked up there with the great deeds of humanity—we'd rigged hidden cameras that kept watch on the ship night and day.

We needed only a computer now, strong enough to make calculations and do the piloting but simple enough to be wiped bare of all data before we got near Earth. The data would be in our own heads and safe from discovery.

I had been given to understand, through Kit's

mind-talk, that getting a computer for the ship wasn't as simple as walking into a shop and walking out with the required computer. It wasn't even as simple as ordering it, special order, from some manufacturer. You see, Kit, and particularly Doc were afraid of subtle sabotage induced by our enemies, if anyone knew the computer was for us.

Have you found it? I asked, as I emerged from the ship to find him leaning against the wall, his hands shoved deep in the pocket of his dark red pants. The tunic he wore with the pants was a bright green that made me think of absinthe, but there was nothing for it, and I'd got used—kind of—to my Cat's taste in clothing. Kit wasn't the worst of it, for that matter. Every Cat I knew had horrible color sense. Kath didn't seem to be able to wear anything not covered with spangles. And at least Kit's tunic matched his eyes. Sort of.

The computer? he asked, straightening and smiling at me while giving me an all-over appreciative look.

I smiled at him and nodded. I'd never expected to be loved. I know what I am and that most people would prefer chewing their own arms off at the elbow to being married to me. But Kit not only loved me. His eyes went all soft and . . . interested, even when I was coming out of a ship with coolant gel all over my hands and wearing sweaty, stained, baggy coveralls.

Doc Bartolomeu thinks he can get it this evening, Kit said. *And we're hoping to leave tomorrow early.*

So soon?

Kit nodded, pressing his lips together. *The sooner we leave, the less time there will be for funny business. Doc thinks that they . . . Castaneda and whoever else, are planning something.*

What would the something be?

Who knows? We thought they meant to sabotage the parts we brought on board, but we've been very sneaky in procuring them… He smiled, a little, and for just a moment looked too young. *At least Doc has been. So sneaky he's left me out of the loop most of the time. It's all high cloak and dagger, and I'm sure he's enjoying himself. The little I've done involves taking a message to so-and-so and bringing a message back and being in a certain place at a certain time.* He shook his head. *I think the Doc is a romantic and is trying to live out one of those adventure books he reads all the time. But I do think we've been secretive enough. Even I have no idea where the parts… or the computer, are coming from.*

At least I wasn't the only one who'd been left out of the loop. I tended to feel left out, but in this case so was Kit himself. *So, why the urgency in leaving?*

Because Doc Bartolomeu is afraid if they can't get in by sneaky means they'll do it bluntly.

Bluntly? I asked. *How… how could they do it bluntly? You mean, they might just kill us? Wouldn't that be murder and set off a blood feud?*

His expression turned momentarily bleak. *Don't ask me how he knows this or who his informant might be, but Doc thinks that the plan, when we landed, was to blow us out of the sky. Since the dock controller forced their hand, they couldn't do that, but there are accidents that can be…* He swallowed. *That could be arranged. A few hours without power during the night and my family compound would contain nothing but corpses. A fleeting smile. Or at least they might think so, though Jean has made arrangements, but*

*all the same . . . The less time we give them to strike,
the less danger we can bring to my family, or to the
people who are helping Doc. Zen's family, fortunately,
immigrated to the Thules a couple of years ago. So
she only had her husband.*

And he's dead, I thought, half to myself and half
projecting. I was not exactly mad-fond of Zenobia. For
one, she didn't give me a chance to be. Sometimes, I
had inklings that there might be a nice, perhaps even
friendly woman under the brittle shell of silence and
distance, but no more than glimpses. It was clear that
for some reason she didn't consider me someone to
confide in. Either this was her normal character, not
unlike Kit's, who sometimes gave the impression one
should pull the words out of him with a corkscrew,
or she was suffering from shock at the death of her
husband.

If she was still in shock at her husband's death,
half the women, at least, would dissolve in garrulous
conversation, confidences and clinging.

Oh, maybe it's a stereotype, but it's always seemed
to me that women seek community more than men.
Not that I was typical in that. And apparently neither
was Zenobia.

Of course, it was always possible that she was madly
in love with Kit—I shielded my thoughts from him
carefully to avoid that leaking—and that she resented
my presence or was only waiting to slip a knife between
my ribs once we were in space.

I smiled. I couldn't help it. Oh, he called her *Zen*
and she called him *Kit*, and they seemed cordial, but
only in the way old friends who didn't have much
in common could be easy with each other. It was

friendly but not personal. Unless she was one hell of an actress, in which case she could have forced herself to fake friendship with me.

Kit had put his arms around me and was looking at me with an odd expression. "Thena!" he said, in voice for once, mingling amusement with just a hint of shock. Which was when I knew my thoughts had leaked.

Before I could play dumb and ask him what had shocked him, Zenobia appeared from inside the ship. "I think we might as well call it quits for the evening," she said. "We can't do any more tonight. Kit, would you mind giving me a ride back to my lodgings? I sold my flyer yesterday and took a cab in."

Kit raised his eyebrows. "Sold...you're not expecting to survive this trip?" He looked genuinely alarmed.

She smiled and shook her head, one of the most natural expressions I'd seen her make. "Oh, no," she said. "Not that. Remember though that I'm newly single. When we come back, I'll just move nearer the Center, so maybe I can meet some nice Cat someday." She sighed. "Not that I really...I don't know how I'll manage, without Len, but I'd like to go to space again..." She shrugged. "I don't...I find I'm not fond of being confined to Eden. I never fit in here, in many ways. Earth is worse, I know, but it is different. Which is part of the reason I volunteered for this."

"Perhaps," Kit said, "you can just find a friend who agrees to go with you to space? There are many people...in your situation right now. Unfortunately."

"What?" She said. "And set all the tongues wagging? No, thank you so much, Cat Sinistra. I note you didn't take a friend to space when you were widowed."

"Not when people thought they were risking life and limb to go out with a potential murderer," Kit said, and his smile had just the hint of bitterness he must have felt at living under suspicion of having killed his first wife. "But you don't have that taint. And besides..." He shrugged again. "I mean, you must know everyone who is free. Surely you'd know if there's anyone you wish to marry."

She gave him a sidelong glance. "No one, unless they're importing Cats from elsewhere," she said, and then quickly added, "If you excuse me, I'll go wash my hands and change."

Part of me wanted to follow her, and not just because I wanted to ask what she meant by importing Cats from elsewhere. Was this a snide remark at my Earth origins, or did she mean something else, perhaps just exasperation at being part of a small group of people for whom necessarily marriage and career were linked? But Zenobia had yet to confide in me on anything.

She shared specs and discussed tools and parts freely—hampered only by the fact that anything that could possibly interest anyone else we typed in a pad and passed back and forth rather than speaking where hidden pickups could catch a word. We were fairly sure there were no hidden sound and vision pickups, but we couldn't be absolutely sure, and it wasn't worth taking a risk.

I washed my hands at a station in the room, and pulled off the coveralls. Under them, I was wore a practical dress of some fabric that fell into perfect folds after being crushed under my coveralls all day. And which had smell-mitigating properties, so I probably wouldn't smell as I should after a day of hot, heavy work.

I was freeing my hair from the pins that held it up during work letting it fall in its natural shoulder-length curls when I felt Kit's arms around me. I turned to face him, within the circle of his arms, and he kissed me. Or I kissed him. It is a minor miracle of telepathy that a married couple can feel when the other means to kiss without either saying anything. Even non-engineered couples.

The kiss was more comforting than sexy, which means Kit had read my mood, and knew what I needed. As I pulled back for breath, he said, "It will be all right, Thena. It really will."

I took a deep breath, realizing how insecure of this I felt, and mind-said, *What if it isn't? What if Jarl didn't have notations that help us grow the trees? What if we can never come back? What if Castaneda takes over Eden and makes it into his little fiefdom? What if everything we have, everything we love, is lost?*

He put his hands on my shoulders and squeezed fractionally. *We'll do it. We'll manage it. We've already cheated death, Thena. We can do it.*

What if the notes don't exist?

They will. Doc said they exist. And we'll find them—if we have to go to another universe for them.

I gave a little gurgle of laughter more out of surprise than humor. *And how do we get around the fact that the Good Men of Earth are either guarding them or very interested in them?*

He grinned at me and kissed my forehead. *Afraid of the Good Men of Earth? Thena, my love, this is not like you. Maybe you need more red meat. They're the ones who should be afraid of you.*

Are you afraid of me?

A chuckle. *No. I wouldn't have you behave any differently.*

We were kissing again when I felt someone else nearby. Zen, of course. Kit must have sensed it too, because he sprang away from me, as I stepped away from him. If I looked as sheepish as he did, we were a sorry sight, like juveniles caught necking. But Zen looked perfectly natural.

She was wiping her hands on a disposable rag. "If it's easier for you two," she said. "I can take a cab from the door. I mean, if you have plans."

I don't know why, but the fact that she said it naturally, without the slightest hint of salacious meaning, made it worse. I felt heat and blush climb from somewhere around my navel to my face. Kit looked away, but smiled and said, in a reasonable imitation of his normal manner, "No, no. It's fine. We have no plans beyond spending the evening with my family. If you want to come with us, and have dinner..." He nodded. "I mean, my parents know you as well as they...I mean, they've seen you grow up and they're very fond of you, and Doc is coming over for dinner anyway. It's by way of being a celebration, or...or a farewell dinner or something."

The "or something" was probably correct, since it never seemed to occur to any of the Denovos that we would not be able to return victorious. So they were celebrating—in anticipation of—our victory, as well as saying goodbye for a time. I felt like this was surely the way ancient adventurers were sent off, when the village had no idea of what dangers they might face but knew, because they were the best of their people, that they couldn't help but succeed.

Zen hesitated. She frowned a little, her eyebrows gathering over her perfectly straight nose. She opened her mouth, closed it, opened it again. Finally, she shook her head, and her eyes acquired that extra hint of reserve that was common around me, even if not always around Kit. "No, thank you," she said. "I appreciate it, but I . . ." A deep breath. "I'm a member of no family. And besides, I have plans for the evening."

There was something so . . . ice-queenish about her, that I couldn't wonder what her plans were. I was sure, in any case, that the stars would burn cold and vacuum swallow the universe before I knew what they were.

Kit lowered his head just a little. "If you're sure," he said, and put his arm around my waist. "But I warn you that there is chocolate cake. Or at least that's what Doc said there would be. Don't complain to us afterwards that you didn't get any. The supply of chocolate we could get on the ship is limited."

For just a second I thought that Zen was going to tell him what he could do with the chocolate cake, and it wouldn't be pleasant. Then her frosty expression melted, and she said, "I promise to hold you harmless of my lack of chocolate, Cat Sinistra," she said.

The ice having melted, we left the room, which both Zen and I verified was closed behind us, and walked along the empty corridor that led to the more populated part of the complex. We didn't talk, because when you're afraid your words are being picked up by listening bugs, noted down and marked for examination, you don't talk. Particularly not when the subject taking up all of your thoughts and all of your concerns is something that you think the powerful people in your society are against. You shut up and walk along.

Kit and I didn't even talk in our minds, partly because one could usually see when Cat and Nav were talking to each other mentally. Or at least I could tell when Kit's family were doing it. There was the expression that seemed to indicate that people were looking inward, or somewhere that no one else could see. And there was the slightest of lags between stimulus and response.

It wouldn't be difficult for anyone watching us to realize that we were talking to each other. And if we did that too much, they'd come to think we were hiding more than we were. In fact, they might think we knew far more than we did know.

So we walked along the dark corridor, all three sets of footsteps echoing over the high, vaulted ceilings and the vast, dusty emptiness.

Because only a patch, corridor-wide and maybe ten feet ahead of us, was lit, while the lights went off behind us, we were in a moving island of light in a sea of darkness, both light and darkness making the other seem more intense.

It is important you know this, because they couldn't have found a more perfect setup.

Zen walked slightly ahead of us, her hands in her pockets, managing to look absurdly graceful and feminine in her baggy coveralls and flat heels.

Kit and I followed behind, holding hands, each lost in his own thoughts. I was thinking that my time in Eden, despite all the trouble, had been the happiest of my lifetime, and hoping I could come back. And hoping Eden would go back to being what it once was.

Which would depend on our succeeding and removing Castaneda's would-be dictatorship from power.

It all happened much too fast. Well, much too fast

for me. I'm not a Cat. Neither is Zen, of course, but she reacted first, stopping ahead of us and reaching into her pocket for... what?

Then Kit shouted "Thena!" And jumped on me, taking me down with him, covering me.

I've said before that Cats move very, very fast but this was something else. They always give the impression, to the untrained eye, of having teleported from one place to the other. You only know that's not what happened, because—even though your eye can't transmit the message to your brain fast enough while it is happening—you retain memories of its happening. You remember the Cat crossing the intervening space.

The minute Kit jumped on me and took me down with him, to the dusty dimatough floor, where my head hit, hard, I entered speeded-up mode, my heart beating madly, my senses sharpening.

When I was very little, and for the time I was on Earth, I didn't know why or how I was different, I just knew I was. When in fear, I would go into what I used to call my "speeded-up state" in which my movements seemed to become too fast for even trained people to follow. It was this, and my general charming and yielding disposition, that had allowed me to survive a childhood beset with military academies, reformatories, and mental hospitals.

I wasn't as fast as an Eden Cat, I knew that. I'd tried it out on Kit, and even after I knew how he was doing it, his speed still seemed to border on supernatural. But I was faster than normal people. Much faster.

I was suddenly aware of people beyond that illuminated square on which we stood. More than one person, moving around, as though... as though maneuvering for attack. I was aware of Zen—though I couldn't see her—taking something from her pocket. And I was aware of a blue ray crossing the air and . . . hitting someone.

I knew it had hit because I could smell singed flesh and hair. Kit tightened his grip on me.

Stop, I said. *Let me go, Kit.* I wriggled out of his grasp and onto the floor, feeling in the pockets of my dress for my burner. Ahead, more rays of light burned. I couldn't see Zen at all, didn't know where she was. Had she gone into the dark space? How, when it was rigged to respond to our heat or movement or sound? But if it was rigged to respond to that, why hadn't it responded to our attackers? *I'm not a child. I can defend myself.*

I'd found my burner. It was a little job, little more than the length of my right hand, and slightly thicker than my index finger.

Eden, in general, was a very safe place. Yeah, okay, so murder was legal, but there were far fewer murders here than anywhere on Earth with the same level of population. Probably because retribution—in the form of a demand for compensation or a blood feud—could come from anywhere at any moment. I thought the latest statistics counted something like a murder a year.

Most duels were carefully announced and arranged days in advance. It wasn't as though anyone wanted to risk their being thought murderers.

So, why was I carrying a burner in my pocket at all? Even if it was a little and thin one?

Listen, if you had grown up as I had, you also wouldn't be able to function without some form of self-defense weapon at hand.

With the burner out, I burned in the general direction the last ray of burner fire had come from, and then someone else shot, and someone else again, and I tried to burn where the light came from as it extinguished.

It was a stupid and futile endeavor. Do I need to spell it out? I was in bright light, while they were in darkness. And I was trying to pick them out. This was one of the most disastrous setups in the history of battle tactics since the Roman army had gone off chasing a herd of cows to which Hannibal's generals had tied lanterns. I couldn't win and they couldn't lose.

Behind me there was a muffled sound, and then "Thena!" in Kit's voice, echoed both mind and voice together.

"Kit," I said, and tried to crawl back to where he was, only right at that moment all the lights cut out, and I wasn't sure where he was.

The corridor echoed, huge and dark, and full of footsteps.

In fact, in the absolute darkness, I couldn't tell if the footsteps were approaching or retreating. I couldn't tell what was happening at all. I could only hear the footsteps and feel at the gritty floor with my bare hands, as I crawled back and forth, calling "Kit!"

He didn't answer, which was bad enough, but there was worse. I couldn't hear him breathe. And that was just wrong.

I'm not going to claim to have supernatural hearing, but as a Mule I did have slightly sharper senses than normal humans and I should have been able to hear him breathe.

Panicked, lost in what had to be just over twenty

square feet of darkened hallway, I felt around, and crawled so fast I felt like I was dragging my knees on sandpaper. I hit something hard. It went skittering into the darkness and then hit something else—possibly, from the high, clanging ring of ceramite on dimatough, the wall of the tunnel.

Steps and the zap of firing weapons distracted me, and I concentrated on ignoring them. I could hear only the loud, pounding, insistent, beating of my heart. And then I tried to ignore that, half sitting up, my fists clenched on my thighs.

"Kit!" *Kit. KIT!* There was no response, but now I could hear it, the very, very faint breathing coming from nearby. I felt in the dark, in that direction, and found Kit's hand. I knew it was Kit's hand, not only because it felt like Kit's hand, but because our wedding ring was on it. We had lost my ring on Earth, but Doc had replaced it, and we both wore broad gold rings with roses cut into the outside and the words *Je Reviens* engraved on the inside. That was archaic French for "I'll return" and the name of the starship that had taken the Mules out of the solar system. Also, incidentally, not a bad motto for a marriage.

Kit's hand felt warm and alive, which was good. By following his arm up with my hand, I reached his shoulder, then by degrees, his chest. It wasn't wet or bloodied, or anything, which was good, and by laying my hand on his chest, I could feel his heartbeat, fast but regular, and then I was following his body up to his shoulder again, and shaking it. "Kit, Kit, Kit?"

There was no response. He didn't move. My hands started, as if of their own accord, examining him.

Something was wrong. Something was very wrong.

Something was terribly wrong. I felt up and down his body, taking note of a wet spot on his inner thigh just up from his knee. A large wet spot which wasn't good, because it was around the area of the femoral artery and the feeling of the wetness was sticky like blood, and besides, I could smell blood, sharp and tangy and metallic.

But no one loses consciousness from being hit on the thigh. Unless...he'd lost consciousness from hitting his head when he'd fallen. No, wait. He'd been down already, having jumped on me to take me down and protect me. Idiot. When he was the one they wanted to get and he was at far greater risk. And yet, if he hadn't done it, he wouldn't have been Kit.

My hands had found the top of his boots and started up again, upwards, fast, feeling his chest, his sides, all the way up. On his arm there was another wet-sticky point, but it didn't seem to be bleeding nearly as fast.

And then up, up, up his neck, with the pulse of life beating fast and decisive at its side, and up up...

I stopped. I stopped before I realized what I was feeling—it was impossible. It couldn't happen. It wouldn't happen. Things like this didn't happen to me. Not to Athena Hera Sinistra, only daughter of Good Man Milton Alexander Sinistra. Not to a Patrician of Earth. Some things had been worse for me, but I'd always been kept from utter catastrophe, which this was.

Kit's temple was not only wet. It seemed to be pouring out blood. My fingers, feeling gingerly, found the edge of a hole on his temple. And blood was pouring out. I could feel it on my bare knees as it pooled on the floor. I refused to believe that was blood, but it felt like blood, warm and viscous.

I put my whole hand down in the puddle by Kit's head, then I brought it up to smell. Blood. It was blood. It was Kit's blood.

Both my hands grabbed at his shoulders and shook him, before I could get control of them. My voice rose high in a sort of wail, as I screamed, "Wake up Kit, wake up. Oh no, oh, no, oh, no. This can't be happening. This isn't happening."

Less than a couple of minutes ago—I was sure of it—we'd been headed out of the Energy Board complex, ready to go to dinner, ready to lift off tomorrow. This couldn't be happening. This wasn't happening. If I closed my eyes...If I wished really hard...we'd still be there, still walking down the hallway. We'd be going home. We were going home. Kit had saved me from near death, and this wasn't going to separate us now. What a stupid way to die when we'd braved Earth and Daddy Dearest.

What a stupid way for him to go when he'd got me back from the brink of death by radiation, when I'd been revived despite having been as nearly cooked from inside out as a human being could be and still live.

From a long, long way away, as if from someone else's head, a thought leaked into my panic. Head wounds bled like the devil, and Kit needed emergency first aid right away. He wasn't dead. I must make sure he didn't die.

I pulled back at my hair, frantically, trying to remove it from my eyes, so I could see the bracelet on my wrist which had a dialer built in. Since an attack on us last year, when I didn't have a communications device in sight, I always made sure to wear at least two. But I couldn't see to dial.

My hair being pulled back made no difference, of course. I wasn't a Cat who could see in the dark. And Kit couldn't dial, and Zen . . . I didn't even have any idea where Zen was. In the dark around me, there was no sound, not even breathing.

I twisted the dialer by feel, blindly. At least Doc's number was easy. It was his personal number, which meant he would have it on whatever receptor he carried. He was supposed to be at the Denovos, he was—

"Hello?" As Doc Bartolomeu's voice answered, loud in the still darkness, I realized I would give my position away by speaking, but it didn't matter. I'd already shouted.

"Doc, Doc, please. This is Thena. Kit was hit. He's bleeding to death. We're—"

"I know where you are," he said. "I'm coming."

"How . . . how?"

"Zen told me," he said. "I'm just outside the complex. Don't worry."

BETWEEN WORLDS

I HAD NOTHING TO DO BUT WORRY. TELLING PEOPLE not to worry while they're in a situation like this was sort of like telling people to stop breathing. It couldn't be done.

I felt the blood spilling from Kit's temple. I knew—had heard—that head wounds bled a lot. The heart pumped a lot of blood up there, of course. It was where the brain was.

I thought of how Kit hadn't reacted, hadn't responded to me even in my mind. He had done it before when he was dying of a chest wound. But now he wasn't. His brain . . .

No. I wouldn't think about it. Just wouldn't. Eden was far more advanced than Earth in all types of genetic engineering and genetics. It came from not forbidding all tampering with human genes for the last three hundred years—as Earth had after the turmoils.

They could repair types of damage that were fatal

on Earth, and I was only starting to suspect—a year after coming to Eden—that people lived far longer here, too. They would be able to heal Kit. He was still alive. He'd survive.

I'd try to do whatever could be done. I crawled around till my knees were under Kit's head, raising it. Raising a wound was always better, right? I tore a piece off my dress and folded it into a kind of pad, and pushed it hard against his temple. Pressure helped reduce bleeding, right?

Then I thought of his thigh, because it didn't matter where the blood was flowing from, right? He could die of exsanguination either way. I tore another piece of the dress with my free hand. It was hard to fold it with a single hand, but it could sort of be done. It wasn't like anyone was going to grade me on my folding. I pushed the rough pad of cloth against his thigh and pressed, pressed as hard as I could.

I don't think I thought of anything. I could barely breathe. All my mind could form coherently was the certainty that Kit couldn't die. I heard my own heartbeat pound with a force that seemed to make my body quiver, and I willed Kit's to beat in unison. It seemed to me that I could feel it, too, echoing just behind mine.

It seemed to me the blood flow diminished and I hoped it was the pressure and not that Kit was dying, and it seemed like no time at all and eternity, all at once, and then there was a wavering light, and then, closer, the doctor, running, with a lantern affixed to his head, in the way that miners used to wear lamps on their foreheads in old period holos.

He ran much better than any man his age should be able to, his movements contrasting with his wrinkled face and his gnomic appearance.

He fell to his knees next to Kit and his breathing was labored and loud. I don't think he even looked at me, as his hand went first to right over Kit's heart, then he sat back on his heels, and reached into his black bag which he'd dropped by his side, and got out the lens implement, and looked through it, then tossed it aside, letting it clatter to the floor of the tunnel and reached into his bag again.

He had to pry my hands away from both Kit's temple and Kit's thigh, and he used something that looked like tiny squares of dimatough, which stuck to the skin, on top of the wound. It looked like he was taping Kit's skin together. The bleeding stopped immediately, and the doctor used an injector on the side of Kit's neck. There was a response from Kit then, a sort of deep sigh, and for a moment I thought he had died, but he continued breathing.

Doc Bartolomeu looked up at me then. "Are you hurt?"

"I . . . don't think so."

He got the examining instrument from the floor. His hand was stained red, from the puddle there. And there was blood on the side of the instrument, but the doctor didn't pay any attention, as he put it to his eye and looked through it. "No," he said, with finality. "You're fine."

I nodded and said, "Kit . . . He . . . bled a lot."

"He won't die from the bleeding," Doc Bartolomeu said. "I've given him something to speed up blood production. He might be a little anemic, but he'll be fine. I need to get him to my flyer soon, though. Ah. There they are."

As though on cue, just then, there were more lights coming down the hallway, the sound of running footsteps. For a moment I thought it was our attackers returning, then recognized Zen, ahead of them, followed by...yes. Jean and Bruno. They had a little antigrav platform between them, and were maneuvering it at about hip high.

Jean turned about as pale as spilt milk when he saw us, but the voice in which he asked Doc, "Okay to move him?" was perfectly calm.

"Yes. We need to get him to my place fast," he said.

Jean and Bruno managed it, though Kit was taller than either of them, and I suspected weighed more than either of them too. They managed it quickly and without seeming to strain, lifting him one at the shoulders and one at the knees and at the same time somehow maneuvering the platform under him.

Zen gathered up tools the doctor had let fall in the blood pool on the floor, and put them in a bag, then inside his big black bag, which she picked up to follow him.

Bruno turned back and said, "Thena?"

I tried to get up. There was no reason I shouldn't have been able to get up. "Are you?" Bruno asked.

"No, she's not," the doctor said, and in his tone of voice there was just the barest hint that I was being a weakling, and weak for no reason.

I managed to get to my feet, but my legs buckled under me, and I heard my teeth chatter, and realized I was shaking, and then I was furious at myself, and felt like I was a weakling and malingering for no reason. Kit was ill. Kit was struggling between life and death, and I was being an idiot and having issues standing up.

"Can you handle it?" Bruno asked, and it was obvious he was talking about the antigrav platform and of course they could, since Zen and Jean were keeping it level and moving, the lights on their foreheads disappearing in the gloom of the hallway.

Then he said "Easy, easy" to me, and took off his coat, and put it around my shoulders. I wanted to tell him I was sure that though I felt cold, I couldn't really be cold, but I couldn't talk and if I tried it, my chattering teeth were going to chop my tongue in half. He put his hand around my waist and led me after the others down the hallway. "It's reaction," he told me. "It's just reaction."

It wasn't till we were outside, and sitting on the back of what I thought was Doc's mobile treatment center flyer, that I looked down at myself and realized I was covered in blood everywhere I could see. Kit's blood.

And then I vomited.

UNDERWORLD

KIT LOOKED GREY AGAIN.

Doc's living space and his treatment facility were one and the same, and going to him for help was much like going into the home of a gnome in a medieval story.

It started at the low door, which was set into what looked like a hill side, and was in fact a very small hill taking up most of the plot he owned. It was covered in low-growing herbs, clover among other things. And the door was almost perfectly round, inset in the side of the hill, made of oak or a good facsimile. A huge iron ring knocker was the only way to call those inside. Not needed this time, as the door opened ahead of us, presumably reacting to some signal from the doctor. Then we were inside, and going past the doctor's long living room, with the walls covered in bookcases, and past the fireplace with large chairs one on each side of it.

And then past the kitchen which despite its modern cooker looked like an ancient kitchen, from the water pump—which poured warm or cold water at a signal—to the cooker which was hidden behind a holo of a cooking fire with a tripod pot over it.

After that opened an area that looked like—and probably was—a private relaxing area. A sofa had a book on top of one of the arms, as though the doctor had been interrupted by our call while reading, though that wasn't possible because he'd never have got to the complex in time. And there was a low table, with a dirty cup on it.

They set Kit on the sofa, looking even paler amid the garish floral pattern of the upholstery. He'd been treated on that sofa before and bled all over it, and I was sure so had other people, but it didn't show. I suspected the sofa, like most other things in this place was an impostor, a biological construct that drank up the blood spilled and remained sterile. The idea of that made me shudder.

But that was just a way to avoid thinking of how ill Kit looked, lying there, pale, and drawn and still.

Kit? I said, mentally, but there was no answer. And it was like everyone else had forgotten I even existed, not that it mattered. I *wanted* them to give Kit all their attention. Bruno had come in the door supporting me and dropped me in one of the chairs next to the fireplace in the living room. Not that I'd stayed there. Now my legs were steady under me, and I could walk.

So I'd come into the back room and leaned against the wall, as close to Kit as I could get, because I couldn't get close enough. Jean and Doc mostly were working on him. Or Doc was, and giving short orders to Jean to clamp this, and use that. I guessed that either Jean had some training, or he was really good at following half-barked orders. Or both. And the doctor's house might look like a cozy cottage, but it was obviously a sophisticated medical intervention center, as well equipped as any Earth hospital.

Bruno and Zen stood a little farther away, handing things to the main combatants. And I—a stranger so new to Eden that I didn't even know the limits of their biotechnology—could do nothing but hamper those who were trying to save Kit's life. I stayed at the periphery, looking on, feeling superfluous and useless, and trying not to think.

Trying not to think I'd gone crawling off, with my burner, looking for trouble, instead of staying and trying to cover Kit, trying to protect him. Trying not to think that he'd been the main target; he'd always been the main target. Trying not to think of where Zen had gone, when she had disappeared all that time.

But most of all, I was trying not to think of why Kit wasn't answering my mental touch. He should be able to. I should be able to *feel* him even if he were in a coma. I'd done so before.

The doctor took measurements and readings, swore softly, did something to the side of Kit's head that involved two tiny needles attached to what looked like a crystal egg, and started putting stickers on Kit's chest. I knew that type of sticker—it was a sensing device that sent info to a computer. Then Doc put something like a transparent helmet connected to other machines on Kit's head and swore some more, then looked up and saw my expression.

"He's not going to die," he told me, gruffly. "I know how awful it looks, but despite the blood loss, it's not nearly as bad as it seems. It's more..." He shrugged. "The brain damage is no more than he would have suffered if he'd had a small stroke. People survive those every day. Their brain reroutes and they go on. Some people don't even notice them. Their speech slurs a little, for a short time, and that's that.

"I'm going to guess it was not the shot your attackers wanted to make. He was probably moving too fast for them. Possibly he was trying to reach you. But the wound is enough to damage his coordination and his capacity to pilot... and judging from where it is, possibly his speech. Not life threatening, mind." Doc bit his lower lip, as though in worry. "He'll slur his words a bit, and his movements might not be as precise as they should be. But for a Cat..."

For a Cat, whose ability to pilot was all-important and built-in, whose speed and coordination were biological gifts he had had since birth, losing those would be like dying. I felt my legs go weak again. "You mean, Kit will never be able to pilot again?"

Doctor Bartolomeu looked at me for a moment as though he'd forgotten who I was, or perhaps as though he didn't understand a word I'd said. "No, no. Of course that's not what I mean. There are ways of recovering, including some very specialized neurosurgery combined with intensive therapy. Our problem is time. None of those methods will allow him to leave with us tomorrow and I can't take everything required for that level of surgery aboard the *Hopper*."

"We can't leave him behind," I said, louder than I intended, as I stared at the still-unconscious Kit and felt my throat closing in panic. "I think they were after him all along."

"Yes. That much is obvious," the doctor said. "No. We can't." Doc looked completely lost and, for a moment, like a little boy on the verge of tears, which was quite a feat when one considered that at the same time he looked hundreds of years old. And was. "Perhaps that's what they wanted. To have us leave without Christopher, which would leave him at their mercy, and would mean we didn't have with us the person they think can interpret Jarl's writings." He frowned. "But even if we just delay we'll be giving them an opportunity to make good on the attempt to kill him. Any time we remain on Eden gives them another chance to kill Christopher or sabotage the ship. We can't do that. It's obvious Castaneda wants him out of the way, though I can't even start to imagine why...unless..." He shook his head as he looked at Kit. "No."

Suddenly, his face seemed to crumple further, his wrinkles multiplying. It was horrifying, like something out of a scary legend, like watching a hundred years fall on a man in minutes. "Oh, damn it, Christopher," he said, under his breath. "Of all the things I didn't want to have to do."

"What?" I asked, because this sounded bad. It sounded very bad.

He paused, looking like he was trying to talk himself into something. "Yes. I'm very much afraid we will have to take drastic measures. And I don't like to do it." He looked up at me, his eyes bleak amid their nest of wrinkles.

THE MAGIC POTION

"NORMALLY I WOULDN'T USE THIS," DOC BARTOLOMEU said. Now I was the one closest to him. Jean had stayed in the other room, monitoring the machines hooked up to Kit. Bruno and Zen were probably there still. I hadn't paid attention. I'd followed the doctor back to his kitchen area, which I knew from before also served as a laboratory.

He had opened a cabinet that looked impossibly deep, and from within it pulled a few vials, muttering to himself as he shook them. After a while, he lifted one of them, frowned at the contents, read the label on it, which was covered in strange symbols that weren't even letters as far as I could tell.

"Is it a poison or something?" I knew that sometimes, for therapeutic reasons, people administered things to patients that would kill them under other circumstances. That was close to the full extent of my medical knowledge.

The doctor turned, still holding the vial in between his fingers, his expression for a moment completely blank, then focusing on me, as though he'd just noticed me. He shrugged. "No. Poisons are part and parcel of any doctor's job...this." He shrugged and suddenly smiled, a genuine smile. "I am old-fashioned, I think. Very old-fashioned, as this technology has existed since before we left Earth. This vial contains nanocytes of a specialized sort. They're repair nanocytes for brain damage." He reached under the counter for one of the bulbous round containers used for administering medicine. He fitted it with an inhaler tip, moving with all the care normally reserved for high explosives.

"What is that?" I asked. "I mean, why...why are you..."

"They're not inherently dangerous." He took a deep breath.

"That's not what I asked."

Doc, holding the inhaler in one hand, looked up at me. Up, though I was a small woman, because he had shrunk with age. Not that he'd ever been very tall, but I'd seen holos. He'd probably been around five foot six or five foot seven. Now his body had collapsed in on itself, unable to bear gravity for the three hundred or so years he'd been alive, even if some parts of him were younger. Growing cloned parts was normal in Eden, but the structure itself knew its age, and showed it.

His eyes showed it too, just now, shadowed with worry and looking very much like he'd rather do anything than tell me the truth. "You know nanocytes are old technology..."

I nodded.

"Well, these...these are just more specialized.

Nanoscale assemblers. They go in and repair brain damage, and restore connections that are supposed to be there. They provide two key functions, leading to neural rehabilitation. First, they provide trophic and metabolic support, to promote stem cell proliferation and replacement of damaged neurons, glia and micro vascular components. But new cells aren't enough, they don't have the proper connections. So the second function is to rebuild those connections by inserting synapsin and receptor proteins to restore neural connection. Does that help?"

"No," I said. "Considering how little of your science I know, and how little I can understand, they're just a sophisticated way of not answering my question."

He blinked at me, and something like a flash of amusement tinged his eyes. I suspected if he weren't so worried about Kit and about what he was doing to Kit, he would have laughed. "You forgot to add *you old fraud*," he said amiably, and the amusement in his eyes deepened, probably at my blushing. "Kit or Kath would have added it. Child, one of the few advantages of having practiced the medical profession since well before your great-grandmother was alive—"

"I didn't have a great-grandmother."

He fixed me with an unwavering look. "Athena Hera Sinistra, one of the advantages of having practiced the medical profession since well before the birth of the great-grandmother you should have had is that I can avoid answering questions without lying."

I stepped in front of him, on the path he would have taken to the room where Kit lay. "Kit is my husband and I have a right to know if anything you're about to do to him is dangerous." I was on shaky ground.

Marriage in Eden is a private contract between two
or more consenting adults, nothing else and nothing
more. It didn't necessarily give you the right to medical
decisions. We'd signed a standard contract, Kit had
said, with the modification that it was for life, but I
couldn't remember—suddenly—if it included right of
mutual medical decisions or not.

Doc Bartolomeu snorted. "Living is dangerous.
We've all been served a death warrant the minute
we drew our first breath."

I didn't answer, just crossed my arms on my chest
to let him know *that* was not even a sophisticated way
to avoid answering.

His gaze wavered and he sighed. He whispered
something that sounded like "I'm too old for this."

"You have some reason to mistrust this treatment," I
said. "Even though, as you say, it is old news."

He shrugged. "A friend of mine trusted on a nanoscale
assembler prophylactic . . . And it didn't work at all or
at least . . ." He frowned. "And Christopher . . ." He
frowned. "Well. It's probably safe, but . . ."

"But . . ."

Doc swallowed hard. "But," he said, speaking very
fast, suddenly, "Jarl Ingemar died of a neural degenerative disease known as Hampson's disease. The NSE/
NSA is useless against it and . . ."

"Jarl died of suicide," I protested.

"Yes, but long after it had become obvious that his
Hampson's was irreversible and that the nanocytes could
do nothing. It is a . . . No standard human on Earth would
even have known about it, since it hits only at what is,
for homo sapiens, an impossibly old age. But Jarl . . ."

But Jarl had been impossibly old in standard human

terms, over three hundred years old. "What does the disease do?" I asked. "And what can it possibly have to do with Kit who is still very young?"

"Well . . . I said that nanocytes could not fix the damage, but . . ."

"But?"

"But in injecting these nanocytes into Christopher . . ."

"Yes?"

"Even though they're of a very different kind from the ones we used on Jarl . . ."

"Yes?"

"They still need to know what the healthy configuration of connections for the neurons, the pattern of the healthy brain is. And I've never taken a pattern of Christopher's. He's young and, that I know, not prone to strokes, and besides . . ."

"Besides?" I asked. I was trying not to think that there was this monster-disease in Kit's genetics that would eventually hit him if we lived that long. In three hundred years, the chances of my darling still putting up with me were close to none. And besides . . . besides . . . Besides there were three hundred years, give or take, before we needed to think of this, and in three hundred years lots of things could happen.

"And besides, I don't like nanocytes. They feel too much like magic. So, I didn't take a pattern of his brain while it was healthy. What the nanocytes do is—in communication with each other—spread out and recreate the pattern of the healthy brain."

"And the brain you imprinted was Jarl's," I said. I can read the writing on the wall when the print is ten feet tall and written in fire.

It seemed like my words relieved Doc immensely.

His body sagged with relief. Had he been so afraid of having to say it? "Yes. Yes. But..."

"But?"

"Even though the imprint was taken in the early stages of Hampson's disease, I want to point out that none of this is relevant. Not really. Look...We're not remaking all of Christopher's brain in the model of Jarl's." His throat worked as he swallowed. "I wouldn't. It would replace Christopher with Jarl. It wouldn't be different at all from what your...what Alexander Sinistra wanted to do with you."

I supposed. Changing the recipient's brain to resemble yours was probably less messy than a transplant, but the result was the same. The original brain would stop existing.

"It's a small, localized dosage, carefully programmed, and too limited to effect any serious change in Christopher's brain."

"But you're afraid."

"Only because Jarl was in the early stages of Hampson's disease when the impression was taken," he said. "I'm afraid it will trigger it in Christopher, and I want to say that it's a superstitious fear, not at all real. But I..."

"Is there some way we can avoid doing this at all?" I asked. Yeah, I'm not superstitious. But I would not willingly drop cold iron in the middle of a Gaian priestess's dance. I would not loudly declare that a computer on which I depended had no personality. And I would not bet my husband's life on a risky treatment, if I could help it.

"Oh, sure. He'll survive on his own. And in six months, with therapy with some micro-targeted surgery, he will be back to normal. But..."

He didn't say *But we don't have six months.* He didn't need to say it. Oh, Kit had six months on the purely biological level. The program the doctor had outlined was safe, secure and... deadly.

People who would ambush us, coming out of the *Hopper*; people who would shoot an unarmed man in cold blood, would not shrink at trying other methods of getting rid of him.

The longer we stayed in Eden, the longer they'd have to try to kill Kit. I couldn't understand why they'd want to kill Kit, or why technologically sophisticated people with knowledge of biological science, would think that Kit had a special gift for understanding Jarl's notes, but they clearly did. And they clearly wanted Kit dead so that they could control energy production and energy access in Eden. And through it, all of Eden, which couldn't *function* without energy.

And in six months... They'd only have to be lucky once, while we, playing defense, had to be lucky every time. And they had all the power in the world, while Doc and I had only the sort of undertow, marginal power that obtains through family and friendship connections, through whispers in the dark, through messages passed in secret.

So far we'd been able to outwit Castaneda and the board, but only because there had been very little time, and they hadn't counted on us even attempting to defend ourselves. We'd had surprise and speed on our side. Not weapons you could deploy twice.

I closed my eyes, feeling as though cold were radiating from somewhere near my stomach and spreading throughout my body. I would not tremble.

Physical courage is easy, and yet each time, before

I attack, each time before I jump in the face of great odds, I'm perfectly conscious of a micro-hesitation before I move, a hesitation that tells me that I know the danger, and I don't like it more than anyone else would.

It's just that when faced with physical threats, as much as I hate the danger of attacking, I know there is also a danger in doing nothing. Adrenalin pumps through my veins and jumping to the attack is easier than sitting still.

When the danger wasn't physical, though, and when it threatened Kit rather than myself, courage was more difficult. Could I live without Kit? Sure I could. I'd lived most of my life without even knowing he existed. I could even live without love. For years, since my surrogate mother had disappeared in the night when I was six, I'd lived without love, my fists clenched against a world that didn't even like me.

Understand. I was my putative father's clone, in almost every way possible except gender. Stuff had been tampered with, of course. I was female, and there were a lot of genes affected by that, all-important change. But that change was not enough to make my basic personality different from Daddy Dearest's.

The gifts I had—of speed, of reasoning, my sense of direction, my effortless and unthinking affinity for mechanics, even the very odd telepathy I shared with Kit—were Mule enhancements. And I'd seen enough of my own basic nature which was often cold, grasping, selfish, and paranoid, to know I wasn't all that different from the late, unlamented Good Man Milton Alexander Sinistra who had been designed, long ago, by humans who should know better, to be a sort of super assassin: a human weapon that could be deployed with complete precision and utter ruthlessness.

Without Kit, would I become like him? Who knew? I didn't.

But to keep this treatment from Kit meant to risk losing him, anyway, and maybe Eden as well and everything I held dear.

What poet was it who had said something about, next to his lady love, considering the world well lost? Life never gives you the same kind of options that poetry gives you.

Give me half a chance to trade this world—both worlds, Eden and Earth, with the Thules thrown in to make up the weight—for Kit's life and happiness and I would do it without hesitation and without blinking.

But no one was giving me that choice. I could risk Kit's mind and life this way. Or I could risk it in a way that would be more dangerous and that might take the world with it.

I felt my fists clenching and opened my eyes, realizing my inner turmoil hadn't taken more than a few seconds. "Do it," I said, stepping aside. "Give him the nanocytes."

Even as I said it, I knew that the doctor didn't need my legal permission. I was Kit's ward not the other way around, and though we were married, because of my lack of legal status, I probably couldn't make decisions for him during his incapacitation. If anyone were legally responsible for Kit, it must be Jean and perhaps Tania.

But the doctor hadn't asked Jean. Or Tania. Or at least not in my hearing. He'd asked me. That was because what he needed wasn't legal permission but something far more complex. He needed moral authority, to salve his own all-too-human conscience, in case it all went wrong.

And while Jean and Tania loved the child they'd adopted while he was still in the biowomb as much as they loved their genetic daughters—if not more, as I'd sometimes suspected—their . . . *being* wasn't intertwined with Kit's, while mine was.

They'd survive his death, if it came to that. Parents do survive the loss of their children, though it's always a sad and terrible thing that by rights should violate some law of nature. I'd probably survive too, physically, at least. But some part of me was intertwined with what Kit *was* and that part would die forever with him.

No, I'm not speaking of souls or spirits. Or perhaps I am. Yes, I know that Nikola Tesla, about whom Kit had made me read, claimed to weigh souls as they left the body. I'm also aware that no one else has been able to prove the existence of such a thing.

But science or even philosophy, is very poor in words to describe what a marriage *is*. In fact, the human mind might be very poor in ways to explain it, which was why Eden did the right thing and treated marriage as a contract between two or more people and nothing more. Social norms should not trespass into the metaphysical.

But if you think about it as Kit and me being joined on some non-metaphorical and deep level that couldn't fully be talked about within the limits of words, you won't be far off. And you'll understand why Doc Bartolomeu asked my permission, not Jean's.

And if you say he didn't ask my permission, you're missing the point. He could have pushed past me, or refused to answer my questions. Jean, Bruno, possibly even Zen, would follow his orders and overpower me if needed.

"You sure?" he said, looking up at me.

I nodded. "Yes. Do it. For us, and... for Eden. Because these people shouldn't get away with what they're trying to do to Eden. Because... I want my children to have Eden as it was, not Eden as a fiefdom where only those in power count."

Kit? I said, a last attempt to reach him before this was done. There was no answer.

"It has to be nasally administered," Doc Bartolomeu said to no one in particular, walking past me, and kneeling beside Kit. "To circumvent the brain-blood barrier." He put the inhaler at Kit's nose and squeezed the bulb, to send the nanocytes into Kit's brain. It was done. Now, whether it triggered Hampson's disease, whether it gave Kit some of Jarl's personality, there was no calling it back.

I felt cold and numb in equal measures.

"No point being scared," the doctor said. "What's done is done."

"I'm not," I said. Partly because I was. I tried to smooth my hair back, but it was a mass of blood. Kit's blood. "He's not responding." I was afraid this data point would tell Doc that which none of us wanted to know: that Kit was gone, that the brain damage had been such, even if small, that the essential personhood was gone, and all that remained of Kit were biological components. *Who can call back the soul once it's flown?* I'm sure some twit of a poet had said that too, but it was true nonetheless. The hospital wards of Earth—at least the wards devoted to the richer patients—were full of patients who were physically well and whole, but who were in a deep coma from which they would never emerge.

"Oh, it takes a while," Doc said.

"He's not responding to my mind-touch!" I said.

"Oh." The exclamation came from Jean, who was hovering over the end of the sofa, near Kit's head. "Don't worry about that. He's in shock. He lost too much blood. And then the doctor sedated him, before he measured the damage, to get an unbiased measurement." He smiled at me. "Poor thing." I wasn't sure which of us he meant. "Thena, you should have asked instead of fretting yourself."

I behaved and refrained from telling him that no one had even let me near Kit, much less let me ask anything. For one, I didn't feel like I had enough energy to explain it, and for another he was now looking at me, and his concerned expression resembled Kit's too much for me to want to give him trouble. For someone who was no biological relation to my husband, he'd certainly served as the model that imprinted Kit's gestures, expressions and behaviors. "Don't let Doc Bartolomeu worry you," Jean said. "He can be stodgy on some things."

"Not stodgy," he said. "I don't like . . . no, I hate tampering with the brain. I don't know where personhood lives, any more than any other scientist or priest for that matter, but the brain seems to be an important part of it." He took a deep breath, and I could see him will what he said to be true, pushing his will power at the world and demanding the world obey. "Christopher will be fine. He has an iron constitution, as you know very well."

I knew. I remembered Kit climbing up the side of a ship while injured, not so long ago.

"Let's leave him alone a while, and then I'll do some readings to see how things are progressing. Mind you, he is unlikely to recover consciousness before we depart. But he will recover shortly afterwards, and I can take the piloting till he does." He hesitated.

"Doc," Jean said. "I think Thena needs to go home and wash and finish packing for herself and Kit." He put a hand on my shoulder. "Come on." He looked up. "Bruno?"

Bruno shook his head, took a deep breath. "If it's all the same to you, Jean . . ." He spoke slowly. "The ones who tried to kill Kit might very well try to do it again. The doctor will need to pack and sleep and . . . I'm armed."

Jean hesitated, then said. "Yes. We should probably also guard the *Hopper.* Yes, I know the compartment is locked, but any lock can be defeated." He looked hesitant. "But Thena—"

He didn't say I needed an escort—and possibly a minder. He didn't have to. I knew I did. I felt so tired that I doubted I could make it to the Denovo compound on my own. I'd probably mumble incoherent instructions to an automated cab, pass out, and be found, when the cab ran out of fuel, in two or three days in the bar levels or the vicinity of the half-g gardens.

"I'll take Thena home," Zen said, very quietly. "I need to go by my home, and pack, also. I'm armed. Thena is armed. And I will call for help if needed." I noted that she looked very pale, too. Like Kit, she turned the curdled milk variety of pale. She looked tired and as though she were awake only by the force of nerves. I didn't protest her offering herself as an escort.

But there was something nagging at me. Doc had

said Zen had contacted him, and now she said she'd call for help if needed. But I hadn't seen her use a link, ever, in the time we worked together. It made no sense.

I waited until we were in the borrowed flyer—Doc's small get-about flyer, not his big surgically equipped one—and halfway to the Denovo's compound. Past Center, while Zen set coordinates and altitude for the autopilot, I felt free to ask, casually, "Can you comlink ahead to the Denovo compound? I'd like Kath to pack Kit's violin."

Busy with the controls and the settings, Zen answered as I hoped, without registering that I could have any ulterior motives for the question, or that I could use the comlink on my bracelet. "Uh? I don't have a link on me."

I leaned back, not sure I liked it. She didn't have a link—at least not one she'd admit to—and yet, she'd called Doc Bartolomeu for help. He'd said so.

Or did she have a link that she didn't want to admit to? Had she joined the other side of the fight, there, in the dark tunnel, where we couldn't see our attackers? And if she had, what had caused her to call Doc? Had she known that Kit was hit? Had she thought he couldn't survive? Had the call for help—on an associate's link—been her way of covering her involvement?

Kit trusted her. Doc Bartolomeu trusted her. But Kit had trusted his first wife, and Doc had been one of Daddy Dearest's best friends back on Earth. Neither of them displayed the best of judgment when it came to people.

Who was Zen? What did she want? Why had she volunteered for this trip?

More importantly—which side was she on?

WHO GOES THERE?

RUN!

Run!

The thought, in my mind, made me jump, before I realized it was Kit's mental voice and so he must be awake, or at least more awake than he'd been for the last day and a half.

We'd just lifted off. Kit was in our bedroom, which had been arranged to look like our bedroom aboard the *Cathouse*, with bed and virtus cabinet and closet.

Kit's mind-touch came when I was fastened in at the control room, calling out coordinates to set our initial route. That route would be changed, needless to say, myriad times en route, to narrow it more and more. But if you started out badly wrong, the adjustments could take more fuel than you had.

The coordinates were charted on a tri-dimensional grid, projected on the screen. I glanced up at it, then at the astrogation map in my head. I'd memorized it long ago, and my sense of direction helped me navigate it. "D–55," I said, as I computed our route for minimum fuel consumption. "Now adjust to P–22–7."

Doc Bartolomeu, piloting, made the final adjustments to our orbit and trajectory, on our way out of Eden, headed for Earth. Normally after this point there would be very little piloting done, unless we met with an asteroid or some other emergency on the way. But the *Hopper* didn't have the normal automatic pilot arrangements, and so someone would need to make course adjustments all along the way. And for the larger adjustments, during the initial liftoff, the navigator was supposed to help with the calculations, re-checking, and adjustments.

The voice in my mind made me jump and, before my rational mind realized what my instinct recognized: that this was Kit, that Kit was still there, even if his body might remain unconscious, I had unsnapped the full-chest seat belt, pulled it off over my head, and was running full tilt towards our bedroom.

Kit lay in bed. He didn't have much choice on that, since he was strapped to it. The doctor had rigged the system of belts—loose enough to allow Kit to turn, but not loose enough to allow him to fall over the side. Which was the whole point. Doc was afraid he would fall, in the sudden, spasmodic movements that had shown up in the last twelve hours or so.

Those movements worried Doc, I could tell that, though I couldn't tell why. I'd tried to research Hampson's disease in the Denovo compound links, in the few minutes I had after packing and before I had to leave. But it wasn't in any database I could find and I started wondering if Doc had made it up.

So I didn't know if those sudden whole-body spasms and shakes were part of the symptoms.

Doc had shrugged and given me more medical double-talk along the lines that each brain was different and that it was entirely possible that all that was happening was Kit was dreaming, having come close enough to consciousness to be dreaming normally, but that the inhibitor of movement during sleep wasn't fully functional—possibly because of the drugs Kit had been given to speed his healing. In other words, Doc had told me that Kit was simply moving in his sleep, a milder version of sleepwalking. I wasn't so sure.

Kit had always been a restless sleeper, turning and shifting and sometimes mumbling. Shortly after we'd gotten married, he'd scared me by sitting up suddenly in the night, grabbing his pillow and flinging it, with intent and force, at the wall across the room. With such force, in fact, that the pillow had burst, letting bioengineered fluff fly all around the room.

But these spasms felt like just that—spasms—involuntary, near-painful seizing and twisting of muscles. It looked more like epileptic seizures than anything else. I didn't like it. I didn't have to like it. There was precious little I could do about it.

And all Doc could do was put belts around Kit's chest, middle, and ankles.

It took me a moment to register that Kit was fully awake, that his eyes were open, that he'd somehow—by force, probably—managed to tear the belt that had been around his chest and that he was now fumbling with the belts which fastened him middle-and-ankles to the bed frame.

The fact that Kit was fumbling with the closures meant that he was still not fully rational, because all such belts had a button that made them retract.

"Wait, Kit, I'll release you!" I said.

He looked at me, and for a moment his eyes were wild and blank with lack of recognition. Then he opened them more and shook his head as though to clear his mind. "Thena!"

The word came out slurred and weirdly twisted, as if it were pronounced by someone who couldn't quite control his mouth, and I froze. "Kit?" Had he got Hampson's disease from the nanocytes? Was this one of the symptoms? Or had the nanocytes done something? Changed something?

Kit tried to speak, and some incoherent sounds came out, and he hissed with frustration. Mentally, he said, *Thena! There's something wrong with my speech. I need to use the fresher!*

The last had the sound of a barely controlled scream in my head, and I grinned, suddenly understanding the wildness in his eyes. Bladder pressure can turn even the most civilized of men into a lunatic. I remembered what had been damaged was his speech center, and I said, "It's all right. I'll explain later." I reached over, pushed the right button, which he could have found if he hadn't been so desperate.

He jumped out of bed and almost fell. "Wha?" came out from his mouth and a more coherent *What's wrong?* From his mind.

"You were lying down for a long time," I said. "Also you have a thigh injury whose healing the doctor isn't speeding up. Here, let me help you."

I supported him to the entrance of the fresher, where he, being male, insisted on going it alone. I let him do so, because the cube used for the fresher was so tiny—between the necessary appliances and the door to the fresher proper—that he could lose consciousness and still remain upright. I don't know how doctors and nurses ever manage to make males accept care—at least males of Kit's type—short of hitting them over the head hard until they lie down. Which would defeat therapeutic intent.

I heard the noises of the fresher functioning, then the sounds of his washing his hands, and he opened the door and stood there, leaning on the door frame on the side of his bad leg. He tried to speak, but only grunts came out and he sighed. *Am I going to be deaf mute the rest of my life?* He asked.

"You're not deaf," I said, and to his frown. "And no. It's just that your speech center was damaged. The doctor has . . . done something to fix it." I crossed my fingers and hoped he wouldn't ask me what. I had a fairly good idea he wouldn't like it. "I can't explain it, but I know it's not instant. I mean, it's much faster than it would otherwise be, but it will still take time. And practice." I grinned at him, because he was looking very serious, and because I was so happy to have him back, in my mind and in body, standing there and glaring. "Which considering how much you talk, could take three or four years."

He snorted. An intentional snort of derision. His speech center might be damaged, but his snorting center was just fine, thank you so much. *What happened?* He asked. *Last I remember I'd picked you up to take you back home for dinner, and then there was a sound in the darkness and I jumped to protect you. And you insisted on . . . scouting on your own.*

"Yeah," I said. There was no point arguing, but I tried anyway. "It was stupid of you to try to protect me," I said. "It wasn't me they wanted. It was you. You know that, or should know that."

He frowned. *They wanted?*

"To kill. How bio-technologically literate people can think that you have your...clone's memories..."

He shook his head. *They probably believe the rumors.*

"What rumors?"

Kit shrugged. *Look, I don't even claim to understand them. There was talk...At least Kath says there is, though of course, people don't discuss these things around me, that I wasn't exactly Jarl's clone, just a... construct, with genes from my...from his wife, and supposed to look like him.*

"But that was the cover story!" I said.

Yes, but...no. They said that I was a construct, not his genetic child, but that he had his brain transplanted into my head.

"What? As a baby?"

I don't know, he said. *It is an inconvenience of rumors that you can't question those who spread them, and they can't explain. I suspect they noticed my... well, there's a resemblance to Jarl that's more than skin deep, you know? I understand we have...largely the same base personality and we're similar in terms of sociability and such. Even a lot of the same gestures and even posture and...If I'd been brought up by him, as had been intended, these things would pass unnoticed. But I wasn't, and people need to explain these things to themselves, and...someone came up with that lovely idea.*

I snorted, in my turn, because there was absolutely nothing wrong with my snorting apparatus, either. "It wouldn't be possible to transplant an adult brain to a baby's cranium," I said didactically. "And you'd think the idiots would know it. Or even to transplant a brain of a Mule into an unmodified homo sapiens body. We're not that different, but we're different enough that it would be rejected. There are genetic differences. It's the whole point." But even as I said it, my certainty wavered. An adult brain into an infant body, no. And besides, I was sure the Denovos wouldn't have lent themselves to such a thing. But an adult brain into a teenage body? Possibly. And though I still knew the Denovos wouldn't lend themselves to such a thing, either, most of Eden might not know it. They might be a powerful and well-known family, but they were also clannish and almost pathologically closed to outside prying. And they were descended from Jarl's own bioengineered servants.

The bond that persisted in Eden between former Mule Lord and the descendants of his servants seemed to me more paternal and almost protective than dictatorial, but who knew? Most, if not all people in Eden would retain family lore about that bond, in the probably stronger form it had exhibited on Earth. Perhaps they believed the Denovos wouldn't have the ability to say no.

Perhaps they thought Jarl's brain had been kept somewhere, then transplanted into Kit.

As for making a Mule brain function in a human body... it would be impossible on Earth, but was it impossible on Eden? "Perhaps in Eden science it is possible. To have a Mule brain in a human body? To pave over the genetic differences?" I said. "I understand near nothing of your science."

He gave a little chuckle, deep in his throat, and put a hand out, tentatively, to touch my wrist. *That makes two of us. I'm just a vacuum-ship-pusher.* Anxiety pulled his features taut, and he raised a hand in front of his eyes, staring intently at it as he wiggled his fingers. *Is Doc sure it will come back? My coordination and speed?*

"Yes," I said. And tried not to think of Hampson's disease, not to let the words pass my mind, much less my thought projecting ability or my mouth. It was much like trying all my best not to think of a pink monkey, but I must have succeeded, at least to the extent of not projecting it, because Kit released breath and lowered his hand slowly.

Good. Though I suspect it will need practice as much as talking. And when I didn't speak, he said, *So you see, I think it's stupid people hearing stupid rumors and believing them that are responsible for our...friends trying to kill me. They're afraid, poor idiots, that I have Jarl's notes stored in my head somewhere, ready to spring back to my consciousness, and make it possible for Eden to plant vast massifs of powertrees.* He shook his head. *As though, if that were true, I wouldn't have done it by now. I wonder if they think our going to look for Jarl's notes is just a cover-up...*

I didn't know and I didn't want to think about it. I don't like it when people behave irrationally. Yes, I'm aware I do it myself on occasion, but that's no excuse. When I'm acting irrationally, I understand my own irrationality. But when others are doing things so far removed from logic that I can't figure out their motives or reasons, it's like being locked out of a machine sequence and unable to understand it. If I can't figure out which buttons were pushed, I can't stop the sequence. And trust me, I longed to stop this particular sequence.

Kit put his hand on the edge of the dresser next to the door to the fresher, and hop-limped along it. *That is a beauty of slice off my thigh.* He said in my mind. *What were they using? Water mining lasers?*

I shook my head, not in denial, but in denial of knowledge. My throat tried to close. Just for a moment I was back in that corridor, with the lasers, smelling charred flesh and hair. *Kit.*

Easy, love. His hand clutched on my arm. *Even if my thigh hurts like hell. I suppose the doctor didn't want to give me anything to fix it that might interfere with whatever is fixing my brain.*

"Right," I said.

And I suspect the old butcher is flying this trap. Or are we far enough away that it doesn't need constant babysitting?

We're a day out of Eden.

So . . . Kit hesitated. *I suppose I should go to him for examination?*

I don't know. I'd left the Nav cage so fast, I hadn't asked anything. It occurred to me belatedly if Kit had been psychotic, uncontrollable, or even sleep walking, I'd have had no idea how to handle it. I knew that one of the spare rooms in the ship was filled with medical equipment, though torture wouldn't have got me to explain why Doc thought he needed it, because I simply didn't know.

When one of the bureaucrats that the Energy Board had designated to hinder the expedition had told Doctor Bartolomeu that he couldn't take medical equipment because it wasn't needed, Doc had growled back that medical equipment had a way of becoming desperately needed if you didn't have it with you. *I heard you in my mind, and I came and I ...* I suddenly remembered what he'd said in my mind. *Kit, what were you dreaming when you woke up?*

Uh? I don't think anything. Why?

Because what you said in my mind was "Run!"

Strange. He wrinkled his forehead. *Perhaps the word was just triggered by my urgency in getting to the fresher, because ... let me tell you, it was urgent.* He gave me an apologetic smile. *But if you ran off to come here, and Doc Bartolomeu didn't come after you, he must know or suspect what happened, and he must be in no hurry to make sure that I'm still compos mentis. I mean, for all he knows, I've killed you and am now hiding the body.*

He wouldn't want to interrupt you at that task. He'd wait until you were done cleaning up the cabin and throwing the pieces into the disposal.

Of course. Otherwise, he'd have to help. Seriously, Thena, don't you find it weird that he didn't come here at all? I could be having some weird symptom. Brain damage is tricky.

I couldn't help it. Laughter bubbled up from my throat before I could stop. *It would be odd,* I said. *If the room com weren't wired for sound and sight so that he could keep track of you while you were unconscious. In case you should suddenly need us.*

Kit looked towards the camera pickup in the room—a standard location as Cats and Navs often used the circuits to keep in touch with each other while working around the ship. This one was high up on the wall of the room farthest from the fresher, so that its sweep took in all of the bedroom and the door to the fresher. The fresher too, if the door were left open. *Well, then I assume that Doc is in no hurry to see me,* Kit said. *Would you tell him, since I can't seem to speak properly, that I'm taking a bath before I go to see him? And that that pickup better be shut in the future, whatever the old perv thinks?*

I said it, aloud, without the color commentary even while Kit wrinkled his nose and spoke on in my mind. *Why didn't you see to it that I got a bath or something? How long has it been? I smell like a chemical plant, and—ew—there's blood on my neck and my suit. How could you stand to be next to me?*

We didn't want to move you!

Of course not. It would waft the smell farther off, he said, as he went into the fresher. I heard him clang the doors shut, heard the sound that meant it was functioning on minimal-water setting.

At least he didn't try to sing. Though he was more likely to hum a version of orchestral pieces, he had a stock of popular songs he'd been known to sing in the fresher, and those would sound very weird given his inability to speak properly.

I stood outside, listening to the hum and splash of water. I wasn't going to blame him for taking a real water shower, rather than a simple vibration one. Yeah, I know. Scientists have proven that vibrations can bathe us as sparkling clean as water. More. They supposedly even clean our teeth and, for all I know, condition and rinse our lungs. But that is not the point. After vibrating yourself clean, you still felt sticky and dirty. With water and soap, you felt clean.

In the same way, though I knew he didn't even have the room to fall in the shower compartment of the fresher, I kept imagining him falling, hitting his head, drowning. The human mind is an odd thing.

Kit, I said, to reassure myself.

Beg your pardon? A mental answer came back and it didn't sound like Kit at all.

Kit? I asked, wondering if I'd somehow got hold of Doc's mind. No, it shouldn't be possible even if we were all endowed with the same type of mind-speech and receptors. Normally you can identify the mind you want to communicate to by feel, and it's not all that hard to keep it contained.

Heck, normally one didn't communicate accidentally even under great stress. It had never happened to me and my friends back on Earth, though since they were all the clones of their Mule "fathers" they all had to be endowed with a similar mental ability.

Who is this? The stranger's mental voice came again, sounding, for all the worlds, like I was the one doing something outrageous. *Irena?*

And that was when I screamed.

VOICES

SEVERAL THINGS HAPPENED, ALMOST INSTANTLY. One, the fresher door opened.

It would have taken Cat speed for Kit to open the door to the fresher that quickly, let alone to turn the shower off—it wouldn't let him open the shower door otherwise—and then open the fresher door and rush out.

But Cat speed or not, Kit forgot he was hurt, and plunged forward towards me, at what would have been a run, except his left leg gave out under him. His knee hit the floor with a sickening thud. A scream escaped him, as he bent over his leg keening in unreasoning pain.

The next thing was a woman's voice, from the door to the cabin, sounding very cold, very clear. "Stay down. Do not go near her."

I turned around. Zen stood in the doorway, in the posture taught in every shooting class, feet slightly apart, arms braced, holding the burner pointed at ... Kit.

141

"He didn't do anything!" I said.

"No?" she said, but didn't stop pointing that burner. Kit glanced up, pale, with tears of pain shining in his eyes. He was naked and wet. Blood covered his thigh. His running must have ripped whatever bandage the doctor had glued on.

"What in all the hells is going on here?" the doctor's voice asked.

"No-nothing," I said. "That is . . . Kit has hurt his leg. You need to help him."

"You screamed like that because he hurt his leg?" the doctor said, and gave Zen one of his patented annoyed glances. "Oh, Zen, for the love of little children, put that damn thing away. Even if Christopher— Just put that thing away. And go get me my bag."

I had the impression of something bitten off hastily after "Christopher" and I also had the impression that Zen knew what it had been. Something I didn't know about Kit? Why? And how?

But she looked reluctant, as she slipped the burner into her pocket and turned to leave.

And while Zen might be reserved, and she might be cold, the one thing she wasn't was completely crazy. She wouldn't have pulled that burner on Kit, while he was fallen over one knee on the floor, unless she had reason to suspect he was dangerous. Dangerous how? Dangerous to me? And why would Zen know that when I didn't? What had Doc told her?

And whose had been that voice in my mind? Who was aboard ship besides us?

Doc had approached Kit, who tried to stand, but was shaking too much and, from the expression on his face in obvious pain. "Idiot boy," Doc Bartolomeu said.

I'd found out long ago that the Doctor tended to scold one and disparage one's mental abilities in proportion to his fondness for the person being addressed. And he was very fond of Kit indeed, probably holding him in as much affection as though Kit had been his son, instead of merely the clone of his childhood friend. "What did you think you were doing, trying to run?"

Kit's mouth worked and sounds emerged, then he took a deep and frustrated breath and managed, slowly, what might have, with some good will, have been interpreted as "Thena. Scream."

"Yes, she screamed," the doctor said. "For no good reason I can imagine. Ah. Thank you." The last was as he turned to receive his familiar black bag from Zen's hands.

"I heard someone," I said, defensively.

"Of course you heard someone," Doc said. "Yourself. You screamed. Let me tell you, girl, they probably heard you on Earth."

"No," I said. I had a feeling he was being purposely obtuse. He didn't want to know. He feared that there was something going on he didn't wish to face, and therefore he would stall me and treat me like an idiot, if I let him. But he had told Zen what he suspected. It was the only thing that explained her overreaction. "No. I heard someone in my mind. Like . . . like mind-talk."

Doc was slathering Kit's wound in something sticky that smelled repulsively sweet. "Kit, were you mind-talking her?"

"No." *I think I fell asleep in the shower,* he said, in my mind. *I only woke up with your scream. Thena, what do you mean you heard someone in your mind?*

"A stranger's voice," I said firmly. "Please don't treat me like an idiot or a child. I know I'm younger than you, but I'm not an infant. There was a stranger's voice in my mind."

This made the doctor frown in my direction. "Are you sure?" he asked. Then he looked at Zen. "I haven't done a sweep of the ship. You have. Could we have a stranger on board?"

Zen shook her head. "You're welcome to double check me," she said. "But no."

Doc was fastening a skin-colored patch across the jagged rent on Kit's thigh. I hadn't seen it clearly or for very long, but I had an impression that cut was almost bone-deep. No wonder Kit couldn't stand fully on that leg, much less run. "If you don't try to run marathons, this should stay in place now, and stimulate your body to heal itself, so that you will be fully able to stand and walk on it in a month or so."

Kit nodded. *I should finish my shower,* he said, in my mind, and I relayed.

"Not..." The doctor looked reluctant, but like he knew he had to do something no matter how unpleasant. "Not yet." He stood, grabbed Kit's forearm. "What were you thinking about in the shower?"

"He says he was asleep," I said.

Or at least not aware of being awake.

"Why did you say *run* earlier?" the Doc asked, and his asking it caused both Kit and I to stare at him openmouthed.

"You can't have heard that," I said. "You can't. The telepathy only works between a bonded pair of—"

"Forget it," Doc said. "You're being irrational. Yeah, Eden telepathy only works between a bonded pair of

Cat and Nav. But Eden telepathy is a different animal, in range and kind from what Mules had. And what you and Kit have is Mule telepathy. And even though we worked very hard at conditioning Kit to believe he could only communicate with his spouse, and even though you don't seem to pick up anyone else, it is possible to. And I heard him clear as day in my head when he woke, saying *run*. So did Zen. Just like I heard Zen before, when she panicked over Kit being hurt and mind-called me back in Eden." He looked at what must have been our equally outraged expressions. At least, Kit looked outraged and I felt outraged. "Don't bother. That was the first time I heard Kit, or at least the first time since he was a toddler. But I'd like to know. Why *run*?"

I don't know, Kit said. *I don't remember thinking it, much less projecting it.*

Doc didn't look like he'd picked up any of that, which was good and bad. Good because I'd really hate to have to kill him, but if that were the alternative to his listening in on every one of Kit's and my private exchanges, then I'd have to face the terrible necessity. And bad because it meant I had to repeat everything in voice to Doctor Bartolomeu.

It didn't help that it made him frown more. He said "I see." And I had the terrible impression that he meant it. And that he didn't like what he saw.

"So?" I said.

"What did he say?" He asked. "That made you scream?"

"He?" I said. "It wasn't Kit's voice!"

Doc waved an impatient hand, much in the way he did when we said something startlingly stupid, and said, "What did he say?"

I noted he didn't have any doubts of the gender of the voice. Curiously, I didn't either. Don't ask me how one can perceive such a thing in a mental voice, which by definition is devoid of sound and timbre and intonation, but it was a male voice.

"He said...he asked who I was," I said. "And he begged my pardon, you know, like people do when they don't know someone."

Are you sure you didn't just dream it? Kit asked. At the same time, I managed to say, "Who is Irena?"

"What?" the doctor said, and looked at Kit as though he'd grown three heads, all of them snake-shaped. Then he looked back at me. "What did he say? All of it?"

I repeated it, slowly, while Doctor Bartolomeu looked at Kit and frowned. "Are you sure you were asleep in there?"

Kit's turn to frown, then shook his head. "Thena. Screamed. I...Wakened?" The words were slurred but understandable.

The doctor took a deep breath, then let out with the longest, lowest, string of profanity I'd ever heard issue from human lips. At least the words I understood were low and vicious and nasty. But I only understood about a third of them. From the sound of it, some of it was ancient languages.

"Doc?" said Kit. His voice shook. *Thena, what's wrong? What is happening? Why does he keep looking at me like that? What have I done wrong?*

I don't know, I said, and then aloud, "Who *is* Irena?"

Irena Alterman—Ingemar, since she took his *name against custom—was my moth...the woman who married my fa...Jarl,* Kit replied. And then, *Thena!*

The last as I felt as if all blood had drained from me, downward, and as if my heart sank somewhere into the floor of the cabin. I looked at Doc Bartolomeu and he looked back. For a moment, we each knew what the other feared, clearly, without words.

"What have you done?" I said, at the same time he said, "What have I done?"

Jarl's brain-pattern had been used for the nanocytes that had been injected into Kit to heal his limited head injury. Doctor Bartolomeu had said that they were neither enough, nor programmed to do anything that would make Kit have any of Jarl's memories or . . . or Jarl's personality. He'd *promised*.

Even as I thought it, I realized that no, he hadn't promised. He hadn't even hinted at promising it. He'd just said it was impossible.

And now he was repeating it, loudly, and in a tone of finality, "Impossible!" And then, snapping, "Christopher, lie down. I need to get some equipment to figure out what's going on."

ALL TOO MORTAL FLESH

"IT'S IMPOSSIBLE," DOCTOR BARTOLOMEU SAID AGAIN. It was the third time in fifteen minutes. He stared at Kit as though he'd not only grown three extra snake heads, but also wings and possibly a pseudopod and some tentacles.

It's been my experience—limited as it is—that when people say that something is impossible that often, they know it's not, but they very much wish it were.

He swallowed, hard. "The brain shows nano assembler activity all over, but..." He swallowed and said again, "That's impossible."

My hands were clenched so tightly that if I pressed just a little harder, they'd form into twin black holes and suck all the contents of the universe into them. My palms hurt where my very close-cut nails bit. "Don't say that," I said. "Word magic doesn't work. Just saying something is impossible doesn't make it so." My voice didn't sound like my own. It sounded low and hard. "I know what you told me before we left. I know what you explained. What could have gone wrong?"

"Nothing," he said. And he sounded defensive, but not so much as though he were trying to convince me. More as if he were trying to convince himself. "Nothing could have gone wrong. Christopher, I swear the nanocytes I gave you had no power to colonize beyond the very limited area to which they were targeted to go. And the only thing they were programmed to do was repair. Not...not..."

Doctor Bartolomeu stepped back and fell into a chair at the foot of the bed. He lowered his head to his hands, and sat like that, for a moment. When he lifted his head, he looked tired, sick, aged and despairing.

Is maternal instinct programmed into the female of the species? Mules too? As far as I knew I was the only female Mule, ever, so there had never been a Mule mother. And yet, I felt like going to Doc, soothing him.

But I wasn't going to. Maternal behavior is part of the expected response from women. No, it didn't mean that Doc was acting helpless on purpose. But it meant if I acted maternal, he might never fully explain himself. Instead, I stayed rooted to the spot, waiting.

He looked at Zen. "Zen, child, would you go to my room and get the bottle of brandy from the cabinet by the bed? Thank you. Medicinal," he said to us, as Zen left, wordlessly. "I am...I will explain, but..."

Zen came back carrying a glass decanter filled with amber liquid, and then I knew that Doctor Bartolomeu was really feeling unlike himself. I'd long ago realized that his behavior was carefully orchestrated and managed, that he kept himself in hand and made himself look human and act human because at the heart of it he was afraid he wasn't.

Genetically, we were close enough to homo sapiens, even if—by design—not cross-fertile. We were human enough, I think. But Doc had not been raised as a human, if what I'd been able to glean about Mules and their childhood was true. And he was still trying to compensate. His entire construct of a house, trying to appear like something out of the Middle Ages, his fondness for adventure books and sugary drinks were ways to reassure himself that he was a human like others, and rooted in a common history; a common fund of legends.

Now he didn't bother with a glass, or any of the other ceremonies that he would normally demand of himself, because it was filed somewhere in his mind under "how humans drink and appreciate liquor."

Instead, he took a swig, directly from the bottle, shook his head, took a deep breath, took another swig and then capped the bottle.

Kit had sat up on the bed. He'd put on the same ratty, violent-green robe he often wore around the *Cathouse*. He hadn't bothered to put clothes on underneath, but, for reasons known only to him, had put on a pair of dress socks, the type he wore with his uniform. They were dark blue, and not at all like something he would normally wear. He was now staring at them as though wondering where they'd come from, but I could tell from the tense set of his shoulders, his almost too impassive expression that his thoughts were occupied with far more than socks. "Doc?" he said.

"Yes," Doctor Bartolomeu said. "Let me tell you about your parents' death."

Kit looked up, frowning. *Thena, tell him this: You've told me. When I was fourteen. At any rate, I think half of Eden knows the story. It was in all the holo recordings. I've seen the recordings.* I repeated.

"No," Doctor Bartolomeu's voice sounded harsh and scratchy, as though he'd been eating gravel for a while. "Oh, no. What the casts say, what everyone knows, what I told you, sensational as it is ... is only half the story. If that."

"Why?" Kit said.

The doctor made a gesture with his hand, as though dismissing the whole question as irrelevant. "Jarl ... I've told Thena, but I don't think I've ever told you, Christopher—I only told Thena when we were faced with ... that is ... I only told her because we had to use nanocytes, and I had a bad feeling. Though, I might say, the bad feeling I had wasn't ... this." Again, a sweeping hand gesture that took in Kit and the small machine clicking on our bedside table, the machine that apparently told him that nano assemblers were active all over Kit's brain.

"Is it possible the readers are malfunctioning?" I asked.

"No." The doctor took another swig of brandy and sighed. "Let me tell it, from the beginning. Jarl had Hampson's disease. We had suspected it for ten years or so, before I was able to diagnose it as Hampson's disease. At first we thought it was Alzheimer's. Alzheimer's poisons brain cells, but if you can detoxify the cells they can function again. So we had tried to treat with nano assemblers, and got some results, but not a complete cure."

What in Hades is Hampson's disease? Kit asked. *And do I have it?*

"You have the genetic markers for it," Doctor Bartolomeu said. "Of course. Whether you'll develop it or not depends on a number of things. We couldn't remove it, because the gene is coupled with others that you need to be...you. But it is also not a gene that is active or activated, necessarily until some... exterior stimulus brings it about."

"But I thought..." I said. "I mean, the Mules were created in a laboratory. Pardon me for speaking frankly." This was one of the things never mentioned openly, in front of Doc. That Doc Bartolomeu, and Jarl Ingemar and my own, unlamented progenitor had been created in a lab, assembled almost DNA strand by DNA strand. It seemed to upset Doctor Bartolomeu, so we didn't mention it. "I thought Mules were designed to the last detail."

"Various labs. National labs. National teams," Doc Bartolomeu said. "Each of us is the culmination of some country's bio expertise and, in their opinion at least, the best their breed had to offer. But they shared knowledge. And if what you mean is that we were created out of clean DNA and that everything that went into us was supposed to have been combed through and got rid of bad genes before our various enhancements were applied, that is true. But this was also the twenty-first century. The dark ages. Genes are coupled, and a lot of them express as junk DNA or were supposed to be junk DNA. They didn't know..." He shrugged. "No one could have known. Though Hampson's disease was discovered in the mid-twenty-first century by R. Edward Hampson, from the University of Aberdeen, they weren't sure what caused it. Some people thought it was a form of Alzheimer's, because of how it presents. Jarl and I thought so ourselves when the symptoms started.

"Wishful thinking, because it was curable. We should have known better. We should have known much better. Alzheimer's genetics were well known by the time we were made, and that would never have been allowed to slip into our makeup." He shrugged and looked at the bottle of brandy as though contemplating drinking more. He must have decided against it, because instead of uncapping it, he sat there, playing with the top, making a sound of glass-on-glass that set my teeth on end. "Hampson's destroys the connectivity between the neurons. Not the cells, but the synapses that store information—all of the memories, skills and experiences. Little by little, it severs them. It doesn't actually liquify the brain, because the brain cells are still there, it just starts breaking down the proteins that form the synapse connections between neurons. It destroys personality and knowledge and mind. It is a disease of extreme old age, though in homo sapiens that can be around a hundred or so. Which is why it wasn't discovered till the mid-twenty-first."

He pulled the decanter's top off, then slammed it back in, and held his palm across the top as though preventing it from jumping out on its own. "It is irreversible. Or at least it is irreversible by any methods that . . . that we could think of. Jarl modified the nanoscale emitter/nanoscale assembler prophylactic treatments we had, in an attempt to stop the illness. They are nanocytes that, once inhaled, can go to work on the brain and modify it to resemble what it once was. It means you lose memories since, since they work according to pattern, but it's better than the alternative. They are programmed to activate stem cells and . . . recreate the brain as it once was. The NSEs—that's the nanoscale emitters—map all of the connections. They were invented as a substitute for medical diagnostic imaging—sort of like a super MRI. The NSAs—the assemblers—read the map and can rebuild it when damaged. It's not . . . it's not as obvious as this, but if you think of the brain as a datagem in which knowledge is stored, where part of it has been erased due to magnetic activity, the NSEs . . . nessies, we call them, can restore the shape that was in the gem before, which restores the memories that were there—anything from the history of Earth memorized in primary instruction, to how to tap dance, learned at eighty."

He waved his hand again, and met Kit's eyes. "We made an imprint of Jarl's brain using nessies." He stopped. "At any rate, it wasn't perfect; by then, he'd suffered some degeneration due to Hampson's. He said he wished he still had the copy of his alpha pattern, but I have no idea what he meant. It was still close enough. Little memories might vanish, like names and faces—in other words, retrograde amnesia. But the means to make new memories and recall what remained was still intact. Enough that if his brain could be made healthy, he could have gone on living without much problem. He might suffer such indignities common to the rest of mankind as having to, occasionally, read over a book that he'd read once, or perhaps lose his codes to some of his locks. But he would be normal otherwise.

"Only we could not make his brain healthy. Just replacing cells was not enough, the *synapses* are where the real memories and skills are stored. The thousands of synapses each neuron makes are why we could never build a computer comparable to the human brain. It's not just the billions of processors that are needed, it's the quadrillions of connections that those processors require. His synapses kept failing, and his brain kept degenerating, faster than we could restore it with the nessies. He kept resetting his memories and losing days, weeks, months, years. And fresh inhalations didn't help, because there is a saturation point. Because the NSAs require a healthy brain map, and the NSEs were working on an already damaged brain. Which is why we came up with another plan."

"Oh, *Light!*" Kit said. It was said with feeling and emphasis, even though a little slurred, and I didn't ask him what he meant, because I thought I knew. Although I couldn't quite see what Doctor meant, I was starting to get the shape of it—the contours, as it were. And I didn't like it any better than Kit did.

The doctor didn't ask what Kit meant, either. He just said, "Quite," and continued. "See, we had figured out, ten or twenty years before, I don't remember, in our research, which we did mostly because his social life was rather limited in Eden, and what there was of it was with people who tended to fawn over him ... Anyway, in our research, we'd figured out the way to clone ourselves, and had in fact created a couple of clone embryos—"

"What?" from Kit.

"We had created a couple of clone embryos of Jarl's. Just to prove we could. They were deep frozen and carefully stored, though I don't think either of us intended on their being used. Not then." He frowned. "The way we were brought up, or perhaps...perhaps something about us...We weren't, then, particularly interested in offspring, or in raising children or..." He shook his head. "It never occurred to us we would eventually die, I think, until Jarl...until Hampson's. And then it seemed too late to start, except...except that Jarl thought he could marry. A pretense marriage. Mostly. He was very fond of Irena, but...She knew who he was, and of course, it would never be a relationship of equals. But he thought he would marry her, and tell her that he wanted to raise his clone, that this would give him a new lease on life. Because everyone in Eden had noticed he wasn't exactly himself those days."

"That's what you told me," I said. "That he did it for a new lease on life. You mean it wasn't the truth?"

"Not...exactly. You see, he planned to introduce the nessies to the womb at a critical point in the development. A modified set of nessies with no mapping capability, only the 'repair' nanocytes. That was part of the reason that we decided Christopher would be a Cat, because that gave us an excuse to introduce a virus to the womb and...and other things could be sneaked in along with it."

"Modified how?" Kit managed to say, in a voice that was all rasp, seeming to issue from his throat without modulation.

"Modified so that as you...as the embryo grew, it would replicate Jarl's brain."

"But it would be the same brain, anyway," I said. "Kit is his clone."

"Don't be puerile, child," Doctor Bartolomeu snapped. "I don't mean his . . . blank brain, the structure of his brain as an infant. I mean Jarl's brain, with all the connections, all the . . . all the data that was in it when we took the impression."

"How? How?" Zen sank to sitting on the carpet, and looked up at Doc. She was taking this much harder than I expected from an uninvolved participant. "The infant brain doesn't have the same structures, the same connections . . ."

"No, that's why the nessies were modified," Doctor Bartolomeu said. "They would lie dormant until the infant brain started to form its own synapses. Jarl had a program to time the actions of the nessies not to make too many changes at once. As Chri—as the child grew, it would slowly change his brain, so that by the time he was thirteen or so, he would effectively be Jarl. During childhood, the nessies would start to work on the prefrontal and parietal cortex, laying down the connections that created the personality, so that the eventual emergence of Jarl's personality would not be sudden. The onset of puberty would trigger the rest of the nessies to start forming the connections that underlay Jarl's memories. Puberty would also provide a perfect mask for the personality change as the child, as . . . Chris—as he turned into Jarl."

"Damn," Kit said. He scooted to the end of the bed and reached for the decanter from Doctor Bartolomeu's hands.

Doctor Bartolomeu extended the liquor, but I intercepted it, my hand around the neck of the decanter. "Is this going to hurt it? To speed up the nessies' actions or . . ."

Doctor Bartolomeu made a face. "Hey, it could even help. Suppress synapse formation for a few hours."

I removed my hold on the decanter, and he passed it to Kit, who took a deep swig from it, swallowed hard as he capped it again and said, *But I'm not Jarl. Or am I?*

Doc Bartolomeu shook his head, smiled a little, then looked grave again. "You are not Jarl. You see, things went wrong, and I swear by all that's holy if I'd known that there was the slightest danger..."

"Never mind that," I snapped. "Why isn't he Jarl?"

"I don't know. I thought it was because Irena found out. I don't know how. Either the house was bugged, something I've started suspecting just lately, or ... or she overheard us accidentally. Her reaction shocked Jarl. It surprised me. It had never occurred to us we were doing anything wrong, let alone immoral. I still don't fully understand it. We grow other body parts via cloning when they break down, or against the possibility of their breaking down. So ... why not a brain? The answer had always been because we couldn't replace the brain and have the same thoughts, personality and memory. But the nessies solved that, so ... why not? And if in the process we could pretend that this was not Jarl's clone, but just another human among humans, why not do it and free him from being known as a Mule throughout Eden? Being known for what he was had made his life odious.

"But Irena went berserk at the thought. She said it was immoral. She said it was wrong. That the child would develop, and then Jarl would just take over and destroy him. Despite being an extremely rational person, smart, really—Jarl wouldn't have chosen her otherwise—she could never give a coherent reason. She could just express disgust and repulsion.

"Because the emb…Christopher was not supposed to be a genetic relation of Jarl's, he was not Jarl's property. Irena had sole proprietorship over the contents of the biowomb, and she could order whatever she wanted done with them. And what she ordered done with them was to have them decanted. Prematurely. Two months of gestation. Killed."

He took the brandy from Kit and took another swig. "I never knew what happened exactly, because it happened, as these things normally do, in the middle of the night. It was…" He compressed his lips, his eyes suspiciously shiny. "It was impossible, to deny, on forensic evidence alone, that Jarl killed Irena, and then he killed himself. Both burner shots through the head. Very thorough. Very final.

"Of course, because there was no doubt he had survived her, and he was her sole heir. He inherited the contents of the womb, and he'd left a note saying Chri—Kit was not to be decanted until term. And because I was his heir, I inherited responsibility for Christopher. I went to the scene as soon as I could, but I couldn't tell what happened. There was a… womb injector on the floor, but part of the contents had dried around it, so I didn't know if any made it into the womb. I didn't know if Christopher had in fact ever been infected with nessies or not. I didn't know if the embryo growing in the womb was a new person or an exact replica of my old friend…and I'd have to wait at least thirteen years to find out." He shrugged. "I arranged for the Denovos to adopt him. I was not married and not in a position to raise a child, and they were the happiest family I knew. I wasn't sure what we'd do if he turned out to be Jarl's replica, but the Denovos stood as much or more chance of hiding that as anyone else. And they might even accept it, at least when there was nothing else they could do. Of all of Jarl's servants and dependents, their family had maintained the most loyalty to him."

"But Kit wasn't Jarl," Zen said.

"No. Christopher wasn't Jarl. By two that was very evident, and it only became more so as he became an adult. So I thought that Jarl hadn't got the fluid into the womb. I swear if I had known..."

"Were you disappointed?" I asked. It sounded vicious and I couldn't help it. The idea of two old Mules, plotting to create a new body and brain for one of them, was too much like what my father and his co-conspirators had done. Oh, okay, so perhaps not, not in a rational light.

After all, my father and his friends, because cloning was illegal on Earth, had to keep up the pretense of normal dynastic succession. They had to let an independent person grow and develop to teenage years, and then commit murder to get the younger body.

I suspected even if the same biological industry—including at nano level—were available on Earth as on Eden, they wouldn't have availed themselves of it. Think about it. If you create a replica of yourself, all you have is an identical twin who shares your memories. It doesn't mean you, as an individual, get to go on living. No, you'll still get old and die, beside your younger replica. Dying of old age was not what Daddy Dearest and his cronies wanted. In fact they changed, normally, before old age, when mild degeneration set in.

What Jarl had wanted, what Doc had helped him do, was more akin to creating an afterlife or a legacy—the sort of thing most normal humans can look for in their normally begotten descendants. The sort of thing that is the foundation of every human society.

Only they weren't considered human, or they had been taught they weren't. Was it so wrong for Jarl not to want to vanish utterly? Was it so wrong for Doc not to have wanted to lose the only friend he had who remembered him as a boy? Given Jarl's gifts, his technological work that few could emulate, was it so wrong, even for him, to wish to be around and continue working? Didn't his work benefit all of humanity?

The two things felt different. One was the killing of a person. The other, simply, the perversion of a new personality forming. And yet, both left a bad taste in the mouth. Both felt wrong in the pit of my stomach.

I understood Irena Alterman Ingemar. The personality would form until age thirteen. Taking it over would be like possession. Corruption of the innocent. Clearly, Doc Bartolomeu hadn't understood it, and he was the only witness surviving. But I could feel the recoil she had felt.

Were Jarl and Doc evil and wrong?

I didn't know. I'd never taken advanced metaphysics. I'd never taken any metaphysics at all. The closest I'd come to metaphysics and solving the unsolvable were late night discussions in my broomers' lair or aboard the *Cathouse*, when all other subjects are exhausted and the mind veered that way. But either with my broomers' lair, or with Kit, we'd been discussing in the absence of reasoned discourse by previous generations.

We'd been trying to figure out these dilemmas armed with nothing but our minds and our life experience, and what felt wrong and what felt right.

In this case all of it felt wrong—anything that Jarl could have done to escape death was wrong. And dying might have been wrong too, considering his knowledge and abilities which Eden desperately needed. Perhaps that's the definition of a tragedy. That there is nothing one can do to find a way out that won't be wrong. Sometimes there isn't even something that is less wrong.

POP GOES THE SHIP

"SO YOU ASSUMED THAT JARL HAD NEVER USED THE nessies?" I asked. I was only channeling the question that Kit had shot at my mind.

"What else could I assume?" Doc asked. "Christopher developed normally, and even though, eventually, I ... well ... Eventually I mourned for Jarl. I missed him. Miss him still. He was my only connection to everything that happened, to everything we were in our childhood. No one else on Eden even knew about Earth, except through historical holos. They ... had no idea. Even those who thought they did. I didn't have anyone to talk to, anymore; anyone who would unquestioningly understand my jokes when they referred to things long past. Of course I missed and miss Jarl but I ... I found out that Mules too could take interest in a new generation. There was Kit and ..." He slid his gaze sideways to Zen.

Zen sighed. She'd been sitting in lotus on the floor,

163

her hands resting on her lap. "I suppose," she said,
"I might as well tell you, Thena." And, as she said
it, I remembered that Doc had said she'd heard the
mental shout in the strange voice. And about her
sending the alarm, when Kit was wounded, via Mule
telepathy. She'd heard it; she'd sent it and so ... She
continued, "Kit and Doc already know, but you don't,
and it's been very difficult spending as much time
working with you as I have, and trying not to fall into
easy conversation because it might all come spilling
out. I've known since I was five or so because my
adoptive parents told me—"

"Your adoptive parents?" I asked. "You're ..." I
remembered Jean saying that Doc Bartolomeu had
suspected I was my father's female clone, because—
and then cutting off abruptly.

"Jarl's other clone. Zenobia. Spirit of Zeus. Christopher. Christ bearer." She flashed me a bright and
embarrassed smile. "I sometimes wonder what Doc
and Jarl were smoking when they came up with this
stuff. It must have been extremely good, and clearly
they weren't sharing. Or did you name us alone, Doc,
in homage to your lost friend? Never mind."

Doctor Bartolomeu blushed, a dusky tone on his
wrinkled skin. "It seemed ... There is such a thing as
folie à deux, and we'd been alone with our own ideas
far too long, talking to each other only. I think other
people ... No. Other people were still real and people,
but we weren't. Or those we could create weren't. The
idea was that each of us would be cloned twice, in
male and female form, and that each of them would
marry the other's clone and then we'd build another
ship and go to the stars, in search of our kind. With

us as sort of avuncular protectors to the young people. Before Hampson's became manifest, of course."

I started to open my mouth, but Doctor Bartolomeu waved his hand. "I said it was insane. A shared folly. The two of us talked too much to each other and too little to anyone else, and both of us so badly wanted to escape. Not Eden, as such. We each wanted to escape who we were. We each wanted to have a future and a family and to be...normal. We..." He shrugged. "It was a dream. I don't think either of us intended to do anything with it, except prove we could do it. Not really. Once we knew the escape hatch was there, we would have no need to take it. But then Jarl became ill and...We started growing Christopher and we thought we might as well grow Zenobia." The blush intensified. "And yes, I named you both, after Jarl's death. I was...grieving."

Kit's mouth worked, making sounds that couldn't be understood, and Doc Bartolomeu said, "No, we never grew the clones of me. We could have. It seemed easier to concentrate on Jarl's first, and then in a year or two...when we knew the pitfalls. The truth is I think I knew, even then, the insanity of it. It would have required us to control those clones, to force them to marry each other. It felt...dirty. It was too much like our upbringing, our...Our controlled lives, our lack of choices."

Did you know this? I asked Kit, sharply.

I knew Zen was my sister. Or at least I was told Zen was my sister when I was so young that I thought I was a normal homo sapiens. Strangely I never questioned it after I found out I wasn't human. Not... Not till this moment. I knew she was my sister, then

I found out I was a Mule, and the two facts didn't seem related or contradictory at all. I suppose if I had thought about it at all, particularly after knowing what you were, I'd have figured it out. But Zen and I rarely saw each other, and you know, she was married and had her own life, and I never thought . . . I rarely thought of her. It wasn't as though we were close. Honestly, I think at the back of my mind, I thought she was my adopted sister, like Kath and Anne, that because her adoptive parents were good friends and unable to have children of their own due to genetic defects Jean or Tania or both had donated genetic material . . . They were very nice to her, treated her as one of us, when she came to play. And Zen and I were both happy where we were. It didn't seem important. She Light! What a mess.

I had to agree on the mess, and I focused again on Doc Bartolomeu, who was saying, "I came to be glad that Jarl had failed. I like Christopher for himself." Doc looked up at Kit and blinked. "I suppose I should say, Christopher, that I love you like a son, or as what I imagine people with normal lives feel for their sons. I've seen you grow, and of course, you have a lot of Jarl's inclinations and dispositions, but you're not . . . Jarl. Not really. You're more like the new and improved model. What Jarl would have been if he . . . if we had been raised normally.

"We always assumed that Mules didn't act human because they weren't born of human parents, in the normal way. Because something in how their—our—genes expressed was different and made it impossible for us to ever be really human. But watching the two of you grow up I've wondered if that's true, or if it was simply the way we were brought up. Knowing we weren't human. Not really."

"So that's why Zen came with us," I said. "Because you thought she, too, might understand Jarl's writings?"

"No. Not because of that. She might understand Jarl's writings better," Doc said. "She... rebelled all along the line, including about her bioing as a Navigator. She studied science for a while, before she fell in love with a Cat and returned to the fold, and decided to learn to be a Navigator. She still graduated with her class, but she brought with her a knowledge of science that Christopher lacks. I stand a better chance of figuring out Jarl's notes than either Christopher or Zenobia. No, they both had to come because Christopher was in danger, and because Zenobia was the one Navigator I could trust implicitly."

"Though I did volunteer," Zen said. "On my own." She expelled air in something between a sigh and a huff. "I don't think I can fully explain it, but see, I knew I was Kit's female clone. With the family who raised me having moved to the Thules, and Len..." She paused. "Len gone... I didn't want to marry again. Maybe I'll never marry again. And Kit was the only... he's my only family. And then he was in danger. I figured even if I died getting him out of this, it would be a life well spent. What else was I doing with it?"

Kit smiled at her, shook his head. "Thank. You. Stupid. Lots. Of. Things. Can. Do."

He took a deep breath and spoke, each word carefully enunciated, though still slurred. "Is... that... why... people... in... Eden... think... I... am... Jarl... in... mind?... They... know... nessies?"

"Yes," Doc Bartolomeu said. "I suspect that so did Athena's fath . . . Alexander, you know? When you landed on Circum . . . No, he probably recognized your voice before you landed, over the com. The ELF-ing has masked your resemblance to Jarl, but your voices are remarkably alike, the same register, the same inflections."

"Not mentally," I said.

"Of course not," Doc said. "That is more like . . . Both of them are violin virtuosos—though we never pushed Kit to it—but the way they play, the . . . expression is completely different. But their voices are almost exactly the same, except for the fact that Jarl had a slight accent. Swedish was his native language. He only learned Glaish at three or four when they brought us together for schooling. He'd have lost the accent, I suppose, but his national trust made sure he spoke and read Swedish fluently. Still, an accent is not a thing of the brain. It's a thing of the ear and the training of throat and mouth. Alexander wouldn't expect those to survive a transplant to a new body, and of course he thought if Jarl had made a clone of himself, it was to replace the clone's brain with his own—"

"Which turns out not to be too far off," I said, perhaps cruelly.

"So, it makes sense that Alexander thought Kit was Jarl, in all but name. And you can imagine his fury, too. Jarl had stolen Alexander's new life, his opportunity to leave the Earth on the *Je Reviens*, and now he'd stolen Alexander's female clone, the culmination of centuries of research, most of it fruitless. It's a wonder he didn't kill you on sight, Kit. He must really have wanted your help with cloning . . .

"It's harder to imagine how people in Eden can have got the idea. But I think . . . I think Irena left recordings. Whatever she heard scared her. Perhaps she was afraid we'd use our modified nessies to tamper with her brain; who knows? It made no sense, since it would only work with a cloned body. But I think she left a cache of recordings or writings somewhere. There was something in Jarl's last note, about people not believing Irena's lies, which makes me believe she told him; warned him. And I think, whatever that was, Castaneda found it? I think he believes Christopher is Jarl and knows all Jarl knew. Hence his wanting Jarl dead. Perhaps not helped"—he bit his lip—"by the fact that Irena was his cousin and they grew up together."

"No, I'd imagine not helped by that at all," I said. "Quite."

For a moment silence reigned, then Kit grabbed the decanter and took another swig. "So . . . How do we stop . . ." He paused and seemed to regroup and started again, still very, very slow and very, very slurred. "How do we stop my brain from becoming Jarl's. I know he was . . . your friend, but . . . I like me. As I am."

Doc closed his eyes, compressing them tight, and then pressed his fingers to his temples, as though trying to contain his thoughts, or perhaps discipline them. "I like you as you are too, Christopher. And besides, the nessies making all these connections, all at once, might very well kill you. The human brain is not made to endure that type of thing. I just hope there isn't enough of the serum active. The problem is that I don't have the . . . necessary computer to create counter-nessies, but an EMP powerful enough to deactivate them all will cripple the ship. We need to create nessies that act like antibodies but only to Jarl nessies. The programming was Jarl's. If we find his notes...and if we can get to Earth and get...if I can get access to the proper machinery to create them, I think I can stop it. Reverse it, even."

"It's three months!"

"Yes. Meanwhile I'll have to find a way to...delay them. Make them slower."

He must have read the horror in Kit's eyes. I did. And I was sure my expression echoed his.

"I'm sorry. If I'd known there were dormant nessies in you, nothing in the universe could have persuaded me to use other nessies on you. Clearly Jarl managed to introduce the nessies, but something went wrong—or right—and they never activated. They were probably just below critical mass. Then I gave you the nanocytes, specifically to heal a brain injury. I'd given them to you before, but..."

"Not brain."

"No. Not inhaled. Not circumventing the blood/brain barrier. And I never thought...when I gave Christopher 'adult' nessies—not the modified juvenile ones that Jarl produced—the presence of the adult-pattern nessies 'matured' the dormant nessies and activated them and now..." He shook his head. "I don't know what to tell you. Except I'll do whatever I can to save you. As much as I miss Jarl, I don't want him back at your expense."

It wasn't the reassurance either of us wanted. Well, it certainly wasn't the reassurance I wanted. I wanted to know that my husband would remain my husband. I wanted Kit. I had nothing against Jarl—other than that he'd apparently killed his wife to get his way, though in the heat of the moment, and while mentally ill, I supposed that could happen—but I didn't want to have him in Kit's body. I appreciated Kit's body, but I loved Kit—the combination of his mind and body, and perhaps soul if there's such a thing.

And Kit looked bleak and scared. *How do I know, Thena?* He asked. *How do I even know if it's me? This is what split personality must feel like.*

I'll know if it's you, I said. *I'll tell you.* And even as I said it, I wondered if that was true, if I would tell him. If we couldn't do anything about it, wouldn't it be better to let him slip into oblivion without burdening him with the knowledge of what he was inexorably losing?

At the thought of his slipping into oblivion, leaving behind his body, still acting as though it were him, and as though he were alive, I felt the hair trying to rise on my head. I don't know what I would have said or done, if at that moment the ship alarms hadn't sounded, loudly, in a range that made all thought stop.

Zen and I were on our feet and running before we had time to reason. And both of us ran, instinctively, straight at the source of trouble. Those alarms could mean only one thing. The steering system of the ship had just failed.

PATCHES AND RAGS

IT TURNED OUT WE WERE RIGHT, UNFORTUNATELY. The steering system had just failed. Oh, no, not just failed. That would be too easy and much too clean. The steering system had disintegrated into powder. As though it had never existed.

"It has to be one of the material-eating bacteria," Zen said, as we were both hip-deep in the bowels of the ship, reconstructing the steering and navigation systems from scavenged parts and bits, and some of the spare parts we'd thought to bring along. Yes, we'd brought spare parts, but we never thought we'd need to rebuild an entire system.

"Bacteria that eat dimatough, ceramite, metal and biolinks?" I asked. "They'd eat us too."

She made a face. "No. A complex of bacteria, I think. But how could anyone have given the infection to anything that came aboard this ship? We had everything that came in scanned, to make sure it was clean."

172

I gave a bitter laugh before I realized what was so funny, and faced with Zen's glare—not improved by the fact she had a dark grease smear on her nose—I had to explain. "Everything we brought in," I said. "What didn't we bring in?"

"Damn," she said, and sounded so much like Kit when he cursed, that I wondered I'd never seen the resemblance before. Only, of course, they were different enough to throw anyone off, between male and female and one bioengineered as a Cat and one as a Nav. The changes to their basic genetics were wide enough. They probably only had as much in common as any brother and sister. "The Hull. The hull of the *Hopper*. It would be almost impenetrable even with bacterial infections because it's made resistant. It's not something a ship can afford to lose so it's well designed. While bacteria would eat through it, it would be so slow they'd eat everything in the ship first." She shook her head. "Of course, I'd never check. It was my ship. They infected my ship to trap me! And the technologies for designing materials-eating bacteria are all forbidden. I mean . . ."

"You mean Eden has no laws, but it's a small enclosed space, and attempting to create these would be something that should set off alarms amid the entire population and make its creator very dead?"

She nodded fiercely, and then disappeared into the engine compartment with an armful of pieces. From the depths came clangings and bangings as she assembled things. We had, of course, sterilized the space and the pieces, first, as well as it was possible to do so aboard.

"I don't think Castaneda is afraid of retribution. I

think he has arranged for layers of protection around himself."

"Yeah," Zen said. "I suspect so too. But all that protection won't be enough when I get back to Eden. I intend to see him die screaming."

"You can kill him after I kill him," I said magnanimously.

"There's something wrong with that reasoning," Zen said, from the depths of the compartment. "But I'm too tired to examine it. I'll arm-wrestle you for first shot at him." There was a long period of silence. "I think I have this on the way to being assembled. Let's hope at least that we got all the infection. Can you figure out how to replace the stabilizer?"

"Sure," I said, as I went in search of a part that would do and hoped this was the end of the infection.

"What burns me," Zen said. "What purely burns me is that Castaneda wants to control the entire world—what we do and what we become."

This seemed like an exaggerated claim and I muttered something about the Energy Board and the riches.

"No. Riches would be easy enough to embezzle from his current position, if that was what he wanted. But he wants to have some lever to make us obey."

"But make us obey to do what?" I said. This was something that hadn't been really clear to me. "I mean, my father got a mansion out of it, and he got, you know . . . He was safe," I said with sudden insight. "I think they never felt fully safe, not, you know, after the riots."

Zen shrugged. She gave me a darkling look from under russet eyelashes. "I don't think so, Thena. I mean, I don't think that's all it is, when people want this sort of control. Perhaps, perhaps it is insecurity, but that's too easy. I think they just want the power to tell everyone else what to do. There's something broken and they see other people as things... as play toys. I don't think he ever thought killing us was murder." She slammed a piece home. "Just that, you know, we needed to be out of the way for his grand plan to go on." I realized she was going to tighten the circuit wrong, because she was using her gestures as counterpoint to her speech. I nudged it aside, and gently pulled two bio circuits together, linking the new ceramite pieces. She nodded at what I'd done, as though approving it, then sighed. "It's like Doc, you know, still not sure why Irena was revolted by his and Jarl's plan. Honestly. They were doing the same thing, treating people as things." Her features softened. "Though, to be honest, in their case it is perhaps more understandable, if not excusable. They were treated as things themselves, weren't they." She checked my work as I linked circuits ahead of her. I wasn't sore. When your life depends on a machine, being checked is good. But I thought of Zen's relationship with her adoptive family, out of nowhere. She never talked about them. She hadn't immigrated with them. And, unlike Kit, I couldn't see she had holos of them anywhere around. "There," she said. "I hope we fixed it."

Only we hadn't. By a week later, when we had assembled the entire steering and navigation systems, it became clear we hadn't, because the air-recycling systems disintegrated suddenly.

This was, of course, a far more urgent job. Without those systems we'd die quickly. We got them patched in time. Just. And then something else broke. Zen and I worked, shift on shift, sleeping maybe four hours before going back to fix and reassemble a neverending succession of systems. Doc worked with Kit, both calculating and correcting courses and trying to stop the infection in Kit's mind.

I wasn't sure how much progress he was making, or what was happening, because I rarely saw Kit, certainly not often enough to be sure of what was going on in his mind.

You see, I only went back to quarters when I was absolutely dead on my feet. And because Kit and Doc were doing not only the piloting, but also the navigation calculations—since Zen and I were busy elsewhere with repairs—plus doing whatever it was that Doc was doing to try to arrest the process by which Jarl was slowly taking over my husband's mind, there was very little time for Kit and I to talk. We usually met only in bed, and only to sleep.

Sometimes Kit would clutch at me in the night, with the despair of a drowning child looking for reassurance. And sometimes...sometimes in the middle of the night I woke up with a stranger's voice in my head asking, *Who are you?*

THE MINOTAUR IN THE LABYRINTH

"WE NEVER INTENDED TO TAKE THE *Hopper* TO Earth," Zen said, for the third time. She looked very tired. She'd been the last one on repair duty. I'd just awakened and let the vibro shake me to awareness, then dragged on my coveralls.

While looking for Zen, who could have been repairing anything anywhere in the ship, I'd found her looking for me. She'd called a council.

This meant pulling the men away from piloting, which was a chancy thing, now that we were so near Earth. We were—in fact—within striking distance of Circum and the powertrees. But it was important, because we'd reached a point we couldn't go on as we'd been.

We sat around the little table in the kitchen, all four of us in the places we'd chosen at the beginning of the trip. Zen and Doc sat across from Kit and me, or at least what I hoped was Kit and me. I

177

didn't know how far gone Kit was. Just before he'd sat down, I'd seen his eyes, and there was a look in them, an odd...not-quite-Kit look.

Kit was no shrinking violet. I think part of what had attracted me to him when we first met, back when I registered my attraction to him as extreme annoyance, was that he was fully confident, as sure of himself and his abilities as I was of mine. I'd never met anyone like that before, and I think that cemented my interest in him.

But what was in his gaze just then was more than that. It was almost a swagger. The confidence of someone not only in what he knows and knows he can do, but in what he is. It looked like how I imagined the eyes of Alexander the Great might have looked when he contemplated invading India.

It had made me recoil a little, and then, looking up again, it was Kit's eyes, looking at me with concern and worry and just a little apologetic at having startled me. So I wasn't sure. It was the weirdest feeling in the world sitting there, right next to my husband, and not being sure he was my husband. Not being sure he wasn't a stranger, the almost mythical Jarl Ingemar. The creature who was killing my husband.

So I wasn't giving my full attention to Zen, either. But the third time she said we couldn't have gone to Earth in the *Hopper*, I sat up and noticed and said, "Of course not. Eden ships aren't prepared for entry into the atmosphere. But we were provisioned for return," I said. "They told us to provision both instruments and parts and...food and all, for the return trip, so they..."

Zen's hiss of desperation told me she'd answered this before, as did the way she turned to me and lowered her eyebrows. "Listen, Thena, why the hell do you care what they thought?"

"The idea," Doc Bartolomeu said, "was for us to set the *Hopper* in geosynchronous orbit. It would be a decaying orbit, of course—we don't have the ability to do much more—but it wouldn't decay that fast in two or three weeks, at most, and I hoped we wouldn't take longer than that on Earth. Then we'd take the lifeboat to Earth proper, and return in it to the *Hopper*."

"And I'm saying," Zen said. "That the *Hopper* will not be in an orbit, decaying or otherwise for more than a couple of weeks, before it becomes so much cosmic dust. At this point, I'm telling you, Doctor Bartolomeu, the *hull* is decaying."

I dragged my hands backward through my hair and thought lovingly of bug juice. No, my personality hadn't changed at all. I still hated bug juice. But the coffee maker had, incongruously, been one of the first things infected with and devoured by the bacteria. And I needed caffeine. But I'd been dragged here, with no time to get any. My head was at that foggy stage that foretells a huge headache. "When did the hull start decaying? I thought you said it was imposs—"

"Not impossible. Very difficult. But these . . . loving organisms were apparently created to become more vicious as generations went on. Lucky, lucky us."

"So we use the lifeboat," Doc said, slowly. "I suppose we'll have to find a ship to return to Eden, but . . ."

"The lifeboat is gone," I said. "It has been cannibalized for parts to keep us going."

"You what?" This was from Kit—or at least I presumed from Kit, in an outraged tone. "Didn't you realize we would need it?"

"Chill it, Highness," said Zen in mordant mode, and either Kit was not quite himself, or Zen believed so, since *Highness* was her nickname for what she called *Jarl Eruptions*. "We realized that without the parts from the lifeboat we'd not be able to keep breathing, which seemed kind of a priority for us at the time. But don't fret," she said condescendingly. "If it makes you feel better, those parts are infected too. More so, even if Thena and I should spend the next two days frantically rebuilding the lifeboat, at the end we'd have a well-organized pile of dust."

I blinked. Even I hadn't realized the situation was that dire.

"Oh, please. There has to be something you can do. Despair is a cover for incompetence," Jarl said, and that time I was sure it was Jarl. My husband was not sweetness and light. Had never been. When cornered and pushed, he was quite capable of behaving like the sphincter of the universe, lashing out first and thinking last. But he would never have said those words. Ever. Kit was a kind man. What was more, he'd been raised in a society of equals. Those were the words of someone who had commanded long enough that he thought he could use his words as a whip upon his serfs and that this would, somehow, magically, bring forth a solution.

I turned a little and saw him open his mouth again, and Doc interrupted. "Not now. You're not adding anything to this conversation, and you can't whistle a solution out of thin air." He paused. "Nor can I. I'll confess I don't see anything for us to do, except perhaps use those nice suicide pills from the—"

"Like fun," I said. It came out of my mouth before

I could stop it. "I'll see Castaneda in the hell of my choice before I kill myself and disappear from his radar letting him do whatever the hell he wants with Eden."

"Well, I'll be damned if I know what else we can do." That was definitely Jarl, too. Or I thought so. Kit would never have said he would be damned. It was not that Edenites were not religious—a lot of them were extremely pious. But the way their minds worked, the idea of being damned would seem odd, as opposed to the idea of damning yourself.

"You probably will be damned," I said, in agreeable tones. "But that does not mean that we have to be as well. What I want you two to do is get us around Circum. Some of the bays at the back are unused or rarely used. Hover there, so we can go into Circum. From there, perhaps we can steal a ship to get to Earth."

"It won't be that easy," I said. I was coming awake despite myself, partly under the influence of the feeling of cold shock and horror of having Kit's body, but not Kit, sitting beside me. Was Kit all gone? Was the battle lost? My heart hammered somewhere near my throat, but I damn well would not cry, not in front of... not in front of whatever remained of Kit. I'd read about split personalities. I'd read a lot about it, since we'd found out about this. Despite the insane work schedules, I'd found time to look through educational holos on split personalities. They had let us bring all kinds of informational holos aboard the *Hopper*, provided they didn't give away anything about Eden. Psychology was one of the subjects most thoroughly covered.

Psychology, of course, had not come into its own

until the twenty-second century, when we'd understood perfectly what the fine tuning of brain and chemicals could do. Anything else, from psychoanalysis to gen-psy had never been more than a faint effort to paste patches of faith over ignorance. Religion by any other name, and, like religion, it had sometimes effected miracle cures, but not with any level of reliability.

Multiple personalities were one of those things that even our psychology couldn't fully explain. It was almost like it required a metaphysical belief in the soul.

Of course, most cases had a physical trigger, and most cases could almost be explained by the physical trigger. But the way the personalities divided the internal space, the access to the senses and modes of communication... I'd read that EEG recordings even revealed that multiple personalities were unique in how they activated the brain. It really was as if two different persons traded off control of mind and body. None of this made any sense in terms of simple physiological mechanics. Something more was needed.

Unexplained though it was, I understood that a secondary personality sometimes persisted, crouched, as it were, within the body, able to hear and see, but not to do anything about it, or at least not until something made the dominant personality hand off control. I didn't know how this would play with the nessies' refashioning of the brain, but even there I remembered that Doc had said something about some of the dosage spilled on the floor of the biowomb center where Jarl and his wife had died.

What if not quite enough had got there? What if the brain would never fully be refashioned? What if enough of Kit remained in there that he could hear me? I didn't dare say anything to increase what must already be unbearable despair. If I conceded the fight lost, if I treated Jarl as a stranger, as though no part of him were Kit, would that contribute to whatever was left of Kit letting go? I didn't know. I didn't want to know.

"It won't be easy to steal a ship from Circum even if there are vast areas that have been abandoned. I believe at some point Circum was a space station, or grew around a space station and into a center of powerpod collection."

"Over the late twenty-first century," Doc and Jarl said in remarkable unison.

"Good. Fine. But what that means is that there are vast abandoned portions. There might be many things in those areas, but one thing I can guarantee is that there will be no ships that we can take to Earth and besides—"

Doc cleared his throat, as though he would speak, but I gave him no time. "And besides," I said, firmly. "If we are really infected with that sort of bacteria that will eat through everything it touches, getting more vicious as its generations multiply, should we do this? I know the rest of you will not be very fond of Earthworms and you have no reason to be. But I visited Circum before..." My voice swelled with tears suddenly, and I had to make an effort to control it. I swallowed hard. "Before Kit rescued me. I made friends with harvesters. They're not the Good Men. They have no power of any sort that could hurt us. They don't deserve to die as Circum fails. Worse than that," I added. "If Circum disintegrates and takes with it all of Earth's ability to collect powerpods—"

"Eden's problems are solved?" Kit's mouth said, and the annoying thing there is that I wasn't utterly sure it wasn't Kit this time. It was the sort of remark he would make to lighten the mood.

"The Earth will starve. They're all depending on this energy. By the time they've retrofitted their technology to take new forms of energy, two-thirds of the Earth will be dead. Or more. And a generation might have passed, and most technology and know-how will be lost. I can't have that on my conscience, any more than I can have failing Eden."

"Are you suggesting we kill ourselves?" Zen asked, unbelievingly.

You know when you look down at an endless abyss and you feel the call to just let go, just let yourself fall? You know death lies there, waiting for you, but just at the moment it seems preferable to whatever else you're facing, whatever else you know you need to do.

In this case, death, for all of us, would leave me without having to wonder who my husband was. Was I even married to him when his body was taken over by someone else? And if I weren't what did it mean? Where had Kit gone? I realized with a shock that my feeling amounted to wanting my husband back and, failing that, taking my toys and going home. For a definition of home.

But I thought of Kath and her children. My death might end it for me—I'd never thought much about life afterwards, and didn't want to think about it now. I'd be out of it. But Kit's family wouldn't. They'd have to live under the whims of a dictator. From what we'd already seen of Castaneda, ranging from energy rationing to trying to kill Kit, once he had power he could rival the worst monsters on Earth. Children would grow up being treated like things.

I knew, in retrospect, that's what had twisted me, being raised as a replacement body for Father. But at least to the rest of the world and in my mind, I'd counted. I'd been human. But these kids would have nowhere to go.

"Thena, that's not like you. You know better than anyone you have to fight. While you can fight, you fight. You know as long as you're alive you have them surrounded."

I turned, and looking at me from the green cat-shaped eyes, was my husband. No two ways about it. "Kit," I said, in a flood or relief that he was still there. That he still existed and was coherent enough to take over, to talk. I stretched my hand on the table, to touch his hand, and he clasped my hand hard. "Don't give up," he said, his voice low. "I haven't. Doc has . . . slowed it down. And I'm still here. I'm still fighting."

"What . . . what does it feel like?" I had no experience of being under siege in my own brain.

"Like being in a labyrinth," he said. "Stumbling around trying to figure out which memories and thoughts are mine and which aren't. There's memory and . . . and knowledge leak. Like when we were linked, Thena, when I was . . . dying . . ." His turn to pause and swallow. "But the best, perhaps the only thing we can do for me is get us all to Earth as fast as possible, so Doc can get Jarl's notes and the access to machines, and figure out how to stop and reverse this. He . . . took an impression of my brain, before it was too . . . too far gone, so it should be possible to restore that,

which means there might be a little voice at the back
of my mind, but not ... this." He paused. "So we need
to get to Earth," his hand squeezed mine. "And we
need to get to Earth fast."

A pause again, and he continued, "There has been
leaking of memories and information, and I know what
the Doctor was about to say. There are vehicles in the
abandoned areas. They were stored there for the last
leg to the *Reviens*. They had intended to take a lot
more people. Not just the Mules who stayed behind,
but some of the ... improved people, who got caught
or trapped and killed before they could make it.
About double the ones who did make it to the ship.
There are fueled, abandoned vehicles no one knows
about, hidden in the abandoned areas." I started to
open my mouth, but he cut me off. "You can't say
we can't do it, Thena. You can't say it. You can't tell
me I have to just let him ... that I have to just die."

"No," I said. "We do have to fight to survive. We
have to find a way. But ... we can't kill Earth. The
price ..."

"The price shouldn't be paid by others?" Kit said.
"I think maybe that's what made Irena Ingemar recoil
from Doc's and Jarl's plan." He rubbed the tip of
his nose with his free hand. It was very much a Kit
gesture. It was a gesture made instead of wiping at
his eyes. I had no idea what in what he'd said had
triggered tears, but it had. Maybe it was the feeling
that he was one of the others paying. Or not. Kit
didn't cry for himself, ever. "I agree with that. I've
seen Earth, and we've been helped, even, on Earth."
A brief smile. "The broomers might be many things,
but they're not worthy of death by starvation. We will

not risk it. I will...There is a way." He swallowed. "We will get to the side of Circum where the boats are stored. We can do that. Then get close enough that we can reach it. And then rope-crawl to it."

Zen was looking at him, intently, her eyes narrowed, as though trying to decide which of them was talking and what it meant. "We'd still take the bacteria with us to Circum," she said.

"No." This was the doctor, frowning. "No. Not if we disinfect carefully, before getting into our suits. We'll need to be in our suits to go across." He frowned. "I take it the suits aren't infected?"

"The suits are, in a way, alive," Zen said. "And so far it hasn't touched living material. Besides, I've disinfected the suit storage every day, just in case. It can only be done thoroughly in a very small area, but fortunately the suit storage is a very small area. They're clean."

"Then we'll get clean ourselves, before we put them on. And we'll disinfect the rope, too."

"But the exterior of the suits," Zen said. "They'll pick up bacteria as we go. They will be teeming by the time we get to Circum. If we can get there through these acrobatics. Who is going to be the first one to go out? I can see that the rest of us will be able to hang onto the rope to get there, but if there's any distance at all, how is the first one to get there?"

"Don't worry," Kit's voice sounded strangely doubled, like he was speaking in unison with himself, one voice reassuring and one supremely confident. He stopped, then resumed with his voice, only. "I'll let him take over for the time. He has more experience in vacuum than I do. Thena, he helped seed the powertrees. All of them did. He...he's not...In other circumstances, I'd go some way to save him. Yes, he's arrogant, and in many ways he's cold, but...his childhood was—" He stopped so abruptly that his lips made a snapping sound. And the tone if not the voice changed, though he didn't let go of my hand. "Touching, but I don't want to be justified. Neither do I wish to die completely, just so some young wastrel can go on with a life he wasn't doing much with. No, he's not bad enough to deserve to die, but you have to ask yourself, which of us is more useful to most people?"

I pulled at my hand, recoiling away from him. "Human lives aren't measured in usefulness." I had been raised to believe I must be useful to justify myself. I must be the perfect Good Man's daughter, the perfect little Patrician. My job was to grow up socially adept, to make a good show of the reasons that the Good Men deserved power. And to marry and have children. Never mind. Those had been lies. Not the children part, but the rest. I'd been a body only, grown to be used. And I felt very strongly that humans couldn't be measured in usefulness, or not that way.

Take my friend Fuse, for instance. He was a poor scrap of humanity. The clone of a Good Man, intended to be used for a transplant, he'd got wind of it and tried to escape. His escape had taken him through an ancient piece of dock machinery, and he'd got caught in it and mangled badly. One of his legs dragged, his whole body was lopsided and twisted. And his mind was, at best, the mind of a six year old.

Poor piece of scrap at best. Our broomers lair looked after him, because they had to have rules to keep the sanity of their members. And one of the rules was that one didn't abandon one's own. And Fuse—broken, seemingly useless Fuse—was one of us.

So we cleaned up after him, and saw that he was fed, and when it became obvious that the accident had turned his incipient pyromania into a full-blown obsession, we made sure that he didn't blow up or set fire to anything too big or too obvious, or which might kill us and him.

But it had been Fuse, late at night, in a despairing time, through a random firing of memories, who had recalled what our fathers were and what they intended to do with all of us. And that moment of lucidity, soon overwhelmed by the wreck that was the rest of Fuse, had made it possible for me to figure out the plot against us and how to circumvent it. It had saved my life and Kit's and probably half a dozen of our fellow broomers—maybe eventually all of them.

Jarl, who couldn't hear my thoughts, laughed at my pronouncement and shrugged. "At any rate, my host in this body and myself are in perfect agreement on one thing. We must get out of this death-trap of a ship and onto a place where our life can sustain itself. And then everything else can be decided. But not if we're dead. Yeah, I can vacuum-swim, and this body is more agile, more...precise than mine ever was. The ELFing, I suppose. I can get your damn rope to Circum."

"We will not infect Circum with bacteria," Zen said, forcefully.

"No. We won't need to. What's the easiest way to sterilize something?" Jarl asked.

"Vacuum," I said, getting it.

"Give the pretty lady a star. Vacuum it is."

I got up. "How long do we have, Zen, and what can we take with us that's not infected?"

She took a breath. "Clothes. We can sterilize them in advance. Anything medical that we're sure is not infected. Kit's"—this with a glare at the direction of the person she, and I, was fairly sure was Jarl—"lenses, because without them he can't take normal light. Other than that, I'd say the suits and the air tanks, and that's it."

"My violin," Jarl said, though it might have been Kit. That violin was after all both of theirs. It had been made by Jarl using the old techniques, the ones that had been lost for centuries and which he had reconstructed by studying violins at a molecular level. And it had been Kit's love. And as he continued, I was sure, suddenly, this was Kit, not Jarl. "Please. I put it in one of the airlocks, vacuum side, as soon as I realized what we were up against. I've been playing it ever since I can remember. It feels like a part of my anatomy. I can't abandon it to space."

I could see Zen relenting before she did. Her eyes softened and she said, "No. Of course not."

I wondered suddenly and irrelevantly if she were the least bit musical, or if it was a coincidence that both Kit and Jarl were violinists.

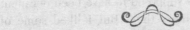

FORTUNE FAVORS THE BOLD

SO HE COULD SWIM IN VACUUM.

"It's not as hard as it seems," Doc said, via helmet communication circuit, as we stood at the edge of the airlock and watched Kit, or Jarl, or at least Kit's body, with just the right amount of push on the skin of our ship, sail away through space, holding a rope.

Circum was maybe fifty feet away. We didn't dare get closer, for fear the bacteria would survive the trip. As it was, we'd cycled the airlock and stood there in the vacuum a long while.

Those parts of the *Hopper* that hadn't fallen apart yet, had been set—on a newly repaired autopilot circuit, which Zen and I had worked on till the last minute when we had to leave—to fly off and into space as soon as we were gone. If it held.

It was almost painfully beautiful to watch Kit fly-swim away, trailing the rope. He'd strapped his violin to his back. From certain angles, it looked as though

191

the violin itself were flying away towards the brilliant circle of metal and lights that was Circum. It looked like something out of a surreal painting from the time just before the turmoils. Yes, I know that art—as well as everything else—is supposed to have been decadent and practically worthless then. But I liked some of those paintings and, in fact, had tracked down a good number of them—going for a song, because current art theory despised them—and taken them home, to my rooms in my father's mansion in Syracuse Seacity.

I watched my husband, or at least his body, grapple for purchase on a thin lip on the other side, then take something out of the toolbelt we'd decided we should all wear, after making sure the tools were clean of course, and use it on the locked airlock in front of him.

The door swung open and he trudged inside, still tugging the rope. For just a moment I wondered what we'd do if Jarl took over and decided he was better off without us; if he let the rope go and left us to our fate. Oh, we'd have time, probably, to find another rope—perhaps even one that was still solid enough—and try again, but it would make life suddenly and painfully interesting.

But Kit had said Jarl was not the enemy. He hadn't set the process of taking over Kit's brain in motion. It wasn't as though he'd done what my father had done: look at a clone with his own personality and his own life, and say, "I can kill him and take it over." No. The process had been started long ago and had been far more ambiguous. It had been a matter of creating a replacement for himself. If it had all worked the way Jarl had planned it, then Kit would never have developed. He'd never have been Kit.

It would just have been Jarl developing, Jarl on his own, a transplant neither of body nor of brain, but of...personality? Soul? Essence? It had been wrong only in the sense that Kit had existed somewhere in potentia, and that Jarl taking over would destroy that potential. But Jarl couldn't be blamed for not thinking of that remote potential. After all, Kit was his clone, created by him, like Jarl had been created for a purpose by the people who had made him. He and Kit, perhaps both—it was hard to tell from Jarl's appearances, because he was not given to telling us anything even remotely introspective—were, to his mind, tools to a purpose. That whole idea of serving humanity. I didn't think Jarl had ever stopped thinking of himself as a thing.

I realized, with a shudder, that was what growing up in a society that cared nothing for the individual and where the individual's duty was supposed to be to exist for the good of society. It wasn't just Jarl. I'd read in the history texts in Eden about such time periods. They all resulted in people that didn't view themselves as human, and therefore didn't view anyone else as human. In fact, in the last stages of such societies, only the leader as the top is supposed to be the human, the individual, the person who embodies that nebulous society for whose benefit everyone lives. In Eden I'd learned of those times with fascination: the Sun King, the mad Red Emperors of the various communist empires. It had been in that light that I'd come to understand the familiar and safe regime of the Good Men was one such. It was just that most Good Men didn't—at this late stage of their control of Earth—bother to convince the peasants that they didn't count, so long as the peasants behaved. Without the constant propaganda, most people on Earth, I thought from the ones I'd met, grumbled about the Good Men. They wouldn't do anything about it, but at least they didn't think of themselves as worthless.

However, Doc had been raised under a much tighter control and under a regime that, being afraid of him, and of the other Mules, *needed* to convince them they were worthless.

I thought of Castaneda. Right now he held Eden hostage with his finger on the energy controls. But, if he succeeded in maintaining control, he'd realize he couldn't do that forever. And the propaganda would start. The children would grow up thinking of themselves and others like themselves as things that could be used for a purpose. And they'd think they should work for the good of the man at the top.

I bit my lip, feeling slightly sick. I returned my mind from that horrific vision to Kit here and now. I had to somehow save Kit and somehow go back, with the secret to replanting the powertrees. But we had Jarl. And we'd never counted on Jarl.

The process had gone wrong, and now Jarl and Kit both were prisoners of the nessies. Neither of them could stop it, even should he wish to, Jarl no more than Kit. At least not till we were near a lab. Worse, stopping it amounted to committing suicide for Jarl. And yes, I was aware that Jarl, or at least the other version of him, had committed suicide. But he had done so while in the grip of an invincible, indestructible disease, which would have killed him, anyway, or perhaps worse than killed him.

Other than that, I expected, sharing the same basic

personality, Jarl was no more likely to embrace suicide than Kit was. And Kit was not likely to do so at all.

These thoughts came and went, seemingly disappearing into the vacuum. I heard my breathing confined in my own helmet, and it seemed to me the air inside it felt stale. It didn't. What was in the tanks was a perfect mix, designed for our breathing. And I didn't think that Eden suits could retain smells. They were made of some biological fabric that felt and stored like a light knit. You could fold them, vibro them, throw them in a small compartment, carry one in your pocket. Even the transparent visor seemed to be no more than part of a head hood, with a transparent front.

But when exposed to vacuum, it solidified and became an impenetrable barrier. Which it was now, sealing me inside its elastic yet airtight confines and making me...claustrophobic. Which was where the sense of staleness came from.

The rope went taut, the end attached to a component part of the ship—a still-solid part—being pulled so that the whole length of rope stayed taut, like a straight line through the intervening space.

Kit, or Jarl, appeared at the airlock door to Circum and moved his hands and arms fast, causing me to blink. The movements were the same thing I knew as broomer language.

Brooms, on Earth—well, beyond the ones used to clean the house, of course—were small antigrav wands. Near untraceable to radar and other detection systems and therefore forbidden in every country—except for limited, short-range use as life-saving devices, in case of a failing flyer—they were nonetheless near-ubiquitous. Lairs of broomers—people who used brooms as their

main and decidedly non-registered, much less traced,
form of transportation—flourished in most seacities of
any size and in many of the large cities on the land
masses, as well.

Many broomer lairs engaged in crime, ranging from
drug trafficking to the smuggling of illegal communication between proscribed groups. The exception was,
perhaps, my own lair, which was, by default, almost
a joke. No. Not a joke. We were illegal broomers
because we were all the sons and daughters of the
upper class—Good Men and their most trusted circle.
The broomers lair was our escape from lives of sti-
fling protocol and maddening restrictions. Mostly we
used it as a place to spend time drinking and having
indiscriminate sex. We rarely committed any crimes,
beyond riding a broom.

In any case, atop brooms, one wore a padded suit,
insulated to keep out the cold—inevitable when flying
at high levels and high speeds—plus an oxygen mask
and goggles. With these in place, it was impossible
to talk coherently, even if it were possible to scream
at each other above the noise of the air rushing past
your face.

But communication had to happen when a broomers lair was flying together. It ranged from the simple
"Up, down, this way" to the complex "Here comes
trouble" or "Not that way, it's dangerous" or "All clear,
come." For that we'd developed hand signals, which
over time—I knew there had been broomers for a
good two hundred years, perhaps longer—became as
complex as any language.

The gestures Kit was making were the ones for
"All Clear. Come. Now."

I heard Doc cackle delightedly, then say, his voice happier than I'd heard it in a long time, "He says to come. It's all clear."

I didn't say anything but wondered how far back the language, and the illegal broomers, went.

About four hundred years, Kit said in my mind. *Since the—*

Kit!

What? he said, seeming puzzled. *Why do you sound so surprised?*

I thought, I said. *He was in control.*

Uh... no. That was mostly me. Oh, him too, but only... after we kicked away from the ship he became caught up in the beauty of Circum and surprise at how big it is. I gather it was much smaller when he last saw it. He also says it looks much cleaner than it was. He paused. *This is really strange, because at the same time he feels like... well, like a part of me. I remember things he remembers and I... I* got the impression of a mental shrug. *On the other hand, it's like a really old man in my mind. In a way older than Doc, though I know they're about the same age. I think Jarl was more isolated and aged more, somehow. It's all "in my day, Sonny..."*

But if you can mind-talk, why the signals? And you don't know the signals!

No, but Jarl does. And the reason to use them is that... well... I needed Doc to see them too, didn't want them to have to come across just on your say-so. I don't know how to use mind-talk to talk to all of you. Only he does.

It made sense, but the impression it gave me, of the two of them squeezed together in the control room of the body, becoming almost chummy, trading reminiscences, made me feel uncomfortable.

I watched Doc make it across, slowly, slowly, hand over hand.

Then Kit's voice in my head. *Now you, Thena.*

I can go last.

You cannot. Your space acrophobia is about to kick in. If you think about it too long you'll go into a panic, and I'll have to come back across and carry you.

I inclined my head, knowing it was true, and told Zen, "Maybe I should go next, before panic sets in. Acrophobia. Space only."

She nodded. "Doc told me you should go second, yes. He said . . . Alexander had acrophobia when working in space and he was worried about you. If I were more sure of the cables around here, I'd tether you."

"No," I said. "I'll be fine. I'll just hurry."

But hurrying wasn't enough. Turns out moving hand over hand on a rope across the vastness of space is a hardship in more ways than one. For one, even though you weigh next to nothing, every movement causes a disproportionate reaction, which you then have to counter, just as carefully. For another, every time you detach your hand, you're aware that the only thing holding you on course and onto your world is this other hand on a rope, and that should you let go, you'll float away into the universe, falling forever, unable—ever—to find your way back.

I'm not afraid of falling off a broom. There's a—rather solid—limit to that. I'm just afraid of falling off into space and never stopping.

Halfway—exactly halfway—between the ship and Circum, it looked and felt as though I was floating in nothingness, with stars above and below, and nothing, nothing to hold me in place. My hands felt numb and as though they didn't quite belong to me. If I let go—If my hands opened of their own accord—

Damn! The voice in my head was almost certainly Jarl's and it jarred me so I might very well have let go of the rope, except that it was followed immediately by Kit, in full, peremptory voice of command, *Thena. Grab that rope. Close your eyes. Do not move. DO NOT move.*

When Kit yelled like that in my mind, it was as though he took direct control of my body. I grasped the rope tight and closed my eyes. With my eyes closed, I could imagine I was only a few inches above a solid ground, in one of the endless and pointless exercises cherished by the boot camps for juvenile delinquents, upon which Daddy had frequently wished me. Like that, I was not afraid of moving my hand over. There was only one problem. The minute my hand lifted, it would have to find the rope again without aid of my eyes. Easy, you say, for a navigator with an inborn sense of direction.

Not this navigator. Not that day, while a part of my mind knew very well where I was and what was happening.

Of all the stupid things for the cloning not to eliminate, even with the sex change, Jarl's voice said in my mind. *Stupid not to have been eliminated with* Alexander *to begin with. What kind of idiots design a superassassin with acrophobia?*

Shut up. Kit's voice. *It's only space acrophobia. Not one more word. Hold on, darling. We're coming.*

He only called me darling when he was afraid I

would die. The rope vibrated, and I realized that Kit or Jarl, or perhaps both, were coming towards me. I risked opening the eye on that side, and saw Kit over-handing it towards me much faster than anyone should be able to. Before I could react, he was on me, and snapping a belt around my mid section, then his. He flashed me a smile, bright and brittle, through his face plate and said *There, I've got you. You can't fall now if you try to. I have you.*

The voice was Jarl's and filled with an odd, echoing tenderness. I tried to hold fast, but he was pulling me, and my hands moved over each other, hand on hand, fast, fast, following the rhythm of his hands, as though they too had been fastened together by invisible wire.

In no time, we were at Circum, my feet touching solid floor, Kit—or Jarl—pulling me along, stumbling. "I'll wait for Zen," the doctor said as we passed, then added, "Good thing you found that belt."

And we were stumbling through two sets of membranes that separated the air lock from what was clearly an air-filled, inner compartment, and Kit's arms were around my shoulders, pulling me close. *I've got you, I've got you.* Jarl's voice, singsong in my mind. *I couldn't have stood to lose you again.*

THE LIVES OF OTHERS

I FROZE. THERE ARE TIMES IN LIFE WHEN YOU suddenly have glimpses that change your life, your perspective, forever. One such glimpse had come when I was very young, maybe three or four. At that age, I had a nanny who was, to me, a figure of authority, a person fully in command of herself and her life, and mine as well.

I no longer remember what she did to displease my mother; my surrogate mother. I only remember that I'd walked in, in one of my more or less aimless rambles through the mansion, and walked on Mother reading the riot act to this poor woman whose name I don't remember. Mother was telling her everything she did wrong, everything she should do differently, and how there were dozens of people willing and able to take her place should she fail to comply with instructions.

At that moment, I'd realized that this woman had a life beyond me, and a face I didn't know.

Jarl's panicked clutching at me, his voice in my ears, had the same effect. Don't ask me how, but I knew, as I knew my own name and my own face, that he was not talking to that Irena whom he sometimes called in his sleep; he was not talking to the woman he'd trusted at least for a time, to help him bring up his clone, the woman he'd probably loved at least a little. No. I was sure, as I was sure of standing there, that he was talking to Daddy Dearest, across the time and space and the centuries of separation.

We wouldn't look that different in the space suit, I realized. Well, I was obviously female, but not if you weren't paying close attention, because the elasticity of the suit tended to flatten and squeeze, giving me the look of a Shakespeare heroine pretending to be a boy.

And I was about Father's height and general size, otherwise. Even what was visible of my face through the visor, just my features, with a few straggles of dark hair that had escaped my ponytail would be close enough. Or at least close to Father when he was very young.

In my mind flashed a holo on Doc's shelves, the image of three young men in summer clothes standing on a beach, the two shorter ones—Doctor Bartolomeu and Father—leaning on the taller one in the middle: Jarl Ingemar.

Thena? What is it? What is it? He let me take over. Asked me to take over. Said you were rigid. In shock. You're safe, love. The arms clutching around me were less desperate and more comforting. *You're with me.*

My . . . Good Man Sinistra and Jarl*! Were they . . . were they?* My mind spun around the affection in Jarl's mental voice, the idea that someone ever had loved the despicable piece of work I'd known as Daddy Dearest. The idea that they might have been more than casual friends, perhaps more than good friends, seemed impossible, bizarre. And yet, there had been the affection and despair in Jarl's voice.

What? Kit's voice, disbelieving. *Uh. I don't think so; not unless he controls his mind sharing far more than I can!* Pause. *It is none of my business. Or yours, Thena. It's long ago and it was their lives.*

But he...he sounded like he liked...loved...Father, like...like he never stopped mourning leaving him behind. Like...like it was a loss.

I think he did love him, Kit said, slowly. *They were so alone, all of them. All these boys, isolated, confined, having no one they could trust but each other. Treated as things, as inhuman. Thena, the things I get from his memory...I hope when Doc reverses it, it will be erased, because they're not memories I want to live with. I used to feel sorry for myself, but now...I think Jarl loved your...loved Sinistra and Doc, like brothers. He felt like an older brother, perhaps, because he was more mature than they were, and larger. I think he tried to protect them and keep them safe. And I think he feels guilty, horribly guilty, that he failed them.*

I almost said that he hadn't failed them. He had, after all, built the *Je Reviens*, or at least designed it and caused it to be built, and he had got Doc Bartolomeu to Eden, where I thought—no, I knew—the Doctor had been happy, despite everything. But he'd left Father behind.

He had to. Father—as I knew him, as I'd seen him act, would not have been safe for an interstellar trip with his kind. Much less would he have been safe for living in Eden, surrounded by humans. Father had been created and, I suspected, trained for killing, inventively and without remorse. I had reason to suspect that at some point he'd taken up doing it for pleasure, and though Doc had never said it, I suspected that had been before the *Je Reviens*.

Father had a complex social life, mostly consisting of being seen publicly and associated with a neverending supply of professional hetairas, dancers, startlets. Less publicly, there had been other things. When I was very young I'd once stumbled onto a locked room.

One of the things that Father had never known about me was that our DNA was close enough for me to open the genlocks he'd locked. He'd never known it, because I'd taken great care not to be caught doing it, and not to be caught where I wasn't supposed to be.

Most of the time, the rooms and compartments I unlocked using this ability contained nothing more interesting than papers or valuables and sometimes, on occasion, strange and marvelous artifacts, collected over the course of a very long life. I'd spent an entire afternoon playing with rare seashells when I was about ten.

But that one time, I'd opened a secret room, and it had almost cured me of my snooping habits. Because Father was in the room I entered. There was someone else too. I think it was a woman. By that point, it was hard to tell. I knew it was human and had once had blond hair, then mostly covered in blood.

I remember the blood, its tang sharp, and I remember the screams—the sort of gasping, high, almost insane screams produced by a throat that can no longer command sound.

Fortunately Father had been absorbed in his work, totally enthralled and concentrating only on it. I had run away fast. Very fast. I'd closed the door behind me. I'd thrown up into a rose bush outside the side entrance. And I'd never again gone to that side of the house. And years later, when I'd found the collection of souvenirs—bits of skin and hair and bone and one single gold tooth—in my Father's desk drawer, I'd tried to forget it. But I still remembered it sometimes in my nightmares.

I suspected Jarl knew of this, was aware of what Father was. At least, Doc Bartolomeu had given me enough reason to suspect that. Which meant that Jarl had done the right thing. You can't pen a wolf with the sheep and expect the results to be good.

But I had heard the emotion in Jarl's voice. He'd loved my father. What type of love didn't matter, but it was real, whatever it was. He'd loved my father, which meant some part of my father must have been lovable in his eyes. I couldn't imagine it, but then when I'd met Father it had been three hundred years later and after the bitter disappointment of seeing his two closest friends leaving Earth, without him, forever. Worse, his two closest friends, the people whom he had trusted, had left him behind in the middle of turmoils and revolt aimed at exterminating his kind. They'd left him to die.

Perhaps Father, despite his unspeakable compulsion, had something good and loveable in him before that. After that, though, there was nothing but the creature I'd come to know. *But what?*

Do you have a need to know? Kit asked, hesitantly, while he held me.

No, I said, truthfully. *No. I'd prefer not to know. My . . . my mother used to say that when you die all debts are paid. My . . . Daddy Dearest is dead. Let his debts be paid. It's none of my business. I just . . .*

Yes? Very gentle, very soft, and weirdly I couldn't tell if it was Kit or Jarl.

I just realized that . . . that you never know. That you can never know everything about someone and that . . . Oh, hell, Kit, I'm not sorry I killed him. As I knew him, he was a despicable bastard, and he died in the process of trying to kill you. And me. But . . .

But?

Was he ever redeemable? Could he have been . . . well . . . not good as such, but like me?

Kit gurgled with laughter at that and said, indulgently, *Thena, you are good.*

No. But . . . I'm not bad. Or not . . . Could he have been like me? Could I have been like him, given the same upbringing? Could I be like him, still, if things . . . if things go very wrong?

There was a long pause, while Kit thought. *Genes aren't destiny. I've told you that before. No, you're not your father. No, you could never be your father. If things had gone differently . . . you'd still be you. I'm not Jarl. Zen is not me. You're not your father.*

But I wasn't so sure. I wasn't sure he was right. In that momentary panic of Jarl's I'd caught a glimpse of a version of Daddy Dearest for whom someone could mourn for hundreds of years. If someone who had even a vague spark of that in him, could become Daddy Dearest, why couldn't I? We had the same genes, and heavens and hells, I'd not been raised with much more love than Daddy Dearest had. Until I'd met Kit and his family, I'd had little experience of normal family and normal love.

Perhaps Kit was intrinsically different from Jarl, because Kit had been raised by a happy and caring family. But I hadn't. My childhood might have been less horrific than that of the original Mules, but it had not been what anyone would call normal or affectionate.

What would it take for my mind to let slip its internal moorings and for me to become capable of caring only for myself and my own needs and desires, and able to look at everyone and everything like things to be disposed of?

I didn't think it would take much. I'd been halfway there when I'd come across Kit. I hadn't changed inside, to tell the truth, until he'd given himself up to Earth to save me. For all he'd known he was giving himself up to death, but he'd done it. For me. There is a love so intense even the emotionally maimed will respond to it. Losing him would put me back in that cold place he'd pulled me from. It would take me back to the path to becoming Daddy Dearest.

I squeezed his hand hard as Doc's voice sounded behind us. "Let's go in," he said. "I think I know the way to where the air-to-spaces were stored."

He looked around the compartment we were in, and to which I'd given no more than a cursory glance. It was a vast, warehouselike space, filled with boxes and bags, most of them covered in thick dust. Soft lights shone from an indeterminate source, and I had a vague idea they'd come on as we entered.

"It hasn't changed at all in three hundred years," Doctor Bartolomeu said, his voice distant. "I wonder how many of those supplies are still good."

"Supplies?" Zen asked.

"For the trip. We ended up only taking about half of them, which was all right, because we only took about half of the people. But we had bags and boxes and compartments of frozen and canned supplies, and anything from tools to animal embryos. Ready to colonize a new world..." He paused. "I wonder if the ones who went on ever found that world; ever colonized. Ah, well, I guess we will never know for sure."

FALLING TO EARTH

FALLING TO EARTH

EXTERMINATOR

THE AIR-TO-SPACES WERE THERE, UNDER MAGNETIC covers, in a vast compartment that might have been a garage. "Strange," Doc said. "You'd think someone would have noticed them in all these centuries."

I shrugged. We'd removed the helmets, and the heavy air bottles. The air in these compartments was perfectly acceptable, if stale. "I don't think so," I said. "There are ... rumors about things in these compartments, the older ones. Some of them are even probably true." I realized they all looked at me, and continued. "Look, this is a very old construction, built around an even older core. I think when it was built, at least judging by the documents I've read, it was an international endeavor, used by many nations, shared in peace. Or as much in peace as ever existed in those days. But the peace didn't last and neither did the accord."

I looked around at the vast, cavernous space. "At

one time or another, it or parts of it has been used as anything from a military encampment to scientific station. But over time many of the areas have also got sealed, because everyone who knew what was in them had died. Or in yours and your friends' case, had left. When you're talking about military equipment and/or scientific materials, you never know how dangerous they've become since they were abandoned. I know the permanent orders for Circum show sectors to avoid at all costs. This is one of them. There are rumors of lizard beings and worse, roaming around these areas. There are rumors of self-willed computers causing death and mayhem. No one wants to risk their lives. Though there are also rumors of scientists who go crazy and drop out and go to hiding here, now and then. But they only add to the danger."

"So this has effectively become no-man's-land?" Doc said, and as he spoke, pulled the cover off an air-to space, showing a gleaming blue vehicle, the finish as clean and perfect as it must have been on the day it left the manufacturing plant. "But why would they keep air and pressure in it?"

"Why not?" Zen said. "It's recycled."

"And at any rate," I said. "If they don't know what's here, how can they know what effect cutting air or pressure would have? You know as well as I do, and I know mostly through association with my friend Fuse, mind, that some explosives are triggered by lowering pressure, and some biological weapons are triggered by lack of oxygen. Why would they risk that? If it's not exploding now, why risk it?"

As we spoke, Kit—or Jarl—had unsnapped the belts that held him to me and moved on, ahead of us, looking at every corner, pulling this cover and that off an air-to-space.

I looked to see where he was, preparing to call him, and—while looking at him—caught movement out the corner of my eye. I turned, and had the impression of a man. He must have been about fifty or perhaps sixty, thin, with long white air, staring at us, openmouthed.

A blue flash cut the air from Kit's direction, and the man gave a sort of odd little sigh. A bloom of blood appeared on his chest. He gurgled, looked surprised and fell in a heap.

"Kit!" I said. He'd killed a man. He'd killed a man without question and without thinking. I'd once seen him go out of his way not to shoot a man who was trying to kill him. Oh, not that he was hesitant about defending himself, at least not normally. But the man was the brother of his late wife, and the only child of grieving parents. Kit had refused to inflict more pain on people already suffering.

Every time I'd seen Kit react violently, it had been against someone who was a clear and present threat to him. The only time I'd seen him kill was when he didn't have time to modulate his shot, to pull his punch.

He hadn't even reacted with lethal force when I'd tried to garrote him after he'd rescued me. "Kit!"

"What?" and though the voice had the same intonation and timbre, I knew it was Jarl speaking. "We didn't need this additional complication."

Zen had gone over and was examining the little man's corpse. He was dressed in what looked like a very old one-piece. "He wasn't armed," she said, looking up.

"I know," Jarl said. "I could tell that. But he could have given the alarm."

"He was probably a hermit here. More scared of us than we of him. I don't think he had been near people in years, much less would give alarm."

Kit's body walked over, and Jarl stood over his victim looking down dispassionately. "Yeah, okay," he finally conceded. "It probably was a waste of burner juice, but it's not like he could have been useful to us in any way, right?" He looked at Zen and me, and finally at Doctor Bartolomeu. "Right?"

The doctor's gaze was pensive, the sort of expression someone shows while trying to solve a particularly difficult math problem. But when he spoke, his voice was perfectly cool and polite. "Let's find a recycler for the body. This air-to-space is in perfect condition and shows a full charge. I'll pilot down. I'll have to do it by memory. Because we never intended to return to Earth, there are no maps of Earth in the vehicle. But I think my memory is still good enough. And, no, thank you, Kit...er...Jarl...we won't need that high a level of coordination to maneuver into Earth space. It's a big globe. We shouldn't have trouble finding a place to land."

EMPTY NEST

WE HAD TROUBLE FINDING A PLACE TO LAND. PART
of this—no, perhaps all of it—was my fault.

I don't claim to be the world's most brilliant person. I have good visual and spacial memory, sure, but
unlike what Doc had said of Jarl, I couldn't claim to
never have forgotten a book I'd read or a code I'd
memorized. In fact, I'd freely admit to having forgotten
lots and lots of things. And if excited or happy, sad
or disturbed, I could forget my own head. Not when
scared, though. When scared I became a machine who
knew and memorized everything.

Why then, in the name of all that's sweet, had I
forgotten the network of alarms and sweeps, of linked
triggers and aimed sensors that covered the entire
surface of the Earth? How could I not even have
made an attempt at disabling whatever transponder
was in this vehicle? What was wrong with me?

I can't tell you for sure, except that seeing Kit

215

shoot someone down in cold blood, even though I knew in my heart of hearts that it wasn't Kit—even though I had no reason to expect sanity of Jarl—had made me forget everything.

The air-to-space was large, larger than Daddy Dearest's which had been a straight four seater. This one was more like a luxury flyer on Earth—or to put it in other words, it looked like a small living room, outfitted with comfortable sofas, a couple of tables, a few cabinets. The only difference between it and, say, the living room in a decent if not spectacular hotel suite was that all the furniture was affixed to the floor, though some of it could be moved via switches.

When we got in, Doc had taken the one chair in front of a screen that was, clearly, the pilot's chair. Kit belted his violin carefully into a chair, then flopped nervelessly onto a sofa. No. Jarl. I'd never seen Kit lie down like that, without the least vestige of control, not even of a controlled fall. And he would never do it in public. Used to being watched, in part because of his family's tragic history and in part because his adopted family was important in the tiny world in which they lived, he could never seem to forget that he must keep up a public face at all times.

Zen sat across from him, with her hands in her pockets, her face grim. I had the impression that she was holding a burner in one of those pockets, and stood ready to fire through it if Jarl made any odd moves. What could I do? I was not married to Jarl, but I was married to Kit. It was an uncomfortable fact that they were shoved into the same body just then. And it was the only body both of them had. It was physically impossible to kill one of them without killing the other. I set about looking in the drawers of the cabinets for something I could use to communicate with Zen.

Yeah, she too had Mule Telepathy. Yeah, she too should have been able to mind-talk me. But I have a theory about that. Unless it's trained and expected from childhood, it won't happen. I'd never mind-talked to any of my broomers lair, though more than half of them were Mules and therefore, presumably, had mind-talk abilities in potentia. For all I was concerned, Doc's mind was perfectly silent. It was a miracle or perhaps an artifact of how tightly wound both Kit and I had been when we'd met that we had happened to listen to each other. I didn't care to find myself in that kind of situation with Zen. Well, not more than inevitable, and hopefully not in the next hour or so. And I needed to warn her. Because I wasn't Jarl. I didn't kill—without warning—people who weren't directly threatening me.

So I looked, until I found a pad. Not like the pads in Eden. No electronic. Just a paper pad, yellowed with age, with an equally aged pencil next to it. I sat down on the sofa next to Zen and printed quickly and clearly, IF YOU SHOOT HIM, I'LL HAVE TO KILL YOU.

She looked at the pad, when I waved it front of her eyes, and frowned at the print, an intent frown, as though trying to decipher foreign writing. It had just occurred to me that she had never, probably in her entire life, read anything even vaguely resembling paper. I wondered if she was puzzled by the concept. Then she grabbed the paper out of my hands, and the pencil with it, and wrote, with remarkable spareness. SO?

Not knowing if she meant she didn't care for my threats, or if she wondered why I would do it, I explained. BECAUSE THAT BODY IS KIT'S. KIT IS IN IT TOO, AND IT'S THE ONLY BODY HE HAS. YOU WILL NOT KILL MY HUSBAND.

Again, the charade with Zen frowning at the page as though it were written in some ancient and unknowable language, then she snatched paper and pencil from my hands. I LIKE KIT, TOO. I CAN'T TRUST JARL.

NO. DON'T CARE. HE'S STILL IN THE SAME BODY WITH KIT. YOU WILL NOT KILL KIT.

MAIM? This was scratched out and followed by. RIGHT. I PROMISE TO DO ONLY THE DAMAGE NEEDED TO STOP HIM DOING SOMETHING STUPID. NOW GO AWAY, YOU'RE MAKING ME NERVOUS.

NO. YOU WILL NOT HURT KIT. ANYTHING THAT REQUIRES TREATMENT MIGHT KILL HIM. WE'RE NOT EQUIPPED TO STOP HEMORRHAGING.

Zen sighed, as though I were totally unreasonable. I'LL TRY NOT TO DAMAGE HIM AT ALL WHILE STOPPING HIM. I WILL NOT LET HIM KILL ME, THOUGH, OR YOU, OR DOC.

I DON'T THINK HE'LL KILL ANYONE.

YOU DON'T KNOW.

And alas, it was true, I didn't. So all I could do was sit across from Zen and keep an eye on her, to make sure she didn't hurt the body in which my husband seemed to be trapped with an amoral genius. Presently, it became obvious that Jarl was asleep. Which might or might not mean anything, since switchovers often seemed to take place while the body slept.

Doc set the autopilot, and then he too colonized one of the long sofas and fell asleep. And Zen and

I sat up right, hands in pockets, each, I was sure, clutching a burner.

Now tell me how I managed to fall asleep? The only excuse I could find, ever, is that it had been a long three months, of too little sleep and too much worry, followed by what was for me a traumatic experience of clutching that rope and following it between the ship and Circum. I'd once read something somewhere about the spirit being willing but the body being weak.

My body was weak. To be exact, my body was so weak that it couldn't stay awake even when my love's life depended on me. Some sentinel I would have made. The only thing I can say in my defense is that Zen, also, fell asleep. And she thought she was keeping vigil for her own life.

I know because when I woke up, with alarms blaring in my ears, it was just a second or so before she woke. And she woke as I expected, withdrawing the burner from her pocket and pointing it. Was that her only answer to everything? Kit wasn't like that at all. Did upbringing and female hormones make the difference in Zen, or had Kit chosen a more reasoned response to emergencies?

Doc and Kit woke at the same time, or close to it, because they both jumped up at the same time. And the person who woke was Kit, because he screamed in my mind *Thena? What?*

Which was when I listened to the words in the alarms. And realized that the screaming words were not coming from the ship, but from somewhere in the comlink. And that the reason they were nearly cacophonic is that they were not one alarm but at least ten, screaming at me madly and at full volume.

I caught enough words in standard Glaish, *violating air space*, for instance, and *identify yourself* to figure out the pickle we were in. I just didn't know for sure what to do about it.

It's always been my fixed policy, when not absolutely sure what to do, to do something anyway. Mostly because in most circumstances where you find yourself faced with life-and-death decisions, no decision at all is more likely to lead to death than a decision no matter how clumsy. Look at it this way: life-and-death situations are rare and desperate. You will find yourself in them only after a series of errors so catastrophically cogent with each other that they brought you to an unlikely spot. It's far more normal to find yourself in a situation where both decisions are wrong or both right.

Those rare life-or-death situations come about so seldom because it takes an extreme of ill luck and a chain of ill luck to bring them about. There is a good chance that any decision you make in that situation will be less bad than the position you're in.

It's possible that it won't be much better. It will only move you away from death a few inches, instead of a comfortable distance. But even that is better than where you were. Burner beams that miss you by inches are as good as burner beams that miss you by miles.

So, first, I decided I didn't need to be screamed at while trying to think. I plunged towards the control panel, found the one for incoming communications and lowered the voices to a dull roar. Only to find that the roar from my three companions panic had climbed, in turn, to very loud.

"Be quiet," I yelled. "All of you be quiet. One of you . . . Kit?"

"Thena?"

"Get in that pilot chair and do what I tell you."

"But—"

"Shut up and do what I tell you."

I'm not normally the type of wife who orders her husband around. All right, maybe I am. But I'm not the type of wife who likes to think of herself as ordering her husband around. And I try to do it more subtly when I have to do it.

So maybe it was the novelty of the situation, or the fact that he was ill, fighting a mind infection. Or perhaps it was the fact that when I yelled like that I did a remarkably good imitation of the old son of a bitch who'd called himself my father.

His behind hit the chair, his hands flew to the controls. I could tell by the way he touched them, tentatively, before disengaging the autopilot, that he was familiarizing himself with the mechanism. His lips moved, soundlessly, as he looked beneath the console. The whole took no more than a couple of minutes, and he looked back at me and nodded.

"Right," I said. "Get ready to take navigation." I touched the portion of the screen that showed communications, and turned the sound to visual waves on the screen: that is, I arranged it so that I could see from where the alarms were emanating and what areas they covered.

What you have to understand is that Earth is not as paranoid as Eden. Not Earth as such. They're not afraid of an invasion from space. They're not afraid of someone from out of the world coming and attacking them. As far as they're concerned, the only populations outside Earth are either in Circum or on the moon, and those are neither in a position nor in numbers sufficient to cause a problem to Earth, with her might and her armies. Perhaps a few of them, certainly a few of the Good Men at the top, know that there is a significant population in Eden. Maybe. Though they don't know where Eden is. They're still not really afraid of Eden. Annoyed by Eden, maybe, but not afraid.

Earth, at last count—and all those counts are always flawed, but they give some indication of how many people are alive at any time—had four billion people. Okay, down from the peak of six billion, but not by far. And even though some of them might be aware that Eden had more advanced technology, barring a mythical superior alien with his inhuman intelligence and weapons, population still counts for a lot. Even the Mules, who might have considered themselves inhuman intelligences, at least according to their legend, were not enough of a threat should they return.

So, there was no Earth defense, and no sensors sweeping the not-so-friendly skies on behalf of united Earth, for the good of humanity.

What there was instead were directorates, principalities, city-states, satrapies, kingdoms, and oligarchies, all loosely assembled into the rational administrative regions, each overseen by one of the Good Men, fifty in all. Each of them deathly afraid of the others. Each of them afraid the others would send armies, or spies or something. Each of them sweeping the sky for threats.

And by *each of them*, I don't mean each of the Good Men. Oh, that too. Though it happened rarely, it had happened before and would probably happen again, that the Good Man of one seacity found no good reason why he shouldn't assimilate another, nearby city as well. Or why someone commanding one half of a continent didn't think he could do a better job if he could also lay claim to the other half. Good Men were nothing if not ambitious.

But it was far more common at a level below that for portions of divisions to fight each other: for kingdom to swallow protectorate, and oligarchy to overtake satrapy. It was even normal for a kingdom or nation to fight...itself. All at the level the local Good Man didn't find serious enough to intervene.

I don't pretend to understand it. I'm just saying it happened. So, everywhere on Earth the scanning was ubiquitous, and the alarms we were listening to were the grown-up, large-territory equivalent of a few broomers flying the edge of their area and signaling to all incoming flyers, "Stay out of our zone."

The fact that we were getting at least six of them at the same time meant that we were not in any particular division yet. This was good, because the grown-up, large-territory equivalent of a few broomer guys beating the living daylights out of trespassers was an explosive or incendiary device, neatly placed amidships.

And my main goal in life remained not to die.

So I looked over Kit's shoulder, at the areas covered by the alarms, and steered by them. Or rather away from them. My goal was to steer so that we avoided all the alarmed regions altogether and landed in an area without screening. An area no one claimed.

Could it be done? Oh, sure. It was something I knew from those occasions when I had been forced to steal, say a flyer that wasn't mine, or perhaps to violate someone's airspace with my lone broom.

Even on Earth, as populated as it was, and as covered in sensors and scanners, there were areas where no one would look for you.

Which is what I was aiming for. I shouted instructions to Kit, in the sort of shorthand we were used to, from the *Cathouse.* "North, north, north, north. Click east. South. South, fast, damn it. Hard east."

We fell onto Earth and into the atmosphere without being shot out of the sky, which was a good thing. For a while it looked like, in my effort to avoid detection, we were going to land in one of the vast, unpopulated oceans. This would be a very bad thing. I could take the ocean, of course, and we could float for a while, trying to find some place that wouldn't shoot us down on sight. Only I didn't know if this gig, being as old as it was, allowed itself to be steered on water, or even if it was waterproof. And besides, I suspected as soon as we hit water the question would become academic. Why?

Because I was the only one there who even had the slightest notion what an ocean was. Oh, fine, maybe Doc did too, but he hadn't seen one in three hundred years, give or take.

Kit and Zen? They would go utterly catatonic the minute they realized we were sitting on that much water. Kit had tried to play it cool when he'd been forcibly submerged in an ocean before, but I remembered the blank panic signal I'd got from his mind then. I did not want to court it again.

So I steered away from oceans too, and eventually, after what seemed like eternity and turned out to be close to five hours, Kit brought us to rest on a desertic area in the heart of old Europe.

I sat down for a while, before I opened the door and looked out. And then I wished I hadn't. The problem with deserted areas is that they are so damn desolate.

There was a ruin somewhere in the distance, and the rest of the landscape looked like someone had let loose with a neutron bomb. There wasn't even a trace of green. Just yellow sands, brownish dirt, and a wind blowing through it all that brought grit with it to scour your face.

Behind me, Kit looked, but it was Jarl's voice that said, "Oh, I'll be damned."

OLD HOME WEEK

DOCTOR BARTOLOMEU CAME UP BEHIND JARL, PUT a hand on his shoulder and looked out, as I retreated from the open door. What he said was less easily transcribed, and might have been a dead language. Jarl smiled, a brief, feral smile. "Isn't it?" he said. "Our own old home."

Doc Bartolomeu cursed again, and this time I understood it, even if the act recommended was physically impossible. Correction: probably physically impossible. It was entirely likely that someone, somewhere, was anatomically freakish enough to do it.

Jarl smiled and shook his head, then looked at me and must have caught the blank look in my eyes. He grabbed my shoulder. He held it loosely and gently enough that I didn't feel the need to struggle as he pulled me forward and pointed out the door at the ruin, "See that? That was the center of a compound where we...ah. The...What did they call us, Bartolomeu?

226

It's been too long. The only thing that stuck was Mules. It stuck in the popular mind, and it stuck in our craws like an insult, and it just stuck. Once upon a time, when we had the ruling, during the war with the seacities, and after we called ourselves biolords. That never stuck. But before that, when they were raising us, raising us to be public servants, they called us something else. What was it?"

"Oligoi," Doc Bartolomeu said, in a tone that made it the equal, if not the worst of all the insults and curses he'd pronounced before. "The few. Apparently, not few enough."

"Ah. Yes. Oligoi. We were Oligoi, and brought here from all over the world to be raised and taught together with the others of our specialty. I think someone had read *Brave New World* and thought it was a manual. We were divided into Alphas and Betas, Deltas, and Gammas and..." He must have noticed that I was once more looking blank. "*Brave New World*? Twentieth century...Oh, I see. My...host informs me Earth has lost most of its literature and history. In the turmoils and after. Probably on purpose." He shrugged. "Never mind. They divided us into classes according to the capabilities we'd been created with and branded us with the Greek alphabet and..."

"I think *branding* us was the only thing they didn't do," Doc Bartolomeu said. "Do you mind horribly if we get out of here, Jarl?"

"No," Jarl said, but narrowed his eyes, looking out at the red and white barrenness upon which dirt that glimmered like glass shards blew. "No, but what happened here? There used to be a city there," he pointed north, into the center of the desolate area. "Or rather an enclave of Mules. What we called Mules, then. Vast numbers of humans who had been created wholesale in laboratories and gestated by animals. They didn't understand enough of biology then, to understand that maturation of a fetus requires exposure to maternal hormones—the proteins in mother's blood that accompany pregnancy. Or they didn't care. In Eden biowombs those are carefully introduced. At different stages of pregnancy, the hormones trigger the stages of maturation of the fetus. Animal hormones have different protein structures. The fetus didn't mature properly because it didn't get the right signals. In fact, most animal brains are nearly mature at birth, while human brains don't finish maturing before age thirteen or so. They used sheep a lot, and the antibodies and mitochondrial DNA weren't compatible. So they injected massive doses of immune suppressants, which also caused a certain amount of mental retardation and impaired functioning, but even after *that* became obvious, they continued making the poor brutish Mules. Had to, because working population was shrinking, as Europe became senescent. The rest of the world too, as the race and religion wars took their tolls. This compound was a compound of laborers. There were . . . two hundred thousand? A vast industrial complex with what amounted to slave labor. They revolted once . . ."

"Jarl, come inside," Doc said, forcefully, and pulled Jarl inside. I stumbled back with him, into the flyer, and Doc shut the door. He sat on one of the nearby chairs and said, "We must get out of here."

"I'm all for that," Zen said. She'd been sitting in the driver's seat, looking at the panel that showed where we were. "But if I understand how Thena steered us..."

"We can't get out of here," I said. "Or not far, and not in this vehicle. This flyer doesn't have the right transponder. It doesn't have any transponder. And that makes it an illegal vehicle. And it's too big to be capable of going under the radar, like a broom would, for instance. You, who commissioned these flyers," I looked at Jarl. "I don't suppose they're equipped with brooms?"

He shook his head. "No. Afraid not. They were supposed to go to the *Je Reviens* and dock." He went and stood behind Zen. I was aware of Zen squaring her shoulders and looking like she'd like to grow eyes at the back of her head, but she didn't turn. "So, we're...at the edge of an area that is without detectors for unauthorized vehicles." He frowned, and it was odd how his expression looked different from Kit's even though the features were the same. He lowered his eyebrows more, I decided, and his chin looked harder edged when he frowned that way. "Why is this area desolate. Bomb? Nuclear?"

"No," I said. "During the turmoils this area got infected with bacteria much like the ones that chased us from the *Hopper*."

Zen looked panicked. "Oh, no. Are we going to need to—"

I shook my head. "No. Neutralized hundreds of years ago. If they hadn't been, they'd have taken over the Earth."

"Ah." Jarl said. "So, we need to find a way out of here or a way to retrofit the flyer, right?"

I nodded. It seemed obvious. "I don't think we can

walk the hundreds of miles into civilization," I said, "though that's an option."

"Well..." he said. "I can't offer other vehicles, but...there used to be a place around here with high communications capabilities that might still allow us to send a signal, if you trust one of your friends to help us." He looked at Doc Bartolomeu, with something like defiance. "What do you think? I don't know if the barriers would have held, but I remember that in my later, paranoid years, I had it insulated against everything, including biowarfare."

"I don't have the slightest idea what you are talking about."

"Yes you do," Jarl said. He turned away from the console his hands deep in his pockets, in a gesture that was so much like Kit that it made my heart clench. "It used to be a resort, when we were kids. The place where..." He paused. "And then I bought it, and made it my own private hiding place."

"Oh," Doc said. "Your bolt-hole. You never allowed us to go there. At least not me."

"Not anyone," Jarl said. "That was part of its charm. It was completely automated for what I needed, which was not much. I wonder if it's still there."

Doc shrugged.

"I say we try to go there. I had a communications room. Had to. It was part of being able to get away, that I had to still be able to keep an eye on things? So...They might still work." He edged towards the pilot seat, lurching, as though unsteady on his feet. "Let me take us there," he told Zen.

Zen turned around in the seat to face him and glowered. "I don't—"

Tell her to let him, Thena, it was Kit in my mind, sounding distant and faded like when he was sedated or hurt or falling asleep. *He doesn't mean anything bad by it. He just wants to get away from here, badly. So does Doc. Horrible memories.*

Kit?

Yes. I'm here. I'm alive. I'm not letting go, but right now you need him in control. I don't know Earth as he does, even after three hundred years. He used to rule most of it, through his influence over the other Mules. He can do things I couldn't.

"Zen, let him do it. Kit says to."

Zen frowned momentarily, then stood up. I noted that Jarl had looked surprised at the mention of Kit, then smiled at me, and dropped into the pilot seat.

He took us off the ground in a smooth glide, but stayed close to the ground as we flew an odd path, straight to the center of the desolate area, past the ruins. Watching him pilot, it was easy to imagine he was Kit. There were the same assured movements, fingers tapping so fast on controls that it was hard for the eye to follow their movement.

After the ruins we took a sharp turn, and there was what looked like a perfectly smooth and flat rut, carved into the ground, hundreds of feet deep and side. Even though it had weathered over what must be centuries, and there was no trace of man made anything around, it was obvious that this space, too, was manmade. Natural canyons were never this even. "It used to be a highway here," Jarl said, as his fingers moved on the controls. "And it led to the big industrial complex where the . . . what even we called Mules labored. And on the edge of it to the resort where visiting managers and vips lodged." He gestured towards the walls, now on either side of us, while his other hand continued minutely correcting the course. "The highway ran across most of Europe. Perhaps it still does, but clearly this part is nonfunctional. Once you got in, you could program your exit, then turn the controls over entirely, while you relaxed. But there... on the walls, on either side, there were advertisements. Tri-D projected advertisements. Since people didn't have to drive, they could lean back and watch..." Doc made a gesture I didn't understand, and Jarl continued, sounding distant, "I used to escape from our lodgings at night and tamper with the controls, so that the displays changed. Tagging, they called it, after an earlier way of defacing public buildings with paint."

"Jarl..." Doc said, the tone hard to interpret.

But Jarl spoke on like someone in a dream. "The authorities who were looking for me called me Angel because my trademark was to project the image of an angel flying away. I have no idea why, except perhaps I often wanted divine rescue, or perhaps to be able to fly away. Anyway, I was out, tagging one evening, and I didn't know all hell had broken loose on the Mule compound and they'd stopped all the flyers in the highway, and I almost got caught, because the police were out and giving instructions to the stranded travelers. And they had this... thing that detected bioed markers in DNA. So they saw me, and tried to catch me, but this woman, traveling alone, let me in her flyer and said I was her boyfriend. I must have been... eighteen? Nineteen? Anyway... she took me to that resort."

"Jarl, if you're going to turn, you need to slow now.

There's no warnings, but the turning is just ahead, to the right."

Jarl shook a little, like a man wakening, and his fingers danced on the panel. We slowed and turned gracefully into a narrower defile.

I was wondering how there could be a resort here. Oh, sure the place had been abandoned for years, and few would brave it to explore. There was nothing there, not even vegetation. But flyers overflew it all the time. If there were a verdant patch, they'd land and look. Or at least it would be known that there was an oasis there and the protective membranes would have been forcibly ruptured. I started to fear Jarl was in for a disappointment. But at the end of the defile I realized there was another possibility.

It was the mouth to a cave. It didn't look natural, though it might have been, but it was vast. And in front of it was the sort of shimmer you see on a road in the middle of summer. In this case, since it was neither hot nor bright, it must be the shimmer of a shield-membrane—soft as cobweb, but impenetrable to radiation and bacteria and any non-authorized life form.

We stopped just short of it, and I was trying to imagine how we'd get in, because most such fields open, automatically, like doors, when the flyer emitting the right code approaches. This flyer wouldn't have the right code.

But instead, Jarl brought us to a gentle stop on the ground, in front of the field, and opened the one window near the front of the flyer touched the same place on the wall.

Something extended from the wall. It looked like a periscope ending in a circle, and in the middle of the circle was the grey membrane of a genlock. "We'll see," Jarl said. "If the genes are close enough. I told you, didn't I, that I'd got a little paranoid—justifiably so—towards the end."

The genes must have been close enough because the periscope thing withdrew and then the membrane retracted and vanished. Jarl closed the window and we flew in to the cavern. The membrane closed behind us.

Only it didn't look like a cavern any more than Eden looked like the interior of a rock. Light must have been piped in from above, and we were flying above what looked like lush forest. At the end of it, a building looked much the worse for the wear—as though the plants around were trying to overtake it.

"Welcome," Jarl said, "to my refuge."

IN A STATE OF NATURE

IN FAIRY TALES, WHICH I'D READ EXHAUSTIVELY shortly after my mom disappeared, there is often an enchanted land, a place where time stops.

This place shouldn't have been like that, and I'm not a gaian priestess nor a nature worshiper. As far as I'm concerned, the best thing about nature is that we can get away from it. And a satisfactory contact with nature is a stroll in a garden from which all harmful pests have been eliminated.

But that was exactly what this place was. A garden, from which all harmful pests had been eliminated, and which had then been allowed to run riot by being unchecked for centuries.

After my time in Eden, it seemed surreal and unlikely. While Eden had vegetation, there were no areas big enough to allow vegetation to grow like this, nor did it have trees this large and old.

Zen stared around in wild-eyed wonder. Kit said in

my mind, *Wow*. And Jarl, himself, stood stock still and blinked. "I'd forgotten what it could get like, if places weren't kept up. I used to have gardening robots, but I turned them on only when I visited, since I might change my mind about their programs and decide to let something grow. Come. We'll go see if the communications work, shall we?"

We followed him along what had doubtless been some sort of path. You could only tell that now, because it remained relatively flat among otherwise broken ground. But if it had been paved, or if the ground had been hardened against plants growing on it, that was gone. Huge roots crossed the path, and a few times we had to detour around large trees or wild bushes.

Birds called overhead, another strange experience since birds in Eden, other than grown for food, were only found in exhibits at aviaries and zoos. Here, you could hear them winging overhead, you could hear their calls, and you could see, sometimes, a flash of color among the branches.

"I'd forgotten what it could be like," Doc said.

"So had I," Jarl answered, ahead of us. "This place was stocked with plants and birds from all over, when I bought it. The fact that it's roofed overhead makes it a constant sixty degrees year round with watering via underground feed, and so species grow here that would never grow in this area."

"I never understood why you bought it or at least why you bought it and closed it to the public. As a resort, it was, of course, a growing concern, and I can understand wanting to buy it and make money from it. But as a private retreat..."

Jarl shrugged. "I bought it because to me it was a vision of paradise. I didn't know how humans, real humans lived. This was the first time I saw something designed for them, the first time I consorted with them, the first time I tasted non-institutional food...the first time I saw women. It was like... in my mind, this is what it was like to be a normal human. I think it still is. So I wanted it to be mine, to be part of what I was and how I lived. And buying it for myself...by the time we were done with the war, I just needed a place to go and be alone. I used to come here and spend days hiking around. You can go to the end there, to the cave wall, in about a day. I would sleep on the ground, return the next day... Sometimes I fished."

I realized suddenly that we were in the equivalent of Doc's gnome-cottage. This was the place where Jarl could convince himself he was normal, a person like any other. I wondered that neither Kit nor I had ever felt that compulsion to act human in order to be human. We'd assumed we were human and we knew, rationally, that a few extra abilities didn't make us something completely different. And then I stopped, arrested by the sudden realization that Jarl had not seen females, either normal or Mule, until he was eighteen or nineteen, the age at which he'd come to this resort the first time.

It made sense, from what I'd seen about the period in holos in Eden. By the time they'd gotten around to creating that variety of Mule they called Oligoi, they'd had twenty years of creating the other Mules. Twenty years where, if the holos I'd seen in Eden were correct, they'd faced countless rampages and rapes of human females by Mules.

At that point they wouldn't have known if the aggression was part of how they were gestated, or part of how their genetics worked, or perhaps just part of the whole package. So, of course they wouldn't have risked raising these young Mules around women.

On the other hand, from the perspective of Jarl and his congeners, it must have been like growing up in jail or a uniquely harsh reformatory, to which they had been condemned without committing a crime.

I suppressed a shudder and realized Jarl was walking ahead, treading the uneven path with certainty. "When I stayed here," he said, "I used part of the hotel. The other part was locked and I had . . ." He shrugged. "Anyway, right at the front are the communication devices. You wouldn't know"—a quick look over his shoulder at me—"whether you still use the same communication systems?"

"My areas of expertise," I said, "related to dressing up and looking good when Daddy Dearest had a party. I also understand that in the future—more so than I thought, frankly—I was supposed to develop an ability to make babies. And meanwhile I learned how to repair machinery and how to keep my lair's brooms flying. Communication just worked or didn't. I knew how to tamper with it, but if you're going to ask me what sort of waves or whatever they used, I don't have a clue."

He smiled, as though my rant amused him, and it was a little odd, because it would have amused Kit too. "Ah, well, then we'll cross our fingers and hope," he said. "Otherwise we'll be making that trek through wasteland to civilization, won't we?"

"We'll have to cross our fingers a lot," Doc said, "because the way this looks, the plant growth will have broken through the walls and crept through the windows and your precious communicators will be covered in sap."

Jarl laughed. "Nah. Not as bad as that," he said. "Ever. Remember it's me you're speaking of. The resort was pretty well built, and when I took over, I had everything reinforced and sealed. There might be some leaks. Three hundred years without maintenance is a long time. But I don't think so. And I think the main things will be fine. Out here..." He gestured with a hand. "Would you think badly of me if I told you I think I like it better this way than when it was kept down and manicured?"

"No," Doc said. "Nor would I be surprised."

The path turned sharply upward and around and we were suddenly at what must, once upon a time, have been one of those grand entrances that are always open—the sort you see in palaces, hotels, and the bigger kind of temple. Someone had outfitted it with a door that clearly was not designed for it, at what had obviously been a later time. I had to assume that had been Jarl, though having heard him extolled as an aesthete among many other things by everyone from Doc to the history videos in Eden, I had to confess myself shocked at the ugly nature of that door, which was panels of dimatough, relieved only by the tiny hole of a genlock in the dead center, where the two halves of the door met.

Jarl slid his finger in, and again, apparently, the lock wasn't sensitive enough to react to the modifications imposed on Kit's body. It made a loud click, then slowly and ponderously, the two halves slid apart and into the walls on either side.

Come in to my lair. I couldn't tell if the voice in my head was Kit's or Jarl's, so I didn't respond, and instead, tried not to shiver as I faced the cavernous and dark interior.

But as Jarl walked in and whistled, the lights came on, also soft, shining from walls and ceiling and even floor in a way that made the entire space seem rich and alive.

It was rich. I hoped it was not alive, because alive would mean that some creatures had sneaked in over the years it had been abandoned. Was it my imagination or was there a skittering like rats from the left? No, it wasn't my imagination, because Jarl had turned his head that way, just momentarily.

But then he didn't say anything, so it must mean that it was nothing, just some function of the way the air circulated. Because if it were unusual or alarming, Jarl would have given it more time. ·

Instead, he turned to a wall, which seemed entirely taken up by a gleaming array of . . . something I couldn't begin to understand. Surely, this whole thing couldn't be a com.

Then I blinked again and suddenly realized what it was. My father had a similar one, in his study. Not his regular study. The one that was behind the genlock I'd learned to circumvent by the time I was three.

When I'd first seen him use it, I had no idea what it was. It wasn't until I was much older I realized it was a center where you could collect and view data from many, many spy cameras. And Father had a lot of spy cameras installed over the centuries—anywhere from the servants quarters of our own house to all the Sinistra properties across the world, to the offices of other Good Men, to places I didn't even know how to identify. Apparently that thing about the Good Man's eyes being everywhere was true. At least when it came to my father.

As I got older, I'd come to view that array of constantly changing screens, through which he could keep track of almost everything on Earth, as a sign of Father's controlling mania and incipient paranoia. Which, apparently, Jarl had in spades and with little bells on. His array was twice as large as Daddy's and twice as complex.

He must have caught something in my eye, because he chuckled. "Yes, well, without it, I'd not have had enough warning of the riots, or that my friends were in peril. And I'd never have been able to give the orders that got a significant portion of those under my care and of my . . . *brothers*, to the *Je Reviens* and unscathed, or relatively so." Then he stepped up to the console, and twisted a button and touched a panel screen, which came to life. "I presume you have someone in mind to contact who will help to get us out of here. What's his code?"

"Simon," I said, and then because I thought that was not good enough explanation I added, "The Good Man of Liberte Seacity, Jean-Batiste Simon Ignace Michelle de Montaigne St. Cyr."

And Jarl's face froze and paled.

MAYDAY

HE FLICKED THE BUTTON BACK. "NO," HE SAID. IT echoed of finality.

"What? He's my closest friend and the leader of my lair, and I—"

"No." Jarl turned around, an almost snarl on his features. "I know you regard me as an invader, an interloper, a creature who is killing your husband, and I even understand that. But I don't feel that way about you. As far as I'm concerned you're the daughter of my old friend Alexander Sinistra. Or if you prefer you're his much younger twin sister. Same thing. I left 'Xander behind because I needed to, not because I wanted to. I left him behind fully conscious that the chances were good he would be dead by the morning after the evening of our departure. It was one of the hardest things I've ever done. For all that 'Xander was...what he was, he was that through design and training, not of his own making. And for that, it was like an illness, a fatal weakness, and Bartolomeu and I had made it our duty, our … responsibility to look out for him, to keep him safe. To keep others safe from him. He was, despite that, a good and … a…."—he swallowed—"a worthy human being. He had the virtues of his faults, in courage and loyalty and … and we betrayed him, and I find that he didn't die, which is worse, and that he became … worse. Because of that, because of what I owe 'Xander and for the betrayal I'll never be able to expunge, I must guard you. And guarding you has no part with letting you go near dear little Jean-Batiste." His jaw set and he put out a hand to touch my chin, but pulled away just before he did. "Remember, those we left behind we left behind for good reason. Overwhelming reason. And you couldn't have *paid* me to let Jean-Batiste aboard, not even if the price you gave me were redeeming 'Xander of his fatal weakness."

"What?" I said again, and swallowed hard. What the hell was he saying about Simon? Simon had been one of my closest friends and the mainstay of our broomers' lair. He'd been the one who made sure that the lair had enough food and drink, the one who made sure we were never caught at anything terribly illegal, the one who cleaned up our messes, and looked after us, in general. Oh, I suppose I'd done some of that too, but not nearly as much as Simon had. I'd never *cared* enough. "Simon is not a danger to me," I said. If he'd been, I'd have known that long ago, since we'd been casual and non-exclusive lovers since our early teens. "Simon is trustworthy. He's helped me in the past."

Jarl lifted a fist, and would have let it fall on the panel of the communicator, if Doctor Bartolomeu hadn't reached for his wrist and held it with improbable and disproportionate strength, as he said, "No, Jarl, listen—"

"Nothing to listen to," Jarl said. "You know what... that worm did. Without his... work in the shadows, most of which we still don't know, the riots would never have happened, nor the turmoils. Oh, we knew that trouble was coming. We knew it and everyone knew it. They put us in charge of the whole Earth, and we were too flawed, too... We couldn't do it. And we'd known it for decades. It was all right while we were generals and in charge of armies. That we could study and that worked. But controlling the economy of a whole world was beyond us then, and we knew there was trouble coming. Which is why we had the *Je Reviens*." He turned towards me, his eyes burning in fury. "But there didn't need to be turmoils. There didn't need to be killings on the street and hunts for everyone even suspected of being bioimproved. It didn't need to come to that. We might have slipped away in the night and not had anyone killed and tortured and... crucified...

"Jean-Batiste was a spy. He was created to be a spy and a... an infiltrator. Which is why they gave him a very ordinary appearance and he looked less... prepossessing than the rest of us. He was designed to pass as human with other humans, to infiltrate. I thought he was working for us. We all did. It wasn't until afterwards that I connected the dots, that I looked for... evidence. There was a slow, steady propaganda movement amid the homo-saps. There was... They were turned against us. Not just against our government but against us. Against the very notion of bioimprovements. Articles, subsidized research, everything... pointed to our very nature being evil. It didn't take much, not after the Mule riots of a century before, where our... less fortunate brethren... killed and burned..." He shrugged. "It took me years, mining the data I'd taken with me to Eden, to realize that behind everything creating hatred against us, stood Jean-Batiste, nudging, pushing. It took me even more years to convince myself that my friend, Jean-Batiste, who'd sat at my table and eaten from my dishes, had done it all so he could get those of us who were not in his little... protected clique... killed, so that he and his friends, his... cohort, could take the *Je Reviens* and leave us out cold. If Bartolomeu hadn't suspected it, from certain of his movements and made him one of those to whom he'd lied about when the *Je Reviens* would be ready; if it had indeed been still two weeks away from being able to liftoff, I'd have died in the turmoils, as would have Bartolomeu, and as would have all of our charges and all of our servants." A muscle worked on the side of his jaw. "No, I cannot allow you to leave us at the mercy of a snake like that. Poisonous snakes should be killed, not coddled."

I took a deep breath. "Simon," I said, emphasizing the name, "is not his father. Or his older clone, or whatever this Jean-Batiste was. He's not..."

"The personality is the same. The personality is there."

"I am not my father," I said, "and Kit is not you." The last was flung out with the intent of hurting, but he only smiled a little.

"He's more like me than you think. I know. I'm in his mind, or he's in mine. Why do you think—"

"Like hell he is," I said. "Kit never killed someone who wasn't directly threatening him. He never said that someone was unimportant because they weren't skilled, or they were ... impaired. He is nothing like you."

Thena, cool it. There's more going on than you think.

All right, then, tell the big moose that Simon is not his father. I trust Simon. You trust Simon, right?

I barely remember Simon. But I trust what I've heard from you. And I know I'd never have got out of Never-Never without his help. And I'm trying to tell the big moose. And what do you mean big moose? Am I a big moose?

You're not this pigheaded. Which is damning with faint praise.

Just then Jarl's eyes went unfocused, as though he were carrying on a mind-conversation with someone. His forehead knit as though he were trying to understand something, then he sighed. "Your ... my ... Christopher tells me that I have it wrong," he said. His voice was slow and stiff, as though he were making a great concession. "He says he has met this ... Simon and that he's trustworthy. For our purposes at least. I suppose if ... if he were to try to betray us, we're forewarned, and at least we'll be nearer civilization." He squinted at our surroundings. "A refuge is good, but it's always easier to hide in the middle of civilization."

He paused, then said, "Liberte Seacity?" And he pressed a couple of spots on the panel. At the other end of the array, a floor-to-ceiling screen came on. And on it, stark naked, coming out of his shower, was Simon.

I was so shocked that I did not react. Someone—I think Zen—gasped behind me, which must have been surprise, because it couldn't have been interest. If, as Jarl said, Simon's ancestor had been made to fit into normal humanity, it made sense, because unlike most of the Good Men he was not particularly powerful looking or extraordinarily handsome. Just a short, slim man with dark hair, an aquiline nose and lively dark eyes. And, at that moment, not just naked, but humming something that sounded martial, as he rubbed at his hair with a towel.

As we watched, he dropped the towel and his walk took on the rhythm of his humming as he crossed a white-carpeted expanse of floor to what I recognized as his dressing room. The camera—was it a camera or some other sort of pickup? Wouldn't Simon's father have noticed a camera in all these hundreds of years? Surely the place had been remodeled or something, and it would have been discovered—followed him around, as he pulled open a curtain and stared, immobile, at an array of suits.

"Simon," I said. "Simon!"

He didn't turn. He didn't even flinch. He just stared on, then made a slow, prolonged "Um…" in a tone of deep consideration and reached for a pair of dark trousers.

"He can't hear us," Jarl said, amusement in his voice. Or rather, amusement burbling at the back of his throat, even as his voice remained steady. "This is how I found out dear Jean-Batiste was working against us."

Suddenly the enormity of it hit me. We were spying on Simon. On Simon who trusted me, as I trusted him. On Simon, who'd been my friend, my associate, my accomplice. Four of us were staring at him while he was naked and vulnerable; while he had no idea of being observed. Three of them were total strangers.

Don't mistake me. As children of Good Men, we grew up knowing privacy happened to other people. We were never fully alone. In houses filled with servants and bursting with retainers, you always had to assume strangers were watching, unless you were up to something pleasantly scandalous and took extraordinary measures. Even then, it wasn't guaranteed.

But we weren't servants or retainers, and we had no right to violate his privacy that way. "Stop," I said. "Turn it off."

Jarl gave me a surprised, not to say puzzled look. He shrugged, reached over and turned the video off, then went back to the original touch screen. "What is his code?"

I gave it to him, and his eyebrows rose, but he said nothing about the facility with which it came to the mind. Which was good. He didn't have a right to. Kit did, but Kit had never asked, never wanted to know, and if he'd inferred the inevitable from my stories about the lair and our adventures, he'd never made a jealous or even ill-tempered remark. He'd known what he was getting, I suppose.

Yes, Kit's voice in my head. *I was getting you. It's all I ever wanted. Who cares who was first, provided I'm last?*

That sounds slightly morbid, and what were you doing in my mind?

Trying to talk to you. Thena, we have to do something. There's something you must understand. Jarl is not . . . himself.

What do you mean? I should hope he's not himself. He's partly you. I don't want it to change in his direction. For him to be himself, you have to stop existing.

No, I mean he's not himself. That violence—

"Thena!" Simon was visible from the shoulders up, enough to see he'd slipped on some sort of a red shirt, and that his hair was still wet and standing on end. "Thena! Are you on Earth?"

He looked so glad to see me, and his question was so casually inane, as though I were a commuter between Earth and Eden, that I wanted to giggle. Instead I said, "Yes, but..."

I gave him a quick rundown of the situation, neglecting only to mention that my husband was possessed by the spirit of his elder clone. Part of the reason I didn't mention it was because well... it was the easiest way to describe it. And yet I knew it wasn't true. And once we got into nessies, Simon would start asking questions. Questions like "So is he Kit or not?" or "What are the chances of ever getting your husband back?" And I really didn't want to answer, even if I could figure out the proper responses.

Simon frowned slightly then nodded. "Weird," he said. "History sometimes parallels itself."

"What?"

"We're in the middle of a fight for freedom ourselves. Liberte, egalite... er... fraternite," he made a halfhearted gesture with his hand that could be interpreted as anything from a high-clap to a fist waved in air. "All very exciting. And deadly dull. Keeps interrupting supplies of wine and wrecking algie farming." His voice was bored and dragging, but his eyes had an interested gleam. I wondered what was really going on and how deep in it Simon was. Simon was always more interested in things than he let on, and deeper in everything going on. I thought of Jarl's description of his ancestor and shuddered. "Look, Earth is not our business. I'm worried about Eden. I just...I'd like to get hold of Jarl's papers and go back as soon as we can, because Eden needs us."

Something like a regretful look flitted across Simon's eyes. "I suppose that is your home now." His gaze flickered to the side, where Jarl stood behind me, probably doing his best imitation of stern guardian.

"I realize there's nothing in it for you, and I hate to bother you," I said, "but without you we're sunk, you see, and I—"

Simon bit his lip. "Ah, well, you're a fellow broomer. Same lair. One has obligations as Max's brother has brought to mind."

"Max's *brother*?" I asked. Max, now dead, had been one of our lair. Like us he was the clone and heir apparent of a Good Man. He had no brothers.

"Long story. Part of the little contretemps we're going through. I can explain later, but it's no big deal." He smiled suddenly, the smile that reassured me because it was so much like the Simon I knew. I should correct my description of him. Simon was unprepossessing and uninteresting until he smiled. That smile was dazzling, like the sun coming out on a cloudy day. There had been a time it made my knees go weak. Now it didn't, which was a good thing, since I suspected Jarl was glowering over my shoulder, but it did make me relax.

"Give me your coordinates, Thena, and I'll come get you. I suspect it's covered under *fraternite*."

I gave him the coordinates, but I'd barely finished when Jarl said, "It's a locked compound. You could bring a whole army, and you can't get in without us letting you in. When you come to the entrance and the lock extrudes, just press the point that says to call within."

Simon frowned up at him, and I wondered if he was confused by Jarl's stern cadences. Had he ever heard Kit talk? Enough to know how different they sounded?

"Mais oui," Simon said, and shrugged. "I won't be there before tomorrow morning anyway. I have to arrange the route. With the rebellion and all, it's become a wee bit difficult to just fly across the sea like that."

"Tomorrow morning," Jarl snarled. "Long enough to set up a treason."

Simon looked so genuinely startled that even Jarl must have seen it and recognized it. "Ah. No. It's just that I greatly dislike being shot to pieces while flying over rebel-held territory, see, and I need to know how that has changed overnight, and if needed, get safe conduct." He gave me a direct look. "Fear not, Thena. You're still one of the lair. I'll come get you, and then we'll try to figure out where your . . . what's his name? Jarl has hidden his notes. I will call on this and leave a message when to expect me." His gaze flickered to Jarl, and then he reached forward, and the screen went blank.

"We have a day," Jarl said. "Let me show you my domains."

I thought it sounded odd. There was some story, in some holy book—not being raised with them, I had trouble remembering which one precisely—about the devil taking a demi-god to a pinnacle and offering him the kingdoms of the Earth. The way Jarl said this, sounded like that.

And then I realized he meant it like that, too. Oh, not that he was offering us the kingdoms of the Earth in return for our subjection, though I suspected he would, if it got him our subjection. But more like he thought what he was showing us were the kingdoms of the Earth . . . or the better part of Earth.

He took us walking up winding paths, to pick only slightly dusty fruit from huge, gnarled, venerable trees. He ate apples with the relish of a child, grinning between bites. "Damn vat-grown in Eden. Or even tree-grown. Might be very healthful and full of vitamins and minerals, but they don't taste the same."

Then he led us to a huge rock, atop a small hill, from which we could contemplate the canopy of trees, with the birds fleeting among them. The air felt like a summer afternoon, and I'd never spent so much time just walking around amid trees. If my husband weren't being held captive, I'd have enjoyed myself greatly.

Kit?

Here, Thena, still here. Don't worry. Just . . . let him enjoy himself.

You like him!

And Kit's voice, slow and thoughtful, *I think . . . it's hard not to like him from inside. I could . . . be him. If I'd had a truly awful life and then been treated like both an object and a threat and a demi-god, all at the same time. Even his achievements weren't his own. They were a reason for his creators to be proud, instead.*

I didn't know what to say. It seemed like a betrayal, like Kit had gone over to Jarl's side, but Kit laughed in my head. *Not on your life. We're going to figure out how to beat this, Thena. We're going to figure out how to defeat it. We'll survive. But he won't. Let him have his fun.*

I realized Jarl was offering me a handful of berries on his palm. "They're very sweet," he said. "I've tasted one."

I looked up into his eyes, and realized he'd been paying more attention to me than to the rest of them. Was it just because he felt guilty over Daddy Dearest? Or was it something else? Had Kit's feelings for me leaked? Behind him, Doc was looking studiously up at the tree canopy or at the ceiling of the cavern up there.

I took the berries and thanked him, with as much reserve as I could put into it, and ate the berries. They were sweeter, and juicier than in Eden, and I conceded this when he asked me. He was enjoying them so enthusiastically his hands were stained with the juice. "The fish tastes better too." He looked over at Doc. "What do you say, Bartolomeu? Should we have a fish dinner by the creek? I have rations stored somewhere...but I'd prefer not to go into the deeper levels here. Also, rations will be good after three hundred years, but they're rations."

Doc made a noncommittal sound, and Jarl turned, giving the impression of sudden, vital energy. He headed for the creek. Zen followed behind me and got beside me. "Do you still hear Kit?" she asked in a whisper.

I told her what Kit had said and she shook her head. "See, that's the difference between us. Kit was always softer. Let's hope he's not too soft." She looked at Jarl's back. "I don't trust him."

"Uh...he's your elder clone, just like Kit is—"

"Did you trust your father?"

"Well, no, but the stories of Jarl in Eden..."

Zen sighed. "He killed his wife to continue with a mad scheme, Thena. I'm not saying he wasn't a wonderful man ... before. Doc seems to think so, and I respect him. But, Thena, when my husband's father started—"

She was interrupted by Jarl turning around from the bank of the creek that ran through the compound and saying, "Oh. My. We won't need fishing rods."

The creek boiled with fish. You could see them through the very clear water, and you could see the pebbled bottom. The creek wasn't at all deep, perhaps waist high.

"I seeded it with fish, and I guess being untouched this long..." Jarl said. "There are filters on the water at the entrance and there's a life-barrier at the exit, which I suppose kept them safe. But I never expected this. Almost a kindness to thin the population." He pulled off his shirt, revealing Kit's muscular chest with its dusting of red-gold hair. He pulled off his shoes. And then he waded into the creek, with his pants still on, and turned in moments, a fish in each hand, and goofy grin on his face. "It's devilish cold, but I've seen nothing like this in three hundred years. Won't any of you join me? Bartolomeu? Thena? Zen?"

"I'll clean the fish," Zen said, catching them as he flung them.

Doc sat a little way away. "I'm too old to go into cold water, Jarl." He looked at me, and I understood the unspoken message and sat by him. I expected the query of whether Kit was still there, but instead what I got was an intent whisper, "When Jarl's brain got imprinted, the pattern already revealed considerable damage from Hampson's. Impossible for it not to show now. And I'm seeing the symptoms. Jarl's brain already showed loss of synapses and some neuron damage. He'd forget a name or a skill or become unexpectedly clumsy. I know these symptoms very well, because every time I treated Jarl again, he would forget everything since the last treatment. He left himself notes, but . . . There are other symptoms, too, harder to pin down. Poor impulse control. Paranoia. Thena, I want you to know that's not who he was." He looked towards the river, where Jarl was throwing a couple more fish at Zen, a happy smile on his face. "This is more like it. He was a kind, generous man, and unlike what happened at Circum, he would no more take life casually than Kit would. The Jarl I knew would never have killed Irena. But . . . he wasn't himself. We figured in the course of the brain growing . . ."

"So you want me to know that not only is Kit being taken over, he is being given a horrible degenerative disease?"

"No, just the symptoms," Doc said. He looked over at me, and chewed his lower lip. "We have to find a solution," he said. Yet, I felt like Kit, he was too likely to think well of the invader.

"Yes, we do," I said. "I don't care how much you miss your old friend, or how worthy Jarl was of living. My husband doesn't deserve the death penalty so Jarl can live."

Doc shivered, and paled a little. "No. No, Thena. We'll find a way. Maybe your friend Simon can give me access to a lab . . ."

"Jarl knows how to build and program the nanocytes

to reverse this, doesn't he?" I asked. "And you don't quite."

Doc sighed. "Jarl designed them, yes. It doesn't mean he knows how to reverse them."

"And he wouldn't tell us if he knew," I said.

Doc frowned, worried. "We have to persuade him, somehow. Or maybe I can reverse engineer it."

DANSE MACABRE

IT WAS NOT THE BEST MEAL I EVER HAD, BECAUSE fish will never be my favorite meal. But it came close to it, with the fresh fish cooked on sticks over the fire and various fruits and berries for dessert. Jarl continued in near manic-mode.

He reminded me of a little boy, trying to show off all his toys at the same time and unwilling to pause long enough to explain why the toys were wonderful. I should have been more alarmed, but I couldn't be.

I could hear Kit's burble of delighted laughter in my mind, and realized with shock that he was enjoying this almost as much as Jarl. Not being in the water. That kept him quiet for a while and I could feel his near-phobia of free running water, born of never having seen so much of it in one place until our last visit to Earth.

But he did enjoy the fish and informed me, *He's right. It does taste different and better. It's more . . . layered.*

After the meal, we lay about on the grass, looking up at the ceiling of the cavern, which was fully dark, now that night had fallen outside and the piped-in sunlight no longer shone. Dark, with a relief of branches waving in the breeze.

Thena, it was Kit in my mind, even though I was almost sure Jarl was asleep on the ground next to the fire.

Yes?

I wish...I wish there were some way for him to live. Just not in my mind, he added, hurriedly.

I felt a surge of alarm again, despite his qualifier. I thought of Zen asking me if I trusted Jarl. Was Jarl, somehow, working on Kit, making him think he should allow Jarl to live, allow him to have Kit's body. *You can't let him,* I said. *You can't let him take over. Kit, I won't let you. I'm in love with you, not him. I have nothing against him, but I will not allow you to sacrifice yourself for him. And he's not well.*

No, Kit admitted. Then said, *And I don't want to sacrifice myself for him, or allow him to take over... me. It's just... You know I love my family.* He paused. *But much as love them, I've known since Doc told me what I was, that I was different, that I wasn't like them. Now I have you, and I suppose Zen, and I always had Doc, but... Jarl is older than I. He's been... he's seen things I haven't, experienced things I haven't. He... feels like a father to me?*

I thought of what a father felt like to me and allowed my exasperation to show, just a little. He laughed in my mind. *Yes, beloved,* he said. *But you didn't know you were different until just recently. You didn't live with it every day of your life from adolescence on. You might*

think that your father was impossible to like or admire.
There was a long silence, and I had a feeling he was
scanning whichever memories of Jarl's he could access
for what my father was like. *All right. Maybe your father
was impossible to like or admire,* he added. *But even so
he might have seemed more tolerable if you knew that
he was the creature closest to you in the world.*

I felt a chill up my spine. What I said, in his mind,
was, *Don't go weak. He can use your emotions too,
Kit. And he wants to live. You have to want to live
just as hard.*

I didn't know if this was true, but I seemed to
remember it from the multiple personality cases I
had read about.

But inside, I wondered if Kit had any idea how
much I feared my similarity to my father, how much
I feared I would grow to be just like him.

Suddenly, Jarl was in control again. I could tell
from the way he jumped up, full of energy, as though
he'd just remembered a toy he'd forgotten to show us.

He came back with the violin. By the light of the
fire, Kit's eyes looked brighter, as if he were feverish.
I realized he—Jarl?—had pulled off his light-mitigating
lenses. He tuned his violin, carefully, a ritual I was
familiar with because Kit always did it before he
played anything.

Then he started playing.

I clenched. I recognized the piece, because it was
one of Kit's favorites, the type of thing he would play
late at night in his room or in the main room of his
parents' compound. It was *Hungarian Dance #4* by
Brahms. But there was something wrong.

I thought it might be just the setting—this old

compound, and the night, and the fire reflecting off Kit's hands and violin and bow while he played, faster then slower again, pleading with the cavern ceiling that obscured the sky and with the unseen stars. But even accounting for those something was wrong. Something was very wrong.

I closed my eyes, and listened, and felt the hair on my head and on my arms rise on end, before I could think what was causing it. And then I realized what it was. Two people were playing that violin. They were handing off, in tiny increments, each perhaps half a minute long. You couldn't perceive where the handoff was, but you knew—you knew—it was happening.

I'm not a musical expert, but I know a difference in style when I hear it. Kit's playing was softer and deeper, and Jarl's more disciplined, curter. And they flowed in and out of each other, seamlessly, like . . .

Like two hands playing the piano together. Like a person picking up something with two hands, like—

I found myself on my feet and running, running madly in no direction in particular, running stumbling in the darkness, running and not caring if small shrubs caught at my clothes, if I fell, and picked myself up, and fell again.

The music pursued me like a living thing, winding around me, changing, enveloping me, choking me, with its seamless, cloying mix.

Once, when I was young, I'd heard my father talk about my mother. I'll remember the words to my dying day. You see, I'd thought they'd been happy, or somewhat happy, even though it had been an arranged marriage. I didn't think it was perfect, clearly, since my mother had left.

But then I overheard Father talking about Mother, and he called her a "stand in" and "disposable" and "the womb." At the time I hadn't understood what he meant. I didn't know she hadn't really been my mother, or really his wife, in any sense of the word. Just the convenient facade of a marriage with which to hide his acquisition of a daughter.

I knew the words hurt though. My mother, such as she'd been, had been the only person who'd shown me affection—personal affection, not the care of those paid to care for me.

The words had cut me to the quick, and I'd found myself running. Running out of Daddy Dearest's home, running out of the gardens, running out of the compound, and, aimlessly, towards the industrial levels of Syracuse Seacity.

I hadn't stopped running till I could no longer move. Father had sent his goons after me, and they found me and carried me home. Because I refused to tell them what had happened, Father thought it was another of my maddening behaviors designed, solely, to drive him insane. The next morning, my governess had found that I had blisters all over my soles.

And I'd found out you couldn't outrun your troubles. They galloped right along with you, waiting to flood your mind and body as soon as you stopped running.

Perhaps that's why this time I stopped sooner. Or perhaps it was because the terrain was broken, full of rocks and trees and roots, and I couldn't run, just run as I'd run as a child, my lungs filling with air, my feet pumping.

Here, I didn't even have the illusion I could outrun

my troubles. Besides, the music stopped, and Jarl's voice called "Thena!" then Kit echoed it mentally: *Thena!*

I stopped and fell to the ground on my knees, trembling, weak, my mind filled only with one overwhelming and horrible thought. I'd been telling Kit he had to survive. I'd been telling him to stand firm and withstand Jarl's attempts to take over wholly. I was sure that, of the two, Jarl was the most determined to live. He'd walked with death for years before his brain imprinting, the part of him, frozen in time, who was trying to take over Kit. He'd know death for the adversary it was and what it meant, and that would make him even more desperate.

I'd thought Kit could fight it, just barely, but I thought he could. I thought he could fight it for my sake. I'd thought he could hold on until I got Doc to a lab, until Doc could concoct something that would keep Kit alive, that would bring Kit back.

I didn't think of the reality of it. No matter how it felt to me, I wasn't dealing with two distinct and separate people, forever apart, or battling it out where one would live and the other die. No. I was dealing with one brain and one creature.

One creature, the love of my life, whose mind was being changed and reshaped by physical means, whose very physical integrity, his body, was being reshaped so that he had the memories and thoughts of another being.

Only there hadn't been quite enough nanocytes in the solution injected in the bio womb. Not enough to start developing when Kit was forming and from what Doc said, probably fewer now, since these things decayed over time. So there was probably just enough to take it halfway, and there the brain would stay, half-changed. Half-Kit, half-Jarl. Some memories from both. Some personality from both.

And because the brain itself wasn't diseased, over time, it would consolidate, it would merge.

I'd thought the choices were to have Kit survive or to have Jarl survive. I hadn't thought of the most likely thing to happen. That they would both survive and merge, till there was only one being in that body, neither Kit nor Jarl, but a hybrid who wasn't either. A hybrid who was not my husband. A stranger in my husband's body.

I walked away in the darkness, and sat down on the ground. I felt cold, though Jarl had said the temperature was constant here.

Something ran over my lap, but I didn't know what it was—a mouse or a rabbit or something else. And I was too tired to even feel my old horror of being outdoors, surrounded by critters.

I leaned against the trunk of a tree.

THENA! Kit in my mind, panicked, and I could hear footsteps, not near, but near enough. He could see in the dark as well as I could in the light, and I was sure I'd left a path of broken twigs and trampled ground as I ran.

I'm here, I said. *Don't come near. No. Don't come. Thena?*

I'm all right. I just can't have you near right now. No. Please.

What . . . what did I do?

Can't explain. Never mind. I'm fine. Just leave me alone. Everything will be fine in the morning.

I felt his reluctance in leaving me, but heard the steps going away and I closed my eyes and prayed.

I'm not religious. I don't even know if I believe in gods as such. But I believe in something. There had to be something, either God or fate or justice. There had to be something out there that listened, that dealt with human needs when our courage brought us so far and then broke, leaving us stranded.

To that distant, nameless force, I begged to have my husband back. And then I threatened. And then I must have fallen asleep.

I woke up in the morning with light in my eyes, a squirrel eyeing me speculatively from a near branch, and Kit—I was sure it was Kit—looking at me with concern from the edge of the little clearing where I'd slept against the trunk of a tree.

"Kit!" I said.

And he smiled a little, and looked sad, then said, "He said it should be me, because he thought he had scared you. Did he scare you?"

"Yes. No. Maybe."

Kit's eyes widened. "Thena!"

"I haven't gone insane," I said. "I know what happened, but I can't tell you." Or I could, but I was afraid both of them would embrace it as a perfect solution. "I can't explain."

His eyebrows rose, and he said nothing, but I felt him draw upon his reserve, a closed look I had rarely seen since our marriage. "Well, at any rate, I thought you'd want to know your friend, Simon, is down by the creek, talking to Doc. He has a brand spanking new, properly registered flyer all sparkling clean and ready to take us to the seacities and civilization."

FRATERNITE

SO I'M VAIN ENOUGH, OR PERHAPS JUST PROUD ENOUGH to stop and wash my face in the creek, a few feet away from where Simon stood, talking with voluble gestures to Doc. Doc and Zen saw us approach, and saw me wash, but Simon had his back to me. Probably on purpose, since he was as much a Mule as I or Kit, meaning he would have more acute hearing than the average homo sapien.

But he waited until I was just a few steps behind him, to turn around and extend both hands at me, "Thena!"

"Simon," I said, and managed a smile. He gave me a peck on either cheek, which was good, because the last time he'd seen me, he'd planted a full open-mouth kiss on me by way of goodbye, and Kit had not liked it then. Now Kit, with his own problems, was wont to like it even less. And I didn't even want to think of what Jarl, with his hatred for Simon's original "twin," and his lack of self control might do.

Simon stepped back. "You're looking very good for someone who has been communing with nature. What a strange thing to find Thena sleeping au plain air." He grinned, sharing the implicit joke that my love for nature had never been great.

But even as he talked to me, I noticed his eyes straying over to Zen with fascination, then he looked back at me, and smiled again, "As I told your friends, we don't have the time to dally because I had to plot both courses coming and going, and if we wait longer, there will be another front in this not quite civil war we're facing, and next thing you know, we will be stranded and shot at. Or perhaps captured and shot at. You know my horror of dying by laser. It's so unsightly and leaves such a mangled body for the public obsequies."

I could see Zen's eyes widening, as Simon slipped into his patented patter. It was as though she were considering whether to run into the night because he was completely insane and she couldn't trust him. Weirdly, it wasn't like the hard expression of distrust and vigilance she aimed at Jarl when he was in control. Instead, it was something stranger, more fluid, part expectancy, part hope and part . . . what was it? I couldn't even tell. Interest, curiosity perhaps, but all of this overlaid with fear of this odd creature and a vague suspicious expression, as though she suspected him of putting her on.

She was right at that, or she was right to an extent. Simon was putting her on, putting all three of them on. But it wasn't a deliberate deception, and I didn't even think he knew when he did it.

When he was young, Simon had inherited, de facto,

his father's responsibilities and honors, after his father had been rendered comatose by an accident. He was brain damaged and unlikely to be able to recover, ever.

Though Simon was the Good Man, even in name, and he fulfilled the function of a Good Man and did all the work of one, he was never treated quite as a Good Man. This had been a source of confusion to us, but at least now I understood that part of it. He wasn't treated as a Good Man, because he wasn't one of the Mules who'd first taken power. And he'd found they suspected him, and any display of intent or intelligence on his part brought resistance and attempts to stop him. So he'd learned to play the inconsequential fool and the clothes-obsessed fop. Only I knew better. I knew how he ran the broomers' lair.

"If you will pardon me," he said, as he opened the door to the large size flyer, "I'd like to tell you this was the best flyer money could buy, but clearly it is not, since it's last year's model, and pardon the distressing color, but they seemed to think this was red, and I was so sad for them I didn't want to have to explain their eyes had gone awry." He continued with voluble nonsense, as we climbed in and strapped on. Kit—or Jarl, I couldn't even tell who was in control— was tightening his jaw shut so hard that it must hurt. Doc looked amused, leading me to wonder if Simon's father had had similar mannerisms. I didn't remember much about him, since I hadn't been very old when he'd fallen comatose. Zen, on the other hand, was frowning at him as though he were a problem that she—personally—must solve and rectify.

Not that he gave her much chance. His flyer was even more comfortable inside than the air-and-space.

There were sofas, all well-upholstered. He waved us to the sofas; we sat down and he took the controls. He proceeded to demonstrate that not only was he bioed with extra gifts of speed and control and movement, but also that he had experience with aerial vehicles. Which I already knew from the way he handled a broom.

I didn't have feelings for Simon. At least not beyond the feelings one has for a childhood friend and teenage lover. I think both of us had assumed we'd be married someday. Then had come the trip to Circum, and Kit and Eden and... finding out what I was.

Now nothing more remained of those vague intentions of marrying Simon someday than a wishful feeling that life should be that simple. But I didn't want Simon. I wanted Kit. And I might not have the choice about getting him back.

I don't remember the trip, partly because the sofa was comfortable, and I'd spent the night on hard ground. I think we all fell asleep.

I woke up as we landed on Liberte Seacity, thereby having missed the excitement of whatever revolution was going on. That was something I had to ask Simon as soon as possible, as well as what had happened with Syracuse Seacity and my father's mansion.

Liberte Seacity is not as vast as Syracuse and it is mostly devoted to algie cultivation, so, by comparison to Syracuse, a bucolic paradise. Their beaches are white and unmarred by factories or construction. Don't take that to mean that Liberte was the seat of a caring and enlightened Good Man. I think Simon's—for lack of a better word—father simply liked pretty beaches. Liberte Seacity was the administrative center of territories that included vast portions of Old Europe, as well as the narcotic-producing city of Shan-gri-la. But Liberte resembled a more carefully—artistically—planned work than Syracuse ever could be. I guess Simon's father was more of an aesthete than mine.

There were personnel waiting for us.

When we stopped, Simon got up and glanced at Kit. "Er . . . keep your eyes down. The hair could be a dye job." Then he walked past and opened the flyer. Onto rows of waiting people.

I felt Zen tense, and tried to signal her that this was not an arrest. I doubted that Simon had even paused to think. We were guests and he was receiving us in the grand style that Good Men hosted friends and equals. He smiled at the six or so men and women waiting. "Ah, I don't believe my guests have luggage, but if you lead them to the rooms you've prepared for them, I'm sure they will give you instructions on what changes of clothing to procure them." He smiled, his disarming, seemingly confused smile. "I'm sure there's clothes in their sizes in house stores, or fabric that can be vibroed or . . . something like that. If you'll lead us to where you set up their rooms, I'll be by, in case they have complaints."

Zen looked from my slight head shake to Doc and, I suppose because Doc looked calm and a little amused, relaxed.

We were led up a vast corridor to a staircase, and from the staircase to what I identified as their best guest wing. I'd been here before, of course, with Daddy Dearest for occasions of state and meetings of Good Men. If you were put on this wing of the house, you knew you were in the good graces of the

Good Man, or possibly vital to his plans. I didn't think this applied, since we were probably the only guests.

I got a room I'd got before, actually the last time I'd stayed here, without Daddy Dearest. Kit got the room next to mine, Doc the room after that, and Zen the room to the other side of mine. It wasn't till Simon had left and the help—two women—were drawing me a bath and bringing in armfuls of clothes I could choose from to wear, that I realized that not only had I been put in a separate room from my husband—not that rare in my class on Earth, but not the normal arrangement—but that there was no connecting door.

Of course, this was entirely appropriate, since I never knew who was in that body at the moment and I was emphatically not married to Jarl, or even to any strange blend that might emerge. On the other hand, I hadn't told Simon this. In fact, I hadn't told Simon anything about Jarl—or the fact that Kit was his clone—beyond telling him we were looking for his notes. And yet I knew, had known for years, that what might be a casual, absentminded slip in another man was usually done for a reason with Simon.

Why had Simon separated me from Kit? Was it his lecherous nature and hopes that I would indulge in a little adultery? This was also not unusual in our class, but I didn't think that Simon had missed me so much he would go to the trouble of setting this up. But what other reason could he have?

I looked for a moment out the broad window of the room, at the ocean beating down below the window, and wondered if the Edenites would find the sight disquieting. Perhaps only Zen. Jarl knew the ocean, and had lived in Seacities most of his life, if his biography was right.

The tones of the sea were picked out in the room, from the elaborate shell-like structure around the bed, designed to maintain an exact microclimate of humidity and warmth in that area, to the soft rugs on the floor. Yet the rugs felt harsh to me, used as I'd become to the bio-rugs in Eden. As did the bed, and the sofa, when I touched them. I couldn't explain why, but biofabric was more yielding, infinitely adaptable.

"Miss," Attendant Number One said, looking out of the bathroom. And I followed her to find they'd run the tub and filled it with bubbles of what had been my favorite fragrance the last time I visited. I thanked them, then chased them from the room as politely as possible. It shocked them, of course. Patricians had attendants bathe them. But I had spent a lot of time bathing myself; I had never really liked having strangers around that much; and besides, I wanted to be alone with my thoughts and to mull everything going on.

I wasn't even surprised by the time I came out of the bath—fortunately wearing a bathrobe since, unlike Edenites, I wasn't comfortable with casual nudity—to find Simon sitting on my bed and the two attendants nowhere near me. The fact that Simon was still fully dressed, and sitting with one leg drawn up and his arms around it—with his boot on the bed, because some men cannot be housebroken—meant he probably wasn't there for amorous purposes. The expression on his face, pensive and puzzled, was not at all seductive.

"Simon," I said, in reproach, "do you wish to set all your employees talking?"

He shrugged. "My employees know better than to talk."

I suspected he was wrong, but it didn't matter.

"At any rate, I didn't tell them who you were, so they can't really talk about you. Oh, you, maybe, personally, but frankly the way the world is just now, with rebellions, and assassinations, demonstrations and..." He grinned. "Even your scandals will be old news. Besides, they always knew what we were up to, didn't they?"

"I wasn't married then," I said.

He put his leg down with deliberate slowness and looked at me intently. "I see. And are you now?"

I opened my mouth, then snapped it shut. "Don't be ridiculous."

"I see," he said again, and I was very much afraid he did.

He paced to the window and opened it, letting in the deafening sound of the sea and the smell of salt, then he turned around, leaning back, posing, framed by the sea, his red shirt against the intense blue green of the sea, his hair dark against the luminous sky. There were creamy lace ruffles, I noted, emerging from the cuffs of his red shirt. Sometimes all you could do was try not to scream at Simon for being Simon. "Don't be afraid to talk," he said. "There's a hush shield outside the window."

I almost told him about the spy cameras that Jarl had set up, but since that compound was now deserted, I didn't bother. "Simon," I said. "I don't want to talk."

This got me the raised eyebrow again. "Thena, my dearest—"

I must have snorted because he suddenly looked

long-suffering. "I said, Thena, my dearest, I don't think you ever realized how much I was in love with you. When I understood, really understood you were married and gone for good, it broke my heart."

"You don't have a heart. You have a Swiss metronome."

He gave me an apologetic smile. "Fine, then it caused the metronome to skip a beat. You know that's not good. We Gallic people have a very passionate nature and—"

"You forgot the 'r' in 'garlic,' you fraud. You don't have any Gallic background. Liberte was founded by a conglomerate of Swiss bankers escaping Old Europe taxes and intrusion, and if I understand properly, your . . . your father was created from spare parts from all Swiss cantons. At best you've got some old European passions or something. Warn me before you start to beat up on yourself."

He sighed. We'd always bantered like that, but he wasn't entering into the spirit of the thing. "I was saying," he said, "that I cared a great deal for you. Perhaps more romantically than you thought, but when you left I assumed I'd never see you again." He examined the lace ruffles on his sleeve. "I'm not going to pretend I didn't . . . well, accept it. I did. And I'm not going to pretend I want to be involved with you. I don't. It's clear you never viewed our relationship as I did. I thought, when I saw you with your Cat man that it was very obvious you were right for each other. You fit, as we never did. So I kissed you goodbye"—a feral grin as the so-and-so probably too well remembered the nature of that kiss—"and let you go. But Thena . . . there's something wrong now.

Something wrong between you and your husband and, if I had to hazard, something wrong with your husband, and I would not like to guess what. I'd like you to tell me, so I can help you, if possible."

"I have no idea what you're talking about," I said.

Spotting the customary refrigerated tray on one of the low tables, away from the window, set with various beverages, I ambled over and picked a fruit juice. I'd just pulled off the top, converting the small bottle into a glass, and taken a sip, when Simon said, "First, your husband is a clone of Jarl Ingemar, isn't he?"

I spit juice across the room, to find Simon slapping my back as I coughed and spluttered. As soon as I could talk, I jumped away from him, "How can you...how do you...how?"

"You're not the only one whose father had holos lying around, and I've been in charge of my father's affairs a very long time, Thena. You know I've always been good with faces. It's not that hard, if you change the eyes and make his hair red, to see it's the same person, really."

"Second, you're not the kind to come to Earth on a jaunt, and certainly not to come with people who are risking themselves, as your redheaded friend—is she one of us? No, don't answer that. You wouldn't have a right to break her privacy even if you wanted to—and the elderly gentleman I presume because your...because Jarl's clone called him Doc Bartolomeu, is Bartolomeu Dias, one of Jarl's inseparable friends, in a remarkable state of preservation for his age." He let go of me and waved me away from trying to mop up the juice with a tissue. "Leave it. My servants need to feel useful every once in a while, or they start wondering why I pay them. The thing is, Thena, that you didn't come here just because it seemed to you a jolly good idea to get Jarl's notes." He looked at me, very seriously. "You're in a bind, and I want to help you."

I realized that I wasn't going to get out of this easily. Simon knew me much too well to be fobbed off with a casual lie or even two. So I sat on the bed, crossed my robe closed and told him the whole thing, from our landing in Eden onward. I omitted only things that weren't mine to tell, though if he, with his ability to recognize faces—a legacy of his ancestor's specialization?—didn't figure out who Zen was, I wasn't going to try to help him. He did stop me when I mentioned Zen and said, "She's a widow? No children?" which might or might not mean he'd inferred her nature.

I explained how important it was that we get Eden back to what it was, where people were free. Even if they seemed to me almost bewilderingly free, it worked, and it was better than a society where individual will counted for nothing compared to the will of the one ruler. "It's not just that Castaneda is making people uncomfortable," I said. "Or arranging the occasional accidental death, even though it's clear he is doing that too. But the attack on Kit was unprecedented for Eden. It was very well hidden and we couldn't find out who did it, thereby precluding revenge of blood geld. Anyone who might have talked, wouldn't, because they were afraid of what Castaneda could do to their power. We knew he was behind the attack, but we couldn't prove it. And we couldn't stop it. If we can't arrest his march to absolute power, no one will dare rebel. As small as Eden is, and as devoid of laws, it will devolve into an absolute tyranny, with Castaneda and whoever succeeds him in charge, forever, and everyone else little more than slaves. It will be much worse than anywhere on Earth."

When I was done, Simon was standing by the bed, very close to me. He pulled me into his arms. Strangely it was both very comforting and completely non-sexual. Strangely, because even two years ago this would have been sexual. "Thena," he said, "listen. I was joking, or . . . not joking but being gallant about . . . wanting to marry you."

I sniffled "I know," which is when I realized that I'd been crying into the shoulder of his red shirt.

"And I don't know what I can do to help you in this, except, of course, make all facilities the doctor might need available to him, which I will do tomorrow morning early. However . . ." He pulled away from me and used the back of his fingers to wipe at my tears. "However, I want you to know this . . . If all else fails and you need . . . refuge with someone who understands you, I'll be here. I can't pretend we are or ever were each other's dream of love, but we're good friends, yes? And if you want that I'm here for you for as long as you want."

"Thank you," I said, and this time hugged him to me, tightly. We were locked in embrace, with me still in my robe, when I saw, over Simon's shoulder, the door open.

Jarl came in. Or perhaps it was Kit. Whichever it was, was not amused. And what he said was, "What is the meaning of this?"

TO HAVE AND TO HOLD

I THINK WHEN BEING CAUGHT IN A COMPROMISING position with a male, a married woman is supposed to feel some sort of panic. But I was never one to do the expected, and besides, for most of my life, most of my friends had been male and I'd never felt compromised by any of them.

I sniffed, and let Simon offer me a handkerchief, into which I blew my nose noisily. And then I said the first thing that came to mind, which happened to be, "I'm not up on comparative semiotics, but I think I was crying on a friend's shoulder."

Jarl stalked into the room, and I was now sure it was Jarl. No, I could never fully describe the difference, except that, as with the violin playing, Jarl walked with more discipline than grace. It occurred to me quickly and irrelevantly that it was perhaps the memory of his body being older and frailer, and having to move cautiously in order not to hurt himself.

Simon turned to face him, with lazy grace, and they stared at each other for a moment, and then Jarl stalked around to the left, while Simon turned that way. They looked like nothing so much as barnyard animals, roosters, engaged in a territorial confrontation. I did not have the time for this.

One of the funniest things in Eden was reading twentieth-century literature, back in the time when they still had faith in the eternal progress—mental, physical, emotional—of mankind, and when they were lousy with philosophies that told them they would eventually become perfect and live in a perfect society. It is funny in a bitter way, because they tended to believe man would become wholly rational and leave behind his animal nature.

I'd like to bring one of those twentieth-century writers face-to-face with the two men in my room—two men who were both created by scientific processes, might I add.

The sad thing was that Simon didn't even want me, and I wasn't sure about Jarl. But I was female and I nominally was married to one of them, or at least to his body. They were going to fight over me at the drop of a hat.

I'd better make sure the hat didn't drop. In fact, I'd better make sure I got their minds away from the possibility of a hat existing, let alone dropping. Knowing Jarl and his lack of control, the last thing I needed was for his old hatred of Simon's... original to come to the fore. There are many many ways to get killed on Earth. Killing a Good Man might be one of the fastest and most painful. And that was before taking in account that Simon might be a bastard, but

I liked him. And I was fairly sure his alleged heart was in the right place.

I jumped from the bed. "Right," I said, standing in front of Jarl. "Would you mind telling me the terms of my captivity?"

"What?"

I could genuinely say I'd taken him by surprise. His eyes flickered from Simon to me. Mentally, I said, *Kit, rein in the troglodyte.*

Should I? To my relief, my husband, or what remained of him sounded more teasing than worried. *What were you doing with the oh-so-suave Simon? What did you tell him that caused him to take you in his arms?* Kit paused, possibly realizing what he'd given away. *Yes, he brought a portable viewer, and yes, the bug, whatever it is, follows Simon. I have no idea how that was done, and he won't tell me.*

But you couldn't hear us?

No. Simon must have some kind of circumventing mechanism in place. It's part of what's driving Jarl insane.

"You're not a captive," Jarl said, and tightened his lips.

"No? Then why are you here asking me about a visitor to my room? What business is it of yours? In Eden, it would be enough to challenge you to a duel."

"A duel! Thena, we're married."

"We are not, Jarl Ingemar."

This caught him out of step. He opened his mouth and said, "But—"

Before he could finish his thought I said, "And even if we were, I would challenge you to a duel for doubting my word. When I married Kit I presumed

fidelity was implied. If he didn't trust my word, why
marry me?"

*Hey! I trust your word. And I don't remember a
promise of fidelity.*

I said implied.

He gave an artistic mental sigh. *Yeah, I suppose it
was, by the laws of your people and all... It's sad,
I'll have to give up my plans to have a harem. And
I'd already picked out ages and body types.*

I stomped on the temptation to tell him he wouldn't
have that chance if he were a figment of Jarl's mind,
and instead turned to Jarl and gave him my best
slow *I'm a patrician of Earth and I've scraped better
looking stuff off my soles* look. "As for you, Mr. ... or
should I call you Patrician, since you're our equal?
Patrician Ingemar, I didn't marry you. Ever. I don't
think I would marry you while compos mentis. I don't
like the way you jump to conclusions."

He looked puzzled. Men aren't very hard to puzzle.
The old-style feminists, the ones who complained
forever about male oppression, must have been the
worst verbal sparrers in the history of mankind.

Something science has shown us is that men aren't
at home with words. Oh, sure, there are exceptions. I'm
almost sure Shakespeare was a little sharper than the
rest. But on average, most men are less verbal than most
women. Heck, most of them get confused with more
than ten words together and if possible would ban them
on the principle of illegal assembly and conspiracy to
confuse. The fact that women have always been better
with words is probably a compensation for the fact men
have the muscles, the size, and the spatial reasoning. If
you ask me, men got the short end of the stick.

"But you married Christopher."

"You are not Kit," I said.

He frowned and came up with a clinching argument which only emphasizes why most men should not get in arguments with most women, "But I have his body."

"I didn't marry him for his body, pleasant though it is."

"But . . . he's not dead."

"No, but neither is he in control of that body. In fact, he might not be able to take control again."

It would take a lot of effort. Thena, we must—

I know.

"And until he does, that body is not married to me. I'm sure that possession by a different entity renders our contract invalid or at least in abeyance." And then I did the dismount and level. "At any rate all this is nonsensical, because all I was doing was telling Simon about Castaneda and the situation in Eden, and why I need access to Jarl's notes so we can go back as soon as possible. There was nothing romantic going on!" And, without giving him time to answer, I went on. "I see that you're dressed. You're probably all dressed. I'm not, because I've had interlopers in my room the whole time. Out. Both of you."

I could see Jarl shape his lips to say "But—" and I gave them no time, physically putting my hands on each of their shoulders and shoving them in the direction of the door.

Then I made sure the door was closed behind them and locked it firmly from the inside. And then I dropped on the bed and let myself have a good cry.

You don't need to tell me tears don't solve anything. All I can tell you is that they're a pressure release valve built into the body for good and sufficient reason. And right then I needed to release pressure.

Once I was done crying, I washed my face and I got dressed.

One of the things I missed about being a Patrician of Earth was the clothes. Yeah, I know Eden has the same kind of freedom in dress as it has in anything else. People dress in whatever pleases their fancy or nothing at all. This was good of course. It was also bad.

It was also bad, because it meant someone designing a new look couldn't reap the benefits of it when the vogue caught on. Most fashions in Eden caught on in a very limited way, anyway.

Since there was no money in it, the best designing minds ignored it completely. On Earth, with fortunes riding on coming up with the next big thing, there were some really good minds working on it. Which allowed me to pick a dress whose top seemed to have been designed by Machiavelli. Or at least, it made my natural endowment seem large and firm enough to be feared. And loved, given men's interest in women's breasts. I didn't have it, but I'd spent most of my life since the age of fourteen or so dressing for those who did. I'd learned how they thought.

The dress was white, the skirt was floaty, and the whole looked pure and innocent. Except that it seemed to add two inches to my height and sculpt my curves into what most men think of when they think of women. It wasn't a bad job. I wondered if I could buy ten in different colors to take back with me to Eden. Kit would like them. They'd be perfect for those nights at the music center. Every man would want me, every woman would hate me, and Kit and

I would enjoy ourselves immensely. And not just with the music.

And that's when I realized that not only did I intend to get Kit back, I intended to get Eden back. I intended to get back to Eden and make damn sure that Eden's freedoms were back to their proper position, even if I had to kill Castaneda and his accomplices, cut them into itty bits and feed them to the hogs.

Correction, I'd *prefer* to kill Castaneda and his accomplices, cut them into itty bits and feed them to the hogs. Even if that meant flying all the way back to Earth to find some hogs.

Yeah, yeah, the situation looked hopeless.

I'd been in impossible situations before. What was I facing now? Jarl taking over my husband's body. The Good Men of Earth, most of whom weren't as compliant as Simon and who, doubtless, would also love to get their hands on Jarl or his clone. And Castaneda back in Eden who would take over if he didn't return.

Bah. I took a deep breath. There was still one of me. I had them surrounded.

HORATIUS AT THE BRIDGE

MY MOOD DIDN'T LAST. IT COULDN'T BECAUSE THE problems I faced were real and serious and not simply a matter of looking at them differently.

Some things went better than I expected that day. Simon cleared a lab in Liberte for Doctor Bartolomeu's use, and Jarl didn't ask why we wanted the lab or what was being done there. I presumed he knew.

He also made no movement to stop his friend, which made me suspect that he knew we wouldn't succeed; else, why allow it? Unless he'd gone altruistic and I strongly doubted that.

Zen, too, seemed to have unwound some and no longer looked at Simon as though she expected him to grow a second head. She still frowned at him, and occasionally looked puzzled by him, but she didn't seem threatened. She told me in a passing conversation that my friend Simon talked a great deal of nonsense. Which I knew was true. I just didn't know what she meant by it.

The problem remained Jarl. He snarled at Simon across the lunch table, interrogated him about the circumstances of his inheriting, then asked him why "you haven't killed the bastard, yet."

To Simon's startled laughing and saying that medical science hadn't ruled out that his father might suddenly wake and recover, and that killing him would be murder, Jarl had mumbled that he'd forgotten about the rules on Earth. I suspected it was rather that they'd never really applied to Mules. At least not since they'd stopped being bureaucrat-servants of the system and taken charge.

In despair, unable to keep peace if Jarl and Simon stayed together any longer, I dragged Jarl out for a walk on the terrace. And there he changed again. Oh, I didn't get Kit. I suspected I couldn't get Kit, though he was still there, and periodically mind-spoke me. But Kit didn't seem to have the ability to control the body, at least not if Jarl wasn't willing to relinquish him.

But suddenly, Jarl became once more what I thought of as Kit's brother—someone I could admit must be related to Kit, with much of the same inclinations, attitude and sense of humor.

He walked to the edge of the terrace. It was surrounded by a wall, into which benches were built at intervals. He stood on one of the benches and looked out onto the setting sun and took a deep breath. "Beautiful," he said. "I'd forgotten how heartbreakingly beautiful Earth can be. I don't think holos do her justice. You know, I was surprised once or twice in Eden by realizing that people born and raised there, even well-educated ones, thought that the ocean was sort of a very large bathtub."

"I know," I said. "Kit got plunged into the sea when I rescued him, when we were on Earth before. I thought he'd gone catatonic. Then he asked me if I knew how rich we could be if we could sell that water in Eden."

Jarl smiled at me, an odd smile. "I don't want to kill Christopher," he said. "I don't want to take over his mind and brain...I..." he opened his hands out, palms displayed, in the ancient gesture of non-aggression. "In other circumstances, I think I would enjoy and...I think he'd be a son to me." A tilted smile. "Not sure Zen would be a daughter, mind. She is...feisty. But I think Christopher and I could have got along. In other circumstances, of course, he'd never have existed. I don't know what to do or say. I'm not sure..." He shrugged. "Perhaps my idea was monstrous as Irena said, because if it had worked, Christopher would never have existed, but I am quite sure this idea is no better. And yet, you can't ask me to commit suicide by helping you reverse it, can you?"

I looked at him, then said, "Yes, I can ask it of you. I want to ask it of you. I want my husband back. But I have no way of compelling you to obey."

We walked around the terrace some more, then went inside, but all the while I was thinking: was there a way of compelling him to obey? It almost seemed to me as though he was saying that he didn't want to commit suicide, but he wouldn't fight too hard. Was that true? I wondered if it would be possible to give the nessies to Jean-Batiste St. Cyr. After all, he was brain dead. Who would care? Then I recoiled.

I liked Jarl, true, but did I want him to have power over Simon's future? Could we trust him when he would never trust Simon? Ideally we'd take Jarl back with us to Eden, but would he agree? Once that was done, he would be Jean-Batiste, with all the powers and rights of the Good Man of Liberte.

When we went inside, Doc and Zen had gone to bed, and I suspected Simon had too. There were servants around, but they were acting as Daddy Dearest's servants acted at this time of night—slinking about, trying to make as little noise as possible and acknowledging your presence only if you called them over.

I didn't call them over. Instead I went to my room, took off my beautiful dress, took another bath because water on Liberte was unlimited, which it certainly wasn't on Eden, then put on soft, flowing pajamas in what felt like black silk. And then I tried to go to bed.

"Tried to" being the operative term. If Jarl knew how to reverse the process, how could I get him to confess? The idea of trying by the world's oldest means presented itself and was dismissed. Then came the idea of trying by force. But what would I threaten him with? Not killing him. He knew I'd never risk killing Kit. And besides, did I want to get into a fight with a man who had demonstrated little to no self-control? And who was built with close to Cat speed and was stronger than I? I had never managed to best Kit in a fight. How could I best Jarl?

I'd turned in bed a dozen times, flipped my pillow over another dozen, and was considering getting up and going for a walk on the beach, which might not be wholly safe in Liberte but was close enough to it, and besides, if some idiot tried to mug me and I got to break his arm it might work off some of the tension bedeviling me. Only the fact that Simon might be upset if I endangered myself like that prevented my doing it. That and the fact that Kit was still somehow aware of what I did and he would be more than upset.

However, after a few more turns the bed became an odious place, where there was no comfortable position and I couldn't manage to rest. I'd just sat up, when I heard the door to Jarl's room close softly.

There are a thousand good reasons for anyone to leave his room in the middle of the night, aren't there? Going for a glass of water. Or going to the bathroom. Or taking a walk because one has too much nervous energy.

But the rooms were equipped with refrigerated trays with all kinds of drinks, including water. The suites each included a bathroom. And if Jarl was going for a walk to use up his nervous energy, he might do something far worse than break a mugger's arm.

No, there was no reasonable explanation for Jarl leaving his room in the middle of the night. Or at least no reasonable explanation I was prepared to accept.

I got off the bed. I gathered the burner I had brought all the way from the *Hopper*. Being without a ¹urner is like being naked in front of strangers: something you should only do if you feel terribly safe. And also more than a little stupid. Slipping it in the pocket of my silk pajamas, I turned off the light in my room, then opened the door. The corridor beyond was not pitch dark, but a stab of light in the semidarkness would still have been visible. Turning off the light first allowed me to open the door without Jarl noticing.

It would have been visible, that is, if he were turned the way of my room. He wasn't. When I emerged from the door, he was down the hallway, walking past Doc's door. I picked the darkest area of the corridor, and, walking as silently as I could, tried to look like I had every right to be there. I hoped—though it was unlikely—that even if he looked my way, he'd not realize I wasn't one of the servants milling around.

I followed him all the way to the end of the corridor, where—warned by no more than a feeling—I had the impression he would turn around. Fortunately all these houses had both staircases and antigrav wells. Normally the wells were used by family or those in a hurry. I bet that Jarl would use the staircase, simply because antigrav wells were not common in his day, and weren't the usual thing in Eden, either. So . . . I would take the antigrav well.

Fortunately there was no question where he was headed—the corridor ended in the stairs, with a slight alcove to the side hiding the antigrav well—and he could only go down, as we were on the uppermost floor.

So I hurried and before he got to the stairs, I got right beside him and, knitting myself with the shadows near the wall, climbed over the little grating preventing accidentally stepping in the well, and stepped over.

As I got to the lower floor, I spread my legs outward, and hit with the tips of my toes, the little lip of floor on the edge of the well. This prevented my falling further and allowed me to stay in the shadows of the alcove, as Jarl got all the way down that flight of stairs and started on the next.

I bit my lip, as I realized he had a burner in his hand and a determined expression in his set face.

Down we went, via antigrav well, all the way to the basement of Simon's mansion. And at that point I started getting a really bad feeling. We'd talked about it at dinner. Simon had casually mentioned his father was in a fully automated room in the basement of the mansion. Doctors checked on him several times a day, of course, but most of the time, he was tended by smart machinery. His needs were, after all, routine and repetitive. Was Jarl going to kill the comatose Good Man St. Cyr?

Why else would Jarl come to the basement with a burner in hand? And why had Simon told him? Had Simon...or was Simon...I didn't want to think about it, but I delayed jumping into the last well just a little.

By the time I hit the basement floor, Jarl was down the hallway. As I dove out into the hallway, he was entering a room at the end. I ran full-tilt after him.

I'd just got the door open when I heard a hiss from within and smelled the peculiar scent of burning hair and flesh I'd last smelled when Kit was hit.

I slammed the door open. "Jarl!"

He turned around. His face was impassive, maybe smiling a little. "Yes?"

I glanced over at a state of the art automated bed, surrounded by machines that hissed softly and one that pinged in a forlorn tone. A glance was all that needed. On the bed lay...well, he had to be Simon's father, because Simon was not that old, nor did he have the peculiar puffy appearance of an invalid who'd been on life support for many years. The life support was redundant now, because someone had burned a neat hole into his left temple. There wasn't as much blood as you'd expect. Someone had set the burner at full power and cauterizing. There probably was an exit wound on the other temple.

I couldn't speak. I was shaking. I looked back at Jarl. He was putting his burner back in his body suit. "You shot a defenseless man," I said. "While he lay unconscious."

"Only because I thought he might someday wake up," he said, and gave me a feral smile.

"You shot a defenseless man. It's murder."

"Centuries ago," Jarl said, and suddenly his voice sounded raspy, as though his throat were scratched, "he was responsible for the death of thousands."

"Years ago!" I said. "He might have repented."

He just looked at me. "I talked to people today," he said. "I asked around. Jean-Batiste remained himself till the unfortunate flyer accident rendered him comatose. Or perhaps the fortunate flyer accident... Fortunate for others."

I couldn't follow what he was saying. I couldn't take my mind away from the dead man on the bed. "It is murder. Even in Eden it would be murder."

"Do you think his...Simon will want blood geld?"

"No. Listen. You killed a defenseless man. You don't kill someone who can't fight back, someone who isn't even aware! You..."

"Of course you do kill someone who can't fight back. Far less messy." From somewhere within him, Kit's mind-voice came, *Thena, you have to stop him.*

How? And why? Yes it was murder. Yes I'm shocked, but Simon's father...

No. You don't understand. It was anger. He was angry at Simon and at you. He...redirected it. But he might not always be able to. He is losing control. But I'm not gaining it. Thena, you must stop him.

Jarl walked past me, seemingly unaware of the voice in his mind, communicating with mine. I plastered myself against the open door as he walked by, not wanting him to touch me.

I'm not squeamish about murder. I not only killed my own father, but I handed my late friend Max's father—and murderer—over to Max's lover, Nat, to be killed. When I handed Good Man Keeva over to Nat I knew it would be murder, and that the death would be neither pleasant nor quick.

On the other hand, I also knew that Max's father had killed Max and taken over Max's body by having his brain transplanted into it. And that killing the murderer might be the only solace Nat would ever get. And I liked Nat.

Still, I knew in handing Good Man Keeva over to Nat, that he was going to be murdered and would have no chance to defend himself. Not unless Nat was in a playful mood and had some failsafe system. However, a failsafe system would mean it was still murder. So . . .

I walked up the stairs, slowly, aware of Jarl's bulk ahead of me, stepping with that carefulness that was definitely not Kit. I didn't think I had the room to throw stones, not even a small hail of pebbles.

Thena!

I didn't answer. I didn't know how long I would be able to communicate with my husband, but I knew that I didn't want to argue with him, in case this was the last time.

Thena, listen. He doesn't like Zen, and if Doc comes

up with a system to ... to take him out of my mind, he might ... I mean, self-defense, right?

It didn't worry you before, I said. *You said you liked him. I think he likes you too, for what it's worth.*

The pause was so long I thought I wasn't going to get an answer. *I do like him,* he said at last. *But I am in his mind. I might be part of his mind. I don't even know how long he will not hear me when I talk to you. And I know that—*

That?

The more control he acquires of the body, the less control he has over his reactions. And knowing he's losing control is making him nervous, which makes it worse. Thena, that was cold-blooded murder. I don't want to be part of it.

I let Nat murder Max's father, I said. And flashed the memory at him.

So? He said. *You did. But I haven't. I have never murdered anyone. I've been accused of murder, and suffered for a murder I never committed. And now he's made a murderer out of me. Yes, I know I killed in Circum—or he did—but it was a quick thing, almost an accident. That man might have been dangerous. But this ... I could tell he was planning it. And I couldn't stop him.*

I stopped, just in front of the door to my room. I don't claim to be a moral genius. Long ago, while engaged in a long argument over the death penalty and the fact that Eden didn't have the ability to condemn anyone to death, Kit had flung something at me that I'd never thought of.

He asked why was it moral for the state to kill if it wasn't for the individual? I'd bitten back with the example of psychopaths and people who killed for sexual pleasure—it's possible Daddy Dearest had been on my thoughts at the time—and that they had to be stopped for the greater good. Then Kit had told me that murder was necessary sometimes, for the greater good. The Eden system of not penalizing murder hinged on that. If someone had no value to anyone and the murder was deserved, chances were the murderer wouldn't pay for it. But the murderer had to make that bet. The individual had to assume that responsibility. There couldn't be hiding behind the collective and saying "well, all of us decided to..."

No, the taking of human life was the ultimate moral or immoral decision, and as such had to be made by someone capable of taking the consequences. Not a crowd. Not a group. A moral conscience. An individual.

I had allowed Max's father to be killed and I supposed if there were consequences, I would have to take them. I might have to ask Simon about that. Had there been consequences? He'd mentioned something about Max's brother, which was a puzzle, since there were no brothers...I mean, none of us had any brothers, that I knew. Sometimes—rarely, it seemed—something happened to a clone, like what had happened to Fuse, and the Good Man made a replacement. But there shouldn't be any brothers, as such. And Simon should have known it.

But if there was something I owed Max's brother, I would have to pay. That was fine. I could accept that.

The problem with what Jarl had done was not that he'd served as Jury, Judge and Executioner. That was what any individual capable of moral sense could and would do when a threat should be removed.

The problem was that there had been no threat.

Oh, yes, Good Man St. Cyr might have wakened. But after fifteen years, it wasn't likely. And if it happened, it was highly unlikely he would be up and shouting orders the next day. If needed, Simon could deal with it. Simon knew what his father had done to previous clones, and I didn't see Simon going quietly into that good night.

That was the first problem, but it got worse. Not only was there good reason to think that Jarl, operating, at most, on half a brain was not fully capable of thinking things through and weighing the pros and cons of his act—Kit said he was acting on impulse. That he had no control. Or little control, and losing that little.

But there was yet a third problem. Jarl had done this while in Kit's body and in a situation where few—including himself, probably—would be able to say where one stopped and the other started. That was in a way to hide behind the collective, to say "we did this."

Judges and juries throughout history have been only one thing: a way to deflect responsibility . . . and vengeance. I doubted Jarl had thought of this in terms of deflecting responsibility and vengeance. And I granted that it was unlikely that word of this murder would ever make it to Eden. But if it did, somehow—say Zen talked, inadvertently—then it would taint Kit with a crime he'd barely been exonerated of before. In the way public opinion worked, Kit would always be at best suspect. In the present circumstances, with the forces arrayed against us, if it ever became known Kit's body had committed a murder, how could we prove it hadn't been Kit's mind. Kit would be a pariah.

I took a deep breath. And if Jarl killed again, say killed a citizen of Eden . . . Even if Kit got back, he could never get his life back. Not his family, not his professional standing, not even his position as an amateur musician with the Music Center.

One of the stories Kit had once insisted on telling me—because men like explaining things to women and I had no objection to letting him improve my rather skimpy education—was that of some Roman or other. It must have been before planes because there was an invasion led by some evil king who had been deposed, and the only way back into the city was through a bridge, and everyone else ran and this man, named Horatius, held the bridge alone against the invaders, until his comrades cut the bridge down.

The story, as Kit told it to me had a happy ending. The young man dove into the river and came out again and was a hero. But I suspect he was changing the story or softening it. No one falls from a bridge to a major river and survives. And besides, since his friends cut down the bridge while he defended it there would be bridge debris. And the way Kit used the expression *Playing Horatius at the Bridge* indicated the end was quite other.

Horatius had defended the bridge, against enormous odds, and known that in the end he would die.

Sometimes one had to do that. If I went up against Jarl, there was a good chance I would die. But there was an even chance, too, taking advantage of the fact the man seemed to like me or love me—perhaps through contagion from Kit's mind and memories—that he would let me live long enough for me to get his notes, and also to figure out the formula for the nanocytes and save Kit.

And all it required was for me to be willing to die. Because I'd never been able to best Kit, much less Jarl. And, Jarl would lash out if he got cornered and his last chance was through me.

Well. I was going to save Kit. Or we were both going to die trying. Jarl would not get through me.

I wasn't doing anything special with the rest of my life, anyway.

But first, I needed to talk to Simon.

BURNING THE BRIDGE

NIGHT TERROR

SIMON WAS STILL SLEEPING IN THE SAME ROOM I'D known as his. Which of course made perfect sense, because he'd moved into his father's room when he'd first inherited, even if it was a conditional inheritance.

The good thing about his being in the same room, was that the genlock was still programmed for my thumbprint. No, we hadn't been that kind of lovers, not the kind who sleep with each other every night. But it had happened, now and then, that I'd decided to drop by after a party or a trip, and go up to his room in the dead of night seen only by servants I thought wouldn't talk.

Apparently my gencode still worked. At any rate, the lock opened, soundlessly, when I put my finger in it, and I stepped in the room and closed the door, equally soundlessly. I could make out the shape of Simon, on his front, on the huge, old fashioned canopied bed. But there was something wrong. Very wrong.

In the middle of Simon's back, just below his neck, was something that looked very much like a hump, and which seemed to be moving slightly up and down, as though breathing, with movements of its own. As I looked, it opened green eyes that glowed in the dark and looked much like Kit's.

I screamed, echoed almost immediately by Simon's scream. The something jumped off his back, and I realized it had been a very large cat, and that he must have taken strips off Simon's back in bouncing off on his claws.

Then Simon said, "Lights!"

The light came on, and he sat on the bed, burner pointed at me. Without my having thought about it or realized what I was doing, I had my burner out, and pointed at him.

His eyes widened in surprise. "You?"

I hesitated, wondering if I should put the burner away. I still liked Simon and of course I trusted him, but I wasn't about to put my burner away when someone had a burner pointed at me. "Me," I said, thinking that was fairly safe to admit.

He frowned. "What the hell are you doing coming into my room with a burner drawn and pointed at me? You used to tell me when I upset you before you tried to kill me!"

"I never tried to kill you!"

"Ah, no? What happened when I accidentally broke your broom?"

"You didn't accidentally break my broom. You put it in the middle of the lair and shot it with a burner. And then looked surprised when it blew up."

"I was drunk," he said sheepishly. "The manufacturer

said it was practically indestructible."

"It wasn't your own damn broom. You could have tried it on your own damn broom."

He frowned. "Well, but that would be ... my broom. You still tried to kill me."

"I hit you with the remains of the broom," I said. "They were on fire."

"That's why I threw water over you afterwards."

"You threw liquor over me," he said, looking full of long suffering patience. "Fortunately not good liquor."

"That was an accident. I thought it was good liquor."

"So you tried to kill me," he said.

"Only a little bit," I admitted reluctantly. I'd been furious.

"And now you're pointing a burner at me."

"Only because you're pointing one at me," I protested.

We both paused, glaring at each other. Then, slowly and ostentatiously, he put his burner down and reached back to shove it under his pillow. Just as slowly, I returned my burner to my pocket. We continued glaring.

He shook his head at me. "What on earth were you doing coming into my room and screaming?"

"I screamed because something opened glowing eyes in the middle of your back."

He sighed, and reached a hand out towards the cat, who was making his cautious way back to the bed. "So I have a cat. Sue me. Come here, Mephy."

"You never had a cat before. Mephy?"

"Short for Mephistopheles. I had to get a cat. You jilted me and broke my heart."

I raised my eyebrows at him. He sighed. "Well, you broke the ... the metronome closest to my heart."

Then he sighed again, looking up at my face. "Still no sale, uh? Okay, I confess, Mephy showed up on the terrace one morning, weighing about ten ounces of sodden fur and pitiful eyes. You know I'm a sucker for sad cases. Look at how I always look after you."

I didn't say anything. He did look after me.

"Oh, come on. You're just going to take that?" He rolled his eyes. Mephy, a big, evil-looking tom who I was sure weighed many times ten ounces and was covered in lustrous, long black fur, climbed onto the bed in one easy leap. He sniffed at Simon's extended fingers, then allowed Simon to pet him.

"Well, if you look at it one way, we've got a lot in common. We both like sleeping with big, male cats."

Simon laughed. "What brings you to my room in the middle of the night? And is the nut case you are perhaps married to likely to follow?"

I had a moment of panic. Was Jarl awake? Was he likely to be looking at whatever portable snooping device he'd brought from his retreat?

Kit!

Yes?

Is Jarl...does he know where I am?

No. I think he's asleep.

But you're not?

No. It's...Thena, we're in trouble.

It's okay, love. I'll take care of it.

A long pause, and then the impression of Kit sighing. *You know, you always worry me when you say things like that.*

When have I let you down?

Never. It's just that you don't have any brakes. Or even speed-moderating mechanisms.

You love me the way I am.

Yes. I do. But it still worries me.

I edged towards the bed, and sat down at the foot of it. Mephy was making a sound like an ill-tuned motor and parading himself back and forth across Simon's legs, rubbing ecstatically against Simon's chest, while Simon petted him. "Who's a good boy?" Simon said, in the idiotic tone people use when talking to their cats. At least cats of the feline variety. Not that some female Navs in Eden didn't sound like the world's own twits while talking to their husbands. He looked up enquiringly. "So, is the wild man going to break in or not? Because I need that burner closer at hand, if there's a chance I'll have to defend myself, or your honor or something."

"No. I asked Kit. He says he's asleep."

"You as— Oh. Mind-talk, that's what you called it right?"

"Right." Simon had always been good at hearing something once, then retaining it. Probably another modification for spying. At least it sounded useful.

"So, in what way can I serve you, my dear?"

I took a deep breath.

"Jarl killed your . . . killed Good Man St. Cyr . . . a few minutes ago."

Simon's hand stopped on Mephy's back. For a moment, he seemed to stop breathing. Then something undefinable flitted across his features, and he said, "I see. So soon?"

It took a moment for this to sink in. "You wanted him to!"

"Not him. I wanted *someone* to. The . . . the surveillance must show it wasn't me." Simon looked more apologetic than he had over my broom on the day he'd blown it up. "With the revolt, the other Good Men—You must understand, I think the only reason they didn't kill me when Father first had the accident was that they might get Daddy back. But now, they don't have that much power anymore. I still couldn't kill Daddy Dearest, because that would bring vengeance, in any case. If they had to kill themselves to do it. But the surveillance reels will show a stranger doing it. And with the war, it is perhaps best if my status as Good Man is unchallenged."

He looked at me, and his expression changed minimally. "Did you expect me not to want him dead? Or do you expect me to grieve? Thena, you know what his plans for me were. What their plans for us were."

"Yes, but..." I thought of the glimpses I'd had of Jarl's friends' life and childhood. Then I took myself firmly in hand. More sinned against than sinning is always a cop out, a way to bring the fuzziness of emotion to a clear-cut decision that should hinge on who the person is and what danger he presents to innocents.

As adults each of us makes his own decisions, and some people with awful childhoods chose well. Good Man St. Cyr had chosen the path that led to his end.

I shook my head. I was sorry Jarl had done it while in Kit's body, but I wasn't sorry Jarl had done it. Someone would have had to kill Good Man St. Cyr, one way or another.

I cleared my throat. "I'm going to need a few things. A large broom, two broom riding suits and oxygen masks. And uh...a burner with a larger charge than I have. Possibly two, in case one fails."

His eyebrows went up as he scritched a point between Mephy's shoulder blades and Mephy's purrs climbed to orgasmic levels. "Is Thena going hunting? May I join in the fun?"

I shook my head. "I'm not sure it's fun. Or that it will be. I have to set this right and I see only one way. There's a very good chance it will end up killing me."

Mephy flopped on his back and Simon reached in to tickle the expanse of fuzz, only to have his hands grasped in all four clawed paws. "Owie," he said, but not like someone who was really hurt, and waiting until Mephy relaxed to remove his hand, which brought Mephy, in a leap, to all four feet, and then quicker than even Kit could move, to swipe a clawed paw across the back of Simon's hand. Simon sucked on the scratches, without comment, then said, "It's not like you, this deciding you might as well die doing something. It's more like you for you to decide someone else must die for you to do something."

I grinned at him, a grin that was only half happy. "Sometimes," I said, "things need to be done. And in this case, I'm the woman to do it."

He returned to petting the cat as if nothing had happened. "You know your business, Thena, I just never expected...Anyway, if you need help. I mean, beyond those trivial items..."

"Well, I'd also appreciate the answer to a couple of questions. One of them might give me a way to achieve at least part of this without... without having to risk my life. The other part might be easier, too."

"Yes?" Simon asked. Mephy stretched so he was within reach, and I petted him, gingerly.

"What happened to Syracuse Seacity?"

"Eh? Oh. I think Lucius is controlling it now. It's part of the rebellious territories or whatever they're calling it."

"Lucius."

"Lucius Dante Maximilian Keeva, Good Man Keeva of Olympus Seacity. He goes by Lucius, like Max's father went by Dante and Max went by Max."

"How could Max have a brother? He was...like us. We don't run to big families, and we don't have accidental children."

Simon frowned a little. "No. It's not...I think it was like Fuse."

"So, Lucius is mentally damaged?"

"No. I think it was like that, only...different. Lucius was in Never-Never. When we broke into Never-Never to get your husband—"

"Lucius escaped?"

"Yeah," Simon petted Mephy's whiskers carefully, as though it were the most important thing in the world. "I don't think Daddy would have been long for this world after that, even if Nat hadn't taken care of it."

"You think Lucius would have taken out Max's Dad?"

The frown became more pronounced. "He was in Never-Never for killing a man, though I wonder if that was the real reason. I wonder if it was because he...was like Max and didn't cover up as well."

I was puzzled. "What difference would that make?" Max and Nat had been lovers since they'd been very young, and Max's father hadn't found out. Even if Lucius had been sexually interested in men, and his father had found out, what difference would it make? Max's father could still have his brain transplanted into Lucius' body, and the brain would still be his. Even if orientation were genetic—no one had ever been able to pinpoint a single gene, though there was a conglomeration of genetic pointers that might indicate it. But it's hard to evaluate because you have to check on not just revealed behavior, and some people are very good at not revealing their behavior, but unspoken and often unacted-upon preference. In any case, the brain would retain its preferences. It had. After old Dante Keeva had his brain transplanted into Max's body, he'd been chasing girls as soon as he was up on Max's feet.

"I don't know," Simon said. "I think he might have thought it was epigenetic."

"Epi...demic?"

"No, epigenetic. It means genes that turn themselves off and on throughout life, as you encounter you know, chemical or environmental influences." He reached over to pet Mephy who was now almost completely on my lap. "I think he might have been afraid it would...you know, turn whatever the gene was on in his brain. Over time."

"What a very stupid idea," I said. "Throwing someone into Never-Never for that."

Simon gave me a sudden grin. "Oh, yes. Without it, he could have got killed and his body stolen. A much better fate."

"When you put it like that," I said.

"I have to put it like that. At least he's alive, and poor Max..." His eyes got unexpectedly shiny. Max had been our friend since we'd all been toddling around in the care of nannies. "At any rate, Lucius...he scares me. He might even scare you. They say he spent fifteen years in solitary. I understand the normal time to break, in solitary, is a few days. Strong-minded people last months. Really strong-minded people last a year."

"Is he broken?"

"If by that you mean insane, no. He seems as sane as you or I. Which"—a voluble shrug—"admittedly might not mean much. But he's intense. Single-focus... I think he scares Nat a little too."

"Nat... knows?"

"Nat is his right hand, in... the rebellion, or perhaps it is the other way around." He made a vague gesture. "There's some council, and religion is involved. Usaians. Sons of liberty. All that."

"I see," I said, having found that was the best thing to say when the matter was, in fact, completely opaque. "So they hold Syracuse. Do you have a way to communicate with them?"

Simon looked around, then sighed, then said, "Not officially, but... yes. Why?"

So, Simon was part of the rebellion. Perhaps supplying them with weapons. Or playing a double game. I thought of what Jarl had said. But I didn't see Simon betraying a fellow broomer. The rest of the world, sure. But Nat was a member of our lair, the Brooms of Doom. Everyone has internal boundaries he won't break; can't break and remain himself. "I need to go to the mansion. I think that Jarl's notes are in the mansion somewhere. Yes, I know a copy was in the lair, and I presume they've disappeared, though it's possible Nat or someone has them. Just not likely, and besides, they're not what I want." Disappearing was the normal thing for anything left unattended in the lair. No, not theft. A society where everyone is unstable and prone to pick fights without warning, is not a society with high levels of theft. It was more likely lost or Fuse used it as a fuse on detonating material. "But the copy in the lair was all about creating a Mule female. We need the rest of Jarl's notes. I'm sure Father would have had them, in paper or in gem. And if I can find it, it's one less thing I'll need to beat out of Jarl."

"Ah. So that's what you're doing." But he looked worried. "Desolate, Thena, but you can't go to the mansion."

"Why? Active fighting? Doesn't worry me."

"No, because it's unlikely to have anything in it like papers or gems, or anything else that will melt under heat and explosion."

"What?"

"When the rebels took it. Incendiary bombs."

Mentally I said goodbye to my paintings, and my dresses and, more painfully, all the books in the library only I read.

"Oh. Well, then it will have to be option two. Just as well, if I get Jarl out of here before he gets worse. Could I have the suits, and the oxygen masks, and a broom suitable for two please. About...as many burners as you can provide me. Oh, also about ten feet or more of sturdy rope and half a dozen rubber balls."

His eyes widened at that, but I smiled at him, an impish smile—I hoped—and said, "Come, I just want to play a nice game of bouncy ball."

His eyes widened again, then he sighed and gave me a sidelong glance. "Thena..."

"Yes?"

"Don't do anything you'll regret."

"I don't think there's any way I can escape what's coming without doing that," I said.

"Well, then," he said, "don't do anything I'll regret. Like getting yourself killed."

"We all have choices to make," I told him, "and mine might not be yours."

Because if it came to my life or Kit's, I'd save Kit's any day.

THE FOX AND THE WOLF

THERE ARE THREE WAYS YOU CAN CAPTURE SOMEONE who is bigger, stronger, faster, and smarter than you. The first one is to make them less effective. Poison or some narcotic can achieve that. The second one is to hit them behind the ear, then they will go unconscious, then you tie them securely. The third is to outwit them.

None of them operated between me and Jarl Ingemar, not while he was occupying Kit's body. With whatever the nanocytes were up to in Kit's brain, the last thing I'd do is introduce a narcotic to the mix. The same for rendering him unconscious with a good thumping. And as for outwitting him...

I have no illusions. Daddy Dearest had been designed to be an assassin. Jarl had been designed to administer a division or a continent or something. It's hard to talk of pure intelligence, and I knew Father had been cunning. Cunning enough to go to ground

313

as a Mule during the turmoils, to escape with his life when less bioimproved people had died horrible deaths because of their mods. Cunning enough to emerge from hiding as the Good Man of Syracuse Seacity with an impeccable natural human pedigree. Cunning enough to remain in power against all challenges for close to three hundred years.

Bully for him. But Jarl was a genius, and—I knew from knowing Kit, who had the same brain—could be just as cunning and twice as effective. The chances of my outwitting him were somewhere below the chances of my moving faster than Kit.

So it would have to be brute force. And the only brute force available, just at the moment, was that contained in a burner. I was all right with that. Weapons are awesome friends. They'll keep you alive even if all your friends turn their backs on you.

In my room, I put on my broomer suit—layered leather and thermal fabric—and boots, attached the broom to my belt loops, made several loops of rope, and put them on my belt. Into the belt pouch that was part of any broomer outfit went the rubber balls and extra burners. Then I bundled the extra suit under my arm and went to Jarl's room.

I'd have been alarmed if the door had opened quietly. It didn't. Locked.

I burned the lock off, while I called mentally, *Kit? How much control do you have over the body?*

Not much. He sounded embarrassed. *Why?*

Because I need him to stay asleep yet a while longer. Can you do that?

I can try. Thena?

Yes?

He has the dresser wedged against the door.

Of course he does. Paranoiacs are always predictable. Particularly by other paranoiacs. How do I get in?

Just push. You should able to slip in. You're stronger than a normal human.

I was indeed, which was good, because it took all my strength to slide the dresser about ten inches with the door pushing on it, once the door lock had been burned out. Ten inches was enough for me to slide sideways, into the darkened room.

Do you have lenses in?

What?

Darkening lenses.

Oh. He sounded surprised, as if he'd never thought about it. He probably hadn't. He wore the lenses for two weeks at a stretch, unless we were in the *Cathouse*, where we kept the lights comfortably—for him—dim, and thus he was able to deal with any tricky jobs of piloting that might be necessary. *Yes,* Kit said. *He put them in in his retreat, in the morning. My eyes bother him. The way he sees things through them. He prefers the vision through the lenses.*

And where are your extras?

Top drawer of the dresser, he said, and as I started edging a drawer out, he must have looked through my eyes, because he said, *No, the left one.* I slid the left one out, found the biopouch that contained Kit's lenses, and put them in my belt pouch. This was part of looking after Kit and I'd gotten used to the idea that nothing would be done, ever, without Kit's lenses being at hand. Because even if we were in darkness, light could come on suddenly. And a Cat's eyes were shockingly easy to damage.

I need you to put a broomer suit on, I said. *And I'm going to remove your lenses.*

Thena?

I could hear the hesitation in his voice. Putting a broomer suit on, if he didn't have full control of his body, would be tricky. Particularly when keeping Jarl asleep. Removing the lenses was insanely risky.

Once they were out, someone could blind him easily enough. Permanently blind him, meaning render him useless for the one trade he'd been designed to work in, for the one job he'd been trained in—so that even if we saved Eden, he'd have no place with it. Cat eyes were almost impossible to regen. Part of being a designed alteration. There were several proverbs in Eden about blind Cats. All of them implied these were pathetic creatures.

I need the lenses to be out and I need him to know they're out. And then I need you to keep your eyes shut. Do you understand? All I need from you is to keep him asleep as long as you can. Can you do that?

I could hear a chuckle behind Kit's mental voice. *It will be tricky.*

Yeah. Very tricky. Because you see, there was no way I could just walk to the bed, peel back Kit's eyelids and pull out the lenses. It's not that this was impossible, but that it was dark in the room. It had to be dark till those lenses were out. I couldn't risk Jarl waking before that. And I'm not a Cat. I don't see that well in the dark. Which meant, I'd have to go over and fumble with Kit's eyes. I don't think anybody—or any body—will remain asleep while someone is poking at his eyes and fumbling with his eyelids.

What then? Well, if Kit could keep him asleep . . .

I had, more than once before, let Kit use my hands and eyes. It was part of that mind-link we shared and just short of full mind-mingling that we'd experienced when he was near-mortally wounded.

I had no idea how this would work with Jarl in the mix, but it was the only chance I had. If I could get Kit's body to reach up and remove his lenses, Kit, presumably, had body-memory of the gesture. I'd seen him do it in nothing flat. Put his lenses in, too.

Brace, I told him. *I'm coming in.*

What? He asked, startled into alarm, and then he must have felt me, willing myself into his mind. *Thena!*

It was . . . different from any mind contact we'd been in. I could feel or sense Kit, as I knew Kit, my husband, the love of my life. And next to him, crouching, I could feel an older, darker presence that definitely tasted of Jarl. And I could feel Kit keeping the Jarl-self quiescent, even as Kit's mind/personality spared mine a brief welcome touch, somewhat like a gentle kiss on the lips.

None of this bears much resemblance to what actually happened, but there is no vocabulary for the mind contact of Eden's Cats and Navs. There was even less vocabulary for what was happening between Kit and Jarl. I hoped there never would be.

I could also feel Jarl hunched over control of the body, but I slipped underneath and wrested the hands and arms from him, without his realizing it. And then the rest of the body.

My own body moved forward and lay the opened suit on the bed. It was one that opened all along the length of each arm and leg, so it lay flat, when I set it on the bed. All I had to do, with my divided mind, was make Kit roll on top of it, then, by touch, close the seams. No boots, but the suit had a sort of socks that would encase the feet.

It took forever. I had to use the mechanisms that allow sleepwalkers to move, and Kit's movements were fumbling and confused. I understood that I was over-riding his control over his body and Kit's personality was providing the sense of dreaming. Once the suit was on, I got it across to his body that he needed to take his lenses off. Projecting discomfort from the lenses in his eyes was enough. The body reacted. His hands seemed to do the thing on their own, going up and lifting one eyelid at a time, and ripping off the lens.

Just as the second lens came off, Kit screamed *Thena!*

The warning was unnecessary. I'd already realized the dark, quiescent presence in his mind had woken and was taking control. I snapped back, fully, into my own body. It felt as though I were an overstretched rubber band letting go of the other end. I came fully to my own mind and body with the sudden, startling feeling of having been slugged.

The feeling was so strong that I reeled back, and braced, even as I pulled a burner from my pocket, and yelled, "Lights!"

Jarl was on his feet by the bed, hands bunched, body bent forward, as though about to spring on me. In the next second the lights came on, full force. Bless the Good Men who programmed the lights in any room to come on at the full intensity and force of the illumination in an operating theater. Good, of course, for spotting intruders and for making sure no one was sneaking up on you, but really not good for Cat eyes.

Jarl screamed and closed his eyes. I hoped he'd closed them fast enough, but I knew even a few seconds of brilliant light were enough to blind Kit for hours.

Kit?

He sounded pained. *Just do what you have to do.*

Jarl still lurched in my direction, his eyes tightly closed. By sound, of course. But he was clumsy and much slower than if he had his vision—Kit's vision—to guide him.

I sprang out of his reach, and took the safety off the burner with an audible click. He stopped. "You wouldn't!"

"Oh, no? Try me."

"You wouldn't kill your husband."

"Why not, if you are?"

"Because you have...hope." His tone of voice gave me a queasy feeling in the pit of the stomach. Clearly he didn't think I should have hope, and he despised me a little for having it. Fine. I'd been known to beat the odds and baffle professional opinion before.

"Right. So I do. But it doesn't take much in the way of a burner ray to disable you, does it? So I won't kill you, but I can burn off your feet, or your hands."

"Even knowing your husband will suffer with me?"

"Oh yes," I told him, and fervently willed certainty into my voice—the most brazen of bluffs. "Yes, I will. If it's what I have to do to do what Kit asked me to do."

"And what did Kit ask you to do?" Jarl asked, half amused.

"Take control of you, because you won't let him, and you can't."

His face set, and his eyebrows descended over his eyes.

"You—"

"Oh, please. I don't have time for this. We're on a tight schedule."

"We . . . what?"

"Turn and put your hands behind you. Both hands," I said. "Together. Quickly. Extend them back as far as you can go. Now. I have a burner and I will use it."

I must be the world's best voice actress. The truth was, even though I knew Jarl was in control of that body, it looked and moved like Kit, and the idea of burning him or of causing him pain made a tight coil of near-pain collect near my stomach. But to save Kit, I might need to hurt him. I had to remember that. And I had to be strong.

Clearly something of my resolve came through, because Jarl turned around slowly, joined his hands behind his back and lifted them to extend them as far as he could.

I think—no, I know—from his bunched shoulders, his tensed legs, that he was ready to spring and grab me if I approached to do anything. After all, he had the advantage of Cat speed and accuracy of movement, even blinded. But I'm not stupid.

First I let him stew. Just a little. I didn't move, and let him stay in what I knew was an uncomfortable position, while I counted slowly to two hundred. He was so aware, so ready to spring, that maintaining both the position and the readiness would, by itself, make him susceptible to overreact and panic.

Very carefully and, I made sure, silently, I took three of the loops of rope and hung them from my arm, where I could easily let them slide down and grab them. I reached into the pouch and got two rubber balls. They were the size to fit one comfortably in my hand, or, less comfortably one in my palm and one held between my fingers. I'd done my share of playing bouncing balls as a child. Like, who hasn't? I think kids in prehistory were playing with rubber balls. There were prints of kids playing with them from six centuries ago.

But this time, I had to throw two of them, as close together in time as possible, and at two wildly divergent locations. You see, I didn't want Jarl to break his position. I needed his wrists together and behind his back.

So the way was to startle him, then startle him again, before he could move. A tall order when dealing with Cat reflexes. But fortunately Jarl was only borrowing the reflexes, and not used to them or the body. With Kit, I wouldn't even have considered this plan.

I threw the first ball, and, without sparing Jarl a full look, registered the minimal shift of his body in that direction, even as I flung the other in front of him, almost immediately.

Given enough time, he'd have understood what had happened. He didn't have time.

As the second ball hit, I made a smooth leap, feet together, behind him, the first rope loop in my hand. And before he could react, I had the loop around his wrists, tightened and secured.

Not as secure as I'd have liked it, but that could be rectified later.

He turned, with a roar, and I already had the second loop of rope in my hands. I jumped back, quickly, and he lurched after me. The tied hands threw him off balance and he brought his feet together. Exactly where I'd placed the next loop on the floor, I pulled it up, tightened and secured.

He tried to hop. Some men refuse to know when they're beat. Kit was one of them, and apparently he came by it all too naturally.

Every broomer knows how to lasso. For one, it's how you rescue a friend whose broom has given out. For another, well . . . there are drug transports and aerial battles with other broomers lairs, and being able to throw a loop of cable and lasso something accurately is essential. Somehow, I didn't think Jarl knew this.

I ran out of his reach—not difficult when he had to hop—and threw the lasso. It slid to his midriff and, as it tightened, attached his arms firmly to his middle. I secured it while he stopped in surprise, and then, quickly, secured the other two ropes, and tied one around his knees too. Look, when dealing with someone like Jarl—or Kit—the better tied, the more trustworthy.

"You!" he started, and then descended rapidly into the gutter in several languages. Or at least I was fairly sure it was the gutter. The few words I did understand were almost low enough to be part of my own vocabulary.

"Very cute," I said. "What am I supposed to do, swoon? You think no one ever called me that? Hell, I've called myself that on occasion."

He looked disoriented. Apparently he really did expect me to swoon. This was the fault of which-ever idiots had raised Mules with no contact with the female of the species. Way too easy to believe poets and filmmakers and the occasional, blinkered, pseudohistorian.

"Now, let's get real," I said. And made sure my movements were noisy enough for him to know what I was doing. "You're blinded. I'm holding a burner on you. I'm going to ask you to climb on a broom. And then we're going for a ride."

His body went very still. Whatever he'd expected, it wasn't this. I wondered if he thought I'd somehow managed to get the nanocytes ready and was about to take his body back. No wonder he refused to stop fighting even while tied up.

"What do you want with me?" he asked.

"Nothing that will hurt you—either of you—if you do as I tell you."

"But—"

"We're going to be flying over the ocean for an extensive amount of time," I said. "*Do* try not to thrash. Because if we fall, remember, Kit has no idea how to swim."

"I do."

"No, your body did. But you're not completely yourself, are you? Swimming, like walking and other actions learned and practiced without thought, are actions stored in the cerebellum and are you sure you control that? You can train, but it will take you time. Like your violin playing. You can impose your style, but Kit knows how to play. How long do you think it would take you to teach the body if he didn't?"

He was quiet. I told him, "Come," and held his arm as I pulled him to the window.

It took me less than a second of fumbling with the window controls to open it. They were slightly different from the ones in Syracuse. Then the windows opened, to the roar of the sea and the chill of the night.

"No," Jarl said. I wasn't sure to what.

"Yes," I said, and dragged him up to the parapet of the window. Thank all the gods and demons, the parapet was broad and made of marble, clearly designed for a bosomy woman to lean into the moonlit night and have a shelf for her endowments. Or perhaps designed for broomers to take off from. All of us seemed to have used a broom, perhaps since the first Mule had become a Good Man. I didn't care. I just cared there was enough space to pull Jarl up, make him kneel sideways on the parapet. I didn't look down. I tried not to think of the sheer drop from the window to rocks below. It wouldn't happen, that was all there was to it. We were going to take off and fly away from here. We were not going to fall.

"I'm going to slide the broom between your legs, but don't get funny. It's a two-person broom and the controls will be behind you."

He was very still. *Thena!* Kit's voice in my mind.

Yes, lover?

Is there a drop on my right?

Straight down to rocks and the sea.

Light! Thena!

Yes, love. Don't let him move.

He's scared stiff, Kit said. *But in his condition fear can go either way: freeze or attack. Be very careful.*

Always, love.

You never are, but do try.

I did try. None of the actions I'd planned were as easy as they should have been. First, you should never, ever, ever, tie someone's legs at the knee, then try to slide a cylinder that was a good five inches diameter into the space directly below his crotch. I went slowly because I knew that Kit was rather attached to those parts of him—in more ways than one—but it wasn't easy. At least, Jarl didn't try to fight, probably because he couldn't see, but he could hear the waves breaking on the rocks right below him.

And then I mounted behind him. The controls were behind me, out of reach of his tied hands, even if he tried. Look. It's not that I didn't trust him . . . Oh, okay, it was exactly that I didn't trust him. Fortunately, I'd done this before and could steer by touch.

Before I did, though, I looped spare rope around his middle and tied him to the broom. "To make sure you don't fall. I'm tying myself too, so the best you can try is to make us crash, while still both attached to the broom. You can't unmount me."

And then I did as I said. He didn't say anything. He didn't try to move. I wondered if he was still in control of his body at all. But the way I saw it, if Jarl went finally and totally batty, maybe Kit could take his own body back.

I had programmed the course into the broom—with certain adjustments Simon had suggested to avoid areas where explosions or armored vehicles flying very fast might make my own route difficult. It would be twelve hours. It was a good thing I'd tied myself to the broom, I thought. Just in case I fell asleep.

But I didn't fall asleep. I have no idea why I'm only acrophobic in space. Perhaps it's the consciousness that I could at any minute fall away, with nothing to moor me, and never be able to return. Or perhaps it was that there was very little to see.

Here, there was the sea below me and the sky above me. Not only hadn't I seen them in almost a year, but there was a good chance, if everything worked well, if I got back to Eden and we got Eden back that I'd never see it again. And we must go back to Eden. We must.

So I flew over the sea, through the night. I know Jarl had his eyes open. I could tell by the way he turned his head, by the way he held himself. But I didn't try to make chit chat. One doesn't become friendly with one's husband's captor and besides I didn't want him to think too much of the beauty of the Earth and everything in it. What would that do, but make him determined to stay alive, and to keep Kit's body?

Five hours later, when we flew over the charred ruins of my childhood home, the sun was a bright glow in the horizon and it made the blackened ceramite and dimatough structure look yet worse—jagged broken walls reaching up to the sky, all of it charred. I had time to register that the area around it was bombed too, and wondered how much of the island was destroyed.

How many of our servants had died in the battle? How many innocent bystanders in Syracuse Seacity? What was this rebellion that Simon had spoken of, this rebellion he was clearly lending support to? Why were people dying? Was it worth it?

Liberte, egalite, fraternite. All very well, but how truthful were those ideals? I had read history in Eden. The revolution that went under that flag had been one of the most bloody, one of the most nakedly insane of all history. The words had cloaked—it turned out—nothing but the usual thirst for power among the usual type of humans. And those who hid behind the words were either monsters or had become monsters, unaware of their own transformation.

I wanted to hope this time was different, but was aware that such a hope, also, had led more civilizations down the primrose path to hell than anything else. It was never different, nice as the hope might be.

After a while we left the sea behind, and flew over Europe. First over populated areas, most of them near the sea. The path that Simon had charted avoided large cities and stayed in those areas where patrols were scant and where the lone broomer would be more or less safe, being, if spotted, assumed to be a disaster victim getting to safety. No one would think of broomers lairs in these small towns and wooded expanses.

I drank water from my bottle and moved my guest's oxygen mask up to allow him to drink some. I expected resistance, but I got none. Instead he drank the water and said nothing.

His silence was only worrisome in the measure that I felt he wouldn't be that quiet if he hadn't made a plan of escape. But surely to make a plan, he would need to know where we were going, right?

As we flew over the deserted, bacteria-ravaged areas of Europe, I thought that he sat up a little straighter, a little more alert.

And when we approached the barrier, I became aware of a problem. The way his hands were tied, even if I tried to move him around and stick his finger in the little genlock-wand, I would have to dislocate his shoulders.

He must have realized it too. His voice sounded raspy and gravely as he spoke. "Untie my hands." And then, "If you want to get in."

I wanted to get in. And look, his middle, knees and feet were still tied. He was still tied to the broom. How much damage could he do with just his hands untied?

I'm not completely stupid. I untied myself first, and got down from the broom, wincing as circulation returned to my dormant legs. Then I reached over, gingerly, with my pocket knife, and cut through the ropes holding his hands.

He brought his hands forward, groaning. "Hell of a position to be tied in that long," he said. He flexed his shoulders, and his arms, then he put a finger in the genlock.

The biodoor retracted.

He was tied to the broom. His middle and legs were tied. He couldn't even reach the broom controls. His eyes had to be closed or else he'd be blinded by too much light. There was no way he could do anything.

He must have used Cat speed and he must be capable of inhumanly good hearing. I suspected nothing till the world went black.

THE FOX IN THE FOREST

I WOKE UP CURSING. YEAH, THIS IS POSSIBLE, AND in this case it might have been the only way I could wake up: halfway through a four-syllable word.

He'd subdued me with a blow to the head. That much was sure from the way my skull felt, bruised and tender, and the way my eyes felt, as though I had a really bad hangover and during my unconsciousness some right bastard had taken advantage of the opportunity to pour fine sand on my eyeballs.

I lay very still and concentrated on breathing, with my eyes closed, until I accessed the situation.

Birds were singing nearby. This meant he hadn't left me on the ground outside the biobarrier. It was confirmed by other impressions—the smell of plants and flowers, and what felt like soft grass beneath me.

So, he'd chosen to bring me inside into his super secret compound, where, in the old days, he hadn't even allowed his friends. Oh, fine and good. But how had he brought me in? And why?

Without moving, I tallied the impressions of my senses. I didn't feel rope on my wrists, and if I moved a little, aimlessly, as though still unconscious, I could pull my hands apart from each other. The same with my legs. Which meant absolutely nothing. There are binds that won't tighten until you move in a certain way.

I didn't know how old that type of bind was, but I suspected old enough for Jarl to have laid in a supply of them.

After a while, with no one pouncing on me, and without Jarl's voice greeting me sarcastically, I risked opening my eyes, a little and looking through my eyelashes. Not enough to let anyone watching me know I was looking, but more than enough to allow me to see that I did in fact seem to be bind-free at wrists and ankles.

I was lying on a patch of grass, in a flat area between two hillocks. And the so and so must like me, because he'd laid me down where there were no rocks. Above me, trees swayed in the wind. There didn't seem to be anyone around me, at least not so far as I could determine by looking and listening.

So I risked opening my eyes fully and turning my head, to look around the entire perimeter of what turned out to be a small clearing.

Not only wasn't I tied, I was fully dressed, though he'd taken my belt with its pouch, and, obviously, the broom. Right. Like I didn't have burners elsewhere. I could feel the pressure from my ankle holster and, by moving my leg a little, tell that the weight of the burner was still on my leg. Other hidden burners were even more intrusive in making their presence known. Which was reassuring.

Still, I was fairly sure that Jarl was not a complete idiot. And even if he didn't know me, he knew Daddy Dearest, right? And knowing Daddy Dearest, who'd been so twisted he could slide down a corkscrew without touching the sides, he couldn't think it was safe to leave me like this, without a thorough search.

Unless...

How bored was Jarl? I tried to think of what his life must have been like in Eden. I'd had hints from other people. Doc Bartolomeu had said that Jarl had had almost no social life. The idea that he wanted to create a clone but not let anyone know it was a clone, because he didn't want him as isolated as Jarl himself had been, was entirely plausible to Kit's family. That meant they must have known how isolated Jarl had been, and that the isolation must have been immense.

I blinked. I had a lot of time to think. Or rather, as much as I felt hungry and thirsty, I had to think. The time I took to think now might not just save me time later. It might save my life.

Besides, what should have been hydraulic pressure wasn't there, the bladder had taken care of itself. The broomer suit I'd worn had arrangements for that. As did Jarl's. I didn't like to use them while awake, but I'd been out for... who knew how long. I'd check and empty the receptacle later.

For now, I concentrated on trying to figure out what Jarl's game was. Because there had to be a game.

As I saw it, the relationship between Mule and his servants had been more distant and perhaps more respectful—certainly more obsequious—than that between Good Man and servants. There had been the belief that Mules were, intrinsically, non human, both more and less than mere homo sapiens. Smarter, better coordinated, all of that, but raised as servants, as . . . things. Useful things that could be used by humanity. Their servants would both respect them, for the well-designed things they were, and despise them for their inability to be normal. And be wary of them, because the stories of Mule riots would be less than a century old for most of the Mules' rule on Earth. They would be fresh in public memory, and make everyone fear them. And no one, not even the Mules themselves, believed them for what they really were: all too human.

Then there was Jarl. If the other Mules were of their own kind, and apart from normal humans, Jarl would be more so. I'd read somewhere in Eden that his genius was accidental.

He'd been created to be brilliant. Of course he had. He'd been created to be—like the other Mules created to rule—very bright and capable of retaining and using unbelievable amounts of information. But he was more brilliant, more capable than any of the other Mules and, more than that, he was a creative genius.

From what I understand, ability to create—like homosexuality—cannot be traced to any particular gene. Perhaps it is the result of a complex set of genes. But it's not something that can either be designed or avoided on purpose. It happens, or—mostly—it doesn't if a combination of factors, lucky or unlucky, depending on how you look at it, happens or doesn't.

All humans have some amount of creativity, of course. Faced with the need to do something in an unusual way, most of us manage it. But most of us manage it in limited and predictable ways. The leaps of genius that take humankind from one state of civilization to the next are always unexpected, unpredictable, and can't be designed.

The man who tamed fire, the genius who created the first wheel, the freak mind who solved the puzzle of gravity: unique, all.

I didn't think anyone designed Jarl to be a creative genius, capable of startling leaps of reasoning. Well, the documents on Eden said no one had. Of course, documents and historians lie. But I could go on the evidence of what else they'd designed, and none of the other Good Men even approached Jarl's creativity. Knowing that he'd worked out both the starship design, and the powertrees, even before realizing he'd designed other things, like a way to turn one brain into another and keep the original information, I'd started to joke that Jarl had invented everything.

This wasn't exactly true, but it wasn't completely wrong either. It was as though Leonardo DaVinci had been endowed with more knowledge than anyone, even relative to a much more advanced time, and the ability to call on scientists and workers to make his dreams come true.

So, Jarl's oddity had been noticed early, if I understood properly. He'd said something about his variety of Mules, the Oligoi, being raised in groups. The Alphas, the Betas, the Gammas... None of the history books I'd found said anything beyond that each particular variety of Mule had been raised according to their abilities and resources.

I'd assume that they'd started from the top, from

those designed to rule. So, they'd be Alphas. But if history was right, then even among the Alphas—most of whom were smart but not creative—Jarl was an oddity and stood out.

I thought of the desolate ruins, where he and Doc Bartolomeu said they'd once grown up. I had nothing to go on, except the vague references to sneaking out, and to not having seen a woman while growing up, and I visualized it as a mid-security prison. Jarl had sneaked out, but Jarl would. I noted he didn't say anyone had gone with him.

So, I thought, Jarl must always have been lonely to some extent. He'd managed, somehow, to make friends and remain friends with Doc Bartolomeu and Daddy Dearest . . . No, not Daddy Dearest. Whatever the old bastard had become by the time I knew him, he couldn't have been that way when Jarl had made friends with him. People can be crazy, but they didn't generally make pets of man-eating sharks. So . . . Alexander Sinistra. I'd guess Doc was also an Alpha, though I could be wrong, but I'd be surprised if Daddy, with his lowly avocation, was anything more than a Beta. Probably a Delta or Gamma. How had Jarl broken protocol to make friends? Who knew?

But the fact he had, meant he had probably had to bend the rules, which meant he had to be lonely enough to do so.

And then there had come Eden, where he'd been both a Mule, and a Mule who was resented for two contradictory facts: for having failed to save every bioengineered person on Earth, and for having left the dangerous Mules behind.

He'd been feared and admired and hated and

cherished, probably all of it in equal measure. It was a mystery he hadn't gone completely around the bend. Or hadn't he?

No. From what Doc said, he might have gone a little strange, but not insane. But he'd been lonely. And, I suspected, he'd been bored too.

So...now he had me to play with.

Great! Be very, very careful. We're hunting crazy geniuses.

I looked all around again, and looked more carefully. Above me, something shimmered. It could be a veil or a net or...some type of web. Something ready to drop on me the minute I moved? Yeah. Almost for sure. So?

So. Most things of this kind were set to be triggered by big, sudden movements. But you could get away with small, incremental movements, the kind of inching away one could do with no problems.

I started inching, until I could see that there was just the edge of the "veil" above me. And then I rolled away, suddenly.

The veil dropped, next to me, the woosh of air blowing on my arm, the grass flattening. Right. Crazy as a broomer high on Oblivium.

I looked very carefully and identified all possible discrepancies in the surroundings. This meant that I edged away from the area on my knees, and didn't stand up till I was a good ways away.

Now the question was, did he have traps set on purpose for me, or had these traps been here when he was young and paranoid? And if so, did he have some way to see me? Like what he kept on Simon? And if he had some way to see me, how would it be activated?

I was going to guess it would be easy.

Simon's was probably set on gen code. If he'd fiddled with his machine, he'd probably have found Simon's father in his basement too. It was the only way I could figure out for the machine to still be active and following a line of clones.

My genes were close enough to Daddy Dearest's to open genlocks. However, those were usually set for one or two salient genes, not the whole sequence. No need for it, particularly for Mules who had no siblings, parents, or other genetic relations. However, I doubted they were close enough for this type of camera or pickup.

And I doubted that one could be programmed that quickly. That meant whatever Jarl had following me was set for x amount of mass, radiating at x degrees. It was also possible that he had set some type of bug on my skin.

For those, fortunately, there was a remedy. I had to make myself colder, and I had to, if possible, wash away skin or clothing probe. Right.

We'd start by removing the broom riding suit. I didn't need it. Under it I was wearing a sweaty and scrunched up but extremely practical one-piece. I rolled the broomer suit—I might need it again—and set it in a hollow between two branches, where it would hopefully stay relatively free of bugs and somewhat clean.

Then I looked around. And sighed. Floating in mid-air above me, was a holo message, one of those cheapy things that are activated if you step on them, and which people often use for clues in children's scavenger games. It read WELL PLAYED, MY DEAR! CATCH ME IF YOU CAN!

Yeah. Bored silly. And I had to endure the silly. But I would catch him.

SHALL WE PLAY A GAME?

I TRIED IT JUST FOR THE SAKE OF COMPLETENESS. *Kit?*

I can't help, he said, his voice sounding distant and muffled, as it did when he was under sedation. *He's not letting me see, and he's not letting me know what he's doing. I gather he's enjoying himself at your expense, though.*

I gritted my teeth. *I bet.* And if he weren't occupying Kit's body, right now, I'd be visualizing really hard which parts of his own anatomy I could make him eat. As it was, I'd have to be careful, and I'd have to be cunning, and I'd have to beat him at his own game, and make him reveal where he'd put the data on the powertrees. And make him explain how to make the nanocytes to restore Kit, which would be harder.

There had to be a way to do that, or he wouldn't be working so hard not to cooperate. As for the first, it really didn't take much thought to know that a paranoid and isolated genius would keep his notes and knowledge in the one place that no one could penetrate, the one place where even his friends weren't allowed to go. That, and of course in his own head. But his head wasn't functioning too well, so it would have to be whatever data gems or papers he had hidden here. He had said there were notes. He'd said it to Doc Bartolomeu when both thought they'd never see Earth again, and when they had no reason to lie.

I knew, though, knowing Kit—and by inference, Jarl—the only way to get those would be to play Jarl's little game and to find him. But I'd be damned if I gave him the advantage of following me on his spying apparatus. At least I'd try to cut out that source of his amusement.

I ran sideways and on an erratic path towards the creek then, from the bank, threw myself in. It wasn't a full dive, because diving in to a shallow, rocky creek is a great way to break one's neck. More of a sideways roll and fling, landing on my hands and toes on the river bottom, under the water, and swimming, still under water, upriver, before surfacing just the minimum to draw breath, then diving in again and swimming.

Thena!

What?

He's lost you. He's scared for you. He thinks something might happen to you.

He should be scared for himself, I said, then added, *If he weren't in your body . . .*

You have my permission to kick him in your favorite spot.

I refused to analyze "favorite spot." Instead, I

mind-disconnected, afraid Jarl could somehow trace it, and swam some more upriver. The river was very cold, which meant I'd probably get hypothermia if I stayed in too long. Maybe that was what Jarl worried about. Let him worry. More likely, he worried that I would find him. And he should.

Fish swam around me, tickling me, and I was sure a couple had got into my boots. If I had a bug in there, I hoped they ate it.

In my mind, I figured out where the building was. He might not be there—he probably wasn't—but I'd bet sooner or later he would go there. He might be following our little so-called game on a remote device, but I'd bet for programming new fun, he'd have to have access to the equipment in the building.

So, I'd go there now.

I got out of the water and ran in the direction I knew the building was. I felt even colder, with the air rushing around me, but that was good. It meant I wasn't radiating at normal temperature.

He says no, don't go there. Not that way.

Right. Well, poor Jarl Ingemar was about to get the surprise of his long and confused lifetime. No matter if he'd been created to rule, no matter how much people had revered him and feared him, his words were not law to me, and he could take his orders and fold them all in corners preparatory to inserting them where—

The ground went out from under me, and I was lifted, up and upside down, to hang from a tree. I'd been captured by a fiendish machine!

But looking up, I realized the fiendish machine was one of those tricks that hunters have been playing on animals since humans first learned they could get easy lunch by setting snares. There had been a bent tree, a carefully positioned rope lasso . . . and I was now hanging from a pine tree by a rope tied of rope binding my feet.

The thing about rabbits and foxes and other creatures who got snared in these traps is that they rarely carried pocket knives. Even more rarely had they been forced by a less-than-sane parent to go through various sorts of bootcamps. That meant they were at a disadvantage, because I had both.

Touching my ankles while standing on my feet had never been difficult. I'll confess more effort was needed to do it against gravity, but it wasn't impossible, and I could sort of grab at my legs and pull myself up that way. With a pocket knife carefully held so I didn't cut myself.

Meanwhile, my mind spun upon itself in disbelief. He'd snared me. What was he? Twelve years old?

This was the sort of ridiculous prank, I thought, as I managed to hold on to the rope above the knot with my free hand and reach up with the knife to saw the loop fastening my calves together, that reminded me of the things boys did to get girls' attention at the various camps I'd attended as a pre-teen.

Had Jarl been so unformed, so isolated, that this was his idea of courting me? I was very much afraid it was. Afraid, because it made me feel almost maternal sympathy, as well as extreme anger. That overgrown, infantile genius needed a spanking. But I very much suspected he would enjoy one way too much and in entirely the wrong manner.

The rope parted, and I was hanging from one hand. I put the knife between my teeth, in manner of pirates in holos, and held with both hands onto the rope, swinging it in increasing arcs until I could reach the branch of a nearby tree, which I leapt to.

I fell straddling it, which was not—probably—the best thing to do. Women might not have the part that Kit called my favorite, but I was still rather attached to the part I did have. I took deep breaths, trying to control the pain, and then stood and inched along that branch to the tree trunk and from that to the end of the next branch—as far as it would support me.

I supposed Jarl could see me. That seemed obvious, considering he'd had Kit scream a warning just before I'd got caught. So the following bug, whatever it was, must be targeted for mass alone. And I couldn't change mass. Well, not that quickly. Give me ten months and enough chocolate, and I could probably double it.

There was nothing for it, then. I'd have to work with that handicap. But it wouldn't stop me from going to the building.

He says you shouldn't go to the building. Not alone.

How convenient, then. Tell him I don't need to be alone. He can join me there.

Thena, are you armed?

Kit, were you hit on the head? Wait. Yes you were. Of course I'm armed.

Oh, good.

Dear lonely hearts columnist, my husband is glad I'm armed against the creature that's occupying his body. What should I do?

Well, I should be about as careful as a sheep at a gathering of wolves, that's what.

So, instead of going to the building over ground, as I'd planned to, I went over the trees. There were these holos very popular when I was a little girl, though

I doubt anyone else, and of course no one in Eden, had ever heard of them. Well, maybe other children my age on Earth. I'd bet Simon remembered them.

They featured a young boy abandoned in the jungle and raised by apes. Somehow—holo writers are not obligated to respect reality, and in fact, they seem to treat it like other men treat hired girls—this gave him special powers to call to animals and to perform the most extraordinary feats.

His normal mode of locomotion through the jungle in which he lived was to swing on climbing vines from branch to branch.

While Jarl's pet forest didn't come equipped with those convenient hanging vines, over the three hundred more years it had been left untrimmed, the trees had grown so close that it wasn't hard to just swing with my whole body from tree to adjacent tree.

I was lucky, no branch broke. Of course, it necessitates a new definition of luck. Before I reached the door to his retreat, my hands were skinned and raw, and my teeth were chattering so hard that Jarl only needed a sound pickup to follow me.

But while he could no doubt hear me, and probably see me, too, it was obvious that he hadn't prepared any fun traps at tree-branch level.

So far, so good. I dropped from the branch directly in front of the door to the building and glared at the genlock.

Kit? Tell the bastard he can either open the door or I'm going to burn his genlock off. And then I'm probably going to burn other things off, too.

Kit's response had a curiously hesitant tone. *He says he'd rather you didn't come in.*

Really? Well, then. I'm going to count backward from ten. If this thing doesn't open by ten, I'm going to burn the genlock.

Thena, don't be too mad. I don't think ... I don't think things are as you believe. He was the one who asked me to ask if you were armed, and said it was good you were.

Oh, I'm sure. He likes to have fun, doesn't he?

I don't think he was the one who trapped you, Thena. It doesn't feel that way. Oh, sure, he enjoyed watching you circumvent the traps, but I don't think they were his. He's very worried about something. He's trying to get into the building, but he's afraid to.

Right. I think he's merely playing you. He's crazy enough to lie to the voice in his own head.

I took a deep breath. *Ten. Nine. Eight. Seven. Six. Five—*

The door slid open. Jarl was bent over his apparatus, and had taken a panel off it. In the holo screen, a small image of me stood, dripping water and shivering, with a burner in each hand.

Jarl turned around. "Good Gaia," he said. "You must be frozen. Let me find you clothes."

"Don't bother," I said. Each syllable was punctuated by chattering teeth. "Don't bother at all. I'll be in the broomer suit again in moments." My hands clenched on the burners. "As soon as you give me every gem you have on the creation, planting and growing of powertrees, or even just a way to transplant a cutting to the vicinity of Eden." The whole concept struck me as funny all of a sudden and I cackled mirthlessly. "Another Eden, another tree."

His eyes—Kit's eyes—went wide with alarm. This

was possibly because the little image reflected on the holo screen and therefore I looked a few power packs short of a full charge, with wild eyes and madly flashing grin. "Oh, yeah, I also need the formula for the nanocytes to get me my husband back."

He backed against the apparatus, with its open panel, his hands held on either side of his body, palm out, in the age old appeasing gesture of "Look, Ma, no weapons at all." He swallowed hard. His Adam's apple bobbed up and down. "Thena, look..."

"Patrician Athena Hera Sinistra to you."

"Athena...Hera? Really?"

"Yeah, your bastard friend had a sense of humor."

"Uh...Patrician," he said, in an apologetic tone. "Uh...Patrician. Madam. Uh..."

"Yes?" I asked.

"You don't understand. I didn't do anything to you."

"Oh, really? Then what made me black out when I untied your hands?"

He sighed, but it was with a sound of exasperation. "I might have done that," he hedged. "But not the rest. You see...there's something..."

"Don't care," I said. Frankly, as confused and scared as he looked, he had to be the world's best actor. "Don't want to know. Doesn't mean a damn thing to me. I just want you to give me the gems and the formula for the nanocytes. And then I'm going to tie you in a way you've never been tied." Oh, no, he hadn't just wagged his eyebrows at me. That had just earned him extra tight ropes. And not in a way he would like. Oh, no. "And then I'm going to take you back, and we're going to give you the nanocytes. And then I get my husband back, and you go the hell away from us forever. Or away from us to hell, for all I care." I was approaching as I spoke, though not so close he could grab my burners. I pointed both burners at a portion of his anatomy that my husband was particularly fond of. He wouldn't like it, and I wouldn't like it, but I could just make the hit painful and not completely damaging. And we were within reach of modern medicine.

He was human enough that his hands went in front of his crotch, in a defensive gesture. He looked up at me. "You don't understand. There are two problems. I can't get in there," he pointed within. "There is something there. I think I know what, but it would take too long to explain. And I don't think it will allow us in. Whatever it is, it's the same thing that created the traps you fell into."

"Right. Why weren't those traps there when we were here before?"

"I think they were, but I think it gen sampled you when you slept in the woods alone before." He gestured wildly at the holo screen. "I swear I never put a tracer on you, though 'Xander—"

I snorted, in rhythm with my chattering teeth. "I don't care. I want the data on the powertrees. And I want my husband back."

"I'll have to figure out a way to get you the data, but I don't think I can give you your husband back. Don't shoot."

THE KINGDOMS OF THE EARTH

"WELL," I SAID, PURPOSELY RELAXING MY DEATH grip on the burner, where my finger had almost flexed on the trigger, "then you'd best explain yourself and quickly. My hands are very cold and they might cramp at any moment, and send a ray through...your hands. And the rest."

He blinked up at me. His mouth said "You wouldn't," but his expression said "you might."

"I don't think," he said, and took a deep breath, almost like a sigh, "that I can in perfect conscience give you your husband back." He lifted his hands, palm out. "Yes, I know you love him, and I think I've told you before that I rather like him, myself. Were we normal unenhanced humans, and were I able to...Had I known him as a son, I think I'd have loved him as a son. He seemed...seems like a good kind of young man, even if too noble and silent for his own good. Perhaps because he's aware of not

346

being . . . quite normal human, and therefore he tries
to be better than he'd otherwise be."

"Kit is human, normal human," I said. "Maybe a little
better, but human." I hadn't meant to say anything. I
meant to have Jarl talk himself out, and then hit him
repeatedly with the butt of the burner until he came
to his senses and gave me what I wanted. Or went out
of his senses. Provided I got what I wanted, I didn't
care how at this point. But the words had come out,
in my voice. Even if my voice sounded shaky and wet
to my own ears.

The hands held in front of his body rose a little,
as though to emphasize the fact that he really, really,
really had no weapons. "No, he's not. He can't be normal human because I'm not normal human. And you
aren't normal human. We're something else. We're . . .
biological machines."

"We are not. We're people. We grow. We can think. We
can love. I can love and Kit can love. Now that I think
about it, I'm not at all sure you even know what love is.
But we can. We can and we can decide what to do, and
use moral sense, so we don't hurt others or ourselves."

He snorted. "You don't do too well at that."

"No one is perfect. It's another way we're standard
humans."

A flicker of something like incomprehension appeared
behind his eyes. "We were created to be perfect, and
I do my best to be. I think, in fact, until Hampson's
struck, I always was."

This bald-faced statement, clear and ringing in the
otherwise empty room, made me lose track of reality
for a few seconds. He really thought he was perfect?
That he had ever been perfect?

I don't know what he said until I tracked again, when he was saying, "So you see, that's why I can't let you reverse what the nanocytes did. I doubt I would have initiated the action on my own—not if I'd met Kit as an adult. But what is done is done. And we must make the best of it. I'm not fully myself, of course. I don't think I'll ever be, but I think Kit and I are coming to some sort of synthesis where, by virtue of my greater knowledge and experience, I'll have the upper hand."

It was what I had feared all along, and now my mouth was dry and my throat hurt and my heart was pounding hard, hard, as though seeking release from my rib cage.

"You can't do that," I said. "You have no right to Kit's body or to Kit's life."

He blinked, seeming genuinely surprised and worried. "But it's not a matter of rights," he said. "Don't you understand? It has nothing to do with what I want. It's what I have to do."

Okay. So he'd now gone completely insane. Heaven deliver us from broomers on Oblivion, Kath in a mood, and an elderly superman who had never grown beyond the emotional age of twelve. "How is it possible for you to be senile and juvenile at the same time?" I asked.

"What? I'm not." The tone was entirely twelve years old. "Don't you understand? I was created and raised to be a perfect ruler for humanity. It is my job to do so. I was made better than normal humans so I could handle the task. Now that I have Kit's memories too, I think I know how to do what the Earth needs. Oh, not the same sort of freedom Eden had. For one, I don't think Eden has it anymore. The complete absence of government only allows other entities to take over. Earth needs a government of some sort to protect it from itself, and what I think it needs is one supreme ruler, sort of an emperor."

"You, I suppose?"

He looked apologetic. "Well, I'm the logical choice, aren't I? I was created for it, and I was the best—by their measurement—of all the Oligoi they created. And now, in this body, I'm young enough that if we use the anti-agiatics available in Eden, I can live for three or four hundred years."

"And after that?" I asked. "You clone yourself and have your brain transplanted into your clone's body?"

"No!" he said, in a voice so horrified that you'd never know he was doing the exact same thing by other means. "Never. I hope . . . I mean, after that, I'd . . . I . . . One has to assume my children will inherit the necessary qualities to be rulers of the Earth."

"Children!" I said raising my eyebrows. "Good luck convincing Zen."

"What? But Zen is my clone!"

"The better to increase the chances of your characteristics being inherited." I said, and went on without giving him time to explain what he meant. "You know you're crazier than a canned cyborg, right? Why do you think your children, if you figure out how to have any, inherit those characteristics that you think are so necessary to governing poor, benighted humanity? Kit is your clone and he didn't. He's nothing like you."

"He's exactly like me. Not as creative, perhaps, but only because no one forced him to cram as much knowledge as I had to cram in my first twenty years

of life. If he applied himself, I'm sure he'd be able
to create on the same level, because his mind works
just like mine."

"Kit," I said, and by now I was so cold I thought
that I'd never be warm again, "is nothing like you.
He doesn't have an insatiable thirst for power."

"Power?" Jarl said.

And suddenly I saw his whole problem. Or the
Earth's whole problem, if he couldn't be stopped and
did take charge.

Earth, in the collective, across the ages, has been
ruled by many people: bureaucrats and generals, busi-
nessmen and visionaries, madmen and greedy despots,
murderers and sadists. I don't think it had ever been
ruled by a saint. It didn't deserve to be ruled by a
saint. And if there were gods, anywhere, they'd save
us from that terrible fate.

Because when Jarl echoed "Power?" and looked
shocked, I realized that he didn't have any desire to
rule. Forget insatiable thirst, he didn't even feel a
mild appetite for power.

And like an echo, in my mind, came Kit's voice, *He
hates ruling. He always did. After the war with the
Seacities, at the end of the twenty-first century, he was
more or less by default, the supreme ruler of half the
world. He either controlled territories directly, or he
controlled them through his proxies. And he hated it.
He really is a lot like me. He doesn't even like social
occasions, unless music is involved. He detested having power. But he feels he has to do this. He feels it's
his duty. You see, he thinks of himself as a machine.
A machine humans created to rule them. So he has
to do it. It was pounded into him when he was too*

*young to think. He was raised to believe that ruling
was his justification for living. He was told he needed
a justification for living.*

Kit sounded sad, and I felt horrified. Humanity
had never met the likes of Jarl, as I said. Not for
apparently more than a brief period at the end of the
twenty-first century. But we'd had several regional and
near-global rulers who felt it was their duty to bring
humanity to some sort of paradise.

Even the rule of the Good Men, corrupt autocrats
who never wanted anything more substantial than to
despoil the Earth, could not compare to the ravages
of well-intentioned people who thought they were
altruistically doing something for the good of humanity.
Because humanity can't be made perfect, people trying to achieve perfection usually managed only blood
baths and massacres on an epic scale. "It didn't work
so well last time, did it?" I said, and my voice was
full of malice. "You didn't become the perfect ruler
you think humanity wants, did you?"

"No, but—"

"No, but, nothing. I seem to remember neverending
wars, mass famines because you misallocated resources,
populations moved willy-nilly from wherever you chose
them to vacate and…"

He shrugged. "It was close on four hundred years
ago," he said, in the tone of someone talking about
errors made when they were under ten. "I didn't
know enough, yet. I didn't know about the Earth as
I should have. All the cultures and all…And besides,
I had to fight with all the other Alphas. They didn't
like me, you know?" A glimmer of paranoia in his
eyes. "None of them liked me, except Bartolomeu.

They resented the fact that I was taken ahead, on an accelerated learning course, that I knew more than they did, that I—"

"Spare me. You might not have to deal with your fellow Mules, but I assure you humanity will still be the same it ever was, and you'll still not understand them."

He gave me an odd smile, that looked far too forced and wooden. "I didn't understand humans because I was alone of my kind."

"I thought you said—" '

"I said there were other Oligoi, other Alphas, but we weren't really a species. There weren't any females of our kind. I couldn't experience what most humans experience: mating with a female of my kind and having children and seeing my children grow and knowing they'll live after me."

Ooh boy. Yeah, I liked the way this was drifting. And I supposed our children, if I were crazy enough to have any with him, would marry their siblings and so forth. By the time we had great-grandchildren, we'd probably be into extra limbs or perhaps additional pairs of eyes. On stalks.

"I don't think," I said slowly and measuredly, "you get what I'm saying. Someone might have made you with the idea you'd rule over the Earth, but I don't think anyone now wants you to rule. There's a whole war against the current rulers going on, and I think if you persist in this nonsense, you won't live long enough to rule over much of anything."

He crossed his arms on his chest. "You underestimate me. We'll give Zen and Bartolomeu the data on the powertrees, and then we'll set about acquiring power. It won't take very long before we rule over the world, my love."

I knew it was coming. I'd caught the drift of what he was saying. I knew what he meant.

Why then, did his words send me absolutely insane?

I think the only reason I didn't shoot him was that I really, really, really, didn't want to damage Kit's body. Instead, I realized I'd pocketed one of the burners, and I was flying at him, hand open. I landed a slap full on his face, hard enough to imprint my fingers on it in glaring red.

I never landed a second, because he'd gripped my wrists, hard, and was making quite sure that the burner was pointed the other way, and he was pulling me, hard, against his body, his heartbeat echoing against mine, as he lowered his mouth to mine.

Should I have expected it? Of course I should. Did I expect it? No, no, I didn't. His lips were sealed over mine, his tongue teasingly venturing into my mouth before I realized what he meant to do, much less what he *was* doing.

Part of my mind commented in a completely irrelevant way that he kissed better than Kit. He damn well should have. He had three hundred years of experience. But it didn't make it right. In fact, it made it very, very wrong. It was Kit's mouth, but not Kit.

I reacted again, or my body did. Honestly, sometimes it was like I, myself, was only a passenger in this body. I realized I'd closed my teeth on his tongue, at the same time my knee went up and hit him squarely between the legs.

He screamed and let go of me. It was only after he did that I realized I tasted blood.

I took off toward the dark interior of the building, running, with only the vague idea that I was going to barricade myself somewhere until I could talk sense into the lunatic megalomaniac.

As I ran into a dank, dark corridor, I heard Jarl's voice calling "Thena, no." It was echoed by Kit's mind-voice. *Don't go in there!*

THE GHOST IN THE MACHINE

ARACHNOPHOBIA

I RAN A LONG WHILE, INTO A DARK HALLWAY. Somewhere, at the back of the hallway, through a high-placed window a sort of cold green light filtered, probably having come through various branches, or maybe mildew on the window. It threw shadows on that space that gave the impression of the whole area being underground.

At the back of my mind was the idea that I must find a defensible place, or perhaps a place from which I could leave the compound. But the first couple of doors I tried were solidly locked, and it slowly dawned on me I couldn't leave.

First, I needed to get the information on how to grow powertrees, because if I didn't we wouldn't be allowed back into Eden, or, if we were, we couldn't save them from Castaneda's clutches, and then Eden would be a tyranny worse than Earth ever was. And second, I was not going anywhere without Kit's body and the means to bring Kit's mind back. Because I wasn't going anywhere without him, but the freedom of Eden depended on us going back.

Yeah, I was fully aware I was up against a superman. That was very sad for the superman, who was against me. I was sure he had absolutely no idea how to surrender gracefully and therefore, he would have to be defeated inch by inch, kicking and screaming the whole way.

I was going to enjoy kicking him and making him scream.

As I realized this, I calmed down enough that I stopped running.

"Thena, come back." It came from the entrance of the hallway, but Ms. Reasonable was not at home for this. Not now. Not today. Not after Jarl had told me how he intended to rule the world and impregnate me. Or something. My skin crawled so much at the idea that I couldn't think straight.

So instead of going back, I thought I'd hide from his sight. He couldn't be without the lenses, because the front room had been fully lit. That meant that if I hid in the shadowy part of the hallway, away from the light coming in through the window, he'd never see me.

I pressed myself against the wall, just as my heartbeat started to slow down and I was thinking over what Jarl had said. His absolute determination that he should serve and rule humanity because he'd been created to do it made me ill, but his clumsy idea of romance with me made me want to cry or laugh. I wasn't sure which, though I was sure I'd eventually figure it out. His kiss itself hadn't been clumsy, but what kind of a genius thought that he could seduce a reluctant woman by kissing her against her will?

Caught between repulsion and pity, between tears and laughter, my heart slowed down and seemed less deafening in my ears.

Which allowed to hear the skittering of...something along the wall on which I was leaning. And then I realized I could hear the same skittering along the floor and the other walls.

I jumped away from the wall, pointing my burner at it, and realized the wall seemed to be moving.

Spiders. Thousands and thousands of little spiders covered the wall in every direction. Here and there were bigger spiders, about the size of mice, and then bigger ones, say the size of a housecat. The entire wall was boiling with them, and as I stepped back in the hallway, my feet crunched on something, and I looked down. Forget the wall. The entire floor, the other wall, the ceiling, all were boiling with spiders.

Only the crunch under my foot had not been bone and shell, or any kind of keratin. It had the distinct metallic-ceramite sound of breaking a piece of electronics.

I blinked, realizing that all the spiders were not creatures, but mechanical constructs—little...machines. But it didn't make it any better that they were all converging on me. All of them. I looked down and saw some climbing my boots.

I had no idea what they'd do, but I knew I didn't want them to do it on me.

I swept them off my boots by stomping, crunching more of them in the effort, then aimed the burner and burned a broad clear swath of floor. I jumped in the middle of it, and, as the mechanical spider things changed course and started towards me again,

I burned behind and around till the wall was clear. Then I burned a swath of the corridor.

But as fast as I burned, more the things came, crawling, creeping towards me. What would they do if they got me? Perhaps they would just walk over me? Or perhaps...

The mind recoiled, and I couldn't entertain a thought of being covered in these creatures without feeling like I'd never be clean enough again.

I couldn't breathe and my finger hurt from being jammed so hard on the trigger.

As I was burning the wall clean, once more, I heard steps and turned, burning a wide swath and just missing Jarl, who'd come to stand by my side, burner in hand.

For a moment, in the heat of battle, I wanted to turn and burn Jarl. But not all the battle-madness in the world could make me forget that this was Kit's body and that if the body were dead Kit could not come back. I burned close to his feet, but not so close I could hurt him.

"You should be glad I didn't burn you," I said, as I clobbered at the bugs with my spent burner, while I reached for another one from within my suit.

"Why would you burn me?" he asked in confusion, as he stood with his back against mine. I could hear his burner zapping, presumably clearing a space on the other side of me.

"Never mind," I said through gritted teeth.

"I'm going to start burning, as we retreat out of the hallway," Jarl said. "Follow me. They can't go into the entrance room."

"No," I said. "What are these things? your pets?"

There was a long silence, while his burner zapped and the smell of charred electronic components filled the room. Then he said, his voice sounding odd, "I suppose. In a way."

"What?" I'd come to think that Jarl was a twelve-year-old emotionally, but that was not an answer I expected, nor one that made any sense. "Then why are you burning them?"

"I'll . . . explain, but . . . not now. Right now, we must get out of here. Now, Thena. When I step this way, you step too. We clear the way and we walk to the door."

He cleared. He stepped. I didn't. "It's Athena Hera Sinistra, Patrician Sinistra to you, you utter bastard, and I'm going nowhere till you explain what these are and why they're attacking me."

There was another long silence. The flashes from both our burners reflected off the walls and made the hallway look like a little piece of some mythical hell. What worried me more is that though we were burning vast quantities of the bugs, there were always more.

Thena, go. Let him explain this in the front room. Just go.

Whose side are you on?

Kit sounded just slightly exasperated as he answered, *Yours. Ours. Trust me, there is no time to explain what these are. He has some sort of barrier which prevents them from going to the front room. Other things can get past, but not these.*

I assessed the situation. It wasn't that I didn't trust Kit. Of course I trusted Kit. The problem was rather that I trusted Kit himself. But Kit wasn't in his right mind. In fact, he was barely in his mind at all.

But one thing I was sure of. Whatever remained

of Kit in Jarl's brain would not side with Jarl to lead
me into a trap. In fact, they both had seemed to col-
laborate before to keep me out of trouble.

And while I still didn't trust Jarl, and I very much
would like to know what was going on with these
things, I would take Kit's word for it that he meant
what he said, and that I should get out of here. Or
at least that was the best of the guesses made by my
husband from what he gleaned from Jarl.

"All right," I said. "Fine. We'll go towards the door.
But then you're going to explain everything to me."

"Yes," he said, in a strangled voice. "Everything."

We turned as one and cleared a space of ground to
the side of us. Then we stepped into it. Then again.
Electronic spiders rushed to take in that space, then
again, but we managed to move, slowly towards the door.

And then suddenly Jarl screamed, "Stop!" I turned
to look the way he was—towards the door.

In front of the door there were yet more spiders, but
these were human-sized, and though Jarl immediately
aimed at them and burned—as did I, though I wasn't
aware of deciding to do it—all it did was make their
carapaces glow. It didn't make them stop. There were
a lot of them, and they were rushing at us.

"Stop firing," I said, scared half to death but prefer-
ring to sound angry. "If you make them all hot, all it
will do is make them burn us when they touch us." And
that's when I realized the things would touch us, and
my mouth went very dry and my throat tried to close.

They were large and rounded, covered in some
sort of circuits that I guessed ended in sensors, which
means they'd have eyes or ears or equivalents. Six of
their legs advanced relentlessly, seemingly not caring

that they were crunching their smaller congeners under foot. And their two front legs had pincers and other instruments I didn't understand.

As the front four or so advanced, I realized there were more behind, dozens of them.

"Thena!" Jarl screamed, and his voice seemed to echo both Kit and Jarl's tones. He burned behind him, towards the wall, and advanced into that spot. I followed him, not because I thought we could escape the electronic things advancing on us, but because I wanted to keep my back pressed against him, to feel human warmth a little longer.

I'm not afraid of insects. Or rather, I'm not afraid of non-poisonous insects. I lived long enough in broomers lairs, where no one is responsible for cleaning, that ants and fliers and spiders don't bother me as much as they would your average patrician. I kill poisonous insects, but that's something else.

But these weren't insects. They might have some biological component—I didn't know, most of Eden's machines did, and these had been designed by Jarl who had been the seminal force in Eden science—but I didn't care about that. They were still machines.

Seeing them advance, I understood the unreasoning fear that many humans have for machines. Not that I'd ever had it. I'm a Nav by trade, which means I have an innate ability with machines. I understand them, and most of them are a lot less troublesome than human beings. Machines have made human life better. Kit says that machines are what allowed humanity to dispense with the age-old evil that was slavery. I believe him. He read a lot more history than I ever did.

So I never feared machines. But these machines were different. What had they been built for, and what did they want with us? What did they think they could achieve? Could they think? What were they designed to do?

In the face of creatures like that, human warmth was a comforting thing, even if the warmth came from my husband's body, which had been taken over by a crazed old genius.

I burned the ground in front of them, even as Jarl burned to the other side—kind enough to clear a space for my feet also—and we retreated into it. Again and again, he burned and we stepped that way. Again and again towards the wall, as the things advanced. I made the ceramite floor glow in front of them, causing the smaller creatures to flame out and become so many piles of charred components.

The giant mechanical spiders didn't care. They kept on coming.

And coming.

As they surrounded us on all sides, save for our backs which were tight against the wall, I felt the smaller spiders climb from the wall into my skull. "What the hell are these things, Jarl? What do they want?"

"They're peripherals," he said. "They were supposed to defend the central computer in this place."

"What? Why?"

I swear he said "Because it was me," before the world went black.

SPARE PARTS

I WOKE UP IN THE DARK, AND I WAS COLD AND NAKED.
My bare bottom was pressed against a flat, dusty surface; my arm had been bent at an odd angle under me, my face was pressed against a hard, cold, vertical surface. And I felt fuzzy-headed and somewhat less than awake. My head hurt. So did my body, at various points, as though I'd been dragged, naked, along a floor. And as though pincerlike claws had tightened hard somewhere near my wrists.

They'd given me some drug.

From somewhere in the direction of my feet came a groan that sounded like the type of sound men make when they've drunk too much and are about to throw up.

Thena? Kit's voice, like a distant murmur.

Here, I said. *Where are we? What have they done to us?*

I don't know, Kit said. Something like an implied chuckle. *When he's unconscious, I can't see or hear.*

365

What did he mean by saying "it was me"? I asked.

Kit said, *He thinks of the computer as himself, which...is weird. I can't explain it, you'll have to ask him.*

The groan came again, low and forlorn, and I thought: Right.

I did not like this situation. I was alone with a man who didn't seem to understand that I didn't view him as my husband, and whose concept of "no" was fuzzy. I was naked. I was fairly sure they'd given me some drug or done something to me that made me still not fully awake or capable of reasoning. And though I had not the slightest idea where I might be, I was fairly sure that I was somewhere within reach and patrol of truly strange electronic "insects." And those were under control of a computer that Jarl said was him...Right.

I didn't have to like the situation. Sometimes, reality must be accepted for what it is. There is no point wiggling and trying to pretend it is something it isn't. People and civilizations who do that usually go under and die while still gallantly clinging to their beautiful illusions.

In the end there are only two types of people: those who survive and those who don't. And I intended to survive.

I forced myself to sit up against the protest of my abraded skin and bruised limbs. A quick inventory showed me that I had no broken bones and the arm hurt only because I'd been thrown into a heap, while unconscious, by things that didn't understand the human body at all. It screamed in pin-prick pains as circulation returned, but it would be fine eventually.

I massaged it slowly, while taking another type of inventory. As far as I could feel, I was disarmed. My burners had been taken from me, even those that were in places where I normally kept them while naked.

This alarmed me more than anything else, because as far my body mass goes I'm a thoroughly non impressive human being. Oh, because of the way I was designed, I'm somewhat stronger than most humans the same size. But in the end without a burner, anyone could take me and hold me hostage—if they had a burner and me without one.

It was like thinking of disarmament efforts of the twenty-first century and before, where people actually believed that groups or individuals would give up on armament that was technologically possible in the name of high mindedness or something. Never happens.

When there's the possibility that a hostile—or whatever you consider a hostile—will get hold of a weapon to use against you, your best bet is to have that weapon or a bigger one in reserve. Counting on other people to be nice to you because you're disarmed and patently peaceful is one of those mistakes that individuals and civilizations only make once. It is a characteristic of the dead that they can no longer make mistakes.

So I liked being disarmed as much as I liked being naked. Which of course, were two problems of the same sort. I lacked protection. Fortunately, I still had me.

I blinked, as my eyes became used to the surroundings. There was a little light starting to filter in, and I identified its source—a window high up to my left—covered in something translucent and green. I'd guess glass obscured by either foliage or a film of green scum.

The light was visibly increasing by the moment, which probably meant that it was morning and the sun was coming up. Which meant more than twelve hours had passed since the fight. Yes, they had to have drugged us. There was no possible way hitting me on the head would make me sleep that long, or wake up this confused.

As more light filtered in, I could see the surroundings, not clearly, but well enough to tell where I was. It was a room, and the door was locked. The windows would be, I guessed, dimatough. And though this might, at one time, have been a resort, before Jarl bought it, and while I assumed the rooms had been minimally taken care of, we were not in something as sophisticated as a bedroom. No. This had all the hallmarks of a high-tech broom closet. It was us and some machinery that looked like robot cleaners—turtlelike vacuums and columnar waiter-robots—thrown together in various states of disarray. The machines were sideways and upside down, as though they'd been flung down, without the least care for their functionality.

Horror made my skin crawl as I realized that it was far, far worse than us being thrown into a broom closet. We were thrown in a broken-broom closet, one in which machinery and things were kept that were no longer used or needed.

I swallowed and looked at the softer heap that I knew was Jarl. Jarl was thrown against another wall, opposite me, also naked, and from the way he'd been flung, I'd have thought he was dead, except for Kit's mental voice reaching me, and for Jarl's occasional groans.

So, he was alive and not well.

I looked around the room again. Broken machinery that was no longer needed. Humans who had been stashed in here because they weren't needed, or had to be kept out of the way.

The fact that we'd been thrown in with machines made me wonder whether the computer controlling the things that had captured us even understood that we were different—that we would need water and food, for instance. Or perhaps the electronic brain behind our troubles thought of us as spare machinery, which could be thrown aside and forgotten until it was needed to be repaired and used.

I squared my shoulders and took a deep breath of the air that felt musty and dusty. It didn't matter, did it? Whatever the computer thought, whatever the computer was, it was, clearly, the key to our getting out of captivity. We were being held prisoner by a machine whose peripherals we couldn't defeat, and which had locked us in a room, away from whatever its plans and interests were. That meant that where we needed to be was out of here. What we needed to do was turn off that computer.

Easier said than done, I know, but if you're going to allow yourself to be defeated by overwhelming odds, you'll...probably not survive, or not in any way you want.

First, to find out what the computer was. If I was very lucky, that would tell me what the computer had been programmed to do and how to defeat it.

Given that I'd have to beat the truth out of Jarl—possibly literally—and that my being naked already put me at a disadvantage with him, I needed a weapon.

I found it in the torn-off arm of one of the servo

robots. Its severed-from-the-body end made a passable club; the other end made a passable stabbing tool.

I grabbed it and turned with it in my hand, ready to hit Jarl over the head and make him confess what kind of monster he'd created when he'd programmed this computer.

And felt immediately guilty. Jarl was pulling himself up to sitting, in the sort of movement people make when everything hurts.

He dragged his back up against the wall, and looked in my direction, as his eyes appeared to be trying to focus. Then his eyes widened. *Thena!* Kit's mental voice said. Jarl just looked shocked.

I repressed an impulse to reassure Kit or comfort Jarl. *No. If you're too kind in this sort of situation, it just means you have to be harsher later.*

"Talk," I told Jarl. "Start by telling me what you mean by the computer *being* you."

THE GALLERY OF
FRACTURED MIRRORS

JARL GROANED AGAIN, THAT DEEP-BODY GROAN THAT speaks both of pain and nausea, and his hand went up to rub his forehead in a gesture that was too much like Kit's for me not to recognize it. It was the gesture that meant "my head is killing me, give me a few hours alone in a quiet room."

This time I couldn't grant him either the quiet or the alone. So, I didn't try to pretend. I just stood there, holding my improvised weapon. "Don't stall," I said. "We don't have time. I think the computer doesn't understand humans aren't machines."

He blinked at me, then cleared his throat. "I'm not stalling. I have no idea what you want to know."

"I want to know why you said the computer was you." I said.

I didn't add that Kit had lent credence to this idea. I wasn't sure how aware he was of Kit, still within him, and I didn't want him to become aware of Kit, if he wasn't.

"Oh." His fingers rubbed at his forehead again, and they must have dragged us over very dusty ground indeed, because even though he looked grimy, as did those parts of myself I could see, his fingers left yet darker marks on his forehead, like symbols of some forgotten religion. "That."

"Yeah, that. How can the computer be you? I've heard of cyborgs but..." I was about to say that Jarl had clearly not canned himself in the computer's machinery, when it occurred to me that I couldn't put it past him to have created a replica of his brain and put it inside the computer, as a cyborg component. I mean, if he could see absolutely nothing wrong with reforming an embryo's brain into his own, then why would he care if he created a replica of his own brain to can?

Cyborgs were one of those concepts the ancients had been fascinated with and which even worked, to an extent. To the extent that adding some biological components and brain cells to computers could make them faster and better. But those components didn't need to be, and usually weren't human in nature. I thought—or I'd been told—that our computers nowadays were almost complex enough to be on the level of mouse-brains. But here was the thing: taking the entire brain of any creature, including mice or birds, and canning it—encasing it in circuits and electronic components, which it controlled—didn't create a supercomputer.

What it did was create insanity. A cyborg created from a whole brain was always insane, regardless of whether the brain had experience of being in a body at any time or not.

Of course, I had no reason to think we were dealing with something sane. And Jarl himself wasn't sane. I suspected he'd started to fracture in his horrible childhood and had, since then, parted company with whatever remaining shreds of sanity he might have held onto.

The idea of his having an additional brain stashed within a machine, growing crazier and crazier through three hundred years out of contact with humans made the hair stand up at the back of my neck. My mouth tried to go dry again, but I wasn't about to give it time, particularly since it was dry anyway—from lack of water and, at a guess, from dust.

"Not a cyborg," he said. "Not . . . really. At least, it wasn't when I made it."

"Explain *not really*."

Jarl blinked at me, in a myopic way which had to be related to headaches, since Kit's eyes are excellent. Then I realized Jarl was squinting against growing light. Which meant he couldn't have his lenses in. What kind of machine was so detailed as to remove his lenses? And why would they? Jarl hadn't worn lenses. Kit did. But Kit was designed in a completely different way. What did the computer know about Kit?

"Well . . ." he said, "there is no real brain in the machine." He smiled a little, at what must have been my reaction. "How could you think I'd do that? Even back then, we knew that those didn't work well in machines."

Work well in machines. That was his criterion. Clearly the idea's monstrous qualities meant nothing

374 Sarah A. Hoyt

to him. I'd grown up hearing that the Mules, raised apart from humans, and created in a way that humans weren't made, had been amoral. I believed they were amoral, but I thought it was how they were raised more than how they were made that caused them to have no moral sense. Kit and I were not amoral, though I sometimes managed to be immoral. I knew where good and evil were. If I crossed the lines, it was only when it was needed.

"Right, so what is this computer? I take it it's not just a supercomputer of the twenty-first century."

Jarl took a deep breath, then hissed it out between his teeth. He looked a little worried, as though he might have to admit to something embarrassing. "It started out as a supercomputer of the twenty-first century," he said. "Then I added . . . biological components and . . . and other things."

"Other things?"

"Peripherals. The machines that you saw are also peripherals, but the ones I gave it initially were . . . well, in one room, and more . . . more restricted. But they did have the capacity to both repair the computer and . . ."

"And improve it. That was where I came up against it, see." His eyes suddenly acquired animation. It was an expression I knew all too well. Father's work often required him to come in contract with scientists of various stripes. And, as his social hostess, I often came in contact with them too. Over the years, I'd arrived at the conclusion a scientist is someone who will speak happily and with great enthusiasm of a cunning method for his own execution.

There was this weird light that came to scientists'

eyes when they described something particularly creative they'd invented or some tricky way they'd found around an eternal problem. The light was in Jarl's eyes now.

"The thing is," he said, "I created a far more efficient, larger and better computer than anything the world had known before, but I had one problem. No one had ever created a computer to be truly creative. Oh, sure, to shuffle and rearrange creative solutions. But truly create? No." He grinned. "So I thought how could I create creativity. I couldn't. No one has managed it. It's not something that can be figured out. So . . ."

His voice trailed off and he was quiet so long I thought he had become lost in the internal dimensions of the problem, again. "So?" I said.

"So . . ." He sighed. "I knew I was creative, right? I'd created things in the past. So I figured I could do it . . . So . . . I increased the complexity of the computer enough to support it, and then I . . ." His eyes shifted side to side, like a thieving servant caught in error. I continued to stare at him, not giving him a respite, or a chance to evade answering. "And then I gave it a brain, but it was a *new* brain and I uploaded my personality and knowledge into it."

I must have made a reflexive movement with the robot arm, because he put his hands over his head and yelled, "Don't."

But I had no intention of hitting his head. The part I hit might be the part that lodged what remained of Kit. It was one thing to be cavalier with my own life, another with Kit's. Instead, and so I wouldn't be tempted, I forced myself to retreat and sit against the opposite wall, with the robot arm by my side.

"I won't ask if you're insane," I said, and he gave me a puzzled look as if I made no sense. "I'll just ask what you thought you were doing."

The smile again, which looked like a rictus in his begrimed face. A bruise ran from the corner of his mouth to his ear, as if one of the machines who'd dragged us here had grabbed his cheek between its pincers. And the other side of his face was abraded, as though they'd rubbed fine sand paper over it. I suspected it was just the way they'd held him. One of his eyelids was swollen. They might have been fine enough instruments to remove his lenses without blinding him, but clearly they hadn't cared if they caused him pain and discomfort.

"No," he said. And I wasn't sure if he was denying insanity or the need to question it. "You see, I was created to serve humanity, but it was becoming obvious..." He cleared his throat. "Humanity is not as easy to serve as you might think." He looked puzzled at the choked laugh that I felt escape me. "They created us first as functionaries. Super bureaucrats? Yeah. You see, the land territories, even though they had much higher resources than the seacities, were bankrupt. They couldn't keep their compact with their own populations, and their brightest and youngest were escaping to the better-off seacities. There was, of course, mismanagement and fraud, and of course they wanted to stop that, so they created us. We weren't human and, in the same way that the church enforced the celibacy rule for priests, back when... Never mind." He must have seen by my expression that history or religious history was not my forte. Gaian priests were not celibate, though ultra-observant ones often had themselves castrated, so that they could more closely approach the feminine nature of their goddess. And they were the only priests I'd ever heard of, in sufficient numbers and in an organized enough church, to have enforced celibacy. "The thing is, because we couldn't have descendants, it was thought we would be free from any interest in...in furthering ourselves or our lines. Because even though we were crammed with every longevity genetic marker possible, it was obvious one day we would die. Everyone does. So it was thought knowing that, we'd just serve people the best we could."

He blinked at me again, and closed his eyes fractionally more. It was possible that the light in this room would never grow bright enough to make him close his eyes, but it was obvious he was starting to feel uncomfortable. "I tried. I know not all of us did, though those of us...well...they found a way to circumvent death, right? But I never did, or..." His eyes wandered again, as he probably became uncomfortably aware that his attempt to take over Kit couldn't be construed as anything else. "Not for a long time. So I took serving humanity seriously, and I did try to be the impartial servant they'd created me to be. Only it became obvious that no matter how much waste and fraud we eliminated, there would always be more." He looked very sad, suddenly, and very young despite the scruffy growth of calico-colored beard on Kit's chin, despite the beauty of a shiner on his cheek, despite his obviously full-grown body. "It's so difficult to govern humans, because humans are so fallible. This is why they created us, of course, to get around their own weaknesses." He nodded, as if to himself. "So you see, we saw that it was our duty to take over, and we did. We stopped their pitiful systems of governance and we took over. We . . . we . . . we called ourselves biolords, but I know everyone called us Mule Lords." He shrugged. "It doesn't matter. Eventually we took over the whole world, including the seacities. And we governed well. There were some of us made by the seacities, even, and they too took over and . . ." He sighed. "But humans don't like to be efficiently governed and their . . . their perverse nature always ended up causing problems and fraud and waste and scarcity. It was impossible to convince humans to live on a rationed diet so other humans at the other end of the world didn't die of famine. It was impossible to convince them to work as hard as they needed to at jobs that provided for everyone, even though it was obvious if they slacked off there would be failures and . . . and lack of things." He rubbed at his nose, and managed to look genuinely perplexed. "And they didn't like us. In fact, they hated us. They . . . there were more and more rebellions, and I realized sooner or later we'd need to leave the Earth." He shook his head, as though at the waste of it all. "But you see, to create the ship and all, and still govern as wisely as I could, I had to create something else, a . . . an additional brain that could take over some of my duties, and so . . ."

"And so, you misguided idiot, you created a cyborg that could think like you did."

He just nodded, and shrugged. "It was really good at helping me with the design and . . . and everything. And when I left, because I left in a hurry . . ."

"Yes?"

"I didn't know if I could survive this or not, if I could even get to the *Je Reviens* in time. I thought I might need to backtrack and hole up here and defend my position. And I didn't want any of the rioters to penetrate and to come here and..." He shrugged. "So...so I you know...programmed the computer to defend this perimeter with its peripherals, and not to let anyone tamper with programming." He sighed. "How was I to know we'd come back centuries later? How would I know it would decide I was an enemy. I tried to talk to it...I tried...It was supposed to recognize my gen signature, and Kit's is good enough for the genlocks, but..."

"But?"

"But the computer seems to be more discriminating when it comes to genes." He sighed again. "When we first came back before, I had some indications that the components had gone rogue, but they didn't seem to be very mobile. I caught glimpses of them here and there, but they didn't mass and attack us—I don't know why, but perhaps because none of us tried approaching the computer—so it thought we were not a threat. Then when we came back...I left you out, in a clearing, and I thought...I thought I'd go to the computer and...uh...see what files there were and...uh..."

"And delete them," I said. I couldn't even manage any anger. What had Kit said once? Or was it Doc? Something about self-defense being enshrined in the law of even the most primitive societies.

Clearly, in healing Kit and thereby getting rid of Jarl's personality and memories, what we'd be doing was killing Jarl. That Jarl was akin to an illness in Kit's brain made no difference. He was alive and sentient and, no matter how he himself might not believe it, clearly human. So if we destroyed him, we would be killing him, and he was within the laws of every civilization to stop us doing it. To defend himself. So, of course, knowing I wanted the knowledge of the nanocytes, if he had anything relating to them on the computer, he'd want to erase them.

His eyes widened a little, in alarm, and he nodded minimally, then added, "Not the ones on the powertrees. I had solved that problem, by the way, just before I . . . just when we had to leave. With the help of the computer, so most of the files were in the computer. So, I figured I would get those on gems, and give them to Zen and Bartolomeu, and get them out of the Earth . . ."

"Oh, yeah, so you could make me your queen of the damned or whatever. Right," I said.

He flinched, but didn't say anything for a while, then spoke in an even voice, as emotionless as though he were discussing the weather, "But I couldn't get near it. I got close enough to realize that it had done something to you . . . that it was playing some game . . ."

"That was your computer alter ego?" I asked. "Charming." No, I didn't doubt it. It was the only way to make sense of what had been, up till then, a bewildering mix of warnings and attacks.

He nodded. "And I tried to stop it, and . . . it attacked me. I managed to erect an . . . electrically disruptive barrier on the way to the front room, so we had access to the communication . . . but then you insisted on running in here."

I didn't say anything. If he didn't understand that

groping and kissing unwilling females might make them insist on running somewhere, I couldn't help him. He remained the same bewildering mixture of aged genius and twelve-year-old boy.

I tried to sound as calm and sane as I could. "So," I said, "that is what is wrong. Now. What are we going to do about it?"

He shook his head. "I don't see that there is anything we can do," he said. "We're stuck in this room and locked down, and we have no tools and no weapons. I couldn't take the peripherals on, even with tools and weapons. Oh, and it's taken my lenses . . . Kit's lenses. We're screwed."

I gritted my teeth. "A fine help you are. Kit would never give up. *You* never give up."

"Oh, yeah? What do you think we could do?"

A CHANCE IN HELL

"WHAT I DON'T THINK WE SHOULD DO IS SHUT UP and die slowly."

"We don't have any way to commit suicide," he said. "No way, at least, that will be a certain thing or less painful than this."

"Stop. Suicide is becoming a habit for you. Considering how hard you're fighting to stay alive when you shouldn't be, I'd think you'd be a little less fond of the notion."

"What? What do you mean?"

I realized that he had no clue what he'd done— how his former body died. He knew about Kit, so the brain impression being restored must have been from after the time when Kit had been created and the nanocytes designed. It was more or less obvious, though, that he couldn't know about his death. Not unless he extracted that knowledge from Kit.

He'd got who I was, and how I'd come from Eden,

I supposed, though frankly he might have got it from our interaction in the *Cathouse* since he'd awakened in Kit's body. I had no idea how sharing information happened or if he could get something Kit wasn't willing to give.

I don't think so, Kit said, in my mind. *At least not if I really fight him on knowing it, and if it's something important. Oh, personal life and such, I think he got instantly. But . . . he hasn't asked how he died, and I didn't want to tell him. I think he thinks it was the Hampson's.*

Jarl's eyes widened. "So, I did put an end to myself, didn't I, when it became obvious I wasn't fully myself anymore? Yes, I had mechanisms in place to commit suicide if needed, but if you think that is a sign of weakness, you're wrong." He looked highly offended at the idea. "You have no idea what it is like to lose who you are and to know there is no way out, or at least no way out of that body. I tried . . ." He opened his hands. "I thought it was my duty to go on living, in another body, even if my . . . ego had to face death in that one. But when death becomes inevitable, suicide is not dishonor."

I glared at him. I couldn't even argue. Oh, I don't think I would do it. Remember, my primary directive was to survive and I'd fought on forlorn odds before. Going down in battle will always, to me, be preferable to surrender.

There might be a paradise after death, though I doubt it. It makes no sense to have perfect happiness, before or after death. The human mind is not designed to be perfectly happy and it could be argued it is—from some angles—the worst form of torture.

As for life after death—real life after real death, not what Jarl was trying for—I refuse to state an opinion. Insufficient facts. On the one hand, we have no way to prove it exists. On the other hand, there does seem to be something, some particle of life and thought that we can't summon at will, though we can get rid of it very quickly and efficiently indeed. Which means... nothing. I'll find out eventually. I see no reason to go exploring that uncertainty until there is absolutely no other option. I know life on this side exists, and that as long as I can keep processing oxygen and food, I can hold that life.

Oh, yeah and water. I really wanted to process some water and soon.

However, I also wasn't about to judge someone else's choices on the matter. Why not? Because I've never been there. Also, because I'm not infallible. Also because I didn't have to. I suspected a lot of the choice between survival and suicide was a personality thing, and I couldn't have someone else's personality for a while to fully judge the matter.

"I'll give you that up against odds like what you faced, it's entirely possible I'd have chosen suicide also," I said. "But we're not up against that kind of odds."

"How not?" he asked. "They threw us in a room with broken machinery and left us to die."

"Right. Have you even tried the door? A machine naive enough not to kill us, but to store us with broken equipment, as though it could pick us up later—" I refused to think of ways in which it could pick up our component parts and use them. "Might very well think that we will not try to get out because it told us not to or something. How much of your knowledge did you upload into it, anyway? If it helped you design the powertrees, how crazy is that design?"

Jarl shrugged. "It had all my knowledge, and initially, it wasn't, as you call it, that naive. But I will grant you that since I left, it might have lost . . . well, its operating memory, the part it uses to . . . The part that feeds the personality, might not remember humans, or that humans are different from machines."

Or given that Jarl had considered himself in many ways a biological machine, built for a purpose, it might never have fully grasped the distinction. "But surely it knows what biological organisms need to survive. There are trees and birds and things outside, as part of its domain."

He shook his head. "Other than tracking you and setting traps, I don't think it has done much outside. I left the maintenance program dormant, and I don't think it has bothered with it. You see, it really is like a human, in that it has various forms of memory and . . . and knowledge. What it doesn't need, or isn't in any way relevant to its . . . essential processes, which are the ones I set, it knows but doesn't think about."

Like Kit not realizing that Zen was his female clone, because he'd never put together the facts that he was a Mule and so couldn't have biological sisters, and that she couldn't be "just" the daughter of his adopted parents because she looked nothing like the Denovos. It hadn't been in any way important or relevant to his life. I nodded. "Fine. So, how do you know it has realized the door needs to be locked? Maybe it thinks that we will simply stay in here because we're programmed to."

He shrugged and shook his head, as though what I

said was too stupid for words. But I dragged myself up, walked to the door.

It didn't have a knob, or anything that could shield a genlock. It was just smooth dimatough, except around the edges where... I squinted. Yeah. Around the edges there was a seam where some... thing had melted ceramite or perhaps dimatough—which required higher temperatures but could be melted—to weld the door to the frame.

I hit it with the robot arm I was carrying. I didn't think about it. I just hit it. Hard. Then again. Then again.

"Thena, please." I became aware that the robot arm had become a few shreds of ceramite and wire and that—from the look of it—Jarl was standing prudently just outside the circle of flying debris, his arms akimbo, saying my name in a plaintive tone. "Please stop. You can't break it."

My arm, holding what remained of the robot arm, was tired. So tired I didn't think I could raise it again. I gave the door a halfhearted kick, that didn't even budge the seal, though it did seem to me to evoke a series of skittering sounds from the outside. Like those horrible spiders.

I swallowed hard. My foot hurt now. It wasn't a good idea to kick ceramite doors with bare feet, a fact you'd think I'd remember. I turned around, to face Jarl, though I wasn't sure what I was going to tell him. It's just as well, because he just opened his arms and hugged me.

All right, we were both naked and it should have scared me, but it didn't. The hug was the most sexless touch I'd ever experienced from that body, and as the warmth of his skin, the uncomfortably tight grip of his arms communicated itself to my mind, I realized that Jarl was that scared, that he wasn't viewing this as hugging a naked female, but just as human comfort.

Still, it was Kit's body, we were both naked, and Jarl had all those funny, funny ideas about us becoming a breeding pair of supermen or something. I pulled back a little, trying to extricate myself from the circle of his arms without being violent or even rude about it. In the situation in which we found ourselves, human unkindness was the last thing we needed.

I shifted my hands from his arms to his shoulders, in order to push gently away.

Movement under my fingers made me look. My first thought was spiders. My second thought was wordless terror as I jumped away. "They're on you," I said. "The little ones are all over you!"

TREMORS

"I KNOW," HE SAID. AND HE WAS COMPLETELY CALM about it. "Are they on you?"

I was already feeling my arms, my body, my head under my hair. As soon as I'd jumped away, I'd started a pat down. I suspect it was instinctive. But I felt no movement anywhere, and shaking my head didn't make anything fall out onto the floor.

I looked back up at Jarl, then stepped back, until I was as far away from him as I could be. "I'm clean," I said, even as my mind processed the fact that we'd both been naked and unconscious in this room, probably for a good dozen hours. Why had they infested him and not me? It couldn't be attraction to body heat, or they'd be on both of us. "Are they all over you?" I asked.

He shook his head. "Mostly my head, though some fall to my shoulders."

It couldn't even be attraction to the very weak

electrical field that human brains generated. They'd be on me too. It had to be the genetics, but if it was the genetics, why would they concentrate on his head? His genes were the same all over his body, right?

No, I wasn't an unlettered savage. I knew that some individuals were chimeras who had different genetics all over their bodies, but Jarl had been a designed individual and Kit was his clone, and I didn't think that kind of makeup would be practical or acceptable. So, Kit was the same all over his body . . . The machines should be interested in his whole body.

I looked up and met with a very weird expression on Jarl's face. It was a smile, I suppose, but it was the sort of smile you'd expect in someone who not only knew he was going to die in an atrocious way, but knew that he would endure the tortures of the damned on the way there, and that there was absolutely nothing he could do to avoid either.

"Don't you understand?" he said. "The nanocytes are still active, and the nanocytes communicate with each other by a method that is used by computers. Electromagnetic communication. They . . . these things are attracted to it, they're possibly trying to communicate with my brain directly. I don't know. I feel . . . very odd. But I've felt very odd since I woke up in the *Hopper*. So I'm not sure they're doing something, but it's entirely possible they are."

"If you think," I told him, my voice more shrill than I intended, "that I'm going to be locked in here with three of you, you have another think coming. It's bad enough that there's you and Kit, but if your computer self is going to join the party, I'm going to do something we'll both regret."

He sighed. "I don't know what you imagine we can do. We're at the mercy of the computer and the peripherals. It's possible it will realize we need to drink and eat if my vital signals go down. Or it's possible it won't. But whether it does or not is not under our control, and there's nothing we can use to escape here. They took everything we had, every weapon."

He was right on that, I thought. But then I looked around at the debris of the robot arm. I was being an idiot. My ability to assemble and create machinery had not only kept me relatively unscathed through my hell-raising childhood and youth, it had made me ultimately welcome in Eden and made it possible for me to travel with Kit. It was instinctive, meaning I could never put it into words. I just knew what worked together. And what didn't.

And here I was in a room full of machinery and parts. Okay, so the light wasn't the best in the world—it was low enough not to hurt Kit's eyes. But there might be a solution for that in this room too. A lot of these server robots had lights, so people who saw them in deserted corridors, late at night, in hotels, didn't just see a dark column moving towards them. Lighting them up tended to avoid collisions with guests who were much the worse for the wear.

At any rate, my throat hurt with dryness, and I was starting to feel distinctly peckish. Which meant that I needed something to distract me. And machines could usually distract me even in the worst circumstances.

I found a light first, in the front of one of the server robots. Extracting it and attaching a battery to it took a little longer, particularly when it came to finding a still-functioning battery.

After a while, Jarl seemed to take an interest in what I was doing, and stood up, as though to walk towards me, but I yelled, "Don't. I don't think those things will transfer to me, not if they are attracted to the nanocyte signals as you say, but I don't want to try it out."

He glowered a little, but as I turned the light on, even if it was aimed at the space in front of me, he seemed to lose any wish to help, and retreated to sit back down again. He rubbed the middle of his forehead with his fingertips, and I thought his head must hurt. Then I wondered if the little machines were causing that pain.

And if they were, what could I do?

I could get out of here.

First of all, I needed to figure out some sort of burner from these components. This was definitely easier said than done. For some reason it didn't seem customary to equip cleaning and serving machinery commonly used in the hospitality industry three hundred years ago with lethal-force lasers. Who knew why? You'd think that one could find all sorts of useful things to do with killing lasers when it came to a resort hotel. Loud guest...zap. Rude customer... zap. Insufficiently clean lodger...zap.

Apparently though and much to my surprise, people who ran hotels were not like me, and weren't interested in eliminating nuisances. Or at least not permanently.

I grumbled a bit at their failure of imagination, mostly because this place was starting to feel like a tomb, with Jarl sitting up against the wall, looking boneless and odd like a broken doll. I wondered if he was asleep or perhaps passed out, but frankly I didn't even want to think about what would happen if the computer took control of him.

He might be emotionally twelve years old, but his personality enshrined in the computer definitely was. And it probably made sense, because not only didn't the machine have human emotions—or at least I didn't think so. No nerves, no instincts, nothing—but it hadn't even been in touch with human behavior for three hundred years. So even if, once upon a time, it had had the memory of Jarl's thoughts and emotions, now the only thing it would have would be very, very attenuated memories, most of them probably not even in that present and obvious part of itself that would be the equivalent of consciousness.

Meaning, once upon a time, since Jarl's personality had been uploaded to it, it might have been able to fake human. Or at least to almost fake human. But now? Now it wouldn't even know in which direction to point to find "human." At best it would manage the more intellectual and detached sort of emotions, like boredom. But it had no gonads and no interest in women, beyond a remembered interest via Jarl. So, a twelve year old trying to make me do interesting stuff.

Think how much more interesting it could get, if he could control Jarl's/Kit's body and get a reaction from me?

I shuddered and I returned my attention to the machinery.

No lasers were no lasers. Again, reality is what it is, and after a certain point one can't change it. One can adapt to reality and use it, or die. I could get some sharp bits of the machines to make passable knives, and bits of wire to make sheaths and straps for my ankles and arms. I wished very much I could make clothes too, but I was aware that this was silly.

Clothes have many uses, from bedazzling the members of the opposite—or same, depending on your preference—sex, to protecting the body in case of collision or abrasion...or of course, the vacuum of space. In this case, given that all I had at hand was wire, and little scraps of fabric that were designed as thermal insulation, and that at best they could be made into three tiny triangles to cover the more usually covered parts of the female body, none of those functions would be served. No, leave clothes alone.

Then I realized that my spectacular barbarian princess knives in their sheaths were quite useless. I couldn't, after all, use them to stab machines. Even the smaller ones would do nothing but break, and let me dull the knife tip on floor or wall.

So I was magnificently equipped to fight off whoever opened our door—and why would they open our door?—provided they were living, breathing creatures, who probably couldn't get in here, unless they had Jarl's genetics, anyway. Right.

Did I ever say I was intelligent? No, I believe I've admitted that, like my late, very unlamented sire, I was cunning. I usually could find my way out of trouble because I could read other people, or know how to scare them. But here, the computer wasn't people. And the chances of its—his?—sending people against us were slim to none. Actually the chances of its sending anything at all to open this door were slim to none, and I still had no idea how to get out of here.

I looked at Jarl again. Right. At least I could fashion something that would get rid of the spiders

.if they should open the door. Or at least something that would kill enough of them to make them stay away from me.

So I set about adding to my fabulous prehistoric weapons with a selection of hammers. Hammers are actually more useful than knives, if you must fight.

Unless you're good at throwing the knives with unerring accuracy, you probably won't get much joy out of them. But a hammer? If you can throw a hammer in the general direction of your foe, it doesn't matter exactly where it hits, nor if the right bit is uppermost. If you hit someone with a heavy enough flung hammer, they will be at the very least distracted. If you manage accuracy of aiming, then you can kill someone.

You can kill someone with knives too, of course, but it's a much more exact craft, and it must be performed up close and personal.

I had just fashioned a belt from wires, and hung it with hammers all around, when I heard Jarl speak.

His voice sounded very young and very scared, and the words echoed, forlorn, in this locked chamber, "Mother, I'm frightened."

MOTHER I'M FRIGHTENED

MY HAIR DID STAND ON END, AND I WAS, FOR A moment, frozen in place.

I didn't think anything about it. Thinking didn't come into it. Two instincts warred in me, the first being to console the creature speaking in that little voice and demanding comfort. The second was to kill it.

I'm not going to justify myself. I don't think I could. I think fear of the mentally ill, like the uncanny valley effect that makes people afraid of things that are almost human but not quite, is one of the oldest instincts of humanity. It was what had made humans create the server bots shaped like columns with extrudable arms, instead of the humanoid creatures of ancient dreams. It was also probably responsible for the survival of the species.

No? Think about it. When a mentally ill proto-human was aggressive to others and large, how hard would it be to exterminate an entire band of hominids? Its own tribe, its own people?

I was sure that most of the legends of possession and were-animals came from incidents like that and were designed to allow people to do what must be done—kill the loved one who had become a danger—and go on living with themselves.

Compassion to the mentally ill and attempts at treatment were much more recent instincts, from a time when population had become so large and science so advanced, that killing those who might become irrationally dangerous was no longer a matter of life and death.

But now I was in a small room with someone who could easily overpower me, and he had clearly gone around the bend.

How did I know he had gone crazy? Easy. The voice that spoke was Jarl's, but Jarl had never had a mother.

I swallowed hard, then said, in a whisper, as though attempting to communicate with a co-conspirator, "Kit?"

There was a little whimper, as Jarl tried to pick himself up off the floor, and seemed to be having trouble controlling his arms and legs. "Mother? Where are we?" And then in a completely different voice, "Irena, is that you?"

Uh uh. I was locked in a small room with six feet plus of crazy. Forget that we didn't have food or drink. Forget that we didn't have any way to get out of here, and that if we managed it, we would have to contend with the devil-machines created by a computer that had also gone around the bend, probably centuries ago, I was locked in a room with someone who could easily take me out for whatever irrational reason it conjured.

Normally it would be a great opportunity to hit him on the head and render him unconscious. No, even I wouldn't have killed someone for going crazy. What can I say? Despite the barbarian princess weapons, I had grown up in a relatively safe and prosperous society. I had the prejudices of the civilized.

Besides, hitting this particular crazy on the head might simply eliminate what remained of my husband. If he wasn't gone already, under the double onslaught of the nanocytes trying to turn him into Jarl and whatever these electronic spiders were telling the nanocytes to turn him into.

I wouldn't think of that, though. I would simply somehow reach the computer and turn it off. But there was that reality thing again. How was I going to reach the computer that these machines were designed to keep safe? More than that, how was I going to get out of this room?

I realized light was decreasing and looked towards the window, and then it hit me. The window!

"Jarl, what are the windows in this compound made of?"

"No one helped me get out," he said, sounding defensive. "You have no reason to punish everyone. It was my doing. No, I didn't do anything. I just wanted to look at the area around here. I didn't... No. Please don't." The last was a scream, and when I looked over, Jarl's eyes were blank, and he seemed to be lost in some dreadful memory. His voice sounded young, but not like a child's, and it didn't take much imagination to picture him defending himself before one of the managers of the home he'd grown up in. I didn't want or need to know any more than that.

I did, however, need to know if that window was breakable.

At some point between the twentieth and the twenty-fifth century, windows had changed from being made of clear transparent glass to being made of ceramite or, in the case of high-tech or high-security applications, of transparent dimatough. Mind you, lots of windows were still made of glass even in my time, because it was so much cheaper than ceramite, but this had been a high-end recreational compound. More than that, it had been taken over by a high-end paranoid, which meant that I could count myself very lucky if the windows weren't made of dimatough.

Here was how things stacked up, though—while glass would be relatively easy to break, ceramite was almost impossible. And dimatough . . . well, you could melt dimatough with very specialized torches, but I didn't have even a laser at hand.

I wished I could remember when transparent ceramite had become viable for windows. I knew the first type of ceramite created had been a sort of gingivitis-pink and smooth. It had been used to create rounded houses which were known as mushrooms. But I didn't know how much longer it had taken for it to replace glass, or for it to become cheap enough to be used for windows.

If I had known how much I'd need it, I'd probably have devoted my misspent adolescence to learning the history of materials science, instead of learning about and exploring new ways to ride an antigrav wand in defiance of the law.

But that was all beside the point, and what did I intend to do about it, right then? I could improvise a way to climb to that window from the shells of machines scattered around me. But what if I got up there and there was nothing doing? What if Jarl, just before leaving in the *Je Reviens*, had replaced the windows with transparent dimatough?

And what if he hadn't? What was I doing sitting around here, besides thinking that I'd really like some steak, anyway?

I forgot the imaginary steak, and the desired bottle of water which for some reason seemed even more attractive. Instead, I started piling up the broken machinery so I could reach the window.

Jarl talked to himself, his voice ranging through his life, from child to adult, his mind seemingly wandering at random through memories—his and Kit's both.

"And if they mean to tell me how to pilot when none of them is a Cat, I'll tell them where to shove it," Kit's voice said, followed by Jarl's. "I was out . . . I was just . . . I was out, you see, and now they're rounding up . . . they said something about escaped Mules. Lady, I'm not a Mule, please, save me. If the police catch me—"

It made my hair rise on end, that voice, the words that didn't refer to anything in this room, anything in reality on Earth for the last few hundred years. I didn't want to hear this, and I didn't want to think about it, but the only way out was through that window, which frankly might be too small for me.

As I managed to reach the top, I decided to try the easiest method first. I took one of the larger hammers, drew back and banged the window hard.

I never expected it to work. Glass seemed the least likely thing for that window to be made of.

The thing is, it wasn't. The window didn't shatter like glass, not even safety glass. Instead, when the hammer first hit it, it seemed completely intact. And then within less than the time it took me to draw breath, it cracked and crazed, and it seemed to... splinter. Like wood under the action of acid, it seemed to disintegrate into its component fibers, until only a few threads of it were attached to the frame.

I felt the threads, which were like steel wool. Ceramite. Ceramite must become fragile with age. At least this type of early, transparent ceramite spun this thin.

I wouldn't know. Again, I didn't spend my adolescence studying materials science. A failure of the imagination, just like the people who had designed hotel machinery and had never thought that killing-force lasers might come in handy. Absent time-travel, neither were remediable.

I knew that the mushrooms made in the twenty-first century still stood. At least those with historical significance still stood. So, I was going to assume that some ceramite didn't disintegrate with age. But this one had, and it was no use complaining about it.

"Sinistra!"

The voice made me jump and turn, but it was Jarl, who remained slumped as he'd been, though he still seemed to be making efforts to get up. It was like his legs didn't both belong to the same person. Hell for all I knew, even a single one of his legs might not belong wholly to the one person. It must be getting crowded in Kit's skull.

"'Xander! What did you do? How could you—"

Among the things I didn't want to know, not wanting to know what Daddy Dearest had done back in the days when Jarl sounded like his voice was just changing from boy to man ranked somewhere pretty high. I could probably think of better things to do, like chewing my nails to the elbow.

But before I left here, I did need information that had to be locked in Jarl's skull. "Jarl!" I called.

"Mother?"

Right. This was going to be fun. I tried, tentatively, the mental reach, *Kit? Kit, my love, I need help.*

There was no answer, which, I realized with a pricking of tears in my eyes, might very well mean that Kit was now and possibly forever beyond the reach of my mental voice. It was entirely possible that he'd gone to find out that answer to what existed after death. Or could one find that out while one's body was alive?

I didn't know, and I didn't want to know. But I knew that Kit, my husband, would never fail to respond when I asked him for help. "Jarl, you loon, what did you improvise to keep that computer from sending peripherals after us in the entrance room?"

"But you see, it's not hard at all to rewire the sign so the hologram is different," he answered, in the tone he used when giving technical instructions. "It's just that making the angel fly away is somewhat difficult. No, the hologram can't work once it's away from the base, so of course the hologram can't really fly away. But I can make it turn, and then diminish in size, and to most people, particularly when it's above their heads, the effect will be the same as flying away."

The effect in this case was for me to realize that I couldn't count on help. Not from Jarl, not from Kit, and certainly not from whatever bit of Jarl had gone into the computer.

I tried to call my husband again. *Kit!*

There was no answer. I didn't expect any answer. So why did it feel so lonely, after all?

I didn't want to ask and I didn't want to know. I arranged the machinery again, so I could climb all the way up.

A head, poked out the window, showed me that there were no skittering electronic spiders outside. Instead, there was a gentle grassy slope amid birch trees. At least, I was almost sure that the trees were birch, though I'd like to point out I also didn't spend my teenage years learning about botany. Frankly, now that I thought about it, I'd more or less wasted my youth.

Wriggling out the window was easier than I thought. I scraped myself pretty badly on the steel-wool-like bits clinging to the window frame, but that was good because it distracted me from the fact that I was starving, dying of thirst and very scared.

I put my hands through the window opening ahead of me, so that when only my feet remained in the room, I could use my hands to break my fall.

To the last moment, I expected Jarl to grab my feet, though of course the only reason he would do that would be if he were in thrall of the computer.

He didn't. From what I could gather from his mumbles and complaints, he hadn't even managed to get up from where he was sitting.

Which was just as well, since if he did he might think he could fit through that window. Who knew, after all, what personal image was in his head from wherever it was that the memories were coming from?.

But there was no way that he could fit through the window when I barely did, so I hoped he didn't try it. He might be crazy. He might even be dangerous. But he was still occupying the only body my husband had. And if he got stuck I would have to find a way to get him out, which might get in the way of my other objectives, which were: figure out a way to keep the spiders away from me, then figure out a way to destroy the computer, or at least to disconnect it from its power source. I didn't want to destroy the knowledge in it if I could help it, since Jarl had more or less admitted that not only did it contain his research on how to grow and transplant powerpods with less than the effort needed for the initial powertrees, but that it contained research on nanocytes of the sort he had used in his forlorn bid at immortality.

I didn't know what those nanocytes would be, exactly. It couldn't be exactly the same he had come up with centuries later. But he thought it was enough to give us a clue, since he'd wanted to erase it. Whether it really was enough or if Jarl was overestimating everyone else, as geniuses tended to do, I didn't know. The chance of something being there was enough to keep the computer safe from me. But its active central, its malevolent personality had to be disconnected. Or maybe not malevolent, just bored and playful. And, yeah, totally insane.

I fell gently on the outer side of the window, got up on shaky legs and walked down the slope.

First things first. Before I undertook to fight a super intelligent computer with my bare hands, some improvised knives and some really nifty hammers, I had a date with river water. And then I was going to find the tree that Jarl had shown us when we were here before, the one loaded with ripe apples. And then I was going to figure out how to rescue Jarl from the computer and Kit from Jarl. And then we were going home. Eden was our home, and we were going to recover it.

BREAKING MIRRORS

WHEN MY IMMEDIATE NEEDS WERE SATISFIED, I TOOK the long way around to the entrance room to the compound. The door was open, as Jarl had left it, which was good. While it was possible to disable a genlock with a laser and then do your best to push the door open by brute force, I doubted it was possible to open a genlock with a prehistoric knife and shove my way into the room when the door wouldn't budge an inch.

I still took care not to walk in through the obvious path, but to sidle up to the door from the side, then inch in.

I know that Jarl—and Kit—had said that he'd made it impossible for the peripherals to come into the entrance room. But I also knew that the peripherals—presumably—had built a trap for me, and ended up with me hanging suspended from a tree. So, while it might have been set before Jarl had blocked its access to the entrance room and through it to outside, how

404

did I know that it hadn't set more traps that I hadn't managed to activate before?

Whatever the machine was doing to Kit's body and Jarl's mind, it was clearly a matter of the greatest urgency that it not be allowed to go on.

I slipped into the front room without incident. It was as we'd left it. Still good.

It took me a moment to assess the room. I'd never paid much attention to it beyond the apparatus that Jarl apparently used to spy on people, but now I noticed that there were other features to it, including what looked like a large desk pushed against the far wall. It had probably, at one time, been a reception desk to the resort this had once been. But it had been pushed out of the way and the things on it looked not at all like something you'd find in a resort. There were gems, a gem reader, a little electronic pad of the sort we still used in Eden centuries later. And there were also piles of paper, a litter of pens and pencils, and a container filled with what looked like little metal spikes whose use I could probably divine, if I had enough time and needed to. Right then, though, I didn't have enough time, and I didn't care.

Instead, I rummaged through the drawers, and the little doors in it, looking for anything that might be useful. Jarl was a packrat. This didn't surprise me. Being untidy must be genetic. Kit had a tendency to throw his dirty clothes around the *Cathouse*, instead of vibroing them. I normally ended up cleaning them in self-defense. He also had collected things, though not as much of a litter as Jarl had in these drawers.

There were pens, pencils, three pocket knives, a box full of what looked like very old currency, more gems.

A letter headed *Dear Jarl*, made me pause because it was Father's handwriting, all pointy and jagged, and for a moment I paused. I didn't read the letter. Reading correspondence from a dead man to a man who was supposed to be dead was no part of my interests. But the first line of it was impossible not to read, as it fell under my eyes, *I've taken care of the little matter you assigned me. Quite an interesting...*

Yes, I was curious. No, I didn't have time for this. I pushed the letter aside, and pushed on. There were three injectors; I wondered for what. Jarl, either in the accounts of him or in the admittedly fractured personality I'd met these last couple of months, didn't strike me as a recreational drug user, even if it had been more or less an acceptable social habit in the twenty-first and twenty-second centuries.

The injectors were completely devoid of inscriptions and the colors were not in any scale I knew—and I'd been very well acquainted with the color scale for medicines, from both some casual trade and from my stay in various institutions. I suspected the color coding had changed, and what was contained in these could be anything from antihistamines to heart medicine. Which was too bad. It was entirely possible some of these could come in handy. You never knew, and it was my policy to keep most drugs I came across in this kind of situation.

Perhaps there was a drug there for using in taking crazy computers and crazy dead geniuses from your husband's head. So, fine. It was unlikely. But a girl could hope.

Another letter, this one from Doc Bartolomeu saying, "Sorry the stomach trouble is back, but I've told you it's just tension. You need to give yourself permission to be only human."

I laughed. Clearly even Doc Bartolomeu had illusions about Jarl.

Under that letter, in the second-to-last drawer, was a tool set. And under that were twin burners. They were things of beauty, with carved silver handles and inlaid mahogany stocks.

I'd heard of ornamental burners, but I'd never owned any. Father had a set with gold-plated stocks, but nothing as fancy as this. By the time I'd become interested in weapons, most burners were completely utilitarian, molded in dimatough.

These had a J and an I, entwined, in fancy script, on the stock. I would guess they had been a gift and possibly, judging by the crazy junk my father had accumulated, a diplomatic gift. More to the point they were both fully loaded and charged. And there was a little holster next to them. I strapped it on, above the war hammers.

In the very last drawer there was nothing but piles and piles of paper written in a distinctly feminine handwriting. If I wasn't going to read the letters of a dead man to a man who should be dead, I also wasn't going to read the letters of a dead woman.

No, I had no reason to know she was dead, but look, what else could she be? It had been three hundred years, she wasn't a Mule, and Earth didn't have the rejuv tech that Eden had. If she were now a cyborg, I didn't want to know either.

I closed the drawer slowly and turned to matters of importance.

First, I needed to figure out where that computer

was. And then I needed to figure out how to keep the stupid spiders away.

Fortunately my facility with machines is truly high and not exactly rational.

To explain, I don't just understand machines I've studied. It would be easier to say I understand the way engineers think, so I can usually figure out how to turn on something and how to prod around and discover what it does.

Even then it took me much longer than I wanted to figure out how to work the spy machine. I'd gone on the assumption that if it could spy on people far away and follow various humans in the compound, it might also be able to look into the unoccupied rooms of the compound.

Once I started poking around I figured that this machine had had its beginning before the place had fallen into Jarl's hands. It had been, I thought, a way for the managers of the hotel to look at various areas. Possibly it had even been used for a little blackmail by recording wealthy guests in compromising positions.

More likely, though, it had been used to make sure no one was vandalizing the rooms and setting fire to the beds. I understand most hotels, even in my day, had something of the sort, though the good hotels didn't activate the system unless there was some emergency, like a guest locked in a room and threatening to commit suicide.

Jarl had expanded the machine, added to it and updated it, but he'd never bothered to extirpate the central components or functionality. And why should he have? After all, Jarl then—and probably now—was paranoid, and this machine gave him the opportunity to look into every nook and cranny of his more or less secret domain, right?

It took me a while to figure out how to focus on the rooms of the resort. The top two floors could be ignored. Nothing but dusty rooms with falling-apart furniture in them. It looked still like a place that had once been expensive and opulent, but now it looked like any ruined, abandoned house. The next floor was the same, though one room was in pristine and clean condition, bed turned down, adjacent fresher done up with marble bathtub, a shimmering shower enclosure with swan-shaped faucets, and polished glimmering floors. Probably Jarl's room when he stayed there. I was going to guess the other rooms had been abandoned in his time. Since he had no intention of having guests there, why wouldn't they have been? I wondered if Jarl had clothes there. I didn't like being naked. Or rather, I didn't like being naked when I had to crawl through tight, scratchy places and drag myself on dirty floors. Clothes for protection would be nice, even if Kit's clothes fit me as well as a spacesuit fit a chicken.

But there was no time for that either. The floor below that—the ground floor where I was at the moment—was well kept, mostly storage rooms. It was also filled with spiderlike things, skittering and chattering all over the walls. One room, on the far end, had a broken outer window. And Jarl. Jarl was still trying to rise and still failing. His lips were moving, his eyes looked panicked, and all I could do was hope that my husband was still in there somewhere.

Then I realized he had somehow managed to reach and get hold of one of the pieces of machinery I'd left strewn around. It wasn't one of those that could be easily made into a knife or a hammer, but it was squarish and had a jagged edge. As I looked, he waved his hand around holding it.

For a moment I thought that he was fighting off an invisible enemy. Then I realized that he was aiming it at himself, and though I had no proof, nor could have it, something about the way he swung that thing around gave me the impressions he was trying to cut his own throat. Fortunately, his aim was as good at that as his ability to get up. So far he'd only managed to give himself light scratches on the forehead and nose.

I thought he would end up putting an eye out, and Cat eyes were near impossible to regenerate even if the optical nerve was intact. I was going to have to make haste.

If I could, I'd go back in there and tie him up to keep him from harming himself. But going there by the window was impossible. There was nothing I could climb on to get to it. And going there through the interior would need a disruptor of some sort. It might be quicker to turn off the computer than to get to Kit.

The computer—in a quick scan of downstairs showed—was in the furthest corner. Its door was sealed, except for small holes through which the tinier peripherals entered and left. The bigger ones mounted guard outside the door.

Uh.

I went to the door of the entrance room to examine what Jarl had done to keep the bugs away from this room. It think I expected something arcane, of the sort used to bar anything alive from outside coming into the resort, unless it were gen unlocked.

Turned out, though, that it was just little wave emitters. Electronic disruptors. Of course. If the peripherals talked to the computer it had to be through electronic, wireless communication. Disrupt those and they would be deactivated.

That I knew how to build, and how to make a little more powerful than the ones on the door. A little more powerful because I'd need to deactivate a wide enough area around me not to waste my time fighting them.

So I rummaged through Jarl's desk again, found the components I needed. Judging from their disarray, he'd done much the same. I used the little tool kit to assemble them.

Assembled, they were spheres about the size of marbles, which I attached to my belt.

I'd go by the room I escaped first, I decided. I'd take the burner to soften the seal and see if I could open it. After all, it would take more time to get to the computer, and I wanted to make sure Jarl didn't kill Kit. The man really did have an unacknowledged passion for suicide.

WELCOME TO THE FUN HOUSE

MAYBE I MADE THOSE EMITTERS A LITTLE TOO powerful. The electronic creatures seemed to become immobile in a wide swath ahead of me, and I crunched over their bodies as I walked. But it was one of those cases where it was better to overdo it than to under do it.

The room where Kit and I had been held prisoner did have a door handle from the outside, and a burner run quickly over the edge of the door made the seal soft enough that it opened with a popping sound.

I jumped into the room and in the next second realized my mistake.

Kit convulsed. Or maybe it was Jarl, but to me it was Kit, convulsing in something like an epileptic seizure, his body trying to bend backwards. I ran to him. It had to be the effect of the electronic disruptors, but it was too late to remove them now.

All I could do was examine Kit, determine he was

still breathing. The peripherals that had been infecting him, though, fell all around as I moved him. I suspected it was disrupting those, and not anything done to Kit himself that had caused Kit to pass out and convulse. No. I *hoped* it was.

I laid him down in what looked like a more comfortable position, but I tied his hands with some wire. If he came to and Jarl controlled him, I didn't want him to indulge in a spot of self-murder. Or at least not the sort of self-murder that would also kill Kit's body.

I hated to leave Kit with hands tied, but right now his worst enemy was within.

As soon as he was secured, I ran off, crunching on peripherals as I went.

Approaching the computer room, a burner ray cut through the air above my head, and I barely had time to realize it had been shot by one of the larger peripherals, before they too were "killed" by the disruptors on my belt. The question was, would they kill the computer? I didn't want them to, and I doubted they were strong enough to. They hadn't hurt the communication device in the front room.

But just in case I divested myself of five of them and left only one attached to my belt, as I softened the seal around the door and went into the room.

I was prepared for everything. Or I thought I was. I was prepared for everything but Jarl's voice coming at me from some unknown speaker.

"'Xander?" it said, in a puzzled adult-Jarl voice. "What happened to you?"

While I'm aware I look like the old bastard who called himself my father, I didn't think I looked *that much* like him. All right, so I have Mediterranean features, perhaps all too well endowed with a rather strong nose. I still don't think I can, in any way, qualify as a male.

So I stopped, totally frozen for a moment. It was a moment too long.

With only one gem on my belt, I was a much smaller zone of total destruction. That meant that there were peripherals active around the wall.

Who knew peripherals could throw lassos? I didn't. Which is how the lasso that came down from my head and started pulling shut around my body almost succeeded in capturing me. Almost but not quite because I lost it. I lost it in the peculiar panicky way that made my movements speed up.

Before the noose could tighten around my middle, I'd cut it through with a knife. My other hand wanted to reach for a burner, but I didn't let it. In this situation, a burner was the least useful of weapons. Instead, I reached for a hammer and flung it, without looking, in the direction of the thing holding the lasso. I heard a satisfying crunch, just as another peripheral raised an arm with some sort of a blade in it. That one too, got it with a hammer, and I used a hammer on one that carried something that looked like a lance before it could get close enough to use it.

The damn things learned fast. Another threw a heavy object of some sort at me. I didn't have time to see what it was, only to duck, fast.

The peripherals surrounded me, circling me, end on end, some with weapons, some just circling. There were a lot more of them than of me. I hit out with hammers, but didn't throw them unless I needed to. When I threw a hammer I lost it. I only had a half-dozen left. Same with knives. And there were hundreds of peripherals here. What did I expect? Did I expect this to be easy? What kind of an idiot was I? Don't answer that. I was an optimistic idiot, who was very tired and just wanted her husband back.

Above the peripherals I could barely see the computer. I had to go for the computer. But the way it was going to work, I was going to have to kill the computer, to completely destroy it. I didn't have time to be subtle.

And then I realized that in the center of the computer was a strange-looking component that I'd never seen in any computer before. It was a rounded thing that looked like an aquarium. I thought of Jarl saying that it had some biological components. I supposed other computers did too, at least a lot of them in Eden. But I didn't know of any that had aquariums in them.

I looked at the thing, which was filled with an odd reddish fluid.

And suddenly I realized that Jarl had lied. No. I don't know how I realized it. You could only see glimpses and pieces through the—glass? dimatough?—that the tank was made of, but it was enough to discern what had to be the contours of a human brain.

A human brain, left attached to a machine for countless years, for centuries, with no human contact. I thought of what Simon had said. Strong people might last a year in solitary. Maybe Lucius Keeva had survived for a whole fifteen years. I suspected there was more to that story than we knew. But this brain—this human mind—had survived alone, in solitary confinement, for the last three hundred years.

Cyborgs were by definition insane, even if they were the cyborgs of mice brains. I'd heard that once they'd used a bird brain hooked to a computer and that had been a disaster, though I suspected birds—at least chickens—were peculiarly insane all on their own.

This brain had started out—I was sure—as an impression of Jarl's brain. It would have started out paranoid. It had grown more so, and more scared. All alone, here, creating its evil little peripherals to protect itself.

Did it—as Jarl seemed to want to half the time—wish to die? Or had it forgotten that it was even alive and become wholly machine? Or was it so completely insane that neither of the concepts applied?

I aimed the burner at it. If that aquarium was ceramite or glass it would explode. If it was dima-tough . . . if it was dimatough, I could still heat it enough to kill the brain.

With the hammer in my right hand, I fended off a thrown object, and used my left—my dominant hand—to aim the burner at the aquarium.

I was killing a living human brain. I hesitated for just a moment. An object aimed at my burner-hand passed close by as I pulled my hand back. But then I thought of the poor thing, locked with its own madness all these centuries.

I don't approve of killing people—or anything sentient—because we feel sorry for them or disapprove of their quality of life. You can't tell how much something is enjoying life, after all.

But this brain, left alive, would cost me my life and Kit's life. Kit's life. Self-defense is everyone's ultimate prerogative.

I aimed and the burner ray flew true. A surprised exclamation through the speakers, and then there was nothing, just the sound of boiling as the liquid in the tank bubbled up. And then a high, high pitch whine as every peripheral around me seemed to seize and malfunction at the same time, frozen in place.

I collapsed to my knees before I realized how weak I felt. I heard someone sobbing and I wasn't sure where it came from. I don't know how long I stayed like that, before I became aware that the tears were falling down my cheeks, so it was probably myself who was making those horrible keening and sobbing sounds.

AN ANCIENT DEMON

I DRAGGED MYSELF BACK TO THE ROOM WHERE I'D left Kit/Jarl. Okay, it was stupid of me to just open the door and go in. You'd think with my varied and disreputable career, I'd have realized going unprotected into a room that might house a mortal enemy was a no-no.

In my defense, I didn't think either of the two people who might be occupying my husband's body could count as a enemy. After all, Jarl had tried to kiss me.

So, it was a very specialized form of female stupidity, right? Also, I was tired, I was in pain, and I just wanted to go in and check on Kit, and perhaps sleep before I got on the com to doc, and find out if Doc had discovered how to reverse Kit's condition.

Most of all, at the back of my mind, I just wanted to go back to Kit. I wanted my husband. And, after all, I'd left him with his hands tied, right?

I didn't have time to realize my mistake. I didn't

have time, because I was hit mid-body and dragged, up against the wall, and by the time I recovered the ability to see clearly, I was staring at a maddened face with Cat eyes.

It was my husband's face, but the eyes were not. The eyes were Jarl's, but worse than I'd ever seen Jarl's eyes look—terrible, burning, filled with a single intent purpose.

I thought, dumbly: I'd tied his hands. Then I looked down. Around his wrists, where the cables had been, were cut deep ruts of bleeding flesh. I realized he'd defeated the binds by main force and regardless of pain.

By that time I was struggling to get away from him. From the force with which his hands were grabbing me, they were going to leave bruises. People talk about insane strength, but they don't know the half of it. It felt like he was crushing my shoulders, and a little more strength would break my bones. I had no idea what he wanted. Whatever it was, he wanted it very much. But from the blankness behind the intentness in his eyes, it might be tomato soup, or really good bunny slippers. Mr. Rational was not at home to anyone.

I lifted my feet together and hit him hard in the part of Kit that both of us prized too much. He made a sound like "urk" and let go a little, but not enough, so I brought my legs apart and kicked both of his knees with my heels, as hard as I could.

He stumbled, letting go for a moment. I rolled away from him, and scrambled, hands and feet on the floor, behind the pile of junk in the corner of the room.

He turned, intent, single-minded, reminding me of the scary monster in holos. He said something in what I presume was ancient Swedish. I don't know. I'm not a comparative linguist, and there's a language that's only studied in some universities these days. But he said it in a sickly sweet voice, and I understood *Athena* in it.

My heart lurched downward and my stomach upward, and I realized what he wanted with me might not be to kill me. And trust me, this was by far the scarier alternative.

And yet he was in my husband's body. I didn't want to use the burner on him. Even for someone with good aim, in the heat of battle, it was too easy for me to kill him with the burner. I grabbed a hammer in one hand, a knife in the other, and I decided that damn it, if needed I would inflict damage and maim. Regen on Earth was expensive but doable, and I'd bully Simon into doing it for Kit. But I was not going to risk killing my husband.

The sickly-sweet words trickled from Jarl's mouth again.

"Don't come any nearer," I said, even then aware that he was coming around the pile, and scuttling around, kicking pieces and stuff out of my way, so I could go around it. "Or I will hurt you, even if you are in Kit's body."

He chuckled. I can't explain it, but that chuckle, bouncing off the walls, was one of the scariest things I'd ever heard.

And then he leapt. He might not have full command of Kit's speed, yet, but he had enough, and as he launched himself around the pile of pieces, I couldn't even see him move, till he had me by the shoulders again, bringing me down, full force, hard against the floor.

The pain where my head hit made my vision swim,

but I blinked moisture—blood? Tears? Sweat? Who cared?—away from my eyes, and tried to twist away from him. Something like a low croaking growl was forming at the back of my throat, leaving it scratchy and raw as it tore itself out. "Bastard," formed itself out of those words, and "Let go, bastard."

He didn't let go. The way he was holding me, I couldn't reach him with my weapons. And he looked at me with those intent and yet blank eyes. He said, "We must have children," his voice sounded almost robotic. It made me wonder how much of the computer-bound-alter-ego had transferred itself into Jarl's head just before I killed him. I was afraid it was a lot. "We must have children. Humanity needs us. The Earth needs us."

And damned if he didn't bring his mouth down on mine and try to kiss me. I bit his tongue again. *Hard.* You'd think he'd learn. Apparently not. He made a sound, backed off. I bit his nose. Then his ear, as he tried to back away. He let go of me. I ran behind a columnar robot. The idea, as far as I had an idea was to leave the room, lock the door, then go to the com, get help.

I didn't get a chance to. He used Cat speed again, and next thing I knew the door was closed, and he was coming towards me. There only so much I could take of dodging him around the stupid server bot. He was bleeding on his nose, and I'd torn a good strip off his ear tip, but he was still coming at me.

I shoved the robot towards him, hard, so he had to hold it to prevent being hit with it, and then I took a fast swipe at his shoulder with the knife. I wished I'd spent more of my youth studying anatomy, and not in the recreational way. I wanted to hurt him, but not in a way that would cause him to bleed out before he could be healed.

But even sinking the knife into his shoulder didn't stop him, and I realized in the state he was in, he might not even feel the pain. There's this state that broomers can get into, a mix of adrenaline and, usually, something illegal and potent, such as Oblivium, where nothing will stop them. I'd seen it happen a few times, fortunately not to a member of my own lair.

Usually broomers who did this were suicidal. But instead of killing themselves cleanly and easily, they'd go out and kill and maim till the authorities brought them down. I thought Jarl was trying a version of this. He wanted to die. He probably had wanted to die since he'd realized he was alive—or at least that he was alive, and what he was. But the same training they had inculcated him with to keep him from committing suicide in childhood was probably still active. They'd convinced the poor bastard he didn't have the right to take his own life. That, in fact, he didn't have the right to his own life, keep it or leave it.

And I had to defeat him mentally. No matter how much I hit him, it was not going to stop him. And I risked accidentally killing the only body my husband had.

Did I mention I'm not a crisis psy-tech? Sure, you could probably surmise that. But I had no choice. I hit him, now with two hammers, one in each hand, trying to get his joints, trying to keep him away from me, trying to keep him from using Cat speed, as I danced backwards away from him around the room, and called out, "Sure. Rule the Earth. Because you did such a great job last time?"

He ducked a hammer blow and came for me, and

his accent was heavier than ever as he said, "This time I know better. This time I've seen the histories of both Earth and Eden. I know what to do."

"Bullshit. You still don't know what every human wants. How can you think you can decide for each of four billion humans?"

"Because I'm older," he said. There was an edge of hysteria to his words. "I'm wiser." He jumped for me, and I realized he was about to use Cat speed. I'd probably gone into my speeded-up state myself, which meant he wasn't that much faster than I as he should be. So I had time to clamber up the robot trash pile.

It wasn't a careful plan, more the idea that I weighed less than he did, and I could dance up the pile, while he—

He fell heavily on it, causing an avalanche of robot parts, and I sang out, my voice purposely imbued with mockery. "Wiser? But humans aren't wiser. They're just human. Take for instance how you're trying to force yourself on me, when I'd rather have anyone, anyone at all than you."

This made him hesitate. He looked up, surprised. "But I am your husband."

"Like hell. Kit might still be in there somewhere, but mostly you're an abused overgrown child crossed with a crazy canned cyborg."

"I am not..." he said. He stood very still, and his hands opened and closed.

"Oh, yes, you are," I said, and realized the words were hurting him more than my physical attacks. "You are part the cyborg Jarl left behind, in the control room of this place, and which went mad from lack of human contact. And you are poor fucked-up Jarl who grew up convinced he wasn't a normal, natural human. And it's all stupid. And you've wanted to die since you knew you were alive, and all you have to do is let go, Jarl. All you have to do is let go."

He looked up at me, and for a second—for just a second—his eyes lost their blank look, and were a little boy's eyes, lost in whatever labyrinth his mind had become. Kit's eyes, perhaps, when he was very small and got hurt. Or Jarl's eyes, when he'd been a child for whom no one cared, a child that people thought wasn't even human.

And then he gave something that might be a growl and rushed for me with such speed, that even as he fell atop me, on top of the pile of robot parts, he didn't let go. He wrapped his arms around me, and we came down, in a pile of parts, as he screamed at me, part in unknown languages, part in Glaish. I couldn't understand half of it, but I got the gist of it. I didn't have the right to refuse him. I wasn't a normal, natural human any more than he was. Humans might have individual wills. But we didn't. He'd been raised to believe neither of us was human. It was deep in his psyche at a level that couldn't be reached rationally. It was my duty to have his children and rule the Earth.

"The humans who created you are dead, Jarl," I said, as I grabbed a pointy robot arm and tried hard to shove it between us, point towards him. "They were stupid. They didn't realize that a few chromosomes don't a super man make. You were never a super man, Jarl. You're just human, all too human, and almost as stupid as those who made you."

"But I must," he said. And his voice was the lost voice of a child, in the resonance and timbre of a grown man. "I must do what I was created to do. Why else am I alive?"

"You don't have to justify being alive. And besides, you're not. You're an inconvenient ghost in my husband's body. I want my husband back. Let go, Jarl. Let go of me. Let go of life. Let go of Kit. Let go. Your time is past and your creators are dead."

"But I'm brighter than they were!"

"What does intelligence have to do with it? Very smart people have been artists and poets and inventors, but some of the smartest leaders were the most horrible and responsible for the worst massacres."

"But I have governed."

"But you didn't *do it well*. Your creators were morons and they created a monster. You might have been a good person, Jarl, but no one can create someone to rule other humans, much less to rule people they don't understand. And you don't understand us. You never did, not even three hundred years ago. You weren't raised to understand normal people."

"People trusted me!" he said. "I did the best I could."

"People trusted Caligula too," I said. I'm not a student of history, as Kit is. But I knew enough to know that people had always had great hopes of the young and bright, even when they turned out to be mad Roman emperors.

At the risk of not making any sense, my fight, both words and physical, reminded me of a story Kit had once told me of one of the ancient mythologies, in which a mortal man had wrestled with an angel all night long, before emerging victorious in the morning.

I felt that I too was wrestling with someone older and better informed, although the only thing that Jarl had in common with an angel was that this had once been his nickname. However, the image in my mind was still of a mortal, all too mortal, human, wrestling with a supernatural being.

He didn't try to kiss me again, which was good, and I have no idea what I told him after a certain point. I pushed the robot arm up, trying to make him let go without hurting him permanently.

And I called him names, and pointed out he didn't belong here, and I wanted Kit back. My mouth tasted of sweat and blood, mine or his, I didn't know.

I'd just told him to let go for what seemed like the thousandth time, and sank my teeth into his arm, where I could reach, when he went very still, and seemed to lose force.

For a moment I was afraid I had done enough damage to really hurt him, that he was bleeding out, about to lose consciousness. And then his eyes shifted.

I can't explain it. They just shifted. Like a holo screen, changing between programs. And a voice, sounding hoarse as if from screaming, said, "Thena?" It was Kit's voice, and his next words were odd and yet infinitely reassuring. "Let go of her, Jarl. Let go. We'll take care of you. We'll arrange for you to go . . . wherever you need to go."

Jarl said something long and complex in the ancient language I thought was Swedish, and then Kit chuckled, unmistakably Kit's chuckle. And Kit's voice was speaking. "But it wasn't your fault. It was never your fault. They created you to fulfill an impossible mission. No one else could have done it. No one can save all of humanity, not anyone who is human."

This time, Jarl's voice broke through in Glaish,

surprised, sounding very young. "But I'm not really human. I was designed to be better at governing."

"What? Because of a few different chromosomes? You're still human, and you were raised by humans. You're still mortal and fallible. Let go, Jarl."

And then Jarl let go of me. Tears fell from Kit's eyes, mingling with sweat and blood. Kit straightened. He took a deep breath. "I'm going to get down this pile," he said. "It's easier for you to climb down on your own. You wouldn't want this body reaching for you now."

And I said, "I always want you reaching for me." And I seemed to be crying too, sobs cutting through my words.

He gave me a weird lopsided smile, and offered me his hand, to help me get up. I took it. Together, we picked our way down the pile, and then Kit seemed to lose all ability to stand, and collapsed to his knees.

"Kit," I said. "Did I wound you beyond—"

But he shook his head and took deep breaths, kneeling there on the floor, as his hands slowly went up to cover his face.

Kit was talking softly through the tears, his voice eerily calm given the emotional storm wracking his body. "You are not responsible for those who don't want you to be responsible for them. Ultimately, each man's ability to save himself or destroy himself is his own. You can't take that away from them. Going to hell in your own way is the ultimate right of every human. It is your right, too, Jarl. In this you can be totally human. You can die."

PICKING UP THE PIECES

A VOICE IN MY MIND, A FAMILIAR AND WELL-BELOVED voice, *Thena? Thena, love?* Kit lowered his hands. There was no doubt that it was Kit behind the eyes.

He looked like hell, naked, bruised, scratched. I probably was doing justice to my image as warrior princess, dressed in wire and weapons, with my hair on end and dirt caked on my tear-streaked face. We looked at each other and I started to cry again.

"Don't cry." It was his voice. Yes. His voice sounded a lot like Jarl's, but his had different inflections.

"Jarl . . . did we get rid . . . ?"

Kit shook his head. "No. He's still in control of most of the body. He's just . . . for now at least, he's accepted . . . The components were . . ." Kit's eyes widened. "I think the computer was trying to change the nanocytes. Reprogram them. Make them into it. He's scared, Thena. And he's shocked. But he accepts that he wants to go. He wants to die. Or at least, he wants to die more than he wants to kill me." He gave me a pitiful, lopsided smile. "It might be the best we can hope for."

I told Kit what I'd seen in the computer room and for a moment I thought Kit was going to throw up, but then his eyes softened. "For what it's worth," he said, "I don't think he did it with ill intent."

"How can you do something like that with good intentions?" I asked.

"I've been..." Kit hesitated, "in his mind more than I wanted to. He was so lonely, Thena. Yes, there were the usual cruelties visited on his kind by the institution that brought them up. Yes, there was separation and being convinced he wasn't human. But most of all, Thena, he was so lonely. There was really nothing but responsibility and duty in his life. I think he created that machine, and I think, in a way, he created Zen and me, not just because he wanted to reproduce himself, or because he wanted to live forever." He paused. "I'm not even sure he wanted to live at all; more that he doesn't know how to die. But... more than that, I think he wanted company. He just wanted company, Thena, and his horrible upbringing had left him with no ability to connect to anyone outside himself."

"Not true. He had Doc and my... and Sinistra. You, yourself, said that they loved each other like brothers."

"Oh, yes. I think Jarl did love them like an older brother. Like an older brother left in charge of younger siblings. Yes, he loved them, and yes, they mitigated his solitude somewhat. But Thena, they were—they were yet more responsibility. That computer and, I believe, probably making me, too, was his attempt to create a friend he wouldn't have to protect. An equal. Thena, he was like a lonely child with imaginary friends."

Men are much softer and more sentimental than women. Don't let anyone tell you differently. This fact is masked by the female ability to cry easily and by our approved emotional displays. But it doesn't mean men are less emotional for being more controlled. On the contrary.

In every couple I know, if presented with a hard case where death and life hang on a decision, she'll vote for death and he for life. He will see some redeeming quality in the most unreformed bastard. She will see the bastard and want him dead.

I think this is because women, evolutionarily, were in charge of protecting the young. We have less room to allow dangerous people to live.

In this case, I think Kit understood Jarl a little better too. I didn't really care. I just wanted Jarl gone. Whatever had happened with the nanocytes had given Kit a chance to look out through the eyes on his body and to talk to me, but Jarl was still there, and his body had curled in a tight fetal position.

Right. I touched his shoulder, gently. One thing Kit was right on, at least; if Jarl was catatonic, I didn't think that being harsh with him would help.

"Jarl," I said, "you must stand. We must get you somewhere where you can bathe, and we must talk. We have to talk. This can't go on..."

Kit shook his head and it was Jarl who spoke. "You killed it?"

"Yes," I said, and braced.

He let out a breath, with every impression of

having held it too long. "Thank you. It was . . ." He shook his head.

Kit's voice came again, "We got . . . all its memories. It was . . . it had gone quite insane."

"Yes," I said. "I suspected as much. Solitary confinement for three hundred years and not being able to die, and having to defend itself as its main imperative."

"Yes." The voice was harsh and raspy and I didn't know if it was Kit or Jarl, and I realized that whoever it was would be severely dehydrated and half-dead of starvation.

"You said there were provisions here," I said. "You need food and water. I'll get you some."

He looked at me, momentarily unfocused, and I got the impression he was talking to himself inside his head, then Kit spoke, "Down the corridor, first door on the right. Should be filled with those ready-made meals that heat themselves. They're warranted for half a millennium. This is where we learn if they're right . . ."

Thank all the gods they were. The dinners, picked up blindly in the growing darkness and self-heated, turned out to be steak and chicken stewed with vegetables and some undefined starch. I'm sure they were as nasty and tasteless as that sort of cookery normally is, but to me it tasted like ambrosia, whatever that is. This was very good.

Jarl managed to use his hands enough to eat and drink. But it had to be one of the weirdest things I'd ever seen. Or heard. It was obvious from the way he was eating that Jarl might control everything from the neck down, but Kit controlled everything from the neck up.

The hand would reach up, and the mouth would intercept the food on the fork, and somehow you knew two different people were involved. He drank more than he ate, a lot of water from convenient dispensers with straws you could suck through.

The strangest thing was that between bites and sips Kit was talking. It was clear he was arguing with Jarl, but Jarl's voice must have been in his head only, because I couldn't hear it. It was like listening to one end of a conversation.

I fell asleep. In the night, I half woke, with Kit next to me. I listened to his breathing. I put out a hand and touched him between his shoulder blades, and he mind-touched me, with an impression of warmth, but he wasn't awake enough for there to be words in the feeling.

Then suddenly, there were words again, Jarl's voice, "Perhaps it would be better, then, to die?" he said. "Just die? Both of them were a misconceived idea, a lost cause. Perhaps resting—"

Kit's voice didn't answer and I woke fully, in a panic, not even sure who Jarl meant by both—himself and Kit? Or himself and me? I couldn't let him. I stood up. He stood there, facing me, and had somehow got hold of one of my knives. There was an odd look in his eyes.

"No," I said. I could have kicked him, but in this case, I didn't know whom it would disturb. "No, Jarl. Perhaps it's your time. I wish it weren't. I will . . . mourn you. Kit will mourn you more, I think. But I think you have run your course, and perhaps it would be impossible to make you sane and whole, even if there were a brain and a body you could inhabit. But Kit isn't you. And I'm not Alexander Milton Sinistra."

He looked at me a long moment, as though he didn't fully understand, then sighed. "Perhaps," he said, "there is indeed something else, hereafter? Perhaps we can start anew, somehow? . . . Not, not in this body or in this life."

"I don't know," I said. "I don't know what to tell you. No one knows. This is the one thing every human must always face alone. Some of us trust prophets and soothsayers and traditions, but in the end, it's one thing everyone must do alone."

Something like the shadow of a smile crossed his lips. "You know," he said, "I always wanted to be wholly normal in something." He raised an eyebrow. "I think I can extract enough information from my poor dead cyborg to make the antidote to these nessies. Would you like to come and observe?"

I would. He might be broken, he might be defeated, but I still wouldn't trust him. Not with Kit's life. I stayed awake through the night, while he hooked things and transferred data and, finally, build an ersatz assembler for something. He put them in an inhaler and inhaled. "These nanocytes will stop the others," Jarl's voice said, "until we can . . . restore Christopher." And of course, I had no way of knowing they were the real thing, but I trusted. He had the look of a man who had run his course. He wouldn't want to start it all again.

"Perhaps 'Xander is there somewhere, and we'll be young again. Perhaps this time we will be brothers and he will be sane?" He looked at me, and must have found no encouragement in my eyes. "No? Well . . . it's a lovely dream in any case."

He used the com and called Doctor Bartolomeu. I was almost sure it was all Jarl, because Kit didn't have the knowledge to do this, but Doc called him Christopher. Perhaps it was wishful thinking. He sent back the template he'd done of Kit's brain after Kit's injury, and Jarl worked on the parts of the computer he could get to function. "He's modifying the model," Kit told me, with a hint of admiration in his voice, "to repair the hole and the damage."

"You trust him?"

"Strangely, yes. Having decided once to...go, though he's not sure what that means, he'll deal straight with me. Thena, you said you thought he liked me too, and I know it is so. He feels about me as though I were his son. That's part of it. You see, he always wanted to have children. Odd, since the very concept should have been alien to him. He grew up knowing he couldn't do so. But he...liked watching children grow up, the children of his servants and retainers, and he always wanted children of his own. I think it is that desire that has given him the strength to allow me to return my brain to what it was. He can't convince himself to sacrifice me to his continued life."

"That's not what he sounded like," I said.

"Don't you see? He thought he had to do it. He thought it was his duty. And even so, he was still trying to get your approval for what he was doing, because it still felt wrong to him."

And then he did more work, and at long last, he built another inhaler, and inhaled that too. "And this," he told me, with a sad smile, "will bring your husband back."

And then somehow I did fall asleep there, with my back against the wall, in the room littered with dead peripherals. I woke up in the morning, and Kit was standing nearby, smiling at me.

IN BETWEEN

"DO YOU HAVE YOUR LENSES IN?" I ASKED, ALARMED because there was way too much light in the room.

"Yes, Mommy," he said, and made a face. I sat up, in panic. Were we back to that? Had he gone around the twist again, confusing his childhood with Jarl's and visiting both in turn.

He shook his head. "No, no, Thena. I was being a brat. Yes, I have my lenses in. They were in Jarl's room, on the bed. Everything that was taken from us, including our clothes, all the burners. I suppose you have your broomer suit somewhere outside?"

"I left it in a tree. I emptied and rinsed the compartment, so it's ready to wear."

That he didn't ask me which compartment, when he knew about as much about brooming as I knew about water mining, probably meant he was preoccupied. He was also, I realized, clean, shaved and wearing a dark blue suit that appeared to be made of natural silk.

435

He grinned at me. He had bandaged himself, and done something to the wounds on his face so they were not as obvious. "If you get yourself upstairs and wash, I'll vibro your suit."

"Jarl?"

"What?" he asked surprised. "He's still here, but—"

"Joking. Kit would never offer to vibro anything."

He gave me a little smile and extended his hand to help me up. "Well," he said, "extraordinary circumstances. I'll explain to you what I've been doing, while you bathe." Then he looked fully at me, as I stood up. "What a picture," he said. "I wish I could record it, to scare the people at home."

I made a face at him, but it wasn't until I was in Jarl's bathroom, while Kit set the bathtub to fill itself, and sprinkled in bath bubbles, that I took a look at myself on a full-length mirror and realized what he meant: my hair, never the most ruly mane of curls in the universe, was now a tangled mess, which had somehow gotten smeared with what I hoped was blood. I didn't know whose blood, though I had a cut in my scalp—I suspected from Jarl's cold-cocking me—and scalp wounds bleed a lot. I was wearing sheaths on wire bands around my arms, my middle and my legs, and most of them contained either a knife or a hammer, save for the fancy holster attached to my waist and sporting two beautiful burners.

Am I paranoid? I don't know. Daddy Dearest was, and apparently some of it is genetic. Kit might be drawing my bath and setting towels at the ready, and he was clearly in control of at least some of him. But he, himself, had told me that he was not in control of the whole body, or at least that Jarl was still there. Yes,

Kit and I might have defeated the angel in night-long combat, but angels are stubborn and ancient creatures and, in this case, loopier than a spiral orbit. Also, Jarl had all the emotional maturity of a twelve year old.

As I divested myself of weapons, I hid them at a corner, behind a potted plant, and made damn sure that Kit couldn't see me, either directly or through the mirrors.

Kit knew I was paranoid, too. Probably because he, himself, had inherited a little bit of the tendencies, despite his much better upbringing. He didn't try to stand by the bathtub, where I'd be forever ready to react to his attempt to pull me under. Not that he made any such attempt, of course, but that's the problem with paranoia. You anticipate both likely threats and unlikely ones.

There was a long stretch of counter and vanities running around under more mirrors, facing the tub. He sat on top of the counter, while I scrubbed and rinsed and scrubbed again, until most of my curls were clean, and my skin was its natural somewhat olive color, and the water in the tub was a dingy grey. Then, while I refilled the tub, he said, "Jarl has agreed that . . . that it's my body and I should have it. I have gems with . . . well . . . with everything he knew about how to reseed the powertrees. He had done the work on nanocytes then, you know. It's what he used on the computer brain, while it was growing. I think that's what he meant when he talked to Doc about the alpha pattern."

I shuddered. "Did he grow the brain in an infant?"

"No, he grew it independently. I think he would have done just that in Eden, when he found out he was ill and got the brain to transplant into his body,

if he'd been fully himself, but he wasn't, and then...
well...I think the lure of being young again and being
able to hide the fact that he was a Mule..."

He was quiet a long time, his face grave. "Don't judge
him too harshly. He was so...lonely and...he still is..."

I nodded. "I know," I said. "I caught a glimpse of
it yesterday. He tried to lift a burden that was too
heavy for any human being, a burden that was too
heavy for a supernatural being even, had there ever
been one. And he refused to bend under it." I took
a deep breath, plunged into the now-clean water,
emerged perfectly rinsed, and said, "Don't take this
the wrong way, but he was...is so much like you.
Neither of you knows your limits. And both of you
feel responsible for things you can't control."

In the past, when I'd told Kit things like this,
he'd argued, but now he just frowned and said, "I'm
sorry. I'll try not to..." I wondered how much he had
changed, and how much things were going to change
between us. It didn't matter, of course. When you
marry someone, or at least when you marry someone
for life, which Kit and I had done, you knew they were
going to change. You rather hoped so, since someone
who stayed in a stage of arrested development all his
life was going to be a disappointment as a husband.

I just wanted my husband back, fully back. I'd deal
with any modifications to the original model as they
revealed themselves.

"I'm going to miss him," Kit said.

"I'm not," I said.

The rueful smile that answered me had a bit of
Jarl in him, and it was Jarl's voice that said, with
something like amusement, "I know."

I looked at Kit for a moment, and wondered if Jarl would ever be fully gone.

"I will leave you both alone, in almost no time," he said, as though reading my mind. "I chose to leave behind some of my knowledge. Kit...allowed me. As few memories as possible to go with it, because my memories are mine, and Kit says that dead men don't owe anyone anything. But as much knowledge as I could leave behind of biology and...and other subjects as I could, I did. Perhaps my life won't have been in vain. I think Eden could use the knowledge, but I don't want to be around to dispense it. We will need to rest for a few hours. I created these nanocytes so they operate very fast, unlike the others which were supposed to operate over months or years. We should be ready to travel tonight."

I didn't like the way he kept saying "we" but then he smiled and said, "Well, Kit will need to rest. I'm sure you won't want to."

Which of course, was right. I stayed awake, while Kit slept. Through the window of the bedroom, I could see what looked like the sun setting in the west. Since this compound was as much underground as all of Eden, it had to be a holo. But it was a beautiful holo, all gold and red tones against the green trees. I sat there and watched it, conscious of Kit on the bed.

Mostly he slept quietly. Once or twice he shuddered, a whole body-long shudder. And, as the shadows of the early evening crept into the room, purple and green and cool, he convulsed once, as badly as he had when the electrical disruption device touched the peripherals on his skull.

I rushed to his side, panicked, but his body had

already relaxed. He whispered, "'Xander! There you are." The whisper was too low to tell which of them had said it. And for just a second it seemed like he'd stop breathing. Then he sighed and his body relaxed completely, and he turned, and the position he took was the way Kit normally slept—on his side, with his right hand under his cheek. And his breathing became regular again.

And I became aware that I had resumed breathing, too.

THE BOOMERANG RETURNS

AND VERY LONESOME HEROS

I WOKE UP IN AN EMPTY BED. THE WINDOW WAS open and sun streamed in, warming my back. There was a smell of flowers in the air, and the birds were singing. But I glared at the pillow with the indentation of Kit's head and got up.

I'd fallen asleep wearing his suit, but it looked better than what I'd worn before. A step into the bathroom reassured me. The clothes Kit had worn the day before were in a pile not three steps from the vibro machine, which was exactly what my husband always did with his dirty clothes.

I washed my face and cleaned my teeth. The window in the bathroom too was wide open, letting in a breeze.

As I turned towards the bedroom again, I heard a sound of steps and glass clinking. I was almost a hundred percent sure that this would be Kit, but note I said almost. I went to the corner where I'd hidden the burners in their holster and I strapped them on.

Then I edged around the door to the bedroom, until I could see Kit. He had a tray in his hand, with what looked like real plates and glasses and silverware and a platter of something.

As I edged out of the bathroom and into view— somewhat reassured, but still wary—he looked up and smiled at me. "I found the butler's pantry and some real eating utensils. They were surprisingly clean. I'm afraid the food is just a couple of the ready-to-eat breakfasts, but I'm hoping their being served in style will make them taste better."

It did taste better, though I doubted it was the plates. I think it was the open windows, the breeze coming in, and the certainty that Kit was back.

He talked as he ate, in between bites. "Doc and Zen and a few of your friends are on their way here."

I stopped chewing on scrambled eggs. "Here?"

"Yeah. I don't fully understand their reasons, but Doc and Zen vouch for them, so I'll have to assume there are reasons. I mean, Doc and Zen need to come, anyway, so we can get back to Circum." He chewed at his lip. A bad habit of his when he was in deep thought. "The fact remains that we have to figure out a ship to go to Eden in. You and Zen will have to retrofit one of these air-to-spaces I think, for greater power and...some amenities. Like bathrooms. We could use someone to guard our back up there, of course, while you do that. One thing is a quick in and out during the night-period of Circum. Another and quite different sitting around and possibly stealing parts and tools. I suppose it could be that all they're coming along for is to guard us while we arrange to leave. But somehow that's not the impression I got."

He'd got the right impression. After we were done eating, and while Kit was doing a very thorough search of Jarl's belongings to see if there was anything that might help us—as he told me, as he finished the search who else would be Jarl's heir but Kit?—the com from outside signaled that someone was at the door waiting to be let in.

There were three of them, not counting Doc and Zen. And one was a stranger, though perhaps it would be an exaggeration to say that he was a complete stranger.

We'll begin with the fact that they were all dressed in one-piece black suits with an odd sheen. I knew these, if Kit didn't. There was such a thing as full head to toe dimatough armor, shining and hard, with view plate and scales that covered the whole body, giving the impression of alien beings. Dimatough armor was near-impenetrable by any means, including targeted laser. You could set a fire underneath the man and cook him in his own shell, but you could not get through the armor.

This meant, of course, that they were very safe— at least if you could avoid having a fire built under you—but they were also heavy, cumbersome and made the wearer clumsy. To outfit an entire army in them would be the equivalent of putting an entire army in tanks. Sure, the enemy would need some highly targeted explosives to circumvent that. On the other hand, your maneuverability and your ability to intercept insurgents and attackers who might run through smaller spaces was zero.

So, most armies on Earth had struck a compromise. These black suits were woven through with dimatough thread, the way cloth had been made of glass thread in the past, though I understood the process of extruding the thread was somewhat more difficult. They were worn by infantry, commandos, and guerillas.

Looking at Doc, who wore the military outfit with the sheepish expression of a gnome who knows he's out of place, I hoped these five idiots had the good sense to wear a cotton singlet and tights under it. I'd worn the thing before. I know how it's advertised. Impenetrable as dimatough, soft as wool. It's not true. Unless they meant wool from sheep bioed to be covered with steel wool.

And fine, I didn't know if they were all idiots, but I knew that Simon, who winked broadly at me, and Nat, who had a large size burner—what we called a ship-killer—on his back, with a bandolier strap crossing his chest, and who gave me just the edge of a smile around one of his eternal cigarettes, were very specialized type of idiots. The type that requires an extremely high IQ and above-normal competency. I suspected Zen and Doc fit that category too. And as for the stranger...

The stranger gave me a turn in my stomach, the sort of funny flip-flop you feel when the eyes see something the mind simply cannot process. Because he looked like Max. Max, aged about twenty years, with wrinkles on the edge of his eyes, but Max nonetheless. He had Max's features and Max's golden-blond hair, his broad shoulders and rather beefy build; not fat, but not exactly spare, either. And he was tall, as Max had been, and moved with the same incongruous grace.

The resemblance was striking enough to make me stop breathing for a minute, but it stopped with those externals. Yeah, his eyes were dark blue, so dark they looked black unless you paid attention, just like Max's eyes had been. But the unholy glint in them was not Max's.

Don't get me wrong. Max was my friend, and I would mourn his miserable, unneeded death the rest of my life. He did not deserve what happened to him, and he was in no way stupid or too trusting.

But he was, at the time of his death, nineteen, blond, good-looking and pampered. His father—to call him that—had never pursued the regime of terror my father or others had engaged in. Perhaps this was because Max engaged in a lot less open rebellion. Or perhaps it was because he had a different approach—spying on and guarding, as opposed to terrifying, the current custodian of his future body into behaving. Max had been a broomer, as the rest of us had, but he never seemed to care much for the greater high jinks of broomer life. Not for him robbing drug transports, or even using drugs or engaging in indiscriminate sex.

Max had been Nat's lover since the two of them had discovered sex, I think, and if they ever, separately or jointly, took anyone else to bed, I'd never heard even the barest rumor of it. Now, while absence of proof is not proof of abstinence, if you knew broomers and their lifestyle as I did, you'd know that there would be absolutely no chance an indiscretion wouldn't come to my ears.

But they were both smart enough to realize it shouldn't come to the ears of Good Man Dante Keeva. Sometimes I thought the only reason they were both broomers was so they could be openly together without worrying.

Still, even with the secrecy, Max had never known strife, nor even disappointment in love. He was an open, innocent and rather self-assured member of the upper class of Earth, the class I'd been raised in.

This creature whose body resembled Max's point by point was a very different proposition. The blond hair that Max wore at most two inches long was now middle-of-the-back long and roughly pulled back into a pony tail. His face might have the same features as Max's and he must use beard inhibitor cream as religiously as Max did. But across the bridge of the stranger's nose, from the bottom of his left eye, and trending towards the right edge of his mouth was a scar. It was obviously an old scar and just obviously he'd done what he could to minimize it. But it showed as a livid thin pink line. I had no idea what had caused it. A blade following that trajectory would have bounced off the bridge of his nose, and a laser beam would have sliced through the bridge of his nose. His dark, dark blue eyes looked barely controlled and feral.

And while he might have been in solitary confinement for fifteen years, the cell had to have been large enough to allow him to exercise, because in that particular suit there was no doubt that he was muscle layered on muscle from his shoulders to the heavy boots that started just below his knees.

I caught myself thinking *sex on two legs* and blushed, both of which were stupid thoughts because if he was like Max, his interest in women would be at best academic. And I was entitled to think whatever I wanted of him. But it didn't help that I was aware of Nat looking at me with a sardonic and appreciative gleam in his eye, even as I examined the stranger.

Just as I felt the blush heat my cheeks, the stranger put a huge hand forward, and engulfed the one that I put forward without noticing what I was doing. "Lucius Dante Maximilian Keeva," he said, with a grin that was partly disarming and partly as feral as the glint in his eyes. "I hear you were one of my little brother's friends, and one of his avengers. Thank you."

Nat mumbled something that sounded like, "Yeah, Thena is a right one."

And then Kit was being similarly greeted by the stranger, who answered Kit's grave "Good Man Keeva" with "Call me Lucius."

We took them down the garden path to the compound.

"I don't understand why you insisted on coming with Zen and Doc," I told Simon, but meaning to include Lucius and Nat. "Is it so you can guard us while we retrofit a ship to take us to Eden?"

"Partly," Nat said, then lit a cigarette from the end of the one he'd just finished.

Simon and Zen traded a look, and Simon sighed. "You could say," he said, "that our interests coincide with yours, in that we...have business in Circum."

"Business?" Kit said.

This time it was Doc who answered. "I'm given to understand that there is a great deal of problems with...the rebellion on Earth. The rebels—on whose side I understand your friends are—have access to communications, but not to the level they can get if they take over Circum. You see, most communication satellites can be controlled from Circum. There are also devices to disable peer-to-peer electronic communications somewhere in Circum—safe, they think, from mutiny and tampering."

"That's part of it," Lucius rumbled. "There's also the powerpods. If you control energy—as your friends from Eden having been telling us—you control the life of an industrial society."

"Of course, we just want to control it so we can set it free," Nat said, but it was too late for me not to feel a twinge of uneasiness.

"Are you sure about this rebellion of yours?" I said, falling back to talk with Nat. The others discussed technical aspects of the trip; Kit explained he'd need help taking some of the stored rations to the air-to-space, since we'd need to eat while traveling to Eden, and our rations were gone with everything else. "I'll remind you that more people have taken power to free others and then——"

He grinned and gave me a sideways look, and I got a truly disquieting feeling that this Nat was almost as different from the Nat I knew as Lucius was from Max.

Nat had always been tightly wound. He came from one of the families that hereditarily served the Good Men. I understood his father was the general manager of Keeva properties, i.e. the person who did all the day-to-day work of directing Keeva farming, manufacturing, and investment operations. He probably also gave instructions to the housekeeper and set menus. At least most general managers did all that, sometimes at a remove, by directing an underling to do it.

Nat was the oldest of seven children and had been trained to follow in his father's footsteps. For most of the time I'd known him, he could easily have passed for the perfect man for that job—a devoted and detail-inclined accountant, with a penchant for following through on everything. He was tall but slim, and though the suit he now wore revealed he was a lot more muscular than I'd have expected, his normal clothes just made him look neat and unremarkable. With emphasis on neat. His hair was pale blond, straight, cut so that every strand fell in place. It was never disarranged. His broomer suit managed to look pressed and neat, even right after our lair had engaged in a mid-air territory-dispute.

In fact, he'd been entirely unremarkable but for three clues which had managed to give away to me, and probably half the world, that Nat was in fact tightly wound. And like all tightly wound springs, he had a lot of kinetic energy just waiting to be released. I'd never been sure where that energy came from, but it revealed itself in the resentful gleam in his almost-black eyes, the always-too-controlled movements, and his chain-smoking, a habit that was fashionable among certain broomers, but certainly not most of them.

Now he looked . . . different. The movements were no longer tightly controlled. They were instead sudden, almost jerky. But the greatest difference was in his eyes, which had gone from resentfully sardonic to amusedly sardonic. He turned those on me now and took a deep puff of his cigarette, before exhaling. "Oh, Thena. Do we expect the revolution to last forever? No. We don't. It never does, does it?"

I blinked at him. "But—No. But what I mean is, if you're going to use power to hold the world hostage . . . I mean . . ."

He inhaled and then exhaled. "What do you think

the Good Men do with the powerpods now? The easy path to power in any society is to control energy supplies." He frowned a little. "We'll have to come up with a way to make that not a monopoly, and perhaps start other forms of energy collection too. I'll have to talk to Lucius about it and get it on the agenda."

"You trust him that much?"

"Uh," he said. Then paused. "Well, yes, and no. I trust him, because he has a deep dislike of authority, even his own. Perhaps particularly his own. I know, all humans are corruptible by power, but I'm not sure Lucius is human." He grinned, and I realized it was a real grin, not the sort of grin that I'd seen from him before. "But I'm not trusting in Lucius alone. Yeah, he sparked the rebellion, but it has been taken up by the vast underground that has been around for three hundred or more years. And I've been a member of that underground a long time." He opened his hands in a gesture of good faith which would have been—probably—more impressive if he'd not been holding a cigarette between the index and ring fingers of his right hand. "You see, I was born into a family of secret Usaians. I've been a member of the Sons of Liberty since I was sixteen."

"I see," I said. It was an automatic response. I was raised in no religion in particular. Daddy Dearest saw his god every morning in the shaving mirror. But the Usaians were one of the forbidden religions, one whose members faced varying but always strict penalties on most of the Earth. I knew very little about their beliefs, except that they believed in a war goddess and a benevolent god-father, and that they believed their god's will could be divined by the will of the people.

The other things they believed were even less rational. Like . . . that all men were born equal and endowed with rights by their creator. Or that those rights included life, liberty, and the pursuit of happiness.

They also believed—or at least I'd heard so—that their benevolent god, who had been the founder of the embodiment of their ideals when they'd been a nation taking up a significant portion of North America, would come back to lead them back to a newly founded Usa. Their prayers—I'd heard—often finished with a plea for the return of the George, which was how they referred to the mythical George Washington. I knew because I'd seen it, that they often wore jewelry and clothes embossed with the image of a cherry tree, which was said to be sacred to the George. In their abodes they often tacked a piece of cloth imprinted with stars and stripes.

I knew the real historical George Washington from Eden texts, but I wasn't sure how he meshed with Usaian theology.

Now Nat pulled back at his sleeve, to reveal a broad silver bracelet with the image of a cherry tree with an ax leaning against it, and said, "As for Lucius, he saved my life, and we are . . ." He shrugged. "But for now, I think I can tell you that half of my co-religionaires think he's the George."

"And is he?"

Nat looked amused and shrugged. "I don't know. If he is, the great architect has a hell of a sense of humor. For now all you need to know—unless you want to stay and fight for the freedom of the people of the Earth—is that both Simon and I trust him to help bring down the Good Men. After that . . . I'll have to see. But to even have half a chance of bringing down the Good Men"—he gave me a rueful smile—"or even to be allowed to live in peace ourselves, we need your help getting to Circum and taking it over."

"What? All three of you?"

"Four. I understand Zen is helping. Also, how much resistance do you expect a bunch of scientists and harvesters to put up?"

At that moment we reached the compound, and Kit organized us to carry supplies to the air-to-space. All the while, he and Doc were discussing what had been in the gems that Jarl stored here, gems my husband had, apparently, looked at this morning and interpreted in the light of the knowledge he had retained from Jarl.

He was explaining that while powerpods could be seeded and we should do so, it would take a very long time and enormous amounts of organic material to do so. And while Eden could mine some of it from nearby asteroids and the Thules could ship enough water, in time—it would take very long to grow enough to support Eden on limited feeding and watering.

Transplanting a branch, on the other hand, would work much better, but it meant that we'd still have a generation of growth before the powerpods could supply Eden and the colonies.

Doc nodded sagely after a while. "I never thought it would be an immediate solution. But just knowing it will be available changes the game. Of course, we still need to get the Castaneda cabal out of power and to resume power runs."

Kit grinned. "I guess Athena and I had best not bioengineer our children as Cats and Navs. The work we've done now will render them unemployed."

But Doc only gave him a jaundiced look. "I don't think that's possible, Christopher. I think we can grow our own powerpods, but as long as Earth has an excess of powerpods, relatively unguarded or even only slightly guarded, they will be one of our sources of energy. It is good to have diverse sources."

Kit looked like he would argue, but then shrugged and headed for the air-to space carrying the final load of provisions. In addition to what we would need for the trip to Eden, we were carrying enough food to sustain Zen and me while we worked on the ship to take us to Eden.

And then Kit made a last trip for his violin.

I DIDN'T SEE NOTHING

THEY DROPPED US AROUND THE UNUSED SIDE OF Circum, Zen and I. There had been a tense moment as the air-to-space pulled into the airlock space, and the door opened and Doc said, "Zen and Thena, good luck. We'll let you know how we fare," where Zen had put her hands on her hips and looked at Simon, who looked sheepish and had opened his mouth as though to apologize.

But he never got a word out, because Lucius intervened. He sounded authoritative, but also somewhat amused as he said, "Zen. Your expertise is needed to see to the ship transformation. Everyone here is more expendable than you or Thena."

"Kit isn't," I said, putting my hands on my hips in turn. "Kit isn't expendable. He has to get back to Eden. If for nothing else, because he has the knowledge he got... Because he understands Jarl's writings."

This got me a very curious look from Zen and an

even more curious one from Simon, but it was Kit who spoke. "Now, Thena, they need my ability to move fast. I undertake to promise you I won't get killed."

"Oh, right," I said, dismissively. "Because you're so good at that."

This brought a burble of laugh to the back of his throat, followed by, "Well...yes. I'm still breathing. So far, so good."

I really wished we were in the exercise room aboard the *Cathouse*, where I could kick him in the ankles for that comment. "So far, so good only because I help."

"I know. Cunning of me, isn't it?"

You can't argue with certain men. Fine, you can argue with most men. What you can't do is make most of those see reason, no matter how hard you try.

"In what time, and how did Kit get briefed on what they're going to do and elect to go with them?" I asked. "We've been with them the whole time. How could they do that? And what is the reasoning behind it? Men have another quarter pound of flesh in a curious place, therefore they're better suited to take Circum Terra, while the little women remain quiet and well behaved?"

Zen was frowning. She had been frowning the whole time, and glaring too. Now she turned that glare on me, and it was amazing how much her eyes looked like Kit's even though his were bioed to act like Cat eyes. "I don't think it's gender. They want to preserve the people with mechanical ability, which will be needed for the ship and also—and Kit will be useful in any fight. They're simply not equipped for his level of speed here, so if we need to make a demonstration of force... You must admit it will be better than allowing Nat to let loose with that damned ship-killer."

You also can't reason with women, I decided. Just when you're furious and want a little cozy confirmation for your fury they will go and become all stupidly rational on you. I muttered this followed by, "Humans. The whole breed!"

And Zen laughed suddenly. "Yeah, all of us."

I thought of Jarl and suddenly choked on words I could never fully say and an understanding I could never fully explain. "It's still better than thinking you're not human. Or that you should be perfect."

Zen seemed to catch something in my expression because she said, "I'm sorry. Was it that bad? Jarl?"

I nodded, then shook my head, then shrugged. "I don't know. It's . . . I'm coming to terms with the fact that I can hate someone but still love him a little at the same time."

She gave me a curious head-tilted look. "You should meet my adoptive—Now, let's look at these ships and see what we can do, shall we? I think turning an air-to-space into an Eden ship is going to be near impossible."

"Uh? Why? They're well-insulated and spacious and—"

"Yes," Zen said, "and that's the problem. They're much heavier than they need to be, with all that insulation weighing them down. And, let's face it, unless we mean to go down through the atmosphere into Earth, it is thoroughly unnecessary. Second, while they have a little space for drinks, they don't have any water aboard, or water-recycling facilities. And third, they don't have a large enough space for a cargo hold to keep the clipping of the powertrees in vacuum and stable, with enough insulation around it to keep the compartment radiation-free."

"Oh. Then what are we supposed to do?"

"One solution," she said, "the one we can be sure of, is to take one of the largest of the harvesters and retrofit it, using some stuff an from air-to-space-to-space. But we can't get to the harvester until we have . . . Until they take over Circum."

"Do you mean they just dropped us off here so that they would not risk us in the fighting?"

"Pretty much," she said, and grinned and looked ridiculously happy. Much, much happier than she had on the trip out. As soon as I got her aboard the Eden ship, she was going to sit down and give me every detail of what had happened to her on Earth. Perhaps Simon had been wrong and Mr. Sex-on-two-legs Lucius was interested in women after all.

But she wasn't exactly telling me the truth. Or at least not the whole truth, because she went on, "The problem with that solution is that it will take months to retrofit, and we'll have to scrub vast portions of it to make it habitable, because previously they've been used to store powerpods. I'd prefer not to do that, and Doc says in this portion of Circum there should be some . . . well . . . they were habitats. Kind of like campers in space, used by workmen while building the *Je Reviens*. They'll have bathrooms and water- and air-recycling systems. What they don't have is a real propulsion or steering system and certainly not one that uses antigrav the way ours does, since at the time antigrav was a very new technology on Earth. He says they used it on the *Je Reviens*, but they weren't sure enough of it to apply it in finer scale."

"And installing those would be much quicker than installing everything else."

"Exactly," Zen said. "Particularly since we had so much practice in the *Hopper*, assembling and reassembling the steering system."

"I could do it in my sleep," I said with feeling. And I meant it, which was good, because I practically would need to.

Have you ever read the diary of some soldier in some great war, say the war between the land states and the seacities? I don't mean the diaries that have been handed over to some narrator who pretties them up and makes them relevant, making sure to introduce the right number of references to famous people, places and events. I'm talking about the day-to-day accounts of foot soldiers involved in wars.

I had, because there were a fair number in my father's now lost library, and eventually I read practically everything. And I'd found that the general tenor of these diaries was just an endless description of long marches and hardships, of sore feet, of insufficient bathing facilities, incompetent officers and commanders, of daily humiliations and discomforts. Even the action these people had seen often managed to come across as an incidental footnote to the real job of enduring a long slog in uncomfortable conditions. You'd get a description of a great battle, but it turned out the foot soldier had only seen a corner of it and was particularly concerned with the fact that his ship had broken down, that the toilet in the troop transport had been clogged, or that—if you went to older wars—his horse had been shot from under him.

The next day felt like that to me. Zen and I found

the accommodations workers had used while building the *Je Reviens*. To begin with they were an odd shape, sort of a rounded V. Second, while they had all the recycling facilities still in place and the dimatough that encased them had not sprung any leaks, each was the barest of quarters. Most of it was taken up with cooking facilities clearly designed to accommodate a full-time cook and assistants, who had fed and looked after a hundred or so men, or with the bunks for a hundred or so men. Spacious, each was. Commodious . . . well, they weren't much better than the *Hopper* had been when we got it.

Zen had named our chosen one, perhaps accidentally, by looking at it a moment then saying, "How appropriate, it's a *Boomerang*. It always comes back."

And I'd been embarrassed, since as an Earth woman I should have known more about boomerangs than Edenites did. But instead, I'd said, waspishly, "Only if you throw them right."

To which she'd grinned and said, "Then let's make sure we do."

But then all humor had turned into a long slog, first as we planned how to retrofit the ship—something at which I was surprised to find I was more adept than Zen, being better able to visualize how the compartments should be laid out and used.

And then we'd started taking apart one of the air-to-spaces—though not the one we'd used—for parts. The antigrav would need to be rigged out of one of the units that gave Circum its artificial gravity. Which meant we had to wait until we had access to those.

The first I knew of how the fight had gone was Simon coming back. He had two burners, one in each hand, and a cut across his forehead that had bled copiously over most of his face. That he hadn't seemed to notice the blood, much less attempted to clean it, told me how very serious the situation was.

"Zen," he said.

And Zen, who had been on her knees, attaching screens to the future control room, had dropped everything and turned, looking anxious. "Yes? What happened?"

"What? Nothing much. We're almost in control. There was . . . some resistance, but Nat has subdued it." When she looked significantly at his burners, he said, "Better safe than sorry, right. Come on."

She stood up. "Come where?"

"With me. We need you to rig the device."

"What device?" I said, in turn.

"A communicator. And . . . stuff . . ." Simon said, barely sparing me a glance. "Nothing that concerns you."

"Right. But I still need to assem—"

"We'll send you Kit," Zen said. "With the stuff for antigrav."

Yeah, I could say that Kit didn't have that kind of expertise. But Kit did okay at assembling things, and he wasn't totally stupid around a screwdriver. And of course he could think three-dimensionally. I wasn't about to say I didn't want him around.

He came in moments later, bearing—as promised—an artificial gravity unit. Actually two, still in packages, ready to be used on the ship.

"What is going on?" I asked, after a quick kiss. "What on Earth do they need Zen for?"

He smiled. I was glad to see that though he looked somewhat rumpled, he, at least, wasn't bleeding anywhere I could see. "Oh, I gather she's been helping the rebellion by creating communication devices and circumventing the ones the Good Men block or create."

"Oh."

"And they needed her. But I'm here. Don't tell me you don't want me around."

"I'd never say that," I said. "Did they take all of Circum?"

"They're still fighting," Kit said. "Mind you, they knew they had ready-made allies. Or at least Nat did. Turns out a lot of the harvester pilots are secret Usaians. Also, a few of the scientists."

Still, I noted that Kit, though he helped me, seemed to also be protecting me. Keeping a continuous eye out for any intruder. I didn't know if that was just his innate paranoia, or if there was real danger.

I didn't know, that is, until Kit suddenly left my side, moving Cat-speed. I barely had time to drop the parts I'd been assembling and turn around.

My eye still couldn't follow his movements. But I did see the man in an Earth-fashion suit get hit on the head with the butt of a burner, and then carefully tied. Or rather, I saw him fall, and I saw him all tied up, and I could sort of remember Kit doing that. Of course, it's entirely possible that my mind had made up the intervening states.

I started breathing again. "You didn't kill him," I said.

"What? No. He is doing what he thought was his duty, keeping Circum in the hands of the people who appointed him. They can later convince him or not allow him to come back here." He shrugged. "I helped them take Circum because it's convenient for us too, but in the end, it's not any of our business. We're not going to stay behind to help rebuild the Earth. They are. The decision on these sort of things is theirs. Eden is our business."

"But Jarl would just have killed him."

Kit frowned a little. "Yeah. You know, he didn't think he was human."

"I gathered."

"No, you don't understand. He really didn't think he was human. They pounded that into him. It wasn't rational, it couldn't be fought and...ate him, inside."

I didn't tell him I'd seen enough of that in that room, while the computer peripherals interfered with the nanocytes. If Kit didn't remember it, I'd be the last person to remind him.

After a while Zen came back, her cheeks glowing, and looking really excited. Doc came back with her, and Doc and Kit set about installing the creature comforts in the *Boomerang*.

Most of it had to be done from materials at hand, which meant there was no real bed we could install— not unless we were interested in moldy workmen pallets. But we could and did assemble something from two chaises that would allow Kit and me to sleep together.

But when they started outfitting a room for Zen, she shook her head. "No. I'm not going."

I saw consternation in Doc's face, but less of it in Kit's and Doc was puzzled. "Zen," Doc said, "you have to come back home."

"No," Zen said. "I don't. I like Earth. I like the open space and the fact I'm not an oddity. I like the fact that I can pick a mate from an endless number and not just from among Cats. I like the fact that I can be myself, and not Navigator Zenobia Sienna. I regret that I won't be helping you with taking Eden back, but I totally trust you to. And I'm sure you'll manage it." She'd smiled, revealing dimples I didn't know she had. "Besides, look at how much food and water you'll save."

And that was that. Doc tried and Kit tried, less convincingly, to talk her into going with us.

I didn't try. I'm not stupid. You can't convince humans to do anything when their hearts and souls are dead set against it, and Zen had made her choice. I suspected she and her adopted family didn't get along and—from her history—that Eden had always felt small and confining to her. Kit loved Eden, but she wasn't Kit any more than I was Milton Alexander Sinistra. Made or born, genetically engineered to be similar or not, the environment and our own choices molded us as much as our genes. Each of us was unique. And Zen had been looking, I think, for a way to run away. Earth was a spectacular way to do that.

I'd become too much of an Edenite to talk someone out of what they'd decided they wanted to do with their lives.

THE FIRE OF THE GODS

IT TOOK US TWO DAYS TO FINISH THE *Boomerang*, and at the last, Zen was the only mechanic working on it, as well as directing Doc and Kit, who were lending manpower, and Simon, who came in for stretches of time before vanishing to "make sure Nat doesn't kill the wrong people."

I didn't want to know how many right people Nat had killed. Though somehow I suspected it was more a figure of speech. Nat seemed oddly mellowed, for given values of mellowing and given values of Nat, at that.

The last day I spent in calculations. You think it is easy to aim a ship with barely enough steering at an asteroid on a variable orbit? Oh, let me tell you something. Normally, Eden used computers that were designed for nothing else, once a Nav had entered coordinates from a predetermined set.

Normally, Kit could make that sort of calculation.

His freakish ability with direction and math—freakish for a Cat, bioengineered into a Nav—had allowed him to travel alone between his first wife's death and finding me, a castaway, in the powertrees.

But without anything more than a computer that amounted to a jumped-up calculator—all we had available—things became more difficult. Oh, there were scientific computers, too, but none of them were preprogrammed to compute routes. It took me twenty-four hours, and most of the time all Kit could do was frown over my shoulder at the calculations and sigh. Once, he corrected one of my assumptions and said, "Jarl. He studied that, for the *Je Reviens*. Your route is slightly askew."

I felt stung, but thanked him. Slightly askew in space could translate into millions of miles away from where you were supposed to be. The *Boomerang*, even without Zen, only had provisions and power for the voyage to Eden. Any more and we'd need another power converter, which would add to the mass and require more power, and next thing you knew we'd be flying something the size of Eden all by itself.

Normally a navigator had to make adjustments as he flew. And while I was good at my job, I hadn't, after all, been trained for it. I supposed Kit was now better than normal navigators.

We said goodbye to the people staying on Earth, or rather on Circum, before leaving. Zen hugged me, Simon hugged me and kissed both my cheeks. "Goodbye, Thena. You take my metronome with you." I believed that like I believed . . . no, wait, I didn't believe it at all.

Then Lucius engulfed my hand in his huge paw

and wished me, "Speedy travel and a good landing." Whatever that meant. And then Nat hugged me, which almost made me pass out. No, not because it was that thrilling an experience, but because it was surprising. I didn't think Nat even liked being touched, except by Max. But he hugged me, then patted me on the shoulder. "You know," he said, as he retrieved one of his eternal cigarettes from his belt pouch and lit it, "it's not going to be easy. People in power, or even on the way to getting power, will fight to keep it."

"I know," I said, still baffled to be the recipient of a hug from Nat.

"Well, then. Success, courage and glory; for all I've learned, courage is often just hiding your fear, and glory is a fickle bitch."

And I decided that Nat was completely insane, but I liked him.

We took off from Circum without incident, though Doc, who was piloting, insisted on evasive maneuvers, in case someone from Circum saw us leaving and was one of the people who'd escaped, and somehow got hold of a ship-killing laser.

"Unlikely," I said. "There are no ship-killing lasers on Circum. Other than Nat's."

"Yes, but there are lasers for scientific applications that could be retrofitted," he said.

But we made it to the powertrees without any problems. By that point, Doc had left to shower and change out of the steel-wool suit, and Kit was the one at the controls. It was just as well, since snipping and harvesting a branch of the powertrees wasn't that much different from harvesting a powerpod. And Kit had been doing that for years.

Still, I held my breath, as we navigated into the vast, convoluted briarlike growth of powerpod plants.

They were called a powertree ring. I understood that once upon a time, when Jarl had designed them, they were rather like a vast ring, a crown of thorns, if you will. Their circular shape with an open middle made it easy to access the powerpods and harvest them.

But in the turmoils Earth's harvesting had become erratic. Powerpods could reseed when they exploded near an area of the powertrees that they could attach to. Beyond that, under the pressures of growing need for energy, Earth had pumped more and more organic waste up its space elevator. The wild over-fertilization had made the trees grow even faster.

Now it looked like nothing so much as a raspberry massif that has been allowed to grow wildly and take up more and more space, while the branches entangle and twist around each other. In this riot of branches, powerpods grew willy-nilly.

Most of Earth's harvesters went around the outside of the powertrees, sometimes penetrating into the outer layer.

But Eden's Cats and Navs were designed to navigate the inner recesses of the powertrees. And did. Our ship, the *Cathouse*—small, black, unreflective—often went tumbling around the inner recesses of the powertree massif, while it was in its dark phase, so no Earth harvester could find us.

The *Boomerang* couldn't go very far. Poor misbegotten thing was not only too large, its shape made it unwieldy.

Fortunately it was in the hands of a master. Or of an Eden Cat, which came to the same. He edged into it sideways, twisting this way and that. The process was kind of like putting a coat hanger through a spider web without breaking a single strand.

"Couldn't we take one of the branches from the outside?" I asked.

"No," he said. "We need one at the right stage of growth and with a powerpod cyst just forming."

I directed him, slowly, from my memory of the powertrees, thinking of where the right growth would be, as I calculated the route through the powertrees. "One left, three right, sharp left now."

And then he'd found it and, because this ship didn't have an automatic pilot, Kit made me take the controls and "hold in place" while he worked with the collection assemblage Zen and I had built.

This meant I was holding my breath on two counts. First, because it's not easy to maintain a ship in place in vacuum, particularly not near two relatively large masses: the powertrees and Circum. And because I wasn't trained for this.

I would have grumbled about it, but I was too busy holding my breath, not sure the collection assemblage would work. Eden's normal powerpod collecting device was a pincerlike instrument that held the powerpod and pulled it aboard. To that, Zen and I had added a scythelike implement that was supposed to cut the stem of a little branch of a powertree. Little because the powertrees were so hard that even a dimatough scythe had trouble cutting through them.

As Kit stowed the branch in storage, I realized I was lightheaded from holding my breath, and started breathing normally. Kit put it carefully into the vacuum compartment, cut-side through a membrane and into a "vase" filled with a special serum that Doc had concocted according to Kit's instructions, retrieved partly from his memory and partly from Jarl's gems.

I gave him the instructions for navigating out of the powertree massif, and once under way, for resuming our route to Eden. This time he did not correct me.

"Won't planting it near Eden give away our position?" I asked.

"We couldn't plant it near Eden," Kit said. "Eden doesn't have enough mass to generate gravity that will keep it in place near it. It would be sad to plant powertrees and then lose them in the vastness of space. We'll plant it *on* a larger asteroid, one large enough to keep it nearby. Preferably, one large enough to have ice and soil from which it can derive some of its nourishment, until we can arrange to feed it."

I lifted an eyebrow at him. "And how will that benefit Eden?"

"A shorter trip to harvest," he said, "and it won't be near Earth and guarded. I do have some locations in mind. Jarl had scouted them out, prior to sending off the *Je Reviens*."

I imagined that little branch in our hold one day growing into a tangled massif, like the existing powertrees, harvested by future generations. "It's a little like stealing fire from the gods," I said.

"It's exactly like stealing fire from the gods," Kit said, as he took us out of the powertrees. "That is Jarl's tragedy, you know. He was Prometheus, who stole the fire of the gods and tried to give it to humanity. Humanity always resents Prometheus figures, because if they knew the fire could be got, they'd have got it themselves, and besides, who do you think you are, bringing them this fire-thing they didn't ask for?"

I frowned at Kit. "I don't know how much...I don't know if Jarl had been changed by the Hampson's so that he wasn't truly himself by the time I knew him. I know parts of him weren't, because he was having trouble with impulse control, but I never thought of Prometheus deciding he'd rule over all of humanity and lead them to true bliss."

Kit tilted his head a little, as he looked at my instructions for how to adjust our route. "Perhaps not," he said. "Perhaps...but what you have to remember is that Jarl didn't think he was human—he'd been trained to think so. He loved humanity—truly loved us, I think. He wanted very much to be human. But he felt he could never be that, or never a normal one, so there was some hatred mixed with the love. And when they rejected his inventions and his gifts to them—"

"They didn't reject the powertrees," I protested.

"They did in the sense of their being a resource that made energy so abundant it was essentially free, or very cheap, at least. As the powertrees came on line, the various governments of the Earth set about making them controlled and restricted."

"He was the government then."

"Not alone. I think, if it helps, Thena, that he was disappointed with all humans, including Mules, even if he didn't think they were human. He tried so hard to give them good things, and they always twisted or misunderstood them. In fact, they rejected him, over and over again. Of course by then he thought the only way to make them understand was for him to take absolute control, more absolute than ever before."

"But he was wrong," I said.

"Of course he was. But having acquired the fire of the gods, having tried his damnedest to make humanity happy and fulfilled and... utopian, he could never understand why they rejected it. The original Prometheus got off lightly," he said. "Jarl got much worse than getting his liver eaten by eagles eternally."

The fact that he spoke so lightly made me sure that other than a few memories nothing remained in him of Jarl. And I was glad that Kit didn't see what I did, as I turned to go inside the ship and take a shower.

Doc must have come in when we were talking. He was leaning against the doorway into the control room, and his face seemed to have collapsed in on itself. Worse, there were tears down his cheeks. I turned hastily and became very busy brushing at the area near the controls, and looking under it for nothing I could think of. Kit was busy entering coordinates and paid no attention.

And Doc's tears were ultimately the best epitaph that Jarl could have. They'd been friends when they were children and the world was young, and Jarl would be remembered fondly. Ultimately, it's all any mortal can hope for.

THE SILENCE OF THE SPHERES

"THIS IS CHRISTOPHER BARTOLOMEU INGEMAR Denovo Klaavil Sinistra," Kit said, "piloting the *Boomerang*, returning from Earth on a mission for Eden. Come in, Eden."

I had no idea why Kit had decided to add every last name he'd ever been entitled to. Yes, his original at-conception last name was Ingemar—because his would-be mother had taken Jarl's name, a rare but not unheard-of arrangement for Eden. The only reason I could imagine for Kit using all the names was to cloak himself in the absolute authority of Eden. He was a legitimate citizen sent out on an errand.

It didn't avail him. There was no answer. Eden, ahead of us, managed to look very potatolike and yet enigmatic, its surface seemingly virgin of any entry point into its populated interior.

"Christopher Bartolomeu Ingemar Denovo Klaavil Sinistra," Kit said, through gritted teeth, "piloting the *Boomerang*, requesting permission to land in Eden."

No answer. "We can't stay in space," Doc said. "We can't. We do not have enough supplies to make it back to Circum and..."

Kit shook his head. "We're not going to stay in space. I thought this might happen though."

"But...what happened in Eden?" I asked. "Are they...dead?"

"No," Kit said. "They are playing possum." And then added, "An Earth animal that I understand to be a near relative of the weasel or perhaps a bird."

"Playing possum," the doctor said, "refers to the possum's main method of self-defense, which consists of pretending it is dead. I imagine in the time since we left, Castaneda has consolidated his power, and that no Dock Operator will admit we exist. At any rate, Christopher, I'd make damn sure to stay out of defensive-fire range, because you know...lasers do go off accidentally and all."

"So, we're going to stay out of reach till we starve?"

"No," Kit said. "I expected this, as did Jarl, and he...I have some idea what to do."

And then he went to a box stored with the food. It must have been carried in when I wasn't looking. Inside was a communicator and a bunch of pieces. "I know Kath's communicator range and frequency," he said, "and I shall try to get her personal com ring."

And then my husband had set about rearranging that Earth-vintage comlink. It shouldn't have made me uncomfortable but it did. Even if there was no Jarl left in him, I hated the thought that he knew things he couldn't have known except through Jarl. Like the expression "playing possum." I knew it was something Jarl had left behind.

When the com was assembled, he dialed Kath and we heard it buzz. Kit spoke as soon as the buzzing stopped, "Kath! Listen, Kath—" And then Kath's voice echoed through the compartment like victory bells. "Kit! Kit! You're alive."

It took a good while for her to quiet down enough to listen to what he was trying to tell her, and when she did, there was a long silence. "I see," she said. "Yes, the landing area is all Castaneda's people. Kit, can I call you back at this frequency? We have to try something. I'm going to ask Eber."

"But if Castaneda controls the land—"

"Wait. I will call back."

I'd expected, and I'm sure the men did too, that she'd call back immediately or close to it.

Instead, hours passed. We waited around the com, while Kit made occasional adjustments to trajectory, to avoid us coming within range of Eden's defense guns. Periodically, desultorily, he called out to Eden, in the forlorn hope that they'd open to us. We had a meal, and then we waited again.

I'd just said, "Well, we can always land and try to blast through one of the landing openings. I know you say it's impossible, but—" when the com crackled to life.

"Kit?" It was Kath's voice.

"Yes?"

"You're going to have to do what we say, and it's going to sound loony. Can you program that thing on autopilot?"

"No. It's not that sophisticated."

"Um . . . Can you set it on a course where it will fly away?"

"Yes. But there's a good chance it will hit something."

"Do you have something aboard you care not to lose, other than your lives?"

"Yes. My violin and a dozen data gems. We had a cutting of the powertree but we planted it near—"

"You did? Good. But you can give us the coordinates later. For now, what you need to do is get your violin and those gems ready to abandon ship, and then stand by with the ship ready to be set on a trajectory... any trajectory, though I suppose it would be good to make it look like you're going back to Earth."

"From here? Hard to tell," Kit said.

"Yeah. So... any trajectory. Eber and I will come and get you. Direct us to a door on the inner side of the V your ship forms. If there is a door there."

"There is," Kit said. "A cargo airlock."

It puzzled me what they intended to do, until I saw what looked like a family flyer—a large family flyer—come out a side of Eden where there shouldn't have been an air lock. It flew in an odd, erratic way. Later I would find that, after long study and some hacking of the surveillance system around Eden, Eber had designed various paths to go into and out of Eden which explored minute faults in the system. At the time I just thought they were having issues maneuvering as they came up behind the *Boomerang*.

Kit directed them, and I opened the cargo door remotely, then closed it, then filled the compartment with air—and then Kath, Eber, and Waldron were there, coming into the control room at a trot. For a moment urgency and rationality had to give away to emotion and rejoicing at seeing each other again.

When we calmed down and Kath had been told that Zen was left on Earth—and nodded with the greatest equanimity, as though this were perfectly normal—we were led back to their flyer. Waldron was left behind to make adjustments to the course at the last minute. He was wearing his space suit, I noted, with the helmet off.

He had the helmet on when he came running into the airlock, after we had bled the air out.

Kit had the time to say, "Kath, you can't take off while the *Boomerang* is pushing off, be—"

And then Kath had done it, erupting out of the cargo hold so fast that she beat the accelerating motion of the *Boomerang* and managed to dive under it and then...towards an area of Eden where—where I knew there were no docks.

It was all so fast, I barely caught my breath, as we plunged into a hole that closed after us.

There was no landing sleeve and no tunnel. Just a sudden drop into a vast room, and air hissing in.

"What is this?" Kit asked. "Why did you rig a flyer for space travel and what—"

Kath turned off the flyer and leaned back against her seat. "We had to, Kit. Mother says we might need to leave for the Thules at any moment. She has water collectors waiting for us not far off. And this is the old landing docks...from a hundred years ago or so. Grandmother remembered. Oh, we needed to retrofit them, but as far as we can tell, everyone thinks they were completely closed out. Well, they were, but they weren't repurposed. So we were able to install the airlocks again and put in the assist computer. It's the only thing we can do, in case our family should not be allowed to leave. Or should be targeted for destruction."

Kit's face had looked increasingly worried through this speech. Now he said, "Light! What is it then? Eden is in civil war?"

Eber shook his head. "Oh, no. It's much worse than that."

THE POINT OF VIEW OF
THE BOILING FROG

THERE IS AN OLD THOUGHT EXPERIMENT. AT LEAST I hope it's a thought experiment, and that no one ever did it. It's repulsive enough as a thought experiment.

The question was—how do you boil a frog? The logical answer is to throw it in a pot of hot water. But then, the frog will feel the heat and jump away with third-degree burns all over its little warty skin, and might survive to be boiled another day.

My solution to this, when first asked, was to say one should hit the frog hard over the head once. At least if there was any reason we really needed to boil amphibians.

But the classical solution was different. It was to put the frog in cold water and then heat it slowly, very slowly. The frog reacted to the warmth by relaxing, and by the time the water got uncomfortable, it was too late to jump out.

As I said, I hope it's a thought experiment. I know many humans who are worthy of being boiled, slow or fast, but animals are—by definition—innocent. They can't be truly evil, because they don't know there is good or evil. The idea of boiling a poor innocent frog made me sick to my stomach for reasons other than frog broth.

But apparently Castaneda had heard of this experiment, because he was boiling the frog really slowly.

"A few of us have experienced cuts in power and water service," Kath said. "Or at least, we should have, only as you know Jean has a rebellious streak a mile wide, and he's long since rigged several back-route fail-safe systems with which we can still get power... But the outages are targeted, as are the Cats and Navs that won't be allowed to go out. Our family and our closest friends and allies are being isolated. Hushers and controllers who won't play along are being cut out, told they can't work for a reason or another. There have been..." She swallowed hard, "a couple of ships that we think went missing through not being allowed back in. We have no proof. We weren't even sure they'd do that, till... well, till now. And we think that... well... There have been odd deaths of people we have reasons to believe were starting to suspect something was wrong. They were either very odd duels, or supposedly self-defense, but the witnesses are always Castaneda partisans. We can't prove anything. And see... everyone else is being treated with kid gloves and getting explanations that we are bad elements who should be frozen out. The cabal are not exerting any openly trespassing power. They're not in any way tipping their hand. Except for doing

things like marginalizing anyone who won't follow
their orders or questions them. But their explanation is always that this person deserves it. They've
undermined our prestige by saying that you deserted.
They seemed very sure you had died. What did they
do to ensure it?"

We told her about the bacteria. She nodded. "That
makes sense, then, because they told everyone you'd
never be back and you'd defected, long before there
could be any hope you would return. People believe
them, more and more as another day passes without
your return."

"Yeah," he said, "I imagine. But we weren't even
on Earth that long. It's just that the ship continuously
falling apart, and Zen and Thena having to rebuild
en route, made us very slow, and the *Boomerang* was
slower on the way back than the *Cathouse* would have
been. Or the *Hopper*."

"I see," Kath said. "Yes, they definitely meant for
you to die en route, so they felt safe in predicting
you'd never return."

"Let's show them we returned!" Kit said. "Let's
make them show themselves for the slime they are."

"No!" Kath said. "No. I have a better plan. First,
let's get you out of here and to a lodging where you'll
be safe."

"And then?"

"And then Mother and I are going to act crazy."

"That at least," Waldron said, tartly, "is the easy
part of the plan."

He barely ducked Kath's playful slap in time.

UNDERGROUND

GETTING US OUT FROM THE LANDING AREA WASN'T too difficult. Since practically no one knew this was a landing area, it was easy enough to come and go from it unobserved. What was hard was getting us anywhere else in Eden without being noticed.

A few people noticed us and saw us, other than Kit's family. At least, when we landed, we had a reception committee composed of Jean, Bruno and half a dozen other Cats and Navs. I remembered Jan and Damon Portago, because, presumably at his parents' request and design—since most people in Eden were thoroughly racially blended—Damon looked like a light-skinned Earth African. A very good-looking one. His Cat eyes didn't look at all strange with his roguish features. And his wife Jan, as olive-skinned as I, was a lively young Nav, always ready to argue with him. With them were their best friends, red-headed Cat Samantha Flanagan and Nav

Zeddadiah Flanagan, much older and nearing the age when Samantha would have to retire. Zed was one of the Navs who'd almost died in the Earth traps, and had the scars to prove it, but he was chomping at the bit to go back. "They can't keep us here," he said. "Eden needs power."

Also with them were a widowed Nav, Kathleen—Kathy—Wormsley, who was dark-haired, with gentle curves and a ready smile, and a widower Cat, Kevin "Fritz" Fotovich, who was a devilishly handsome man, and for some reason preferred to go by Fritz. I wondered if their being here together meant there was something in the offing. However much Zen had hated the idea of a restricted mating pool, enough to want to leave Eden forever, Cats and Navs tended to pair up.

They were, I gathered, reassured to see us. I think that was why Kit's family allowed them to be there. Some people needed to know that whatever Kath and Tania's plan was, it was not nearly as crazy as it sounded. Enough people needed to know.

We were subjected to hugs and pats on the back, a little disconcerting for me, since I'd not grown up as a Nav and was only a marginal member of the fraternity. Probably a little disconcerting for Kit, too, because he was not the most sociable person around.

And then they took us to some lodgings, taking advantage of two things—the fact that people look less closely to each person in a group, and the fact that Eden's fashions and attire were always free form. Any Edenite might be wearing anything at any time, from fully covered in something resembling a blanket to completely nude. I got completely covered and also two of the Cats put their arms over me, so I was almost invisible between their much greater heights.

Kit on the other hand, I regret to say will never, ever, ever look natural in a bright blue shoulder-length wig and a subdued grey suit. However, I suspect that the very fact the hair was outlandish and the clothes something no Cat in his right mind—or vision—would wear, kept him from being recognized.

Doc had been given something that looked rather like a monk's costume with cowl, which meant that he was still perfectly himself and in character as some sort of medieval gnome. But I doubted many people had realized that Doc thought he would fit perfectly well in the Middle Ages. His house notwithstanding, he was so matter-of-fact and practical on everything else, that I didn't think most people realized his obsession.

We got safely into someone's flyer—a small flyer with the biostuffing torn out of one of the seats; I think the owner was one of Waldron's friends—and were taken to a nondescript lodging in an area of town I didn't remember visiting. The place was Damon and Jan's, a starter home, on a tiny plot. Living room, bedroom and kitchen, the quarters were smaller than the ones we enjoyed aboard the *Cathouse*. How they managed to live there with Javier, their toddler, was beyond me, though of course, in normal times, they'd be spending most of their time aboard their ship, the *Manolo*. But it had plenty of water for showers, and we could cook food. Jan and Damon were double-bunking with Sam and Zed for the duration.

Kit's family couldn't all crowd into the place, even if it had been safe, but they managed to straggle in, by ones and twos in the wee hours of the morning, until all the adults were crowded into the tiny living room, sitting on the single, spectacularly uncomfortable sofa, and on pillows taken from the bed, and on the floor.

"What did you mean about acting crazy?" Kit said. "I don't think they're going to suggest you should be put down for being mentally defective, and failing that, how do you expect them to tip their hand?"

"Oh, easily enough," Kath said and grinned. "You see, we've demanded that they submit to hypnotics in the Judicial Center."

"What?" Kit said. "On charges of planning to take over Eden?"

"No, of course not, silly. On charges of murdering you."

"What? But I'm alive."

"Well, yes," Tania answered in turn. "And have I told you how happy I am about that, my dear? But they don't know that."

"It doesn't matter," Doc Bartolomeu said. "You can't prove they even attempted anything against Kit. If you never found out who shot him, though I'm sure the assassins were attached to Castaneda, there is no way to know for sure."

"No," Kath said. "We never could prove it. As in the other incidents in which people *did* die, there is nothing concrete to say it wasn't even self-defense. And often there are witnesses that the dead person attacked first. A lot of witnesses, all with the same exact story."

"No," Jean said, "but that's part of the beauty of it. You see, we expect them to say there is no proof you were murdered. And then Tania and Kath say they just know. And then..."

"And then?" Doc said. "It seems like a dangerous game."

"Not really. Then they're going to demand we submit to hypnotics, to see if we have any proof Kit was murdered. Or even attempted against. Not just by them, but attempted against in general. Because you see, they say our family is crazy and troublemakers for saying Kit was attacked. They're using the fact that you left ahead of schedule as proof that you were trying to betray Eden all along."

"That doesn't even make any sense. How would leaving ahead of schedule make me more likely to betray Eden?"

"It wouldn't, of course," Kath said. "But they say you left that quickly lest they discover you'd made arrangements to stay on Earth."

"Right…" Kit said. "Such as provisioning for the trip to Earth. Or perhaps…what? Trying to make sure we got there in one piece?"

Kath shrugged. "Who knows. There are rumors that you smuggled Eden technology to give you a safe passage on Earth."

"I see. So…you two submit to questioning," I said. "But that's a problem, because neither of you even saw Kit shot. All you saw was blood on me when I came to pack."

Kath nodded. "Of course. That's the beauty of it."

TICKLING TROUTS

ONCE, IN DADDY DEAREST'S LIBRARY, I FOUND MYSELF reading a book on hand fishing. To be precise, about something called trout tickling, apparently possible in unspoiled wildernesses, where the unsuspecting trouts didn't expect treason.

If right about now you're thinking I spent a lot of my youth reading about cruelty to animals, you're probably right, and my only defense is that I much rather preferred to read about cruelty to humans. But sometimes you have to go with what's available.

However, as far as I understood the trout-tickling technique, it went like this: First you went in and made nice to the trout. You made that trout feel you were a friend and you were there to give it a really good massage and perhaps a fin-cleaning or whatever it is that trouts like to have done to them.

And then when the poor trout least expected it, you grabbed it behind the gills, got a good hold, and threw it out of the water and onto the bank, to be cooked for dinner.

As Kath's plan started to become obvious, I realized that was exactly what we intended to do with Castaneda and his allies. Except for the cooking for dinner part. I didn't think Eden had a food shortage yet. But that would inevitably come, if we allowed tyranny to take hold, at least if Earth's history told the truth. Particularly this type of tyranny which restricted access to sources of energy. There were three families involved, about half of the Energy Board, and all of them closely related: the Castanedas, the Altermans, and the Fergusons.

By great good fortune, the only Cats related to these families were much older than Kath, and probably older than Tania. This meant that no one could legitimately play the duel card and attempt to take the two of them out that way. Well, I suspect there were a Cat or two who might be bribed or coerced into dueling them but for one thing—Kath was a noted markswoman. And besides, most active-duty Cats were on our side, openly or not. They didn't like not being able to take runs as often as they were willing.

You have to understand, Cats and Navs in Eden endured high risk for high pay, but they were used to the high pay, and also believed that the limit of what they could earn should be determined solely by how many runs they were willing to make, not by the board. They didn't like someone else deciding it was too unsafe to travel. And even when they didn't complain, because they didn't see a way to win the fight, they didn't like it, and wanted someone to remove the restrictions.

And so, Tania and Kath publicly and privately accused the three families of having murdered their darling son and brother. They gave lurid descriptions of possible fates for Kit. And they invented the most outlandish slanders. In other words, the most outrageous members of the Denovo clan were having more fun than should be legal.

But despite their enjoyment of the process, and despite a growing hubbub of rumors, gleefully reported by our visitors, there was no official movement to respond to the supposed—and some of them real—calumnies.

I was starting to suspect I'd live the rest of my life, alone with Kit and Doc, in our little borrowed hideout. Or else, we'd have to figure out a way to steal a ship and go back to Earth.

This was starting to look appealing. I was so nervous and cabin-feverish I kept throwing up and felt tired all the time.

Of course, Kath had the retrofitted family-flyer and Tania said that with three days' notice, she could get some people from the Thules to meet us in space. They had supposedly been waiting and spelling each other, in striking distance of Eden. But the truth was that Kit and I didn't want to go to the Thules or to Earth and leave Eden to its fate. We'd gone to Earth in search of the fire of the gods, to save Eden from tyranny. And now, no one even cared about the little powertree we'd left growing on a larger asteroid.

Sometimes I dreamed that the poor little plant had died, ignored. And sometimes I dreamed we'd died too, that the *Hopper* had disintegrated and that we'd suffocated in space.

Perhaps it was the spectacularly uncomfortable bed Kit and I shared. Though the sofa Doc slept on was worse.

We didn't exactly start to bicker. Well, not Kit and I. We were used to spending time in space together alone, in cramped quarters. But Kit and Doc seemed to argue for amusement, and if I heard just once more, "Christopher, don't be an idiot," I was going to sit down and have a good scream.

Kit must have been fairly close to it too, no matter how much the two of us knew that the doctor only insulted those people he liked.

When Kath came in on what I thought was the month anniversary of our captivity, Kit said, "Look, nothing can be served by this. I say we emerge and tell them about the powertree. For one, though it should remain alive and dormant for a while, it's going to need water soon."

"I know, but that's fine, because Castaneda and his friends have issued a complaint against us for slander, and a demand that we appear in the Judicial Center to be interrogated under hypnotics, to ascertain if we truly are deluded and believe there is any reality to our accusations, or if we are in fact simply malicious."

Kit hugged her. And then I hugged her. And then we planned.

Two days after, when the hearing had been set, we were smuggled out of the lodgings and into the Judicial Center. This was a little more complex than smuggling us out of the landing dock, because we had to get in near the end of the questioning. This was to minimize the risk of someone recognizing us. But the Judicial Center was as full as in the two other cases involving Kit and me.

Fortunately our allies had a streak of conspirator in them. Or perhaps Doc orchestrated it. I say this because we all seemed to end up in cowled outfits. We also left separately.

I was taken by Jan and Damon, who smuggled me into a side door and, with the help of confederates, onto a seat at the side of the amphitheater, with Zed and Sam on either side for cushioning. Even I didn't know where Doc and Kit were.

All I knew is that they were somewhere there.

Tania was being interrogated. She was the second one to submit to questioning, as Sam explained. And her deposition had so far been negative on proof. As had Kath's.

Now, in response to a question she said, "No, I didn't see my son wounded, and I have no proof his life was attempted against."

And then Castaneda got up, from the audience, up front, full of righteous indignation and noble suffering. "I say the two of them have spread calumnies against me and my family, as I've tried to steer the world through this crisis and the truth is that Christopher and Athena Sinistra, perhaps without the knowledge of Doctor Bartolomeu Dias or Nav Sienna, always intended to defect to Earth. The truth is, I am doing what I'm doing for the good of society and my aims are society's and I—"

I thought to myself that I'd been right. He was equating his own good with the good of society, and if he succeeded, no one else's rights or wishes would count, but only those of "society," read to mean Castaneda. Or rather, I didn't think at all, I just stood up. Kit anticipated me, though.

My darling has a turn for the dramatic. I thought he looked pretty dramatic the very first time I saw him, coming into the airlock of the *Cathouse*, burner in hand. Now he stood, with a fluid movement, removing the disguising garment, saying "You lie."

And Doc Bartolomeu stood also, from where he'd sat. It wasn't nearly as impressive, because he'd never been a tall man, and age had shrunk him further, but he stood up anyway, and his voice carried and crackled with indignation as he said, "You lie."

What is a girl to do when handed that sort of entrance line? I stood up, cast off the cloak with hood that I was wearing and said, ringingly and in what was for Eden a truly weird accent, "You lie."

For a moment there was complete silence, and then the crowd went wild.

Far, far wilder than I'd expected. As everyone got up, talking, arguing, I saw the burner ray cut through the crowd. I screamed "Kit!" and threw myself in his direction, which tells you how worried I was, because there was no possible way I could reach him, not when he was on the other side of the amphitheater. There had to be a couple hundred people between us.

But I saw Kit duck out of the way, and then a few of our Cat friends, including Fritz, closed ranks around him. The seemingly random movement of the crowd wielded a few Cats and Navs who seemed to be directed by Kathy and who closed ranks around me, as well.

I presumed Doc had his own honor guard. The rest of the room boiled in pandemonium, and Fritz, who had been one of our more frequent visitors, had jumped the shooter and was holding him on the ground and seemed to be tying him up. Kathy Wormsley seemed to be helping, but it was hard to see through the crowd.

Kit spoke as though the room were in perfect calm, his voice so loud it carried above the babble. "I," he said, "Cat Christopher Bartolomeu Ingemar Denovo Klaavil Sinistra, accuse you, Fergus Castaneda, as well as unknown accomplices and abettors, of trying to kill me three times, and my companions, Doctor Bartolomeu Dias, Athena Hera Sinistra, and Zenobia Diana Sienna, twice. And I will be deposed on the matter, under hypnotics if you so choose."

The noise increased. Some people tried to leave the hall, and I gathered our friends detained them, but it was hard to see. I didn't know if the frog was boiling, but the auditorium was. There were three or four fights, full-blown fistfights, just in my immediate vicinity, and burners fired and people screamed, and you couldn't tell what was happening through the press of people and the movement. Were people dying? Or wounded? I couldn't tell. For a while, I couldn't even see Kit's family or Kit.

And yet, Kit and Doc Bartolomeu and I got pushed up front and towards the stage. The doctor who had administered the hypnotics to Tania insisted on doing it to Kit, probably because he was afraid that Doc would cheat. Or perhaps because he wanted to avoid even the appearance of impropriety.

Doc, of course, had to intervene twice because he wanted to make sure that Kit survived it, despite his allergy. Kit didn't show any reluctance, except for grabbing my hand and squeezing hard.

And then, he was sitting and the auditorium suddenly went quiet, and Doc was asking questions. Of course, we had no proof that Castaneda had done anything. But there was inference that could be made, and Eden was very good at inference. Guided by Doc, questions were asked about whom the scarcity of powerpods could possibly benefit and Kit answered with his best guess.

More devastating was his describing the attempts against his life, the shooting, and the bacteria that ate the *Hopper*, and finally the attempt to make us stay in space and die there. Meanwhile the shooters were presumably being questioned, and our people moved through the crowd, staking positions for the real fight to come. There was a sob from the audience at this, and I wondered if it was the reaction of a family member of one of the people who had disappeared en route...if they now suspected their relative had died locked out of Eden.

Fritz, who, at the best of times looked like an impudent rogue, grinned at me, winked, and blew me a kiss as he took a position at the foot of the stage, presumably defending us. I winked back.

Yeah, this was probably dangerous as he was one of the Cats who had been widowed in the traps set by Earth. On the other hand, Kit had never shown any jealousy of him, and Kit was very good at detecting true predatory intentions. I assumed Fritz was one of those people who enjoyed flirting with everyone, married or not, and whether he was interested or not. People like that, unless you take it too seriously, can brighten your day by making you feel wildly seductive, even when you know you're not.

"You have no proof that I was behind any of this," Castaneda said, as Doc signaled that Kit had had all he could have, and the other doctor administered the antidote to the hypnotics. "This is nothing but more calumny and slander orchestrated by the Denovos. So, their son is alive, but how do we know who attempted against him? It's not the first time someone tried to kill Cat Kla—Sinistra. His personality lends itself to making people wish to kill him. And spreading lies about me, while I try to do what is best for Eden, is just another facet of his antisocial—"

"I can prove it," Doc Bartolomeu said, "and so can Nav Sinistra. We can prove there was only one person with the kind of access to the *Hopper* that would allow them to have infected the hull. I traced the progression of the infection while Nav—"

I saw the burner ray, aimed straight at Doc, but it was too late for me to react and do anything. But a Cat could. Fritz seemed to dematerialize at the foot of the stage and reappear at the top, in front of Doc, just as the burner ray pierced Fritz's chest.

Fritz looked very surprised, but he was still moving fast, even if no longer Cat speed, and he managed to get his burner out of his holster and shoot at his assassin, an elder man with Cat eyes, in the crowd. They fell at the same time.

As Fritz folded to the stage, he muttered something that could be interpreted as "damn tyrants." Not eloquent perhaps, but I'll say it's as good a set of last words as anyone could hope for.

And then a dark-haired Nav, John Ringo, stood up, drawing a burner from somewhere beneath his red kilt, and shouted, "Live free or die," before shooting another man aiming a burner at Kit. Ringo lived for maybe three seconds, afterwards, as one of Castaneda's associates burned him in the middle of the chest.

Kathy Wormsley avenged him immediately, shooting the man who had shot Ringo before Ringo had fallen to the ground. And then someone shot her. While this happened, the crowd seemed to have frozen. But eventually the sense that this was no longer a normal enquiry started to penetrate.

And then all hell broke loose, and burner rays shot everywhere. Kit was the only person not involved, still strapped to the interrogation seat, shaking himself back to his senses.

I guess someone viewed him a sitting duck, and perhaps a sitting duck that still knew too much. He had, after all, told them there was a new seedling to powertrees, but not where, and that could still be averted.

I jumped to block the laser, but Doc got there before me and brought the seat and Kit down onto the floor of the stage with him. Then he pulled out a burner, shot the man who'd shot at Kit, and loudly started naming names and the reasons he had to associate them with the plot. I knew how he had got the names. He'd spent the month tracing people who were doing favors for and covering for Castaneda. He'd also taken some names from Kath who had traced them the other way, from the people she was sure, from circumstantial evidence, had been the ones to attempt against Kit's life.

As the named were caught in various stages of attempting against us, or of trying to escape, the confusion in the hall resolved itself. Edenites finally realized what had almost happened to their vaunted liberty, and reacted—at last—as we hoped they would.

When calm was restored, Kit had stopped shaking and no longer looked sick.

And Castaneda was gone.

PAYING THE PIPER

TRACING CASTANEDA WASN'T HARD. FINDING SOMEONE in Eden was never that hard. There were plenty of people who knew of several places he could be, and from there, there were enough of his associates who had been along for the ride, in either the full assumption of his innocence, or because they'd thought he'd win and wanted to be on the side of the winners.

Now that it looked as though public opinion had turned against him, and everyone loyal to him could end up at the wrong end of a set of challenges, a lot of people had suddenly become positively chatty.

How on Earth Sam and Zed, Jan and Damon, Kit and I and Doc, ended up in a loose group, outside Castaneda's office, I can't explain. It seemed like people went off in different groups, in flyers, to find him, and we hit the jackpot.

Of course, at the time we didn't know that it was

the jackpot, just that it was one of the possible locations where he might be.

We stood around the door, which was, in Eden fashion, on the ground. Kit had the battle light in his eyes, and stomped hard on the door twice, calling out, "Come out, Castaneda. Now. Come out or we break in."

Doc, who knew Kit and his temper, cleared his throat. "Christopher," he said. "He's likely to have rigged the whole thing to go up in flames if we break in."

"Fine, so we go up in flames, too, but it takes him with us," Kit said, because when he's like that, there's no reasoning with him.

Doc knew there was no arguing with Kit in that mood, so he gave him a patient look and a slightly less patient sigh, then moved to the side of the door, where there was the button you could press with your foot, which would allow him to talk to those inside. If there was anyone inside, though our source had sworn there would be.

Pushing the button, Doc spoke in his best diction and his calmest manner. "Mr. Castaneda," he said, "for attempts against my life and the life of my friends Christopher Sinistra and—"

I realized what Doc was doing. He was challenging Castaneda to a duel. If Castaneda did not accept, then we'd have the option of striking him down anywhere, because public opinion would be against him. But I thought that Doc was not the person to do it. Yes, Doc was a Mule and almost as fast as Kit, certainly as fast or faster than I was. But Castaneda, whether he knew that or not, could claim not to know it. He could claim to be attempting to spare a doddering old man and that was why he'd refused the duel. It might not turn public opinion completely in his favor, but there would always be those who thought that he was less guilty than claimed. There would be a seed of future problems.

Kit couldn't challenge him, either. Castaneda wasn't a Cat, and Cats were forbidden from challenging non-Cats.

I edged Doc aside, gently. "Fergus Castaneda," I said, "for attempts against me, against my family, against the integrity of Eden, I challenge you to a duel to the death."

"Thena!" Kit said, and I didn't know if he was afraid or upset at my conditions.

And for a moment there was no reply, but then the com crackled. "I accept."

After some time the door opened. We stepped back away from the door, onto a patch of ground in front of it—a recently dug patch planted with rose bushes, one of which was poking me intrusively on the behind. I didn't like that it had taken this long for the door to open. I could hear my friends ranging themselves behind me. Three of Castaneda's five friends—or perhaps relatives, as they all looked like him—walked behind him.

Castaneda looked dour. He looked at me from under lowered eyebrows. When he spoke, his voice sounded like each word had been rehearsed in advance. "I accepted under protest. I have reason to think that you have been bioengineered for higher speed. Not as high, perhaps, as a Cat's, but significantly above that of normal humans. I'm registering my protest and the right for my family to collect blood geld, should you kill me." He thinned his lips and glared at me.

Doc Bartolomeu counted off.

"This is absurd," I said. "This is utterly insane. You have used your assassins to kill anyone who opposed you while you manipulated the Energy Board to ration power and thus give power to only the favored few. You have tried to obtain power over the lives of everyone in Eden. You've constituted yourself a tyrant over the free citizens of—"

"Careful there, Nav Sinistra. None of these charges are proven." Castaneda looked at his finger, as though something about it held his attention as he spoke. Some people had time-telling devices embedded into the index fingertip, but what could he be looking at the time for? "I would demand you substantiate your charges or pay for damage to my reputation."

I frowned at him. If I killed him, and I was fairly sure I could kill him with minimal effort, would Kit and I have increased our debt to the point we would be indentured for life? Could anything ever be proven about Castaneda's actions?

Kit had accused him under hypnotics. We'd proven he'd lied about our deserting, but did that prove his intentions towards Eden? Sure, the crowd had reacted emotionally to the revelation of his lie, but what could be proven, calmly and in discussion? Could we prove he'd killed or tried to kill anyone? Could we make any of his crimes stick? Could we make it in any way obvious he'd been behind disappearances and deaths and pseudoaccidental losses of power and failures to let darkships back into Eden? There was no positive material proof of any of this. Deaths had been dismissed as self-defense. Even Kit's accusations were just Kit's belief.

Standing there, blood rushing past my ears, I realized that even with the fight in the Judicial Center, unless one or more of his minions confessed and implicated him, Castaneda could rebuild his reputation.

This meant that I had to kill him in duel. But Kit and I might very well end up economically enslaved for the rest of our lives.

He was still looking at his finger. "Well," he said again, urbanely. "Nav Sinistra?"

His finger must be fascinating. I felt angry, but realized all too well he wanted me angry. He wanted me to lash out without thinking. Clearly my husband was thinking also, because he said in my mind, *Don't do anything rash.*

I cleared my throat. "Given that I have a certain superiority of speed, but not to the level of a Cat, how about we equalize the odds by having me face any three of you."

Thena, Kit said. *They might have enhancements, too. You're not as fast as I am.*

I heard flyers land on the road behind us, but I didn't turn, because I was afraid of taking my eyes off Castaneda for any time. Instead, I snapped at Kit, mentally: *I'm fast enough.*

As the doors of flyers slammed shut, and I wondered for whom the reinforcements had come, us or Castaneda, whose expression gave nothing away, a familiar voice shouted, "Thena, *move!* Move, all of you!" I relaxed because it was Waldron, then tensed as I wondered what he meant.

Castaneda and his friends turned and ran away from us. I started to run. Someone hit me and pushed me, mid-body, stopping me from following, then shoved Kit into me, shouting, "Get her out of here. All of you run." Someone—Waldron?—a Cat, moving very fast, was picking up our friends and shoving them backwards, towards the parked flyers—throwing the smaller people out of the area.

Kit grabbed me under one arm, and Waldron put his arm around me from the other side, and they jumped. We hit the ground next to the flyers and—with Waldron shoving us and screaming "Don't stand up"—Kit and I crawled forward to the side of the flyers. I had no idea why, but I got the idea we should get behind them—or in them?—but before we could, there was a roar.

And then we were pummeled with hot...fragments. Hard. It felt like fist-sized lumps of something hot and hard, and Waldron took a leap, and landed half on top of me, and Kit tried to protect me from the other side.

"What—What—" I said, as the bombardment stopped.

"They had it set to explode. The chamber beneath the place just in front of you. They kept you talking, because they figured when they ran, on time, you would chase and then—Oh, shit."

The "oh, shit" was because Castaneda and his friends had come back. Perhaps they'd figured they couldn't run. Or perhaps they hoped we were disoriented enough. I saw one of his friends shoot at Jan, who fired back. I tried to sit up but I felt bruised, and Kit was patting himself down and seemed to have lost his burner.

Waldron bent to pull his burner from the holster, but he must have been winded because he never hit Cat speed. He just had his hand on his burner's hilt, when the ray hit him through the heart.

I thought *no. Never. Not Waldron.* Even as I saw him fall. I heard the same disbelief in Kit's thoughts. I felt as if I'd gone frozen. Waldron was the oldest of the grandchildren in Kit's family, and both a source of pride and amusement to everyone older. He was recently married. He—

My hand was not frozen. As Waldron fell, I grabbed the burner from his suddenly lax hand, and shot in the direction from which the killing ray had come.

I didn't know if I'd hit anyone, until the ray came that told me I hadn't. I felt the ray hit my shoulder before I could sidestep. It didn't hurt. It just felt cold.

I must have gone into my speeded-up mode, because everyone and everything around me went very slow.

Suddenly I was aware of everyone else around me being engaged in firefights. There were more than five of Castaneda's people shooting at us. Either Castaneda had sent his allies out earlier, or he'd also got reinforcements. But I felt like I was in a dream, and I couldn't focus on anything but Castaneda standing in the middle of the group, aiming at Kit, who was trying to get Waldron's other burner from its sheath.

I jumped into the line of Castaneda's fire, and let a laser ray fly at him. He ducked. I saw what Kit meant, that Castaneda might be enhanced. He moved as fast as I could. Of course in Eden, anyone could be enhanced if their parents paid enough, and I suspected there were retroactive enhancements, too.

I fired again and ducked. He retreated, interposing his friends between us. I pursued. My entire vision, almost my entire thought was bent on him.

He was destroying Eden. If I let him escape, he'd find a way to exonerate himself and finish the job. He'd killed Waldron, and if he got half a chance he would kill Kit and my entire family. He would at least try to indenture Kit. And our only choice would be to run away, to give up Eden forever.

I had to kill him.

I realized three of Castaneda's friends were arranging themselves around him, shooting at me, protecting him. But they mustn't be hitting me because it didn't hurt. Kit was involved in a single fight with someone who had gone after him. I could see through the corner of my eye as the two wove and shot around the flyers.

I aimed carefully and picked off Castaneda's right-side bodyguard.

Doc stepped in beside me and said, "You can't go it alone, Sinistra." I wondered if he was talking to me, or the wraith of Daddy Dearest.

He relieved me by distracting Castaneda's remaining bodyguards and allowing me to aim at Castaneda. I hit him over the heads of his friends, on the small slide of hair and forehead I could see between the two still-standing bodyguards.

For a moment it looked like I hadn't hit him. Then blood and brains erupted in an explosion, and Doc hit Castaneda's left-side bodyguard.

When it all cleared, Castanedas were on the ground, dead or wounded. On our own side, only Waldron was down, and Jennie was kneeling by him, holding his hand. When she looked up, she seemed to have aged a hundred years. Her eyes looked immensely sad. "We found out," she said, "about the trap Castaneda had set to blow up anyone coming after him. His second cousin told us. He thought—" She seemed unable to continue and sat on her ankles, rocking back and forth.

Kit limped from behind the flyers, looking cut and bruised. Jan came from the other side, limping.

Doc, standing beside me, whimpered. It was such

an uncharacteristic sound for him, I turned to look him fully on.

And Doc was very pale. Standing, but very pale.

I noticed the sleeve of his arm was dripping blood. "Doc," I said. And then I realized that he'd been hit twice. The shoulder shot was just the one bleeding the most. He'd also taken a shot through the stomach. "You're wounded."

Doc Bartolomeu turned to me, his face so pale that he looked like an animated wax doll, and contorted in a rictus of pain that lent itself ill to the smile he superimposed on it. "Hush, child. It's all right. It's time. I won't make Jarl's mistake. My time is all in the past. And perhaps..." He smiled a little and seemed to look behind my shoulder. "Why... perhaps a few hundred years of separation is expiation enough," he said softly. At least it sounded like that was what he said. "Do you believe in ghosts, Thena?"

"No," I said.

"Pity. Ghosts would work, as an explanation."

"No. We need you."

"No. You and Christopher and... and your children will be fine."

And then he died.

I started to kneel down beside him, to try to... I don't know what I wanted to try to do, but there must be something, there must. I couldn't take losing both Waldron and Doc.

But I couldn't see him clearly; it was as if everything had gone foggy and dark. I put my hand up to rub my eyes, but I fell forward, across Doc.

Thena, Kit said in my mind. *Thena. Light. That is all your blood. Thena, don't die.*

ALMOST THE END OF THE WORLD

WE ALMOST HAD A CIVIL WAR THEN. I KNOW NOTH-
ing about it, because I was unconscious and in a
regen tank. I'd got shot three times, most of my
hair burned away, and without regen I'd have been
one-armed forever. I was out for a week, but I heard
about it afterwards.

I think the only reason war didn't happen is that
everything had been so public. No one could say we'd
accused Castaneda in secret, or that it had been us
who had shot Doc.

There were many duels in the coming days, and
two of them took out the two men who'd shot Doc
Bartolomeu. Kath took care of one, and Kit another.

Kit had been quiet and detached through everything.
He'd helped prepare Doc's funeral. He'd gone through
Doc's belongings and closed Doc's house, leaving in it
anything that couldn't be sold. He stood as principal
mourner at the funeral while Doc was cremated and

507

his ashes deposited in the rose garden where the Denovos' dead were placed.

Kit didn't cry or even look sad, and I suppose most people thought he didn't feel much. But Waldron's death had left a hole in the family, and most people didn't hear Kit play his violin at night, the lonely notes crying like lost souls, until he grew too tired to play anymore. I came back from the regen center in time to hear this. I came back in time to go with him to the reproductive center, accompanying Jennie to consult about the baby she and Waldron had in the biowombs. I'm glad she decided to keep him and that she has that consolation. Right now it looks like she'll never get over her grief, but Kit says it passes. Maybe it will. I don't know. Maybe everyone will heal, too.

While at the center, we found that Doc had left two embryos in deep-freeze. We think they're his own male and female clones. Kit has inherited control of these. We think we'll gestate them soon and raise them with our children. No, they won't be Doc, but a little of him should be allowed to go forward into the future. Something of his should have a chance at a normal life.

I wasn't aware that Kit had challenged one of Doc's killers who had escaped. The first I knew of it was when Kit came back, looking grey and haggard, and put the engraved burners we'd brought from Earth in their storage case in our room, then sat on the bed. "It is done," he said. "He is avenged. In the end, whatever Jarl intended for me, I was Doc's son, as much as I was anyone's. He loved me for what I was and raised me, and wanted me to be happy. I was the repository of his hopes for the future. And I owed him a son's duty."

And then he covered his face with his hands and cried.

Over the next few weeks, things worked themselves out. Most of the people in the conspiracy were either quasi-innocent or misguided. A few truly bad apples were told they could choose to either leave for the Thules or continue to live in Eden under public shunning. Or fight duels for their honor. A few fought duels, but most of them left for Ultima Thule, where I was given to understand by Tania the locals had ways to deal with anyone who tried to make a grab for power. At any rate, the most power they were likely to get was over a couple hundred people, if that.

Some of the Thule colonists decided to feed the powertree in exchange for a share in its eventual fruit.

You see, it had been decided that the powertree would be private property and not common. Part of this was because everyone had finally looked at the Energy Board and the Water Board. Institutions of Eden, they'd been around so long that no one had ever questioned on whose authority they levied fines, or hired people, or decided who could and couldn't fly.

I guess everyone had assumed they were some form of shared proprietorship among the hereditary members of the board. Turned out they were wrong. Going far enough back in the history of the two, it became obvious that they had originated from emergency panels and that the first collector ships from which the fleet grew had in fact been common property, owned by all citizens of Eden.

And that ultimately was the problem, because when

something belongs to everyone, it belongs to no one, and those who administer it in a supposedly selfless manner end up being the ones who own it.

Over the centuries, the families in charge of the boards had enriched themselves under the cover of public service. It had never caused much problem because greed was a relatively clean desire, like lust. It was for something that people wanted to have, to acquire, to enjoy, and which might affect other people but didn't enslave them.

But then there had been Fergus Castaneda and his desire for power, which he'd decided to gratify by means of the Energy Board. Desire for power is not clean. It doesn't stop till you've stripped power from everyone else, and made them your slaves.

And now, we're going to have three water companies and two energy companies, and the powertree that is growing nearby but not too near will be owned by Kit and the people who tend it.

The water companies were formed by people who bought the ships at public auction, the profit to be distributed to each Edenite. Now Cats and Navs can choose which company they want to work for; companies will have their independent training programs, and if a Cat and Nav want to fly independently, that's all right too, provided they own their own ship and pay dock fees—and arrange with an energy company to buy their powerpods.

Kit and I are not working independently. Yes, eventually the little powertree will grow, the fruits will ripen, and people who harvest them will pay us a share. Eventually, our children will be wealthy beyond the dreams of avarice. But right now we owe really quite a lot of money to the Energy Board, which got transferred as debt to the people whose ships we damaged.

Doc's estate had come to Kit. We'll keep it for Doc's children; Kit thought we owed it to them. So, we barely had money to purchase even the *Cathouse*. Fortunately Kit's family decided to buy half a dozen ships, including the *Cathouse*, and start their own family enterprise. Which is how we came to be in the *Cathouse*, a month later, headed for the powertrees.

WHERE THE HEART IS

KIT WAS PLAYING THE VIOLIN. I LIKED THAT. IT reassured me every time he played it, because it was so obvious that he was alone in his skull.

I knew there were memories there that had nothing to do with science or knowledge, memories that he would never share with me. And his playing tended to the sadder melodies. But that was fine. As long as he was the only one playing that violin.

We were in the bedroom, and he stood, playing, while I reclined on the bed and listened to him.

As the last plaintive note sounded, I said, "Kit."

He lowered the bow. "Yes? Hey, want to go to the exercise room? You haven't wanted to mock-fight for a while."

"I don't feel like it," I said.

"You're getting fat," he said, but grinned.

"Am not. Okay, maybe a little. Do you mind terribly?"

He sat on the edge of the bed, and patted my hair. "No. You have a while to go before I mind."

"Yeah," I said. And as I thought of our last trip to Earth, I thought of Doc and Jarl. "I think we'll name our firstborn Jarl Bartolomeu."

"What?" Kit said. "What if it's a girl?"

"Especially if it's a girl. Think of the surprise."

He laughed and kissed me and said, "Well, no reason to worry about that. I'm sure in the next few years I can convince you to come up with a more sensible girl name."

And he probably could at that.

I'm just glad to be home.

You're very strange, and we're not home, Kit said. *We're in the* Cathouse.

Which is home, I said, and explained, slowly, because I could see he didn't get it. *Home, Kit, is wherever you are.*

The following is an excerpt from:

MARS, inc.
THE BILLIONAIRE'S CLUB
BEN BOVA

Available from Baen Books
December 2013
hardcover

1
SAN FRANCISCO

"Well, somebody's got to do it. The goddamned government isn't going to."

Charles Kahn smiled tolerantly as he reached for his half-finished glass of manzanilla. He had never heard Art Thrasher speak the word "government" without preceding it with "goddamned."

The two men were sitting in a pair of wingchairs in a quiet corner of the Kensington Club's Men's Bar, a haven of restful luxury, leather upholstery and dark cherrywood paneling. Through the gracefully-draped window beyond Thrasher's chair, Kahn could see the club's lovely little private garden and, beyond its carefully-tended trees, the Bay Bridge arching over the surging waters.

The trouble is, Kahn thought, that no place on Earth is placid or quiet when Art's in it. I should never have invited the little toothache to come here for a drink with me. He's small potatoes, him and his electronics gadgets; he's not even worth a billion. Nowhere near it. Why am I putting up with this aggravation?

Kahn reached for his wine again; the little stemmed glass rested on the elegantly-styled sherry table standing between their two chairs. Thrasher's mug of ginger

517

beer was beside it, untouched. Ginger beer, Kahn thought; how infantile.

Mistaking Kahn's silence for tacit approval, Thrasher continued, "We can do it! You, me, and a handful of others. We can get to Mars!"

"Really, now, Art."

"Really," Thrasher insisted.

The two men were a study in contrasts. Thrasher was short, paunchy, with big round light hazel eyes made even more owlish by his rimless eyeglasses. He wore his sandy hair boyishly short despite his receding hairline. His tan sports coat and darker chinos barely passed the club's dress code, Kahn knew. Instead of a tie he was wearing one of those ridiculous Texas string things. Even sitting in the capacious wingchair he fidgeted and squirmed restlessly, like a little boy yearning to go outside and play in the mud.

Compared to him, Kahn was a monument to calm dignity in his gray three-piece suit and chiseled ruggedly handsome features, the very best that modern cosmetic surgery could provide.

"And just how much would this mission to Mars cost?" Kahn asked.

Thrasher hesitated, rolled his eyes ceilingward, pursed his lips, then finally replied, "About a hundred billion, tops."

"A hundred billion?" Kahn almost dropped his drink.

"That's over five years, Charlie. That's twenty billion a year. Peanuts, really."

Kahn sipped at his manzanilla before replying, "You have a strange concept of peanuts."

"Come on, Charlie, we both know you're making indecent profits. What's the price of gasoline at the pump? Nine bucks a gallon? Going up to ten, eleven here in California, isn't it?"

Kahn shrugged noncommittally.

Thrasher went on, "You and your brother can put up a billion per year, each. You make that much in interest on your holdings every year, don't you? Take it off your taxes as a charitable donation."

"Really," Kahn muttered.

"Think of the publicity you'll earn! The good will! You could use some good will. I hear you're getting death threats on Twitter."

With a sigh, Kahn said, "I have PR people to handle things like that. And security people, as well."

"Give the people Mars and they'll love you! They'll build statues to you."

"There's no profit in such a mission."

"Only the profit of knowing that you've helped advance humankind's frontier. Mars, for chrissakes! The red planet! The scientists are dying to explore it, find out if there's life there."

"And why should I spend my hard-earned money on such a venture?"

"Come on, Charlie, this is me you're talking to. The hardest work you've done in the past fifteen years is reading *Forbes* magazine to see where you stand on the billionaire's list."

"Why isn't NASA—"

"Because the goddamned government has slashed their budget, that's why! Those fartbrains in the White House have no interest in human space flight anymore."

Kahn said nothing. He had contributed generously to the superpac that had helped get the current president into the White House. And Thrasher knew it.

Scrunching up closer on the wingchair, Thrasher coaxed, "Look, the Chinese are sending a man to the Moon in five years or so. America's going to look like a chump."

"You want to upstage the Chinese."

"It'd be great, wouldn't it? Leave those commies in the dust by going to Mars. Make *them* look like chumps."

"That's what John Kennedy did to the Soviets back in the Sixties," Kahn mused. "He leapfrogged their space efforts by putting Americans on the Moon first."

"And we can leapfrog the Peoples Republic of China! With private enterprise! Capitalism beats the communists!"

"A billion a year," Kahn murmured.

"For five years."

Leaning back in the warmly embracing wingchair, Kahn eyed Thrasher for a long moment, then said, "Tell you what, Art. You go to New York and see my brother. If you can talk David into doing this, then I'll come along, too."

Thrasher jumped to his feet, pumped Kahn's hand vigorously, and dashed out of the bar. Heads turned as he raced out. Several of he elder members shot disapproving glances at Kahn.

As if I'm responsible for the little ass, Kahn grumbled to himself. Then he reached for his sherry again. Let him talk to David. My brother will swat him like the annoying little mosquito that he is.

2
HOUSTON

The flight from San Francisco to Houston took just a tad over three hours, in Art Thrasher's executive Learjet. The plane's interior was luxuriously outfitted with swiveling plush reclinable seats, leather covered bulkheads and a full bar. Thrasher ignored all the amenities and split the time between phone calls and text messaging, while wondering in the back of his mind if he should get himself a supersonic jet.

Naah, he decided. The goddamned government doesn't allow supersonic flight over land. People complain about the sonic boom. As he hunched over his notepad's keyboard, pecking away, he thought: Maybe a rocket, like Branson's flying out of New Mexico. Cut the travel time to half an hour or less.

He cleared his screen, then texted his secretary in Houston to look into the idea. Branson's Virgin Galactic was making money, at last, flying tourists to the edge of space for a few minutes of experiencing weightlessness. Could the same technology be adapted to fly from point to point on Earth at hypersonic speed? That could make as big an impact on commercial air transportation as the transition from piston engines to jets, over a half a century earlier.

The pilot's voice came through the intercom speaker. "Making our approach to Houston, Mr. Thrasher."

Home sweet home, Thrasher thought, tightening his seat belt. But not for long. Gotta get to New York and see Charlie's big brother. They say he's got balls that clank.

Leaning back in the commodious chair, Thrasher thought, I've got to come up with something that'll get him interested. He won't go for scientific interest or national pride; not him. It's got to be something that'll make money for him. Let's see . . . he's into real estate, banking, what else?

As offices of corporate moguls go, Arthur Thrasher's was minimalist. No swanky overdecorated suite filled with underlings and paper shufflers. No airport-sized executive desk to overawe visitors. No art treasures on the walls.

Thrasher Digital Corporation had a modest suite of offices on the top floor of one of Houston's least gaudy high-rise towers. One flight up, on the building's roof, was a helicopter pad. Thrasher made the commute from the airport to his office in half an hour or less.

He hustled down the spiral staircase from the roof to the reception area of Thrasher Digital, briefcase in hand. With a nod to the two young women seated at their desks, he dashed into his suite's outer office. His executive assistant, Linda Ursina, was standing just inside the door with a frosted mug of ginger beer in her hand.

"Thanks, sweetie," Thrasher said as he took the drink from her with his free hand and headed for his private office. "Got me a date with Dave Kahn yet?"

Linda was just a few millimeters taller than Thrasher, with the slim, graceful figure of a dancer. Long legs that showed nicely in her midthigh skirt. The face of an Aztec princess: high cheekbones, olive complexion, dark almond-shaped eyes and sleek midnight hair that she wore tied up on the top of her head, making her look even taller.

"Mr. Kahn says he's free tonight," she replied, in a smooth contralto voice, "but not again until next Wednesday afternoon."

Thrasher grunted as he pushed through the door to his private office. It was large enough to hold his teak and chrome desk, a round conference table in one corner, and a trio of comfortable armchairs, upholstered in burgundy faux leather. One entire wall was a sweeping window that looked out on the city. The other walls held flat screens that showed priceless art treasures from the world's finest museums. Thrasher appreciated fine art, he just didn't want to have to pay for it.

The screens on the walls were showing High Renaissance works from Italian masters: Da Vinci, Michelangelo, Rafael.

His one concession to vanity was a small sculpture sitting on a credenza against the office's back wall. It was bust of Thrasher himself, sculpted by his second wife, back in those early days when he thought she loved him.

Sliding into his padded, high-backed desk chair, Thrasher slammed his mug of ginger beer on the desk's cermet coaster as he muttered, "If I run out there tonight Dave'll think I'm pretty damned desperate to see him. If I let it slide into next week..." He snapped his fingers. "Get Will Portal on the phone."

Linda's full lips curved into a slight smile.

"I know, I know," Thrasher said, peeling off his jacket. "Portal doesn't come running to the phone just because I've called him. You just explain to whichever flunky you talk to that this is the chance of a lifetime and it can't wait."

Looking less than impressed, Linda asked, "May I tell him what it's all about?"

"Hell no!"

"Would you kindly tell *me* what it's all about?"

"Mars, what else?"

"Oh, that."

It was nearly seven p.m. when Linda stepped into Thrasher's office and said, "If there's nothing else you need, I'll be going home now."

He glanced at his empty mug, but nodded. "Yeah, sure, go on home, kid."

"Portal hasn't returned your call," she said.

"It's two hours earlier out in Seattle. He'll call."

"You're going to wait here until he does?"

"Yep."

"You'll miss dinner."

He sighed. "As General Grant once said, I intend to fight it out along these lines if it takes all summer."

Linda said, "If I recall my history lessons, Grant didn't win until the following spring."

Thrasher grinned at her. "Go on home, smartass."

The phone jingled.

Linda started for the desk, but Thrasher stopped her with an upraised hand, waited for the second ring, then punched the speaker button.

One of the wall screens flicked from a Renaissance

Madonna to the youthful, slightly bemused face of Willard Portal.

Thrasher broke into a wide grin as he said, "Hello, Will. Good of you to call back."

With a lopsided smile, Portal said, "Your message said it's a matter of life and death."

Leaning back in his leather-covered desk chair, Thrasher said, quite seriously, "It is, Will. It is. The life or death of human space flight in America."

"Oh?"

"We've got to put together a human mission to Mars, Will. There's nothing more important, absolutely nothing."

Linda went to one of the armchairs and sat down, fascinated, as Thrasher spent the next hour and a half cajoling another billionaire.

3
HOME SWEET HOME

It was nearly nine o'clock when Portal finally said, "Okay, Art, okay. I'll think about it."

His bolo tie pulled loose, Thrasher tilted his padded chair back and planted his booted feet on his desk top. "Think of the tax break you can get out of this, Will. Think of the publicity and good will."

"I said I'll think about it," Portal repeated, his thin voice rising slightly.

"Fine, wonderful."

"Now can I go to dinner?" Portal's face took on a sardonic little grin.

"Sure," said Thrasher magnanimously. "Sorry to have kept you so long. I appreciate your time, Will, I really do."

"Good night, Art."

"'Night, Will."

The wall screen went back to the displaying the Madonna. Thrasher sighed heavily, then took off his glasses and rubbed his eyes. He was surprised to see Linda still sitting there, her chin on her fists.

"I thought you were going home."

"I am," she said, getting to her feet. "Goodness, look at the time."

Replacing his glasses, Thrasher said, "Just because I work crazy hours doesn't mean you have to."

She smiled. "Have you made any plans for your own dinner?"

"I'll grab something out of the freezer."

Linda gave him a critical look. "You ought to take better care of yourself."

Getting up from behind the desk, Thrasher said, "Yes, Mommy. Now go home."

"Make sure you get some food into you."

"And be back here at eight sharp."

"Right, boss." She turned and left the office.

Admiring her form, Thrasher recognized that Linda was really a very beautiful young woman. What is it the Catholics call it? he mused. Then he remembered, She's a near occasion of sin. A very tempting morsel indeed. He shook his head and said to himself sternly, You do *not* come on to employees. It's very unfair to them. And you could get sued up to your eyeballs.

The intercom buzzed.

"What?" he demanded.

Linda's voice asked, "Should I tell Carlo to meet you in the lobby?"

"Naw. Tell him to go home. I'll stay here tonight."

"You're sure?"

"Stop mothering me, kid. And go home yourself."

A hesitation, then she said, "Goodnight, then."

"Goodnight, already."

Thrasher's home was far out in the posh suburbs, a mansion he had built for his second wife, the sculptress. But he maintained a modest apartment on the other side of the corridor from his office suite. Nothing very fancy, just a couple of bedrooms, kitchen, sitting room, and a book-lined study. Plus a walk-in shower in the master bathroom. He had spent some very special hours, sharing that shower.

But tonight he was alone. He pulled a dinner package from the freezer, microwaved it, then sat at the kitchen counter and nibbled at it while he watched television, switching from CNN to Fox News to MSNBC and back again at every commercial break.

Pouring himself a ginger beer, he briefly thought about adding a dollop of brandy to it. Brandy and dry, the Aussies called it. He decided against the brandy and walked slowly to his study, then out onto the balcony that overlooked the garish lights of downtown Houston.

Can't see the stars, they keep it so goddamned bright, he complained silently. Not like Arizona. Not at all.

His mother had died in childbirth and Thrasher was raised by his embittered father, a dry husk of an astronomy professor at the University of Arizona's Steward Observatory. Dad worked all his life and what did he get for it? Bubkiss. A lousy pension and his name on a couple of boxfuls of research papers.

His father had accomplished one other thing, though. He had instilled in young Arthur D. Thrasher a love of astronomy, a fascination with the grandeur and mystery of the stars.

Not that Art followed his father's footsteps. The chalkdust classrooms and genteel poverty of academic life were not for Art. To his father's despair, Arthur took the university's business curriculum, then won a partial scholarship for an MBA at Wharton. He covered his expenses with the money he'd made from his first entrepreneurial venture: a bicycle repair shop on the edge of the UA campus.

His father died the year Art made his first million. Art married, divorced, married and divorced again. By the time he was worth a hundred million, he had given up on marriage—but not on women.

Leaning against the balcony railing, Art took off his glasses, folded them carefully into his shirt pocket, then peered at the sky. He was farsighted, he didn't need the glasses to see the stars. Farsighted. He laughed to himself. At least that's better than being myopic. His second wife had gotten him to try contact lenses, but Art hated to insert them, felt uncomfortable with them, always feared one of them would pop out at an embarrassing moment.

There was talk of new surgical techniques to alleviate hypermetropia, the medical term for farsightedness. Art shook his head at the thought of it. Maybe after I'm sixty-five and eligible for Medicare, he decided. Let the goddamned government pay for it.

Then he reminded himself that it wasn't the goddamned government's money, it was the taxpayers'. With a sigh, he realized that sixty-five wasn't that far away: thirteen years. Lucky thirteen.

He ducked back into his study for a moment and pulled what looked like binoculars from his desk drawer. Actually, they were nothing more than a pair of toilet-paper rollers, duct taped together. Out on the balcony again, Art put the contraption to his eyes and searched the sky. The tubes blocked some of the glare from the city's lights.

He saw a reddish dot through the glow and smog. Mars? Might be Antares. But no, the dot wasn't twinkling, the way stars do. It was a steady beacon. The planet Mars. He remembered the first time his father had shown him Mars, rising bright and clear over the rugged mountains ringing Tucson. I couldn't have been more than five years old. And the lurid adventure tales set on Mars that he'd read in his teen years; his father shook his head with disdain at his son's choice of literature.

"Mars," Thrasher breathed, staring at the red dot in the sky. Thirty-five million miles away at its closest. But we'll get there. We'll get there.

Why? he asked himself. Because it's there? He laughed. Because we can make money from it? I doubt that. Because I want to show my father that I'm not just a money-grubbing Philistine?

None of the above.

Or maybe, he thought, it's all of the above. And more.

And he remembered his father's dying words, as he lay in the hospital, withering away before Thrasher's tear-filled eyes:

"Make something of yourself, Arthur. There's more to life than money. Do something you can be proud of, something worth doing."

Something, Thrasher thought bitterly. Something you could never do, Dad.

We'll get to Mars because it's worth doing. Something I can be proud of. It's that simple. It's something I can be proud of. Something to make my father proud of me.

4
JOHNSON SPACE CENTER

"But I'm a NASA employee, Mr. Thrasher—"

"Art. Call me Art."

Jessie Margulis looked distinctly uncomfortable. Thrasher had driven out to the NASA center specifically to meet the engineer, but Margulis had refused to bring him inside, to where the offices and laboratories were. They sat next to each other in the spacious visitor's center reception area.

Margulis hunched close to Thrasher, his eyes worriedly following every salesmen and bureaucrat and engineer that paraded past. He even glanced cautiously every few seconds at the four receptionists sitting behind the big curving desk in the center of the room. Christ, Thrasher thought, he acts like we're planning a bank heist.

Thrasher's chief engineer, Vince Egan, had identified Margulis as one of NASA's top engineers, the man who headed Johnson Space Center's advanced planning department.

"I'm a government employee," Margulis repeated. "I shouldn't even be talking to you."

"Why not?" Thrasher countered, "I'm a citizen and a taxpayer; that makes me your boss, kind of." Then, with a grin, he added, "It's not like we're plotting to blow up the place."

Margulis winced. He's sweating, Thrasher noticed. They air-condition this barn cold enough to put icicles on your *cojones* and he's sweating.

Thrasher went on, "We're just having a friendly little chat about what a manned spacecraft—"

"Crewed," Margulis corrected.

"Crude?"

"Cre-we*d*." The engineer emphasized the second syllable. "We don't say 'manned.' It's not politically correct."

Thrasher nodded. "I gotcha. And besides, we'll have women among the crew for the Mars mission."

Margulis winced again at the word "Mars." He was a bland-faced man in his forties: receding hairline, little fuzz of a goatee hiding a weak chin, a pot belly, shirt pocket stuffed with pens. Put him in a party with six hundred guests and ask any one of 'em to find the engineer, they'd go straight to him, Thrasher thought.

Still, the headhunters claimed he was a brilliant engineer. And more than that, he was a leader among engineers. The rest of them respected him.

But Margulis was saying, "NASA has been directed to shelve its plans for a crewed Mars mission. There's no money in the budget for it."

"And all the work you've done on the project has been scrapped," said Thrasher.

"Mothballed," Margulis corrected. Thrasher thought he detected some resentment there.

"So what are you working on now?"

The engineer tracked with his eyes an older man in his shirtsleeves and a NASA employee's badge dangling from a chain around his neck. The guy glared disapprovingly at Margulis as he walked past.

"What are you working on now?" Thrasher repeated. "Is it a secret?"

"No, we don't work on classified projects. We're completely open."

"So what're you doing now?"

Margulis shrugged. "Robotic planetary probes, mostly. Another mission to Europa. Conceptual studies of a probe to land on Titan."

"That's a moon of Saturn, right?"

"Right."

"And manned . . . I mean, crewed missions?"

"Nothing."

Brightening, Thrasher said, "Well, I've got a crewed mission for you to work on. Mars."

"I can't discuss that with you," Margulis hissed, almost pleading. "I'm a NASA employee."

"You're not allowed to consult with a private citizen?"

"No. That'd be a conflict of interest, in the government's eyes."

"Then quit the goddamned government and come to work for me. I'll double whatever you're making now."

Margulis' mouth popped open, but no words came out.

"I want you to head my Mars project."

"I . . . In another couple of years I'll have put in my twenty. I've got a pension coming, and there's the health care insurance . . ."

"I'll equal or better it."

"Could you wait two years?"

"No."

Margulis was clearly torn. Tempted.

Thrasher coaxed, "You'll be head of the project, free to run it any way you like."

The engineer blinked twice, then asked, "Suppose I want to use a nuclear propulsion system."

"Nuclear?"

"A nuclear rocket would be a helluva lot better than chemical rockets. More efficient, capable of moving a much bigger payload. But NASA's stopped all work on nukes. Too much anti-nuke pressure."

Thrasher saw an opening. With a shrug, he said, "You're the tech leader. If you think nuclear is the way to go, we'll go nuclear."

"There'll be a lot of opposition," Margulis warned.

"I'll take care of the opposition. You do the engineering."

For a long moment Margulis said nothing. Then, "The problem is . . . Art, your project might go belly-up. You might not get the funding you need. Or the anti-nuke people will stop you. Or the money might run out. With the government, I've got a steady job. I've got security. I have a wife and three kids to think about."

"Jessie, I will personally fund a pension and health care insurance plan for you. Fully fund them both. Put the money into a separate account, where it'll be safe."

"I . . ."

"I want you Jessie. You're the best man to run this project, everyone I've talked with agrees on that. I *need* you."

"I'd have to quit NASA. Leave all my benefits."

"Can't you take a leave of absence? For a year, say? Then, if my project doesn't work out, you can come back to NASA and no harm's been done."

"Maybe . . ."

"You think about it, pal." Thrasher popped to his feet. Margulis remained seated, his expression somewhere between thoughtful and frightened.

At last he got slowly to his feet, too.

"I will think about it, Mr. Thrasher."

"Art."

"Art."

"Double your salary. Full pension and health insurance." Thrasher started to turn toward the door, hesitated, and turned back to Margulis.

"Oh, I almost forgot the most important point of all."

"What's that?"

"You'll be working on a mission to Mars, by damn. A nuclear-propelled crewed mission to Mars. You'll never get to do that as an employee of the goddamned government."

—end excerpt—

from *Mars, Inc.*
available in hardcover,
December 2013, from Baen Books